LIZZIE

Also by EVAN HUNTER

NOVELS

The Blackboard Jungle
Second Ending
Strangers When We Meet
A Matter of Conviction
Mothers and Daughters
Buddwing
The Paper Dragon
A Horse's Head
Last Summer

Sons
Nobody Knew They Were
  There
Every Little Crook and Nanny
Come Winter
Streets of Gold
The Chisholms
Love, Dad
Far From the Sea

SHORT STORY COLLECTIONS

Happy New Year, Herbie

The Easter Man

CHILDREN'S BOOKS

Find the Feathered Serpent
The Remarkable Harry

The Wonderful Button
Me and Mr. Stenner

SCREENPLAYS

Strangers When We Meet
The Birds

Fuzz
Walk Proud

TELEPLAYS

The Chisholms

The Legend of Walks Far
  Woman

LIZZIE

A NOVEL BY
EVAN HUNTER

HAMISH HAMILTON

London

First published in Great Britain 1984
by Hamish Hamilton Ltd
Garden House 57–59 Long Acre London WC2E 9JZ

British Library Cataloguing in Publication Data
Hunter, Evan
  Lizzie.
  I. Title
  813′.54[F]   PS3515.U585
  ISBN 0–241–11172–2

Printed and bound in Great Britain by
Richard Clay (The Chaucer Press) Ltd, Bungay, Suffolk

THIS IS FOR ROGER MACHELL
AND
CHRISTOPHER SINCLAIR-STEVENSON

Lizzie Borden took an ax,
And gave her mother forty whacks.
When she saw what she had done,
She gave her father forty-one.

LIZZIE

1: LIVERPOOL AND LONDON— 1890

There was, for Lizzie, a sense of discovery—no, of homecoming. Standing at the ship's railing, listening to the groaning and hissing of the steam machinery as it hoisted the trunks and valises from belowdecks, she felt less a foreigner than she did a returning native. This England, this sceptered isle—today wreathed in ominously shifting gray clouds that promised rain—called to her from more than two centuries past, when a man named John Borden left his home in Kent to seek his fortune in the colonies.

Had he felt, upon his arrival in Boston, the same keen anticipation she felt today in this vast and sprawling harbor? Had the skies over that alien port seemed as utterly appropriate to him as did these leaden skies above Liverpool now? Appropriate, yes; sunshine would have been a disappointment, a contradiction of expectations.

The heat in Fall River a week ago had been intolerable. New York City had been even less hospitable, its temperatures hovering in the mid-nineties, the noise and confusion of the docks miraculously disappearing the moment the women boarded the *Teutonic* and found their cabins. But for all its splendor and

1

speed, the great Ocean Greyhound, as it had been advertised, had seemed only another necessary delay, five days—almost six—before this moment, this already cherished instant, when she could stand here, the wind wet and raw on her face, the harbor crowded with hundreds of ships and boats defying the waves, and glimpse there in the distance the rooftops of an England recalled as though she had been here countless times before.

The transatlantic journey had not been shortened by the fact that Anna had been seasick almost every moment. They had invited her along, after months of preparation and consultation, only because first-cabin accommodations were so dreadfully expensive ($60 to $140, depending upon the location!) and none of them could afford the luxury of travel in an unshared room. It had been Lizzie's misfortune—and she hoped to correct this as concerned future hotel arrangements—to have drawn a short straw similar to Anna's from a hat belonging to Rebecca Welles, the chance draw determining exactly how the ladies would be traveling *au paire*, as Rebecca had put it in her somewhat strained French.

Even under the best of circumstances, Anna Borden was a dour, pale-faced woman, entirely humorless, and given to wearing a veil day and night, perhaps to hide her plainness, perhaps to ward off unwanted glances from foreign men, of which there had been many on the voyage out. The fact that they were both named Borden had encouraged far too many people to ask, "Oh, are you related?" which they weren't—except perhaps for some common ancestor in the dim, distant past: there were now something more than four hundred Bordens in Fall River, most of whom Lizzie didn't even know. She claimed to the other two women in their party that she had never seen Anna without a veil covering her face except when she was vomiting in the ship's toilet, but this was an exaggeration. Anna slept with her face naked to the night airs. And snored loudly, as though to dispel whatever evil spirits might be tempted to invade her nostrils when the veil was tucked away in her dressing case. She stood veiled and shivering beside Lizzie now, clutching the rail for dear life although the ship was virtually motionless, breathing deeply as though in imminent danger of vomiting again.

2

Of the three women traveling with her, Lizzie liked Rebecca Welles best. Somewhat younger than Lizzie—she was twenty-seven or -eight, Lizzie wasn't quite sure—she was a well read and quite attractive young woman with a passable knowledge of French and a smattering of German as well, which Lizzie hoped would stand the party in good stead on the final leg of their journey. They had met the way so many unmarried women in Fall River did, at a church function, and it was Lizzie who had convinced her to join the church's Chinese department, where they struggled side by side teaching English to the sons and daughters of the town's laundrymen. In many respects Rebecca—though her forebears were mixed Welsh and English—looked Chinese herself, with masses of straight black hair and eyes the color of loam, somewhat slanted over prominent cheekbones.

The Liverpool harbor resembled nothing so much as a giant canal—miles long and a thousand feet wide, Lizzie guessed—lined with great walls of heavy cut stone divided into berths large enough to accommodate any seagoing vessel. Everywhere she looked, she could see ships and smaller boats disgorging cargo, the markings and flags on the vessels indicating they had come from ports everywhere on the face of—there now! The tenders that would carry them to the customhouse were approaching the ship. Further along the railing, Felicity Chambers, her blond locks blowing in the wind, waved at one of the approaching boats, or rather at the *pilot* guiding it alongside; she could not imagine how Felicity could even *see* the man through the grimy window of the pilothouse, but waving she was, and in a thoroughly unladylike manner that caused Rebecca, by her side, to give her an equally unladylike poke with her elbow. Felicity was twenty-four years old, destined one day to become the wife of one of Fall River's businessmen, Lizzie guessed, a dimpled, curly-headed little thing quite remarkably endowed by nature and possessed of all the cute mannerisms Europeans expected of small-town American girls traveling abroad.

One day, strolling the deck in bright sunshine on the voyage out, Lizzie had chanced to overhear a remark made by an Englishwoman returning to her native land. As Felicity flitted past, the woman said, "So American. Beautiful, rich—and vulgar." Lizzie had taken this as a comment less directed at Felic-

3

ity's blond, blue-eyed good looks and extravagant figure than at the particularly lavish way she was dressed for a daytime, topside constitutional. And whereas she quite agreed that her traveling companion had looked overdressed and inappropriately bejeweled in contrast to the Europeans making the homeward voyage, she nonetheless felt a fierce, protective loyalty. Staring the Englishwoman down, letting her know with her penetrating gaze that she'd been overheard, she had deliberately gone to Felicity, embraced her, kissed her on the cheek, and walked arm in arm with her into the grand saloon.

"Oh, it's England, it's *England!*" Felicity said now, and waved this time at the distant anonymous shore.

At the booking office in the Birkenhead Station, Lizzie was informed (and she was already beginning to regret her role as elected treasurer) that the distance from Liverpool to London was two hundred miles, and that a first-class ticket would cost one pound, eight shillings, which she clumsily calculated as seven U.S. dollars, or approximately three and a half cents a mile, which she supposed was something of a bargain. They followed a porter in blue livery to the luggage van (they called it *luggage* here, she noticed, and not *baggage*) and watched as he labeled each piece Paddington and then hefted the lot of them inside; he was a giant of a man, who tossed their trunks into the van with little effort and even less care. Lizzie waited in vain for a receipt of some sort, but apparently the British confidence in human nature was sublime, and when she saw that none was forthcoming, she began rummaging in her purse for the expected tip.

An Englishman was standing nearby, tipping a porter who had performed a similar service for him only moments before. Lizzie detected at once that only a single bronze coin changed hands—twopence, as she reckoned in the swift exchange. Had she grossly overtipped the custom-shed porter? She fished in her purse, found what she hoped was a half shilling, and handed the silver coin to the porter. He gave her a baleful look until she added several bronze coins to the one in his palm, and then his craggy face broke into a wide gap-toothed grin, and he murmured, "God bless, madam," and led them immediately to the first-class compartment of the nearest passenger car, where he stood by the steps and bowed them aboard, his cap in his hand.

No sooner were they seated than a freckle-faced, towheaded newsboy wearing a cap tilted over half his face, a loose baggy sweater that came almost to his thighs, and kneebreeches falling loose over equally fallen stockings, came along the platform crying, "Papers, papers!" and stopped at the open door to the compartment. "Papers, ladies?" he asked, and Felicity, making herself comfortable in the seat next to the window, looked at the array of newspapers he proffered, rolled her blue eyes, and said, "Oh, my, whichever one shall we read?"

"Depends on your politics, miss," the newsboy said. "If you're Gladstonian, I'd advise the *News*. If on the other hand you're Tory, you might do well to take either the *Times* or the *Standard*."

"We'll have the *Times*," Lizzie said.

"Are we Tory?" Felicity asked.

"Y'could be worse, miss," the newsboy said, grinning, and counted out the change for the coin Lizzie handed him. "Thank you, ma'am," he said, and Lizzie wondered when *"miss"* became *"ma'am"* in Europe. In Fall River, she was Miss Lizzie. Here in England, Felicity was miss, but she herself had been ma'am or madam on more than one occasion now. She had celebrated her thirtieth birthday on the nineteenth day of July, three days before they'd boarded the *Teutonic*. Felicity was twenty-four. Did those six years make such a difference here? Vaguely troubled, she opened her purse and was dropping the loose change into it when the door on the corridor side suddenly opened.

A man with the word Inspector stamped onto a round brass plate pinned to his cap stepped into the compartment and said, "Tickets, please, tickets." She rummaged in her purse for the tickets she had purchased, regretting more and more the chore the others had imposed upon her. The uniformed man took the tickets, and with a heavy punch gouged into each of them a pie-shaped wedge. "Have a pleasant journey," he said, and touched the peak of his cap. Outside on the platform, there was a sudden bustle of activity as uniformed men ran along slamming the doors of the cars. Just as suddenly, the train began to move.

She sat opposite Felicity in the narrow compartment, their skirted knees almost touching, and began reading the London *Times*.

5

They learned soon enough that the train offered none of the comforts or conveniences to which they were accustomed on American railroad coaches. Not anywhere in the car was there a toilet stand, a closet, a heating apparatus or a drinking-water cylinder. The weather was brisk compared to what they were used to in July, and with the windows closed, the compartment was quite close. Anna complained of a headache. Felicity, after a tour of the car and a search for toilet facilities, indelicately suggested that had she known such accommodations would be lacking, she would have carried along her own slop pail. Rebecca, now reading the *Times* Lizzie had already read from first page to last, visibly winced at Felicity's comment.

It was with considerable relief, therefore, that they learned from the inspector, who flung open the corridor door again just as the train was pulling into the Chester station, that they would be stopping here for twenty minutes should the ladies care to stretch their legs. He assured them he would make certain that no one occupied their seats, and Lizzie wondered if he expected a tip for his concern. As if to confirm her surmise, the inspector returned just as the train was pulling into the station, carrying a narrow strip of paper dripping with paste. The paper, Lizzie saw as he affixed it to the window of their compartment, was a printed form that he had filled in with pencil. It read:

ENGAGED

From *Liverpool*

To *London*

July 27, 1890

What then to tip this great grinning ape who now backed away from the window and stood beaming with pride at his primitive accomplishment? According to Lizzie's calculations, a shilling was the equivalent of twenty-five cents. But surely even

6

a man with the word Inspector emblazoned in brass on his cap would not expect so exorbitant a fee for posting his simple bill and insuring his vigilance. Would a half shilling suffice? She glanced across the compartment to Rebecca and by the look on her face saw that she was engaged in the same process of calculation. Rebecca shrugged behind the waiting inspector's back. Lizzie dug into her purse and handed the man a shilling after all. He seemed satisfied; at any rate, he touched the peak of his cap before he left the compartment.

His little sign, in fact, worked remarkably well almost all the way to London. But as the train was pulling out of the Oxford station, the door on the corridor side was yanked open, and a man peered into the compartment and said, "Excuse me, ladies, may we join you? The other first-class sections are fully occupied."

She wondered for a moment who the "we" might be; she had no desire to share the compartment with two strange men. But the man seemed to be utterly alone, a tall, brown-eyed Englishman (judging from his speech), wearing a single-breasted lounge jacket cut to button four but worn to button one, the sleeves short enough to show his fashionable, colored linen cuffs, his close, small-buttoned trousers cut well up to reveal his fancy patent leather buttoned boots. He wore beneath the jacket a vest with a small check repeated in the fabric of his hat, which in every other respect resembled a bowler. Like most of the other men Lizzie had seen here in England (and it was a relief from the bearded men at home), he was clean-shaven except for short side-whiskers and a mustache. Without waiting for their reply, he threw the small valise he was carrying up onto the overhead rack, said, "Thank you," and then ducked out into the corridor again and called, "Allie! I've found us some spaces!" and backed away a few steps, waiting.

The woman who appeared in the doorframe was quite the most beautiful woman Lizzie had ever seen in her life. She stood almost as tall as her companion, some five feet eight or nine inches, Lizzie guessed, her extraordinary height exaggerated by the modest gabled toque she wore, a close-fitting hat trimmed with velvet and feathers, its inverted V-front exposing a fringe of frizzed blond hair. The toque was green, echoing the green of her eyes, as deep as any forest glade, perfectly match-

7

ing the Norfolk jacket bodice and plain-fronted skirt she wore. Her face was as pale as milk, a perfect oval with a generous mouth and an aquiline nose. Her eyebrows lifted slightly when she saw how nearly full the compartment already was. "I do hope we shan't be crowding you," she said, and behind her the man nodded a belated apology.

"Please join us," Lizzie said graciously, and first the woman and then the man entered the compartment. She had given her window seat to Rebecca when the train left Warwick. The woman sat beside her now on her right—Lizzie noticed with relief that her bustle was small and fashionable—the faintest scent of eau de cologne wafting about her as she smoothed her skirt. She was wearing black stockings, Lizzie saw, and laced shoes with rounded toes and low heels. The man sat diagonally across from Lizzie, beside Felicity, who had swapped her window seat with Anna.

"This is so very kind of you," the woman said.

Her voice was pitched rather low, sounding more like an adolescent boy's than a woman's, somewhat breathless now after her supposed dash for the train and the struggle to find a seat. The man, Lizzie noticed, though he was in the company of ladies, had not yet removed his absurd checked bowler. She immediately assumed he was ill-mannered. And yet, the woman seemed so fashionably dressed. And, certainly, their speech hadn't sounded at all like what Lizzie had expected of lower-class Englishmen. Both of them were silent now. The man shifted his weight and stretched his long legs. The woman stared directly ahead of her, her slender, gloved hands folded in her lap.

"Allow me to introduce ourselves," Lizzie said, turning to the woman and seeming to take her quite by surprise. "I'm Lizzie Borden, and these are my friends. Felicity Chambers . . ."

"Charmed," Felicity said.

"Rebecca Welles . . ."

"How do you do?"

"And Anna Borden . . . there by the window."

Anna nodded behind her veil.

"Americans, of course," the man said, and smiled.

"Yes," Lizzie said, and returned the smile.

8

"How often would you say I've taken this train in the past five years, Allie?" he asked the woman.

"Countless times," she said.

"Countless times," he agreed, nodding. "And never has anyone but an American spoken to me."

"*Nôtre sang-froid habituel*," the woman said, and added in explanation, "We English, you know," and smiled.

"Even if you hadn't been so kind as to speak first," the man said, "I'd have known you were American."

"Oh?" Lizzie said. "How?"

"Only lords, fools and Americans ride first-class," the man said, and laughed.

"Since you, my dear Albert, are neither an American nor a lord . . ." the woman said, and airily waved aside the rest of the sentence.

"A fool for certain," the man said, shaking his head. "The smoking compartment's packed full, you know. Book a first-class ticket and ride all the way to London without a cigar."

"Please don't ask the ladies if they'd mind," the woman said.

"*Would* you mind?" the man asked, looking across at Lizzie.

"Anna isn't feeling well," Lizzie said apologetically.

"Oh, what a pity," the woman said, and glanced about at the other women, as though trying to recall which of them was Anna. Her glance settled unerringly on the veiled figure huddled beside Felicity in the window seat on the other side of the compartment. "Forgive me," she said, "I'm Alison Newbury. This is my husband, Albert."

"Allie and Albie," the man said.

"The 'Albie,' of course, is to distinguish him from our late and eternally lamented prince consort," Alison said drily.

"Who *but* a prince would book first-class?" Albert said. "Is the 'Lizzie' short for Elizabeth?"

"No, that's my full name," Lizzie said. "Or rather, part of it. It's Lizzie Andrew, the whole of it."

"Are you and the other lady related?" Alison asked.

"No, we're not."

"Small world then, isn't it?" Albert said. "*Andrew,* did you say?"

"I think my father was hoping for a boy."

9

"Oh, dear," Alison said, "how dreadful for you," and patted Lizzie's hand.

"I rather like that, actually," Albert said. "The Andrew part. If ever we were to have any children . . ."

"Bite your tongue," Alison said.

"I'd choose to name him Andrew," Albert said, and shrugged.

"Please note the male posture," Alison said.

"Posture?" Albert said.

"The certainty that *if* and *when* we ever had a child, God forbid, it would be a boy." She smiled at Lizzie. "Is your father's name Andrew?"

"Yes. Andrew Jackson Borden."

"After one of your presidents?" Albert asked.

"I would imagine. He's never said."

"Have you been traveling long in England?" Alison asked.

"We just arrived this morning," Felicity said brightly. "From New York."

"Oh, you poor dears," Alison said. "You must be *utterly* exhausted!"

"Not really," Rebecca said. "It was a very comfortable crossing."

"I was seasick most of the time," Anna said from behind her veil.

"You poor dear," Alison said.

"Do you make your home in New York?" Albert asked.

"No, we're from Massachusetts," Rebecca said.

"Ah, yes," Albert said.

"Fall River," Felicity said.

"Afraid I don't know it," Albert said. "Where will you be staying in London?"

"Don't be cheeky, darling," Alison said.

"A perfectly proper question," Albert said, and stroked his mustache. "Surely the ladies are staying *somewhere*."

"The Albemarle Hotel," Lizzie said.

"The *Hotel* Albemarle," he corrected. "One must be exceedingly careful in London. I once asked a cabbie to take me to the Victoria Hotel, which any fool knows is on Northumberland Avenue. He pulled up in front of what seemed a gin palace, bearing the sign plain enough—Victoria Hotel. I told him I wanted the one on Northumberland, and he promptly said, 'Then why didn't you say *Hotel* Victoria?' I might add that he charged me a fare and a half to emphasize the distinction."

"You mustn't frighten the ladies," Alison said. "That's just reopened, hasn't it? The Albemarle?"

"Rebuilt it from top to bottom," Albert said, nodding. "Did a handsome job of it, too."

"Near St. James's Street, isn't it?"

"Corner of Piccadilly and Albemarle Street," Albert said. "Choice location, very fine indeed. Made it over in the French style. I fancy you'll like it. But why on earth have you taken *this* train?"

"Isn't this the train to London?" Anna said, alarmed.

"Indeed it is," Albert said, "but one of the others might have been more convenient for you."

He went on to explain that four different railway companies ran trains from Liverpool to London. The train they were on, operated by the Great Western Railway, had taken them through Chester, Birmingham, Warwick and Oxford and was now on its way to Paddington Station, which was rather more distant from their hotel than some of the London stations the other lines went into. Moreover, because of the many stops along the way, the rail journey was lengthier than it might have been; two of the other lines offered shorter, swifter routes.

"But this route is scenic," Alison said.

"If you enjoy looking at the rooftops of middle-class English homes," Albert said.

"Besides, we never would have met otherwise, would we?" Alison said, and again patted Lizzie's hand.

It was Albert who also informed them that they could have had their luggage shipped directly to the hotel rather than having it knocked about from pillar to post all the way to London and then from Paddington Station where they might, on a Sunday, have difficulty getting transportation on to the hotel. Lizzie was grateful when the conversation shifted to less dismaying ground. The Newburys, she learned, made their home in London, to which they were returning after a weekend visit to Alison's cousin in Oxford, a trip necessitated by the fact that they were leaving for a holiday on the Continent next Wednesday. This led to a discussion of the itinerary the women

11

had planned for their *own* holiday (Lizzie repeated the British word with great pleasure, and hoped she didn't sound affected) and the Newburys, who turned out to be widely traveled, helpfully pointed out the tourist attractions and restaurants that shouldn't be missed.

She was surprised when, at the end of an acquaintance that had seemed entirely pleasant but altogether too brief, Alison offered her a visting card upon which was imprinted her name, address and telephone number, and asked her to be in touch should they need any sort of assistance in London. Albert reminded his wife that they were leaving for Paris next Wednesday, and Alison said, "Hush, darling, I meant *until* then, surely." To Lizzie's greater surprise, it was Albert who made certain that their baggage was transported from the luggage van to a large waiting vehicle, and then hailed another four-wheeler for the ladies themselves. When he tipped the porter for his services, Lizzie protested vigorously but in vain. When he advised the cabman to keep an eye out for the luggage carrier ahead, and gave him the number of the vehicle, Lizzie wondered aloud how they might have managed without him, and Albert—pleased and flushing—assured her it was no trouble at all. The women shook hands all around. Just before the Newburys' hansom cab pulled away, Alison smiled and waved. Her eyes looked intensely green in the slanting ray of sunshine that touched her exquisite face.

Standing by the open fourth-floor windows in her nightdress, looking down at Piccadilly, Lizzie listened to what could only be considered a roar in comparison to last night's hush.

In the early morning sunshine there was even more traffic below than she had seen on her several visits to New York. Looking down at the cabs and hansoms flying about below in such a hot and reckless fashion, she wondered how she would ever get from one side of the street to the other without being crushed beneath the thundering hooves of the horses.

In one of the beds across the room, Rebecca murmured in her sleep and then rolled over. Lizzie had suggested, when the women were registering for their rooms in the ornate Renaissance lobby below, that perhaps they should share the accommodations throughout Europe on a rotating basis (this to avoid

Anna's snoring, though she made no mention of it) and the others had readily agreed. They had paired off haphazardly, too tired to give any thought to contriving a system that would serve them all through Europe, and then had gone upstairs to unpack before taking their evening meal in the ground-floor dining room, which the headwaiter proudly informed them had been decorated in the style of Francis I. He blinked politely when Felicity asked him if that had been a British king.

The long day, which had started when they'd been awakened aboard ship at dawn, had finally caught up with them midway during their supper. Only Felicity ordered dessert; perhaps she had noticed that the predominant style of beauty among Englishwomen seemed to consist of a heavy bust, a narrow, corseted waist and a large bottom, and was determined to go back to Fall River looking as much like one of them as was possible: Anna, who'd scarcely eaten a bite anyway, abruptly excused herself and went directly upstairs to the room she would be sharing with Felicity. Rebecca, her eyes looking somewhat glazed, excused herself shortly afterwards; she was already asleep when Lizzie went up to their room at a little before nine.

She changed into her nightdress, padding quietly about the room so as not to awaken Rebecca, and then went to stand by the open windows, surprised by the utter calm of the city. A hush, rather, broken only by the muffled sound of distant vehicles. The scent of flowers and of freshly cut hay wafted through the open windows. Smiling she went to her bed and sat on the edge of it, savoring the silence. And then she lay down and pulled the covers to her chin, and the hush was broken suddenly by the sound of Big Ben tolling the hour, echoed by the liquid chiming of yet more bells on the muzzle of the night. She listened to the tolling of the bells in all the clock towers, and when they had faded, and when the hush was complete again, she drifted off into a deep and peaceful sleep.

"Is it morning?" Rebecca asked from the bed behind her, blinking at the sunshine.

"Oh, *yes!*" Lizzie said.

She might have been in Boston, the two cities seemed that similar. Not those sections of Boston that had been rebuilt since the Great Fire, certainly not, but those that had survived.

13

London, like Boston, seemed to be a city of three-story buildings, a third of them stucco painted drab, the remainder fashioned of brick or stone. There was a quiet modesty to the buildings, an air of substance and dignity. The similarity startled her; perhaps it had to do with the fact that Boston, before the Revolution, had never been anything *but* British.

The soot! Dirt of the dirtiest sort! Corinthian columns with one side of them a pale gray and the other a black as deep as midnight. St. Paul's, and Westminster Abbey and the squat Bank of England wearing robes of black soot except for their very tops, where the stonework stood out mysteriously pristine. Rebecca explained that this was because the British burned soft coal. Anna was certain that all those flying black globules would bring on a congestion of the nose, the throat and the lungs. Felicity, as only she might have noticed, commented that even the collars of the men's shirts appeared black.

On their first morning in London, they went to the Tower, of course, and then the National Gallery, and took their midday meal in one of the precious few luncheon places recommended for ladies. The guide books had suggested the Criterion in Piccadilly Circus as convenient to the art galleries, and Gatti's in the Strand for a meal that was not too costly. They settled on the Criterion and ate in the basement room as the guide books had advised, rather than upstairs where the same dishes were served at higher prices. As it was *le diner Parisien* would have cost them five shillings had they chosen it; they did not, because they intended to be in France within a fortnight. Instead they selected the *table d'hôte* bill of fare at three and six, which Lizzie calculated to be something close to a dollar in American money.

Two things struck her as decidedly odd during lunch. The first of these was that although this was certainly a first-class restaurant, the men not only carried their hats into the dining room but carried them on their *heads* until they took their seats, this despite the presence of so many ladies in the room. The observation caused her to reevaluate her first impression of Albert Newbury, who'd kept his hat on his head all during the ride from Oxford to London. The second thing was that it was impossible to get a glass of water. The ladies were quick to learn that they were *expected* to order wine with their meal. As Alison

14

Newbury would later tell her, the English people, when thirsty, drank wine, beer "or something stronger." The simple white wine they ordered added an additional shilling and sixpence to their bill. Neither Lizzie nor Anna touched a drop of it.

After lunch Anna went back to the hotel for a nap, and the three other women—freed from her hypochondriacal tyranny —simply wandered the narrow streets at will, as they had read unescorted young ladies might do if they dressed sedately, walked fast and looked directly ahead of them. This was the part of their day, thus far, that most pleased Lizzie, although she was uncommonly aware of her frank and level gaze which, the guide books had warned, could easily be misinterpreted by foreigners. American girls—and she had never honestly thought about it before—had a habit, it seemed, of directly meeting the eyes of strangers, and she had no desire to be followed by any man eager for the chance of possible amusement. But, oh, so much to see in this marvelous city! Was she to walk with her head lowered and her eyes averted like a nun on her way to vespers?

Everything was new to the women, everything excited their interest. Like children deposited suddenly in a magic kingdom with unexpected treasures, they marveled at the simplest things that met their receptive eyes, chattering gaily, disregarding the warnings in the guidebooks, pointing and staring and rushing on to the next unimaginably clever wonder! The streetlamps here were taller than the ones at home (gas illuminated, of course, although the Hotel Albemarle was fully electrified), and each of them was equipped with a long, thin ladder resting against it, presumably to facilitate the lamplighter's task. The large iron cylinders on virtually every street corner were entirely alien to them, and when Lizzie timidly asked a policeman what they might be, he answered, "Why, pillar posts, ma'am!" and when he saw her bewildered expression, added, "In which to post your letters, ma'am." In almost the very next moment, a letter carrier dressed like a toy soldier in a little cap and blue sack suit with a red collar unlocked the cylinder and relieved it of its contents, carrying a stack of letters and parcels to a waiting mail wagon that resembled nothing so much as a little red circus cart on wheels, the letters *V.R.* painted on the side of it in gold.

15

"For Victoria *Regina!*" Rebecca translated triumphantly, and the women giggled and rushed off the pavement, having learned that crossing a London street was done in two stages. First you ran to a granite-block, oval-shaped platform in the middle of the roadway, a lamppost sprouting in its center, its circumference fortified by stout iron posts to ward off wagons. Next you caught your breath there while an avalanche of cabs, hansoms and horse-drawn vehicles of every shape and size thundered past, and then you rushed from the island to the other side of the street. If you were fortunate, a bobby would dash courageously into the maelstrom, raise up his gloved hand and, as if by silent proclamation, cause the horses and the rigs behind them to stop miraculously in their tracks. There were more policemen in London than Lizzie had ever seen anywhere! Wherever she looked, there seemed to be another bobby. ("Quite handsome, too," Felicity remarked.)

Crowds, oh, my Lord, the crowds! They seemed endless, rushing along the pavements (they were called pavements here, the women had learned from a bobby, and not sidewalks as they were at home), darting in and out of the various shops and restaurants, hurrying by in quadruple procession, risking life and limb as they raced the horse-drawn traffic in the streets, dashing from curb to island to the safety of curb again, six million people (though they seemed far more) going about their daily business as if there were not these ogling, overwhelmed, confused and delighted Americans in their very midst.

And the street cries, oh, the marvelous street cries! Everywhere about them there was a babble of voices as the vendors hawked their wares in a veritable operatic chorus. Here stood a bootblack shouting, "Clean yer boots, shine 'em, sir?" And just beside him was a man standing behind a tray of nuts bawling, "Jaw-work, up and under jaw-work, a whole pot for a ha'penny, hazel nuts!" And then, should the hazel nuts not appeal, "Warnuts, a penny for ten!" There were chimney sweeps whose faces were soiled a black as deep as their garments, shouting "Soot!" and "Sweep, ho!" and then turning to see that their equally begrimed apprentices were following close behind. On one corner stood a man selling meat on a skewer, and when Felicity wondered aloud what sort of meat it was, the man said, "Cat's meat, miss, you eat it without no salt!" and then bellowed

16

to a passing gentleman, "Cat's meat, sir?" A man, carrying his tools and apparatus buckled in a leather bag, shouted, "Mend yer bellows, mend 'em well!" and just beside him stood a frail young woman dressed in tatters and piping in a high, clear voice, "Come buy me fine myrtles and roses!"

The chorus became a blend of sound that was not at all unpleasant—"Stinkin' shrimps! Lor', 'ow they *do* stink today!"—a constant reminder of the rush of tumbling humanity in this city—"Buy my windmills, ha'penny a piece!"—male and female voices, aged men and withered crones, young boys and fresh-faced girls, "All a-growin', all a-blowin'! Knives, combs and inkhorns! Six bunches a penny, sweet lavender! Quick periwinkles! Sheep's trotters, hot! Cherries-o, ripe cherries-o! Lily-white mussels, penny a quart! Doormats, want? Brick dust today? Buy any clove water? Hot rolls! Rhubarb! Songs, three yards a penny! New Yorkshire cakes! Buy my matches, maids, my nice small, pointed matches! Buy a Beaupot! Buy a broom! Hot cross buns! Young lambs to sell! Tuppence a hundred, cockles! New-laid eggs, eight a groat! Samphire!"

The language these people spoke was English—but it was not English. And this had nothing to do with the words the women heard not only on the streets but everywhere around them (*tumbler* for *glass* in the restaurant, *basin* for *bowl* in the lavatory) or saw posted in shop windows, *print* for *calico*, and *cotton cloth* for *muslin*, *frock* or *gown* for *dress*, and *stays* for *corsets*. In one of the shops Rebecca learned that a writing pad was called a block of paper here, and when she said—in all innocence and intending a compliment—"Such a fine store, it must be very old indeed," the proprietor promptly said, "It's not a store at *all*, it's a *shop*, miss. I call a *store* a place for the sale of a miscellaneous lot of goods. *This* is a *shop*, miss!"

But more than that, more than the words that fell like Greek upon their American ears, there was the curious lilt and tone of the speech. Lizzie would later hear Alison define British as opposed to American English in terms of colors. "American English is yellow," she said. "British English is brown." And surely the British voice did seem pitched somewhat lower than the American. Moreover the average Englishman seemed to speak in a monotone until he reached the end of a sentence, at which point the voice rose to a higher note. It was Rebecca who commented (and she was a skillful pianist) that Englishwomen sounded as if they were speaking liquid music.

All was new and strange and fascinating in this bustling cosmopolis where a livery stable was adorned with a sign that read Job and Fly Master, or where men's clothing stores were distinguished by signs such as Hosier and Glover or Outfitters. Even the bakery windows, brimming with dishes of cakes and pastries, displayed tiny little cards identifying each exotic delicacy, the words alien to their eyes: Banbury Buns and Eccles Cakes, Sally Lunns and Scones. The confectionary stores carried items with names like Rocks and Jujubes and Voice Lozenges, and dozens more that were unfamiliar to the women. All of London seemed an exotic bazaar brimming with merchandise of the queerest sort: coats of arms and heraldic devices, cast-off jewelry, stones taken from fob seals and rings, secondhand books, tarnished silver, hand-me-down clothes. In a drugstore, where Rebecca had thought to buy a draught of iron and quinine to bolster her flagging energy, the druggist (chemist, as he was called here) said, "Oh, we can't give you that without a prescription, you know."

"We can buy it in America without one," Lizzie said.

"Aye, perhaps, ma'am," the druggist said. "But not here."

"Well," Lizzie said, "can you give my friend an ounce of tincture of iron?"

"Yes, ma'am."

"And a pair of two-grain quinine pills?"

"Yes, ma'am."

"And could you lend her a glass—a tumbler, that is—with a little water in it?"

"Why, yes, ma'am," the druggist said, looking extremely puzzled. When he brought the requested items to the counter, Lizzie added a dozen drops of iron to the water, and then held out the two quinine pellets to Rebecca, who swallowed them in a wink. The druggist was amazed.

"Now that is what I call clever," he said. "Very clever indeed."

She learned from Alison later on that whereas the man might indeed have been amazed by Lizzie's American ingenuity, he would have been even more confounded by the American penchant for patent medicines and the ease with which they were purchased in the United States. An English chemist—although he might offer for sale such items as face powder (which the fashionable London ladies were not wearing that year) or cologne and soap and toothbrushes—was almost exclusively in the business of putting up prescriptions, and was unfamiliar with a clientele who might walk in off the street to ask for a little aromatic spirits of ammonia after a reckless night of libation, or acid phosphate to counteract the aftereffects of nicotine or a glass (or a tumbler, or whatever one chose to call it) of Calisaya tonic. So whereas his refusal to honor Rebecca's request had seemed decidedly odd to the ladies, it was no odder to him than had been the request itself.

But Lizzie learned this only later, and for the moment it all seemed bewildering and strange and marvelously exciting, and she was as much exhausted by her own tumultuous reactions to this new world (imagine them calling *America* the New World!) as she was by the physical exertion of exploring it. When at last they made their way home—how odd that they already considered it "home"—to the Albemarle, she slipped out of her dress, corset and shoes, and lay down on the bed instantly, wearing only her underclothing and stockings, hoping for a short rejuvenating nap before the hush of evening descended upon this stimulating city. She was just beginning to doze—Rebecca was already asleep in the other bed—when the telephone rang, startling her out of her wits. There were telephones back in Fall River, of course, but certainly none in the Borden household, and none of them were quite like this one on the bedside table, with its short urgent ring sounding more like a warning than a summons. She groped for the instrument in the near gloom—Rebecca had drawn the curtains before they'd retired—brought the receiver to her ear, and mumbled, "Hello?"

"Miss Borden, this is the hall porter," a male voice said. "Will you accept a telephone call from Mrs. Newbury?"

"Mrs. Newbury?" Lizzie said, puzzled for the moment. "Oh, yes. Put her through, please."

She waited.

Alison's voice came onto the line, deep and rich and liquidly musical. "My dear Lizzie," she said, "I hope I'm not catching you at an awkward moment."

"No, no," Lizzie said. "Not at all."

19

"I tried ringing you earlier, but I suppose you and your friends were out on the town. Have you been enjoying our dismal little city?"

"We love it," Lizzie said.

"Ah, do you?" Alison said. "How nice. Is there anything at all we can do to help you get settled?"

"I can't think of anything," Lizzie said. "But it's very kind of you to ask."

"Well then, directly to the point," Alison said. "We *did* so enjoy our conversation with you on the train yesterday. Albert and I," she said. "And your friends, of course. Has Anna overcome her malaise? I do hope she has. We were wondering, Albert and I, if you might be free for tea this afternoon. I know it's rather the last minute, isn't it, but I promise I did try you earlier. We're in Kensington, just near the Cromwell Road—how silly of me, you don't know London, do you? But if you think you're able to come, I'll send my coachman round to collect you, say, at half-past four, a quarter to five. Albert should be home by then, and I know he'll be happy to see you again; he so admires Americans. Do you think you might possibly come? With your friends, of course, if you choose."

The "if you choose" made it sound, suddenly, as though Lizzie alone were being invited. She considered the propriety of abandoning her friends, wondered how long she was expected to stay for tea, wondered, too, if she could catch up with the others later for their evening meal. Rebecca had said something about asking the concierge (she was still unaccustomed to the term *hall porter*) to book some tickets for the D'Oyly Carte, which was performing *The Gondoliers* at the Savoy Theatre. Had Rebecca meant for tonight? If so, was there indeed time for tea and then supper before going to the theater?

"Lizzie? Are you there?"

"Yes, I am," Lizzie said.

"Have I quite overwhelmed you, my dear? I know I must sound rash and impulsive—but then again, Kate, nice customs curtsy to great kings."

The "Kate" confused Lizzie until she realized that Alison was quoting from one of the Shakespeare plays, though she couldn't exactly pinpoint which one. She thought to awaken Rebecca, who was sleeping peacefully in the other bed, a smile

20

on her face, to ask whether she would care to accompany her to tea at the Newburys—the prospect of going there alone frankly frightened her.

"I'm afraid I've made a dreadful mistake, haven't I?" Alison said. "Forgive me, do. And, Lizzie, if you *should* need any assistance, please don't hesitate to ask. I was quite sincere about my earlier . . ."

"I'd be delighted to come to tea," Lizzie said.

2: FALL RIVER—
1892

And of course the townspeople were crying for blood.

Blood insisted on more blood. Five full days since the murders, and even yet the crowds continued to gather in the dust, expecting a lightning bolt from above to dissipate the stifling heat together with the horror of what had happened. Murder and heat, Knowlton thought, a fine, shimmering pair.

He looked down at the square below.

The watering carts had already passed this way twice today, but there was no way of properly laying the dust in the summertime when the westerly wind drove it roiling up the hillside. In the spring, when there was rain in abundance, Fall River's roadways turned to dust to mud to dust again within hours. Today he would infinitely have preferred rain. Rain would have kept down the dust—and the crowds outside.

From where he stood at the open, second-story window of the old courthouse, Hosea Knowlton could smell the dust and hear the murmurings of the crowd below. The people had begun gathering before ten this morning, awaiting the arrival of the servant girl—he would have to remember to refer to her as "Maggie," the way the sisters did. This morning, when he'd questioned her, it had been Bridget Sullivan. Miss Sullivan this, or Miss Sullivan that. This afternoon, it would be Maggie. The *previous* servant girl had been a Maggie, apparently, and both sisters—either through indolence or indifference, he knew not which—preferred calling *this* one by the same name. Rather like replacing a beloved pet who's wandered off or died, he thought, and looked off to the south, from which direction the carriage would come. Masses of people were standing along the curbing for as far as he could see, thronging the approach streets to Court Square, waiting. For *what*? he wondered. For deliverance, of course. God give us some answers this afternoon.

He could remember a time when things seemed so much simpler. He had spent his boyhood in Maine, moving with his family to New Bedford when he was nineteen years old and his father, the Reverend Isaac Case Knowlton, accepted the position of pastor at the Universalist Church in that city. A scarce ten miles apart, Fall River was as familiar to him as was his adopted city of New Bedford. The courtroom in which he stood today might have been the sitting room of his own house on Cottage Street, so many times had he appeared here since his appointment as district attorney three years ago. The building itself never failed to please his eye: a stately piece of architecture it was, the entrance flanked with somewhat Grecian pillars supporting the pediment, the whole fashioned entirely of native granite. He felt at home in this building, in this room. If only there were not the baffling murders to contend with. If only the townspeople did not expect a hero today.

He scarcely thought of himself as a hero. He was, in his own eyes, a man of not more than medium height, somewhat portly at the age of forty-five, his sandy hair graying at the temples and receding somewhat higher on his forehead with each passing year, strands of gray threaded through his close-cropped beard as well. The beard felt decidedly uncomfortable on a day like today; the temperature at noon had stood at only seventy-nine degrees, but combined with the humidity that was enough to cause distress. Sweltering in black English worsted, high linen collar and black silk scarf, Hosea Knowlton, the people's *hero*, district attorney for the Second District, waited for Lizzie Borden—and perhaps a ray of hope.

There was an expectant hush from the crowd below. Knowlton looked toward South Main. Not a sign of the hack yet. The city marshal had served the summons this morning, and she was scheduled to appear at two. It was now almost that. He expected her attorney would arrive at about the same time; Jennings had already made it known that he intended to apply for permission to be present at the inquest. The Borden house on Second Street was less than an eighth of a mile away. The hack, when it came, would undoubtedly avoid Main Street, preferring instead to cross Pleasant and approach the court-house by the easterly side of Market Square.

Someone had sighted the hack. There! Drawn by two horses, with two ladies on the back seat and two police officers in civilian clothing up front. Men, women and children began scurrying for the narrow alleyway, choking the square. The driver laid his whip on the horses. The crowd cleared a way, and the hack veered in toward the curb in front of the court-house. The two officers stepped down first, Marshal Hilliard and another he did not recognize. He heard someone shout, "Stand back, stand back!" and then she stepped down out of the carriage, and Knowlton had his first glimpse of her.

She was wearing a blue dress of some sort, a blue hat. Her hair was as red as the heat itself, caught in a bun at the back of her head, stray ringlets spilling from beneath the wide brim of the hat. Odd that she isn't in mourning, he thought. Head held high as she moved through the silent crowd, followed now by the other woman who'd been in the hack, a friend, no doubt. He had heard them speak of Lizzie Borden's eyes. Gray, they had said. Steady, they had said, almost staring. Cold, they had said. Penetrating. He could not see her eyes from where he stood above. Nor could he any longer see her as she passed between the pillars and into the building.

God give us answers this afternoon, he thought.

Andrew Jackson Jennings had celebrated his forty-third birthday on the day before the murders; Knowlton could just imagine what a joy it had been for him, as the Borden attorney, to be summoned to the family's aid almost immediately after-wards. He listened to Jennings's argument before Judge Blaisdell, knowing full well his plea would be denied but none-theless admiring the man's talent and tenacity. Although he was

24

not very much taller than Knowlton himself, Jennings somehow affected the bearing of a man of considerable height, the impression fortified by a bristling gray mustache and a silvery mane of receding hair. Knowlton's notes told him only that the man was a graduate of Brown University—where he'd pitched for the Varsity baseball team—and later of the Boston University School of Law. Knowlton's observation told him that the man was skilled in the law and would be a formidable adversary should his client be charged with the murders and the case eventually come to trial. But his request for attendance at the inquest was argued to no avail. Judge Blaisdell listened soberly, intently and patiently, and then ruled against it.

On this Tuesday afternoon, August 9, there were only six people in the courtroom. The wooden doors were locked on the inside and guarded on the outside. The judge sat behind his bench, chin resting on his left hand, his right hand holding a large straw fan he moved occasionally in defense against the heat, his left hand now moving from his chin to seat his pince-nez more securely on the bridge of his nose. Before the bench sat Clerk Leonard, balding head and weary eyes, looking much like Father Time himself with his long white beard spilling over the front of his suit jacket, a Bible on the desk before him. To the right and somewhat apart was City Marshal Hilliard, sitting erect and attentive, shoulders back, his hand reaching up now to touch his handlebar mustache and then to run his fingers over his sloping forehead and short-cropped hair. Sitting near the witness chair, sharpened pencil poised over her open pad, was the court stenographer, Miss Annie White.

"Please make yourself comfortable, Miss Borden," Blaisdell said. "You understand, do you not, that we are here today only to make inquiry into the terrible tragedy that overtook us this past Thursday, and neither to accuse nor to incriminate."

Lizzie Borden said nothing. She sat quite still in the wooden chair, her hands clasped in her lap. She was still wearing hat and gloves. The courtroom shutters had been drawn against the glaring afternoon sun, but the room was still unbearably hot, and yet she had not taken off her gloves and, indeed, looked cool and implacable. Knowlton saw her eyes as she raised them to meet Blaisdell's. There was, indeed, something unsettling about her steady gray gaze, her stony silence now in response to

25

the judge's placating words. She might have been attractive, Knowlton thought, were it not for a plumpness about the jaw, only partially hidden by the ruffled collar about her neck. A good mouth, with a firm upper lip and a somewhat pouting lower, grimly set now as she continued to stare silently at the judge, not a trace of nervousness about her, sitting rather like a member of royalty called to account by her own retinue.

"Well, then," Blaisdell said. "Mr. Leonard, would you administer the oath, please?"

Knowlton watched as Clerk Leonard rose from where he was sitting, the Bible in his hand, and approached the witness. Good, churchgoing woman, he thought. Member of the Central Congregational Church for the past five or six years, member of the Christian Endeavor Society, did charity work at the Fall River Hospital—a decent, upright woman. *Could* she have killed her own father and stepmother? The Reverend W. Walker Jubb, of her own church, had taken for his sermon this Sunday past the first chapter of Ecclesiastes, ninth verse. *The thing that hath been is that which shall be; and that which is done is that which shall be done; and there is no new thing under the sun.* Perhaps not, Knowlton thought. Perhaps there *is* nothing new under the sun.

At the end of his sermon, Mr. Jubb had stepped to the side of the pulpit, or so the newspaper account had reported, and said, "I cannot close my sermon this morning without speaking of the horrible crime that has startled our beloved city this week, ruthlessly taking from our church household two respected and esteemed members. I cannot close without referring to my pain and surprise at the atrocity of the outrage. A more brutal, cunning, daring and fiendish murder I never heard of in all my life. What must have been the person who could have been guilty of such a revolting crime? One to commit such a murder must have been without heart, without soul, a fiend incarnate, the very vilest of degraded and depraved humanity, or he must have been a maniac. The circumstances, execution and all the surroundings cover it with mystery profound."

Lizzie Borden took off the glove on her left hand. She placed that hand on the extended Bible and then raised her right hand.

"I think I have the right," Mr. Jubb had said, "to ask for the prayers of this church and of my own congregation. The murdered husband and wife were members of this church, and a daughter now stands in the same relation to each one of you, as you—as church members—do to each other. God help and comfort her. Poor stricken girls, may they both be comforted, and may they both realize how fully God is their refuge."

She did not look too terribly stricken now, Knowlton thought, listening as she swore to tell the truth, the whole truth and nothing but the truth, so help her God. She put on her glove again as Leonard went back to his chair before the bench.

"Mr. Knowlton?" Blaisdell said.

Knowlton rose. "Your Honor?"

"May we begin, please?"

He walked to where she was sitting.

On Saturday last week he had been summoned from his home in New Bedford for a meeting with City Marshal Hilliard, State Officer Seaver, Medical Examiner Dolan, and Mayor Coughlin. He had recognized from the start the need to proceed with extreme caution, and had voiced his feelings to the others even before they explained what they had done by way of interrogation and investigation. The marshal showed him all the evidence he had collected, spreading notes, papers and documents on the tabletop, reporting on the various conversations with those who had first arrived at the scene of the crime and—most importantly—detailing the conversations with Bridget Sullivan and Lizzie Borden, the only two people who had been in or about the premises when the murders were committed. By the end of their consultation, Knowlton was convinced that an inquest was in order, and he announced to the reporters gathered outside the Mellen House that such inquest would be held immediately before Judge Josiah C. Blaisdell of the Second District Court of Bristol, in Fall River.

This was that court; this was that inquest.

He had listened this morning to the testimony of the servant girl, Bridget Sullivan. He had made copious notes at the Mellen House meeting, and had carefully read Miss White's transcript of the morning's testimony. His notes and the transcript were on the table behind him. He did not think he would need to refer to them; the facts, as he knew them, were firmly rooted in his mind. He wanted to learn now, firsthand, exactly how Lizzie Borden's version of what had happened differed from what he already knew.

27

He looked directly into her eyes.

"Give me your full name," he said.

"Lizzie Andrew Borden."

"Is it Lizzie or Elizabeth?"

"Lizzie."

"You were so christened?"

"I was so christened."

"What is your age, please?"

"Thirty-two."

"Your mother is not living?"

"No, sir."

"When did she die?"

"She died when I was two and a half years old."

"You do not remember her, then?"

"No, sir."

"What was your father's age?"

"He was seventy next month."

"What was his whole name?"

"Andrew Jackson Borden."

"And your stepmother? What is her whole name?"

"Abby Durfee Borden."

"How long had your father been married to your stepmother?"

"I think about twenty-seven years."

"How much of that time have they lived in that house on Second Street?"

"I think . . . I'm not sure . . . but I think about twenty years last May."

"Always occupied the whole house?"

"Yes, sir."

"Somebody told me it was once fitted up for two tenements."

"When we bought it, it was for two tenements, and the man we bought it of stayed there a few months until he finished his own house. After he finished his own house and moved into it, there was no one else ever moved in. We always had the whole."

He nodded. He walked deliberately and slowly away from her, back to his table, picked up a sheet of paper there and glanced at it, though he had no need to. On the day after the murders, Andrew Borden's brother-in-law had said in an interview, "Yes, there were family dissensions, although it has always been kept

28

very quiet. For nearly ten years there have been constant disputes between the daughters and their father and stepmother. It arose, of course, with regard to the stepmother. Mr. Borden gave her some bank stock, and the girls thought they ought to be treated as evenly as the mother. I guess Mr. Borden *did* try to do it, for he deeded to the daughters, Emma L. and Lizzie A., the homestead on Ferry Street, an estate of one hundred twenty rods of land, with a house and barn, all valued at three thousand dollars. This was in 1887." Knowlton meant to ask her about this now. There are no murders without motives, he reminded himself, and put the sheet of paper back on the table again, and walked again to where she was sitting.

"Have you any idea how much your father was worth?" he asked.

"No, sir."

"Have you ever heard him say?"

"No, sir."

"Have you ever formed any *opinion*?"

"No, sir."

"Do you know something about his real estate?"

"About what?"

"His real estate."

"I know what real estate he owned, part of it. I don't know whether I know it all or not."

"Tell me what you know of."

"He owns two farms in Swanzey . . . the place on Second Street and the A.J. Borden building and corner . . . and the land on South Main Street where McMannus is . . . and then, a short time ago, he bought some real estate up further south that, formerly he said, belonged to a Mr. Birch."

"Did *you* ever deed him any property?"

"He gave us, some years ago, Grandfather Borden's house on Ferry Street. And he bought that back from us some weeks ago, I don't know just how many."

"As near as you can tell," Knowlton said.

"Well, I should say in June, but I'm not sure."

"What do you mean by 'bought it back'?"

She turned from Knowlton and looked at the judge, as though questioning whether or not she had given her previous answer

29

in the English language. Somewhat testily, she said, "He *bought* it of us, and gave us the *money* for it."

"How much was it?"

"How much money?" she said, her voice still carrying a note of irritation. "He gave us five thousand dollars for it."

"Did *you* pay him anything when you took a deed from him?"

Again she looked at the judge. "*Pay* him anything?" she said, and turned back to Knowlton. "No, sir."

"How long ago was it you took a deed from him?"

"When he *gave* it to us?"

"Yes."

"I can't tell you. I should think five years."

"Did you have any other business transactions with him besides that?"

"No, sir."

"In real estate?"

"No, sir."

"Or in personal property?"

"No, sir."

"Never?"

"Never."

"No transfer of property one way or the other?"

"No, sir."

"At no time?"

"No, sir."

"And I understand he paid you the cash for this property."

"Yes, sir."

"You and Emma equally?"

"Yes, sir."

Knowlton nodded. He went back to his table, took what he hoped would seem a long time consulting the same sheet of paper, and then turned back to her. This time he held the paper in his hand. It was a transcript of the interview the brother-in-law had given last Friday. It read: "In spite of all this, the dispute about their not being allowed enough went on with equal bitterness. Lizzie did most of the demonstrative contention, as Emma is very quiet and unassuming and would feel very deeply any disparaging or angry word from her father."

"How many children has your father?" Knowlton asked.

30

"Only two."

"Only you two."

"Yes, sir."

"Any others ever?"

"One that died."

Knowlton nodded. Judge Blaisdell had begun fanning himself again. The court stenographer had caught up with the previous exchange. Her pencil stopped. She looked at the witness. Back to motive, Knowlton thought. On the day after the murders, Andrew J. Jennings had said that he had no particular desire to talk about the family affairs of the Bordens, but he admitted that as far as he knew, the murdered man had left no will. The estate would, as a matter of course, go to the daughters.

"Did you ever know of your father making a will?" Knowlton asked.

"No, sir . . . except I heard somebody say once that there was one several years ago. That is all I ever heard."

"Who did you hear say so?"

"I think it was Mr. Morse."

"What Morse?"

"Uncle John V. Morse."

John Vinicum Morse, Knowlton thought. About whom lawyer Jennings, in that same interview, when asked about the possibility of the murders having been committed by a member of the family, said, "Well, there are but two women of the household, and this man Morse. He accounts so satisfactorily for every hour of that morning, showing him to be out of the house, that there seems to be no ground to base a reasonable suspicion. Further than that, he appeared on the scene almost immediately after the discovery, from the outside, and in the same clothes that he had worn in the morning. Now, it is almost impossible that this frightful work could have been done without the clothes of the person who did it being bespattered with blood."

"How long ago?" Knowlton asked.

"How long ago I heard him say it? I haven't any idea."

"What did he say about it?"

"Nothing, except just that."

"What?"

"That Mr. Borden had a will."

31

"Did you ask your father?"

"I did not."

"Did he ever mention the subject of will to you?"

"He did not."

"He never told you that he had made a will, or had not?"

"No, sir.

"Did he have a marriage settlement with your stepmother? That you knew of?"

"I never knew of any."

"Had you heard anything of his *proposing* to make a will?"

"No, sir."

Which, of course, was the proper answer *if* she'd murdered him. And if her motive had been to murder him *before* he could draw a will, thereby insuring that his estate would go to her and her sister, as her own attorney had pointed out. He reminded himself that this was an inquest, not a trial. An inquest—by definition and by law—was a judicial inquiry, an investigation. He was here today to make inquiry, to investigate—not to accuse, not to judge. Perhaps, as the Reverend Jubb had postulated, the murderer might, after all, have been some fiend incarnate, the very vilest of degraded and depraved humanity, a maniac.

"Do you know of anybody that your father was on bad terms with?" he asked.

"There was a man that came there that he had trouble with. I don't know who the man was."

"When?"

"I can't locate the time exactly. It was within two weeks. That is . . . I don't know the date or day of the month."

"Tell all you saw and heard."

"I didn't *see* anything. I heard the bell ring, and father went to the door and let him in. I didn't hear anything for some time, except just the voices. Then I heard the man say, 'I would like to have that place, I would like to have that store.' Father said, 'I'm not willing to let your business go in there.' And the man said, 'I thought with your reputation for liking money, you'd let your store for anything.' Father said, 'You're mistaken.' Then they talked awhile, and then their voices were louder, and I heard father order him out, and went to the front door with him."

"What did he say?"

32

"He said that he'd stayed long enough, and he would thank him to go."

"Did he say anything about coming again?"

"No, sir."

"Did your *father* say anything about coming again? Or did *he*?"

"No, sir."

"Have you any idea who that was?"

"No, sir. I think it was a man from out of town, because he said he was going home to see his partner."

"Have you had any efforts made to find him?"

"We've had a detective. That's all I know."

"You haven't found him?"

"Not that I know of."

"You can't give us any other idea about it?"

"Nothing but what I've told you."

"Beside that, do you know of anybody that your father had bad feelings toward? Or who had bad feelings toward your father?"

"I know of one man that hasn't been friendly with him. They haven't been friendly for years."

"Who?"

"Mr. Hiram C. Harrington."

The very man who, in last Friday's interview, had said, among many other things, "Lizzie, on the contrary, was haughty and domineering, with the stubborn will of her father, and bound to contest for her rights. There were many animated interviews between father and daughter on this point. Lizzie is of a repellent disposition, and, after an unsuccessful passage with her father, would become sulky and refuse to speak to him for days at a time."

"What relation is he to him?" Knowlton asked, though he knew full well.

"He's my father's brother-in-law."

"Your mother's brother?"

"My father's only sister married Mr. Harrington."

Which noble in-law had *also* said, "Her father's constant refusal to allow her to entertain lavishly angered her. I've heard many bitter things she's said of her father, and know she was deeply resentful of her father's maintained stand in this matter."

A fine, true relative for a woman suspected of murder, Knowlton thought.

"Anybody else that was on bad terms with your father?" he asked. "Or that your father was on bad terms with?"

"Not that I know of."

"You have no reason to suppose that man you speak of—a week or two ago—had ever seen your father before? Or has since?"

"No, sir."

"Do you know of anybody who was on bad terms with your *stepmother*?"

"No, sir."

"Or that your stepmother was on bad terms with?"

"No, sir."

"Had your stepmother any property?"

"I don't know—only that she had half the house that belonged to her father."

"Where was that?"

"On Fourth Street."

"Who lives in it?"

"Her half sister."

"Any other property beside that? That you know of?"

"I don't know."

"Did you *ever* know of any?"

"No, sir."

"Did you understand that she was worth anything more than that?"

"I never knew."

"Did *you* ever have any trouble with your stepmother?"

"No, sir."

"Have you . . . within six months . . . had any words with her?"

"No, sir."

"Within a year?"

"No, sir."

"Within *two* years?"

"I think not."

"When last? That you know of?"

"About five years ago."

"What about?"

34

"Her stepsister. *Half* sister."

"What name?"

"Her name *now* is Mrs. George W. Whitehead."

"Nothing more than hard words?"

"No, sir, they were *not* hard words. It was simply a difference of opinion."

"You have been on pleasant terms with your stepmother since then?"

"Yes, sir."

"Cordial?"

Lizzie smiled. The smile quite transformed her face, startling him, the gray eyes softening, her mouth relaxing from its grim, set position of a moment earlier. "It depends on one's idea of cordiality, perhaps," she said.

Knowlton returned the smile. "According to *your* idea of cordiality," he said.

"Quite so," Lizzie said. She was still smiling.

"What do you mean by 'quite so'?"

"Quite cordial. I don't mean the *dearest* of friends in the world," she said, and leaned forward a bit, as though taking him into her confidence, "but very kindly feelings. And pleasant." The smile widened. "I don't know how to answer you any better than that."

"You didn't regard her as a mother," Knowlton said flatly, and the smile dropped from her face.

"Not exactly, no," she said, and paused. "Although she came here when I was very young."

"Was your relation toward her that of mother and daughter?"

"In some ways it was, and in some it wasn't."

"In what ways *was* it?" Knowlton asked.

"I decline to answer," Lizzie said.

Knowlton looked at her as though he hadn't quite heard her. He glanced at the stenographer. He looked at Blaisdell. Then he turned back to Lizzie.

"Why?" he asked.

"Because I don't know how to answer it."

Knowlton kept looking at her. At last, he said, "In what ways was it *not*?"

"I didn't call her mother," Lizzie said.

"What name *did* she go by?"

35

"Mrs. Borden."

"When did you begin to call her Mrs. Borden?"

"I should think five or six years ago."

"Before that time you'd called her mother?"

"Yes, sir."

"What led to the change?"

"The affair with her stepsister."

"So then the affair *was* serious enough to have you change from calling her mother, do you mean?"

"I didn't choose to call her mother," Lizzie said.

"Have you ever called her mother since?"

"Yes, occasionally."

"To her *face*, I mean."

"Yes."

"Often?"

"No, sir."

"Seldom?"

"Seldom."

"Your usual address was Mrs. Borden."

"Yes, sir."

"Did your sister *Emma* call her mother?"

"She always called her Abby. From the time she came into the family."

"Is your sister Emma older than you?"

"Yes, sir."

"What is *her* age?"

"She's ten years older than I am. She was somewhere about fourteen when she came there."

"What was your stepmother's age?"

"I don't know. I asked her sister Saturday, and she said sixty-four. I told them sixty-seven. I didn't know. I told as nearly as I know. I didn't know there was so much difference between she and father."

"Why did you leave off calling her mother?"

"Because I *wanted* to," Lizzie said.

"Is that all the reason you have to give me?"

"I haven't any other answer."

"Can't you give me any better reason than that?"

"I haven't any reason to give, except that I didn't *want* to."

"In what other respect were the relations between you and

36

her not that of mother and daughter? Besides not calling her mother?"

"I don't know that any of the relations were changes. I'd never been to her as a mother in many things. I always went to my sister. Because she was older and had the care of me after my mother died."

"In what respects *were* the relations between you and her that of mother and daughter?"

"That's the same question you asked before," Lizzie said. "I can't answer you any better now than I did before."

"You didn't say before you could *not* answer, but that you *declined* to answer."

"I decline to answer because I don't know what to say."

"That's the only reason?"

"Yes, sir."

Knowlton nodded. He moved closer to her chair, and—almost in a whisper, almost as though he were sharing a secret with her—said "You called your father . . . father?"

"Always."

"Were your father and mother happily united?"

Lizzie did not answer for several seconds. Then she said, "Why, I don't know but that they were."

"Why do you hesitate?" Knowlton asked.

"Because I don't know but that they were, and I'm telling the truth as nearly as I know it."

"Do you mean me to understand that they were *happy* entirely? Or *not*?"

"So far as I know, they were."

"Why did you hesitate then?"

"Because I didn't know how to answer you any better than what came into my mind. I was trying to think if I was telling it as I should. That's all."

"Do you have any difficulty in telling it as you should? Any difficulty in answering my questions?"

"Some of your questions I have difficulty in answering. Because I don't know just how you mean them."

Knowlton paused as though trying to frame his next question so that she would understand completely and without doubt *exactly* how he meant it. Slowly and deliberately he said, "*Did* you ever know of any difficulty between her and your father?"

37

"No, sir."

"Did he seem to be affectionate?"

"I think so."

"As man and woman who are married ought to be?"

"So far as I have ever had any chance of judging," she said, and lowered her eyes. He thought she was making reference to the fact that she was still unmarried at the age of thirty-two, and felt faintly reprimanded. For a moment, he was flustered. He said, as if in summary, "They were."

"Yes," she said simply.

Their eyes met, and held.

Abruptly, he asked, "What dress did you wear the day they were killed?"

"I had on a navy blue," she answered without hesitation, "sort of a bengaline. Or India silk skirt, with a navy blue blouse. In the afternoon, they thought I'd better change it." She paused. "I put on a pink wrapper."

"Did you change your clothing *before* the afternoon?" Knowlton asked.

"No, sir."

"You dressed in the morning—as you have described—and kept that clothing on until afternoon."

"Yes, sir."

A fly was buzzing somewhere in the courtroom above his head, near the gas fixture above his head. It distracted his attention. He looked up with some annoyance and recognized all at once how suffocatingly hot it was in this room. The heat still seemed not to affect her. She sat quite motionless, her gloved hands folded in her lap, her head erect watching him, waiting for his next question. For a moment he himself wondered what the next question might be. He had as yet uncovered no reasonable motive for her having committed the murders. As for the means, the only possible weapons found in the Borden house had not yet been delivered to Professor Wood of Cambridge for his examination and report. The only remaining avenue, for the time being, was to question her regarding opportunity. Her uncle, John Vinicum Morse, had unquestionably been away from the house on the morning of the murders. Had she *known* he would be gone? Had she indeed expected his arrival the day before?

38

The fly continued buzzing in the overhead fixture.

"When did Morse come there first?" Knowlton asked, rather more abruptly than he'd intended. "I don't mean *this* visit. I mean as a visitor. John V. Morse."

"Do you mean this day that he came and stayed all night?"

"No. Was this visit his *first* to your house?"

"He's been in the East a year or more."

"Since he's been in the East, has he been in the habit of coming to your house?"

"Yes. Came in any time he wanted to."

"Before that, has he been at your house? Before he came East?"

"Yes, he's been here . . . do you remember the winter that the river was frozen over and they went across? He was here that winter. Some fourteen years ago, was it not?"

"I'm not *answering* questions, but *asking* them," Knowlton said.

"I don't remember the date," Lizzie said, and in her voice there was as much ice as there must have been in that river fourteen years ago. "He was here that winter."

"Has he been here since?" Knowlton asked.

"He's been here once since. I don't know whether he has or not since."

"How many times this last year has he been at your house?"

"None at all, to speak of. Nothing more than a night or two at a time."

"How often did he come to spend a night or two?"

"Really, I don't know. I'm away so much myself."

"How much have you been away the last year?"

"I've been away a great deal in the daytime. Occasionally at night."

"Where in the daytime? Any particular place?"

"No. Around town."

"When you go off nights, where?"

"Never unless I've been off on a visit."

"When was the last time you've been away for more than a night or two before this affair?"

"I don't think I've been away to stay more than a night to two since I came from abroad. Except about three or four weeks ago, I was in New Bedford for three or four days."

39

"Where at New Bedford?"

"At Twenty Madison Street."

"How long ago were you abroad?"

"I was abroad in 1890."

Knowlton nodded impatiently. Her trip abroad was of absolutely no consequence to him, and he wondered why he'd even asked the question. He was determined to learn the whys and wherefores of John Vinicum Morse's visit. *Had* it been expected? *Had* she known he'd be leaving the house on the morning of the murders? And had she seized upon this circumstance as the opportunity for bloody mayhem?

"When did he come to the house?" he persisted. "The last time before your father and mother were killed?"

"He stayed there all night Wednesday night."

"My question is when he *came* there."

"I don't know. I wasn't at home when he came. I was out."

"When did you first *see* him there?"

"I didn't see him at all."

"How did you know he *was* there?"

"I heard his voice."

"You didn't see him Wednesday evening?"

"I did not. I was out Wednesday evening."

"You didn't see him Thursday morning?"

"I did not. He was out when I came downstairs."

"When was the *first* time you saw him?"

"Thursday noon."

"You had never seen him before that?"

"No, sir."

"Where were you Wednesday evening?"

"I spent the evening with Miss Russell."

"As near as you can remember, when did you return?"

"About nine o'clock that night."

"The family had then retired?"

"I don't know whether they had or not. I went right to my room. I don't remember."

"You didn't look to see?"

"No, sir."

"Which door did you come in at?"

"The front door."

"Did you lock it?"

"Yes, sir."

"For the night?"

"Yes, sir."

"And went right upstairs to your room?"

"Yes, sir."

He still had no information as to what she had known or not known of John Vinicum Morse's comings and goings, projected or otherwise. He moved closer to her. He put one hand on the witness chair. He leaned into her.

"When you came back at nine o'clock, you didn't look in to see if the family were up?"

"No, sir."

"Why not?"

"I very rarely do when I come in."

"You go right to your room."

"Yes, sir."

"Did you have a night key?"

"Yes, sir."

"How did you know it was right to lock the front door?"

"That was always my business."

"How many locks did you fasten?"

"The spring locks itself. And there's a key to turn. And you manipulate the bolts."

"You manipulated all those?"

"I used them all."

"Then you went to bed."

"Yes, directly."

"When you got up the next morning, did you see Mr. Morse?"

"I did not."

"Had the family breakfasted when you came down?"

"Yes, sir."

"What time did you come downstairs?"

"As near as I can remember, it was a few minutes before nine."

"Who did you find downstairs when you came down?"

"Maggie and Mrs. Borden."

"Did you inquire for Mr. Morse?"

"No, sir."

"Did you suppose he had gone?"

"I didn't know whether he had or not. He wasn't there."

41

"Your father was there?"

"Yes, sir."

"Then you found *him*?"

"Yes, sir."

"Did you speak to either your father or Mrs. Borden?"

"I spoke to all of them."

"About Mr. Morse?"

"I didn't mention him."

"Didn't inquire anything about him?"

"No, sir."

And *still* not the trace of a hint that she'd *known* who would or would not be in that house on that fateful morning. Why hadn't she gone to Marion as she'd planned? Had she stayed behind by design? To do the awful thing that had to be done in that house?

"Why didn't you go to Marion with the party that went?" he asked aloud, surprised when the thought found voice.

"Because they went sooner than I could. And I was going on Monday."

"Why did they go sooner than you could? What was there to keep you?"

"I had taken the secretaryship and treasurer of our C.E. society . . . had the charge . . . and the roll call was the first Sunday in August. And I felt I must be there and attend to that part of the business."

"Where was your sister Emma that day?"

"What day?"

"The day your father and Mrs. Borden were killed."

"She'd been in Fairhaven."

"Had you written to her?"

"Yes, sir."

"When was the last time you wrote to her?"

"Thursday morning. And my father mailed the letter for me."

"Did she get it at Fairhaven?"

"No, sir, it was sent back. She didn't get it at Fairhaven. For we telegraphed for her . . . and she got home here Thursday afternoon . . . and the letter was sent back to this post office."

"How long had she been in Fairhaven?"

"Just two weeks to a day."

"You did not visit her in Fairhaven?"

"No, sir."

42

"Had there been anybody else around the house that week? Or premises?"

"No, sir, not that I know of."

"Nobody had access to the house—so far as you know—during that time?"

"No, sir."

"I ask you once more how it happened that, knowing Mr. Morse was at your house, you did not step in and greet him before you retired."

"I have no reason. Except that I wasn't feeling well Wednesday, and so did not come down."

"No, you *were* down. When you came in from out."

"Do you mean Wednesday night?"

"Yes."

"Because I hardly ever *do* go in," Lizzie said. "I generally went right up to my room. And I did that night."

"Could you then get to your room from the back hall?" Knowlton asked.

"No, sir."

"From the back stairs?"

"No, sir."

"Why not? What would hinder?"

"Father's bedroom door was kept locked, and his door into my room was locked and hooked, I think. And I had no keys."

"That was the custom of the establishment?"

"It has always been so."

"It was so Wednesday? And so Thursday?"

"It was so Wednesday. But Thursday, they broke the door open."

"That was *after* the crowd came. Before the crowd came?"

"It was so."

"There was no access, except one had a key. And one would have to have *two* keys," Knowlton said.

"They would have to have two keys, if they went up the back way, to get into my room. If they were in my room, they would have to have a key to get into his room, and another to get in the back stairs."

Knowlton went back to his table. He sorted through the papers there and found the upstairs floor plan one of the police officers had made at the scene.

43

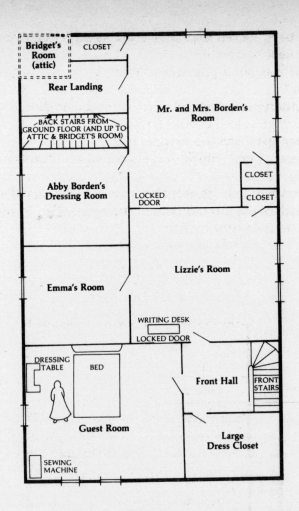

Studying the sketch, he walked back to the witness chair.
"Where did Mr. Morse sleep?"
"In the guest room, over the parlor in front of the stairs."
"Right up the same stairs that your room was?"
"Yes, sir."
"How far from your room?"
"A door opened into it."
"The two rooms connected directly?"
"By one door, that's all."
"Not through the hall?"
"No, sir."
"Was the door locked?"

"It has been locked and bolted, and a large writing desk in my room kept against it."

"Then it was not a practical opening."

"No, sir."

"How otherwise do you get from your room to the next room?"

"I have to go into the front hall."

"How far apart are the two doors?"

"Very near. I don't think more than so far." She spread her hands.

Knowlton nodded. He went back to his table and found the police sketch of the ground floor of the house. He carried it back with him to the witness chair.

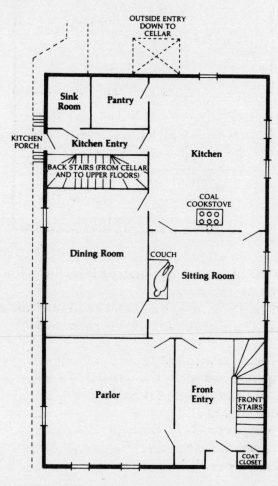

"Where was your father when you came down Thursday morning?" he asked.

"Sitting in the sitting room in his large chair, reading the *Providence Journal*," Lizzie said.

"Where was your mother?" Knowlton asked, and then immediately said, "Do you prefer me to call her Mrs. Borden?"

"I had as soon you called her mother," Lizzie said, and looked him directly in the eye. "She was in the dining room with a feather duster, dusting."

"When she dusted, did she wear something over her hair?"

"Sometimes when she swept. But not when dusting."

"Where was Maggie?"

"Just come in the back door with the long pole, brush, and put the brush on the handle, and getting her pail of water. She was going to wash the windows around the house. She said Mrs. Borden wanted her to."

"Did *you* get your breakfast that morning?"

"I didn't eat any breakfast. I didn't feel as though I wanted any."

"Did you get *any* breakfast that morning?"

"I don't know whether I ate half a banana. I don't think I did."

"You drank no tea or coffee that morning?"

"No, sir."

"And ate no cookies?"

"I don't know whether I did or not. We had some molasses cookies; I don't know whether I ate any that morning or not."

"Were the breakfast things put away when you got down?"

"Everything except the coffee pot. I'm not sure whether that was on the stove or not."

"You said nothing about Mr. Morse to your father or mother?"

"No, sir."

"What was the next thing that happened after you got down?"

"Maggie went out of doors to wash the windows, and father came out into the kitchen and said he didn't know whether he'd go down to the post office or not. And then I sprinkled some handkerchiefs to iron."

"Tell me again what time you came downstairs."

"It was a little before nine—I should say about a quarter. I don't know sure."

46

"*Did* your father go downtown?"

"He went down later."

"What time did he start away?"

"I don't know."

"What were you doing when he started away?"

"I was in the dining room, I think. Yes. I had just commenced, I think, to iron."

"It may seem a foolish question," Knowlton said, and smiled. "How *much* of an ironing did you have?"

"I only had about eight or ten of my best handkerchiefs."

"Did *you* let your father out?"

"No, sir. He went out himself."

"Did you fasten the door after him?"

"No, sir."

"Did Maggie?"

"I don't know. When she went upstairs, she always locked the door. She had charge of the back door."

"Did she go out after a brush *before* your father went away?"

"I think so."

"Did you say anything to Maggie?"

"I did not."

"Did you say anything about washing the windows?"

"No, sir."

"Did you speak to her?"

"I think I told her I didn't want any breakfast."

"You don't remember of talking about washing the windows?"

"I don't remember whether I did or not . . . I don't remember it. Yes, I remember. Yes. I asked her to shut the parlor blinds when she got through. Because the sun was so hot."

Knowlton nodded. The first question he had put to Bridget Sullivan this morning had been in regard to her whereabouts all through the morning of Thursday, August 4, up to the time of the murder. She testified that she'd been doing her regular work in the kitchen on the first floor. She had washed the breakfast dishes. She saw Miss Lizzie pass through the kitchen after breakfast time, and the young lady might have passed through again. She said she had finished up her work downstairs and resumed window washing on the third floor, which had been begun the preceding day. She *might* have seen Mrs.

47

Borden as she went upstairs; she could hardly remember. Mr. Borden had already left the house.

"About what time did you think your father went downtown?" Knowlton asked.

"I don't know. It must have been after nine o'clock. I don't know what time it was."

"You think at that time you'd begun to iron your handkerchiefs?"

"Yes, sir."

"How long a job was that?"

"I didn't finish them. My flats weren't hot enough."

"How long a job *would* it have been? If the flats had been right?"

"If they'd been hot . . . not more than twenty minutes, perhaps."

"How long *did* you work on the job?"

"I don't know, sir."

"How long was your father gone?"

"I don't know that."

"Where were you when he returned?"

"I was down in the kitchen."

"What doing?"

"Reading an old magazine that had been left in the cupboard. An old *Harper's Magazine*."

"Had you got through ironing?"

"No, sir."

"Had you *stopped* ironing?"

"Stopped for the flats."

"Were you waiting for them to be hot?"

"Yes, sir."

"Was there a fire in the stove?"

"Yes, sir."

"When your father went away . . . you were ironing them."

"I hadn't commenced. But I was getting the little ironing board and the flats."

Knowlton hesitated before putting his next question. This morning Bridget Sullivan had testified under oath that she'd heard Miss Lizzie on the *stairs* when she was letting Mr. Borden in after his walk downtown. Lizzie had just told him she was down in the kitchen when he returned.

48

"Are you *sure* you were in the kitchen when your father returned?" he asked.

"I'm not sure whether I was there or in the dining room."

"Did you go back to your room before your father returned?"

"I think I did carry up some clean clothes."

"Did you *stay* there?"

"No, sir."

"Did you spend *any* time up the front stairs before your father returned?"

"No, sir."

"Or *after* he returned?"

"No, sir. I did stay in my room long enough when I went up to sew a little piece of tape on a garment."

"What was the time when your father came home?"

"He came home after I came downstairs."

"You were not *upstairs* when he came home?"

"I was not upstairs when he came home. No, sir."

"What was Maggie doing when your father came home?"

"I don't know whether she was there or whether she'd gone upstairs. I can't remember."

"Who let your father in?"

"I think he came to the front door and rang the bell. And I think Maggie let him in. And he said he'd forgotten his key. So I think she must have been downstairs."

"His key would have done him no good if the locks were left as you left them," Knowlton said.

"But they were always unbolted in the morning," Lizzie said.

"Who unbolted them that morning?"

"I don't think they'd *been* unbolted. Maggie can tell you."

"If he hadn't forgotten his key, it would have been no good."

"No. He had his key and couldn't get in. I understood Maggie to say he said he'd forgotten his key."

"You didn't hear *him* say anything about it."

"I heard his voice. But I don't know what he said."

"I understood you to say *he* said he'd forgotten his key."

"No. It was *Maggie* said he said he'd forgotten the key."

"Where was Maggie when the bell rang?"

"I don't know, sir."

"Where were *you* when the bell rang?"

"I think in my room upstairs."

49

"Then you *were* upstairs when your father came home."

"I don't know sure. But I think I was."

"What were you doing?"

"As I say, I took up these clean clothes, and stopped and basted a little piece of tape on a garment."

"Did you come down before your father was let in?"

"I was on the stairs coming down when she let him in."

"Then you were *upstairs* when your father came to the house on his return."

"I think I was."

"How long had you been up there?"

"I had only been upstairs long enough to take the clothes up and baste the little loop on the sleeve. I don't think I'd been up there over five minutes."

"Was Maggie still engaged in washing windows when your father got back?"

"I don't know."

"You remember, Miss Borden—I will call your attention to it so as to see if I have any misunderstanding, not for the purpose of confusing you. You remember that you told me several times that you were *downstairs*, and not *upstairs*, when your father came home. You've forgotten, perhaps."

"I don't know *what* I've said," Lizzie answered, shaking her head violently from side to side. "I've answered so *many* questions, and I'm so *confused* I don't know one thing from another!" She took a deep breath. Her eyes met his again. "I'm telling you just as nearly as I know," she said.

"Calling your attention to what you said about that a few minutes ago," he said calmly, "and now *again* to the circumstance, you've said you were *upstairs* when the bell rang, and were on the stairs when Maggie let your father in. Which—*now*—is your recollection of the *true* statement of the matter? That you were *downstairs* when the bell rang and your father came?"

"I think I was downstairs in the kitchen."

"And then you were *not* upstairs."

"I think I was not. Because I went up almost immediately . . . as soon as I went down . . . and then came down again and stayed down."

50

"What had you in your mind when you said you were on the stairs as Maggie let your father in?"

"The other day, somebody came there and she let them in, and I was on the stairs. I don't know . . . whether the morning before or when it was."

"You understood I was asking you exactly and explicitly about this fatal day?"

"Yes, sir."

"I now call your attention to the fact that you had specifically told me you'd gone *upstairs*, and had been there about five minutes when the bell rang, and were on your way *down*, and were on the *stairs* when Maggie let your father in that day."

"Yes, I said that. And then I said I didn't *know* whether I was on the stairs or in the kitchen."

"*Now* how will you have it?"

"I think . . . as nearly as I know . . . I think I was in the kitchen."

He knew he would not, at the moment, get more from her on that single important point. She seemed to have lost control back then, but only for the briefest instant, and she'd recovered again almost at once. The most *telling* thing about her testimony, he realized all at once, was that from the very start she had adopted an adversary position. Small wonder when Mayor Coughlin had bluntly and inadvisedly told her, on the very day they'd put her father and stepmother in the ground, that she herself was suspected of having committed the murders. But given this advance warning, as it were, should she not now have been more eager to assist, in every way possible, toward finding a solution that pointed to someone *other* than herself? Why had she adopted this oddly belligerent posture—the stubborn set of mouth and jaw, the pale fire in her gray eyes—unless she herself was indeed the "maniac" the Reverend Jubb had described?

"How long was your father gone?" Knowlton asked, his voice softer. There was no sense bullying her now. She was composed again, and she would only resist such an approach.

"I don't know, sir. Not very long."

"An hour?"

"I shouldn't think so."

51

"Will you give me the best story you can, so far as your recollection serves you, of your time while he was gone?"

"I sprinkled my handkerchiefs. And got my ironing boards. And took them in the dining room. And left the handkerchiefs in the kitchen on the table, and . . . whether I ate any cookies or not, I don't remember. Then I sat down looking at the magazine, waiting for the flats to heat. Then I went in the sitting room and got the *Providence Journal* and took that into the kitchen. I don't recollect of doing anything else."

"What did you read first? The *Journal* or the magazine?"

"The magazine."

"You told me you were reading the magazine when your father came back."

"I said in the kitchen, yes."

"Was that so?"

"Yes. I took the *Journal* out to read, and hadn't read it. I had it near me."

"You said a minute or two ago you read the magazine awhile, and then went and got the *Journal* and took it out to read."

"I did. But I didn't read it. I tried my flats then."

"And went back to reading the magazine?"

"I took the magazine up again, yes."

"When did you last see your mother?"

"I didn't see her after . . . when I went down in the morning and she was dusting the dining room."

"Where did you or she go then?"

"I don't know where *she* went. I know where *I* was."

"Did *you* or *she* leave the dining room first?"

"I think I did. I left her in the dining room."

"You never saw her or heard her afterwards?"

"No, sir."

"Did she say anything about making the bed?"

"She said she'd been up and made the bed up fresh, and had dusted the room and left it all in order. She was going to put some fresh pillow slips on the small pillows at the foot of the bed, and was going to close the room because she was going to have company Monday and she wanted everything in order."

"How long would it take to put on the pillow slips?"

"About two minutes."

"How long to do the rest of the things?"

52

"She'd done that when I came down."

"All that was left was *what*?"

"To put on the pillow slips."

"Can you give me any suggestions as to what occupied her when she was up there? When she was struck dead?"

"I don't know of anything. Except she had some cotton-cloth pillowcases up there, and she said she was going to commence to work on them. That's all I know. And the sewing machine was up there."

"Whereabouts was the sewing machine?"

"In the corner between the north and west side."

"Did you hear the sewing machine going?"

"I did not."

"Did you see anything to indicate that the sewing machine had been used that morning?"

"I had not. I didn't go in there until after everybody had been in there, and the room had been overhauled."

"If she'd remained downstairs, you would undoubtedly have seen her."

"If she'd remained downstairs, I should have. If she'd remained in her *room*, I should not have."

"You didn't see her at all?"

"No, sir. Not after the dining room."

"After that time," Knowlton said thoughtfully, "she must have remained in the guest chamber."

"I don't know."

"So far as you can judge."

"So far as I can judge, she might have been out of the house. Or in the house."

"Had you any knowledge of her going *out* of the house?"

"No, sir."

"*Had* you any knowledge of her going out of the house?" Knowlton asked again.

"She told me she'd had a note. Somebody was sick. And said, 'I am going to get dinner on the way.' And asked me what I wanted for dinner."

"Did you tell her?"

"Yes. I told her I didn't want anything."

"Then why did you not suppose she'd gone?"

"I supposed she'd gone."

53

"Did you hear her come back?"

"I didn't hear her go or come back, but I supposed she went."

"When you found your father dead," Knowlton said, and paused. "You supposed your mother had gone?"

"I didn't know. I said to the people who came in, 'I don't know whether Mrs. Borden is out or in. I wish you'd see if she's in her room.'"

"You supposed she was out at the time?"

"I understood so. I didn't *suppose* about anything."

"Did she tell you where she was going?"

"No, sir."

"Did she tell you who the note was from?"

"No, sir."

"Did you ever *see* the note?"

"No, sir."

"Do you know where it is now?"

"No, sir."

"She said she was going out that morning?"

"Yes, sir."

Judge Blaisdell cleared his throat. Knowlton turned toward the bench.

"Your Honor?" he said.

"Mr. Knowlton, the hour's almost six, and Miss Borden appears a trifle weary. I wonder if we might continue this in the morning."

"Yes, of course," Knowlton said at once.

"Miss Borden?" Blaisdell said. "Would ten o'clock be a convenient hour for you?"

"Yes, sir," Lizzie said.

"This hearing is adjourned till ten tomorrow morning," Blaisdell said.

3: LONDON—1890

The Newbury house looked rather forbidding.

Surrounded by a tall iron fence (the coachman stepped down to open the gilded gate), approached by a driveway that circled round a grassy oval, it resembled nothing so much as the courthouse back home in Fall River, with its Grecian columns and solid gray stonework. She climbed two low, flat steps to the massive wooden front door, lifted the handsome brass knocker fashioned in the shape of a Medusa with snaky locks, let the knocker fall, and waited. The door opened almost at once. A pretty young woman, wearing a black dress, a white apron and a lacey black cap, smiled out at Lizzie, and in an Irish accent said, "Miss Borden, mum? Do come in, please, mistress is expecting you."

The interior of the house came as something of a surprise. The floor of the vestibule was paved in alternating squares of black and white marble. Immediately facing the entrance door was a mantelpiece upon which stood a pair of terra-cotta vases. To one side of the mantel was a carved oaken bench; to the other was a Gothic-style chair that looked like a king's throne. An ornately designed bronze umbrella stand, its supporting rod

55

decorated with sculpted flowers and flanked by sculpted birds resembling flamingos, stood to one side of an opening beyond which a short flight of steps led downward to another area. Plant stands and pedestals surrounded the umbrella stand, creating a flowering arbor in which the sculpted birds seemed quite at home. On the other side of the opening was a statue of a voluptuous nude woman, surely Italian in origin, its marble illuminated by the soft light of the gas fixture overhead. Beyond the steps was a paneled wall. One of the huge doors in that wall opened, and Alison came through it, a smile on her face, her hand extended.

"Do forgive our monstrous home," she said at once. "It's Palladian, I fear, and quite out of fashion at the moment."

She was wearing a satin tea apron over a skirt and blouse, the apron edged with embroidery and pastel satin ribbons. Her blond hair, frizzed onto her forehead in front, was swept straight back into a French twist and a bun worn rather higher than American women were wearing them.

"Moira," she said to the maid, "do bring in the tea, won't you? Come in, dear Lizzie, come in," she said, and took Lizzie's hand in both her own and led her into a room that quite took her breath away.

"You'll find the drawing room a bit cluttered," Alison said. "Albert *so* loves clutter. Please sit down, my dear. Tea will be here in a moment."

She had called it a drawing room, and Lizzie assumed it was the equivalent of what at home would have been either their parlor or sitting room. But, oh, the immensity of it! A fireplace dominated the room, a carved wooden mantel above it—stained the same darkish brown as the woodwork and the bookshelves—a brass coal scuttle beside it, a huge mirror in a gilded frame above it. The bookshelves ran around all four walls of the room, standing as tall as Lizzie herself did, brimming with books bound in red and green leather. The wallpaper above the bookshelves echoed the books themselves, a leafy green embossed upon a deep red field. The carpeting on the floor looked to be Oriental, with glowing reds and muted beiges and here and there a touch of blue that complemented the jungle green of the wallpaper's embossing. The green was again repeated in the plush velvet upholstery on a buttoned, padded sofa

56

and the armchairs beside it. As in the vestibule outside, there were any number of stands topped with blooming flowers and ferny plants, as well as lower inlaid tables bearing porcelain and glass. In one corner of the room—

A knock sounded at the door. The maid came in and placed the tea tray on a gateleg table flanked by a smaller sofa (again done in the green plush velvet) and two chairs upholstered in red.

"Thank you, Moira," Alison said, and the maid curtsied and soundlessly left the room.

"Now then," Alison said, "would you prefer lemon or milk?"

"Milk, please," Lizzie said, and sat in one of the armchairs facing the sofa.

"We've all sorts of goodies to tempt you," Alison said, and began pouring from a richly ornamented silver pot.

In one corner of the room was a small, upright piano with music spread on its rack and a piano stool before it. There was a needlework cushion on the stool's seat, and all about the room were framed needlework samplers. Lizzie wondered all at once if the handiwork was Alison's. She wondered, too, if the predominately green theme of the upholstery and heavy draperies had been deliberately selected to complement Alison's eyes. Behind the drapes on each window were white lace curtains that seemed a trifle gray from London's interminable soot. A writing desk stood against a wall upon which hung framed water colors of nude women frolicking in a vernal—

". . . to be making your first trip abroad *now*," Alison was saying.

"Pardon?" Lizzie said.

"Our clutter has overwhelmed you," Alison said, smiling.

"No, it's . . . beautiful," Lizzie said. "Forgive me, I was simply admiring everything."

"The cottage is Albert's," Alison said.

"The cottage?"

"The small piano. He plays abominably, but it relaxes him after a day of coping with high finance. He should be here by now, but undoubtedly he's been buttonholed by one of his money-worshiping cronies. Sugar?"

"Yes, please," Lizzie said. "You were saying earlier?"

"Only that you're fortunate to be making your first trip

abroad *now*, and not ten years ago—or even *five*, for that matter."

"How do you mean?" Lizzie asked.

She considered herself fortunate to be making the trip at any time, and she could scarcely believe the stroke of good luck that had led first to their chance encounter on the train, and now *this*—to be invited into an English home! And *such* a home! As Alison continued speaking, Lizzie's eyes roamed the room in wonder, touching upon the silver everywhere about, and the framed paintings and drawings, the cut-glass decanters, the bric-a-brac, the dark mahogany cabinet with its glass doors and its fine china within, the iridescent globes on the unlighted gas fixture overhead, the—

". . . convenience, of course. Until last year, the only London hotel offering separate tables for dining in public was the St. James—quite near you, in fact—on the corner of Piccadilly and Berkeley Street. Now there's the Savoy, of course, and many other such establishments where a well-bred *lady*" (and she rolled her eyes) "can dare to dine in public with a friend of her own sex, and without the fortifying presence of family or spouse. One can even dine at the Savoy on a *Sunday* now, rather than rushing off to Evensong, or wherever it is religious people are always scurrying to in the fog. You're quite fortunate, truly."

There was in Alison's voice, as a counterpoint to its low and typically English musicality, a note of—mockery, was it?—and Lizzie felt somewhat uncomfortable in her presence. She could not imagine any respectable woman of her acquaintance making sport, first, of the cherished precepts of ladylike expectation, and next—not a moment later—of religion, which Lizzie considered the mainstay of her life in Fall River. Nor could she imagine that Alison would have dared to speak so boldly in the presence of her husband. And yet, hadn't there been that same challenging tone on the train when Albert was talking about naming a child? "Note the male posture," Alison had said, with the same slight raising of her eyebrows, the same half smile on her mouth, the same liltingly derisive edge to her voice.

"Not too many years ago, had you been a woman traveling alone," she said now, "and I include your friends, of course—*women* traveling alone—you'd have taken a hotel in Bond Street, most likely, or perhaps Cork Street, and your accommodations

58

would have included a dining room of your own. *Horrors* to have thought that a proper *lady* would have rubbed elbows with strangers at a common table in the coffee room below! Nor would you have enjoyed, as I'm sure you do at the Albemarle, the conveniences of running water and a gas fire, though I imagine the Albemarle has those new electric radiators, has it not?"

"Yes, it does," Lizzie said. She was thinking that she herself would not have enjoyed dining with strangers, either, and she was grateful for the separate tables offered at the Albemarle last night and at the Criterion this noon.

"You'll find things have changed on the Continent as well," Alison said, "though most of the women there still consider any visiting American girl an opportunist."

"Opportunist?" Lizzie said.

"Yes. Setting her cap for marriage to a titled foreigner with scads of money. *You're* not looking for a French or Italian nobleman, are you?"

"No, of course not," Lizzie said, and lowered her eyes.

"Am I embarrassing you?" Alison asked.

"Why would you be?"

"I shouldn't think I was, but nowadays so *much* pressure is put upon young women to marry—how old *are* you, Lizzie?"

"Thirty," Lizzie said. "Just."

"I would have thought much younger."

"Thank you."

"There's something so . . . fresh about you," Alison said.

"Well . . . thank you," Lizzie said again.

"Which could be said about *most* American girls, I suppose. Forgive me, I had no desire to dilute my compliment. It's just that here in the Old World, we've become so accustomed to the sort of woman we see everywhere about us that American girls take us quite by storm. So open and frank, so—well, fresh *is* the word for it, after all. Now I *am* embarrassing you, do forgive me."

"I'm flattered," Lizzie said.

"One grows *so* weary of our young English girls, with their horsey ways, their lack of elegance and their brusque manner of walking," Alison said. "And how tiresome the French girls are, those humble violets of supposed femininity. The American

59

girl is more like an orchid, I would say, blooming in a way that surprises me incessantly. Beautiful, dazzling, it first charms by its strangeness, and then intoxicates with its subtle perfume. It lives on air, an orchid, and needs none of the material conditions of existence for other plants. The surprise is that it often comes from a gnarled stem which seems to defy beauty. Yet from this hideous stem, it blossoms frequently—with singular, but always incomparable, attractiveness. The American girl is surely the orchid among all feminine flowers."

Lizzie was struck speechless.

"Considering the more than eleven thousand virgins who migrate semiannually from America to the shores of England and France," Alison said, "one might be compelled to argue that there *is* no such creature as *the* American girl, since—like the orchid—she comes in many different species and varieties. And, certainly, I've met or observed a great many American girls who commit the commonest sins—or *supposed* sins," she added, "against public manners, like loud laughing and talking in hotel parlors or *salles à manger*. But rarely is she badly dressed, however unmusical her cackle, however much slang may pepper her speech. Her stylishness, of course, may be due either to the quickness of her eye or the length of her purse; one has no way of judging. But surely Paris dresses her *à ravir*, and she wears her clothes like a queen—or, rather, as queens but seldom do."

Lizzie was staring at her now, quite overwhelmed.

"Here in the Old World," Alison said, "the American girl is certain of attracting any young man who's abused life, who's a little blasé, and who—to be captivated—has need of what we call *du montant*. But, surely, it's the same for you at home, is it not? Your father must be plagued by gentlemen callers ringing your doorbell day and night."

"Well . . . no," Lizzie said.

"No?" Alison said. "I'm surprised, truly. I should have thought just the opposite. You have such marvelous color, Lizzie, that wonderfully fiery hair, and those incredible gray eyes. It's a pity cosmetics are so frowned upon these days—oh, a little pearl powder, perhaps, or a faint dusting from a *papier poudré*, but only for *married* women, of course," she said, and again rolled her eyes. "But how I would love to rouge your cheeks—or my *own*, for that matter—as many dotty dowagers do, or daub a

60

bit of lip salve on your mouth, or line your eyes with kohl as black as Cleopatra must have used. How silly of me, you're quite beautiful enough without any artifice."

"I've . . . never considered myself beautiful," Lizzie said, and realized she was blushing.

"Are there no looking glasses in all of Fall River then?" Alison asked, and smiled.

"You're too kind."

"Too honest, perhaps. I had no intention of making you blush."

"I fear I am," Lizzie said.

"But that is part of your American charm, dear Lizzie," Alison said, and leaned across the low table between them to pat her hand as she had done on the train.

"I'm not sure I've ever had a conversation quite like this one," Lizzie said, and smiled.

"The broadening influence of travel," Alison said, and returned the smile. "But surely you have female companions at home."

"Yes, but . . ."

"Well, what do you talk about *there*?"

"I'm not certain, actually. We talk about various matters, I suppose."

"Matters such as . . ."

"Well . . . matters that might interest us."

"And what might interest you, Lizzie?"

"The same things that might interest any woman my age. The church, of course . . ."

"Are you a regular churchgoer then?"

"I am."

"Then you must forgive my earlier reference to Evensong."

"I took no notice of it," Lizzie said politely.

"And what other matters? Other than church matters?"

"The things that interest women most."

"Such as?"

"Well, I'm sure it's the same here in England."

"I'm sure. But tell me."

"Well, cooking, of course . . . I suppose we discuss recipes a great deal. And needlework . . . all sorts of needlework. I see you have some about. Is it your own handiwork?"

61

"Perish the thought," Alison said. "I should sooner dig ditches."

"Well . . . as I say . . . embroidery and knitting and common sewing. And other things, of course."

"What other things?"

"Flowers . . . our gardens. And books we've read . . . or magazine articles. The same as here, I'm sure."

"Which magazines do you read, Lizzie?"

"*Harper's Bazaar*, of course. And *Peterson's Magazine*, and *Godey's Lady's Book*, and *Frank Leslie's Gazette of Fashion* . . ."

"Fashion interests you, I can tell. You dress so beautifully."

"Well, thank you," Lizzie said again. She could not imagine such wild compliments—or was it simply European flattery?—from a woman herself so beautiful. Again she felt herself blushing.

"How prettily you blush," Alison said. "And the books you read? What of those?"

"I can scarcely recall, I've read so many. Let me see. This past spring, I think it was, I read *The American Commonwealth* . . ."

"Ah, by one of ours, an Oxford professor."

"Yes, James Bryce."

"Why such a learned volume?"

"I was interested in his views on the United States."

"'Sailing a summer sea,' wasn't that his metaphor? 'And setting a course of responsible liberty that will be a model for the world.'"

"He perhaps flattered us too much," Lizzie said, and her eyes met Alison's directly.

"As *I* flatter *you*, do you mean?" she said, picking up the challenge at once. "But surely there's a line between honest praise and flattery, is there not? And equally as certain, one who denies a compliment only seeks the same compliment twice."

"Well, I . . . I really wasn't . . ."

"And now I've flustered my Lizzie," Alison said. "Forgive me. Tell me what else you've been reading."

"*Time and Free Will* . . ."

"Ah, yes, *Essai sur les données*, et cetera, et cetera. I read it in the French. Did it interest you?"

"I found it . . . difficult."

62

"Perhaps something was lost in translation," Alison said.

"Perhaps."

"What else? Do you read many novels?"

"Those that are proper for me to read, yes."

"Proper?"

"Morally acceptable."

"Such as?"

"I've just finished *A Connecticut Yankee in King Arthur's Court.*"

"Ah, your clever Mark Twain, yes. Did you read it as preparation?"

"Preparation?"

"For your journey here?"

"Oh, no. Only for pleasure."

"And was it morally acceptable?"

"I would say so."

"And what else? For pleasure."

"*Looking Backward,*" Lizzie said. "Are you familiar with it?"

"I'm afraid not."

"It's a sort of Utopian novel about the United States in the year 2000. It describes how all industry has been nationalized and all wealth equally distributed, and it . . ."

"How perfectly horrible!" Alison said, "I'm sure I shouldn't want *my* wealth distributed, equally or otherwise. Are you wealthy, Lizzie?"

"I wouldn't call ourselves wealthy, no. We're comfortable, I suppose . . ."

"Ah, that delicious American word, 'comfortable.' What sort of work does your father do?"

"He's a banker," Lizzie said. "That is, he's involved with several banks in Fall River. And he owns property here and there. But I shouldn't say we're wealthy, no."

"Do you live in a grand old house on a hill somewhere? I *love* those photographs of American houses high on hilltops."

"No, we're close to the center of town, actually. And the house isn't grand at all."

"Fully electrified, I'm sure."

"We don't even have gas illumination."

"But, my poor darling, how do you *see*? To read all these *books* you've been telling me about?"

"We have lamps, of course. And candles."

"Like your Abraham Lincoln."

"Well, we don't use candles unless we're out of lamp oil."

"Great big candles in heavy brass candlesticks, I'm sure."

"Some of them, yes. And some of them rather old. One particularly handsome one used to belong to my mother's mother. We keep it in the spare room across the hall. Emma says it's eighteenth century. I would suppose it came from England."

"Emma?"

"My sister."

"And your mother? What sort of woman is she, Lizzie?"

"My mother is dead," Lizzie said. "She died when I was two years old. I don't remember her at all."

"Has your father remarried?"

"Yes," Lizzie said, and paused. "How did you know that?"

"Well, they *all* do, don't they?" Alison said, and smiled. "And in this candlelit house of yours . . ."

"Lamps, usually," Lizzie said.

". . . are there many servants?"

"We have only one. A girl from Ireland. Her name is Bridget Sullivan, but we call her Maggie. My sister and I."

"Maggie? But how odd."

"Our previous girl was named Maggie."

"You must have been very fond of her. The previous girl."

"No, it's just . . . habit, I suppose. Calling her Maggie."

"Is she comely, your Maggie?"

"I would guess. I never really noticed. She's young and healthy, and we get along quite well with her."

"How young?"

"Maggie? Twenty-three, I would suppose. Twenty-four. Somewhere in there."

"Do many people in your town have servants?"

"Some. Not all. Not very many, I guess." She paused, and then said, "How many servants do you have?"

"Far too many, I'm sure," Alison said, and laughed. "You met George, of course, who was kind enough to fetch you, and Moira, who deigned to interrupt her nap when you rapped on the door, and later served our tea. We've a gardener and a cook, but I don't employ a personal maid, and Albert is quite capable of buttoning his own shoes. Neither have we any need for a nursemaid, thank heavens."

"A person who employed such a staff would be considered very wealthy in America," Lizzie said.

"Oh, we're not half so wealthy as Albert would *wish* us to be," Alison said, and again laughed. "There are families here in London—high society, don't you know—who keep a staff of twenty or more, scurrying about underfoot. I should expect it costs them a quarter of their income annually—Lizzie dear, you *must* forgive me! We British haven't the slightest qualm about discussing personal finance. In ten minutes' time, a British stranger will ask you how large your fortune is. And, moreover, he'll expect a reply. There's nothing rude about it; it's merely a national trait, our obsession with money. How large *is* your fortune?" she asked, and unexpectedly winked. "I don't expect an answer, I'm pulling your leg. I'm *so* enjoying this, Lizzie, aren't you? Have you tried the clotted cream? You haven't touched a bite!"

"Clotted?"

"The most sinful concoction ever devised by man. Or *woman*, as I'm sure the case actually was. Try it with the berries. Spread it on one of the scones. It's from Devon, and my dairyman assures me it came into London fresh this morning."

"I shall become fat as a horse," Lizzie said.

"In which case, you'd be perfectly in fashion," Alison said. "Here, let me help you."

"I'm far too plump as it is," Lizzie said.

"Plump? No, no," Alison said. "You're what my mother might have called *wollüstig*."

"Is that German?"

"Yes."

"Is your mother German?"

"*Was*. She's been dead for quite some time now."

"Oh, I'm sorry," Lizzie said.

She watched in silence as Alison sliced one of the scones in half and then spread each half first with cream as thick as butter and next spooned onto them the tiniest strawberries Lizzie had ever seen.

"Thank you," Lizzie said, accepting the plate. "What does it mean? The German word you used?"

"*Wollüstig*? Well, I suppose it would translate as 'voluptuous.'"

65

"Oh, my," Lizzie said. "Voluptuous, indeed!"

"Have your read *The Book of the Thousand Nights and a Night*?" Alison asked.

"I wouldn't read that, no," Lizzie said.

"Why not?"

"It would not be in keeping with serious piety."

"Are you seriously pious then?"

"I should hope so."

"And you would consider that book improper? Morally unacceptable?"

"From what I've heard of it, yes."

"What have you heard of it?"

"Only that the Persian monarch has many wives . . ."

"And you disapprove?"

"It's beyond my ken. And that one of them . . ."

"Scheherazade, yes."

". . . tells stories that are bawdy."

"Have you read *The Golden Bough*?"

"I've never heard of it."

"It's only recently been published. I was wondering if you might consider *that* morally acceptable."

"I have no way of knowing."

"Are you familiar with the work of Krafft-Ebing?"

"I'm afraid not."

"He hasn't been translated into English yet," Alison said. "I found a copy of his book on our last visit to Germany." She hesitated, and then said, "*Psychopathia Sexualis*."

"Oh, my," Lizzie said.

"You should look for it when it comes to America. I'm sure it'll be widely translated. Or does the title frighten you?"

"If it means what I think it does," Lizzie said.

"What do you think it means?"

"I'm not sure it would be polite for me to say."

"It deals with sexual aberration," Alison said.

"Which is what I imagined."

"Now I've shocked you."

"I do not shock easily," Lizzie said.

"You're blushing to your toes," Alison said, and smiled.

There was an uncomfortable silence.

"This cream *is* sinful, you're right," Lizzie said.

"I warned you," Alison said.

The silence lengthened.

"When you're with your friends," Alison said, "do you talk about anything more intimate than cooking or sewing, or books and plays . . . *do* you enjoy theater, by the way?"

"Yes, I do. Whenever I'm in Boston, I try to see what's on."

"I shall have to give you a list of things to see here in London."

"Rebecca is trying for *The Gondoliers*."

"Bless D'Oyly Carte. He built the Savoy, you know."

"I didn't know."

"She seems a clever sort, your Rebecca."

"Yes, she is."

"Your Felicity is a twit, though, isn't she? Quite lovely, but oh, *my*!"

Lizzie said nothing.

"Now I've offended you," Alison said.

"She *is* a friend," Lizzie said.

"Forgive me, how rude of me. Do you ever discuss more meaningful things with *her* then?"

"More meaningful than what?"

"Sewing or cooking or . . ."

"Well, not with Felicity, no."

"With some of your other friends then?"

"Yes, I would say we're quite open and honest with each other."

"As good friends should be," Alison said.

"Yes," Lizzie said.

"So I'm sure you discuss marriage and . . ."

"No, I don't think I shall ever be married," Lizzie said.

"Which, I assure you, is no great loss," Alison said, and smiled. "Men are fun to discuss, but it becomes awfully tiresome when one has to *live* with them. *Him*, I should say. Singular rather than plural. Albert certainly is singular," she said, and rolled her eyes. "You *do* discuss men, don't you? With your close friends?"

"Hardly ever. We're much beyond the age when such talk would seem appropriate."

"Ah? *Was* it appropriate at one time?"

"When I was a girl, certainly. Oh, my, we discussed boys day and night."

"Ah, didn't we all?" Alison said, and again smiled. "What sort of talk, Lizzie?"

"The usual nonsense," Lizzie said. "Gossip about beaux . . ."

"Have you had many beaux?"

"Not very many. And none for a long time now."

"This gossip . . ."

"Oh, the usual sort. We talked about—mind you, this was when I was much younger . . ."

"Yes?"

". . . their good looks or their homeliness . . . whether they were conceited or not . . . when they planned their next visit to Fall River . . . whether or not a suitor was serious or merely . . ."

"*Were* any of them serious?"

"One. That is . . ."

"Yes?"

"I'm not sure we should be discussing this."

"Why not?"

"Well, we scarcely know each other, for one thing. And for another . . ."

"I feel I know you very well," Alison said.

"Well, I do, too, of course. Feel I know you. But . . ."

"But you just said otherwise."

"I meant . . . on such short acquaintance . . ."

"I had hoped we might become good friends, Lizzie."

"I would hope so, too. But . . ."

"Then can't you be as open and as honest with me as you are with your other good friends?"

"I've been nothing *but*, believe me," Lizzie said. "I only meant to say that . . . well, surely you know this . . . talking about past romances is a matter more suitable for discussion by someone like Felicity."

"Ah, then you *do* agree with me!" Alison said.

"Well, she *is* something of a twit, I suppose," Lizzie said, and smiled.

"How old *is* she?" Alison asked.

"Twenty-four. Just twenty-four, I believe."

"A lovely age," Alison said. "And so beautiful. But, oh, so empty-headed."

"Well, yes," Lizzie said.

"She has a marvelous figure; she'll be the envy of every woman on the Continent," Alison said. "Just make sure she keeps her pretty mouth tightly shut and shows her breasts to good advantage."

Lizzie raised her eyebrows.

"Well, surely," Alison said, "*breasts* are a suitable topic of conversation for women, are they not? Morally acceptable, I'm certain, and—at least when hands are clasped over them in prayer—seriously pious."

"She does have a good figure, yes," Lizzie said, somewhat curtly.

"And who, after all, is better equipped—if you'll forgive the pun—to discuss those lovely appendages of which we are the sole possessors? Although, I might add, when considering my *own* scant equipment, I sincerely and in all serious piety pray that 'less is more' may be more than idle supposition. I keep shocking you, Lizzie, I pray your forgiveness. I'm far too outspoken, I know, my worst failing. The Hastings Curse, actually, inherited by both my brother and me. Hastings was my maiden name—Alison *Lydia* Hastings, to be precise—and my father was quite the most outspoken man alive. I'm sure I'll never be invited to Buckingham Palace, where our dear mourning monarch much resembles a pouter pigeon in Trafalgar Square. Moreover, I'm sure that if I *were* invited, I should politely decline. More tea?"

"Yes, thank you," Lizzie said, and watched as she poured. "You think I'm terribly provincial, don't you?" she asked, surprised when the words found voice.

"No," Alison said.

"Then why do you mock me?"

"Mock you? No. But yes, I *do* admit to my feeble attempts at *shocking* you, Lord knows why. In the face of my incessant barrage, you've remained as unflappable as a cavalry captain. But you see, dear Lizzie, I am sick unto death of idle chatter . . ."

"If you think . . ."

"I *could*, if you prefer, advise you not to miss St. Stephen's

Crypt in Westminster Hall. Or I could offer a critique on *The Sign of Four*, if Mr. Doyle's new novel is on your list of morally acceptable books . . ."

"That's the mockery I spoke of," Lizzie said.

"Is it? I'm sorry, it shan't happen again. But, my dear, *would* you truly be interested in learning that a statue will be going up on the Thames Embankment this Thursday, in honor of the late Mr. W. E. Forster, and that Lord Cranbrook will do the unveiling? Shall we talk about the Lord Dunlo trial, and the interminably long time he's been in court petitioning for a divorce from his wife? Shall we babble on about inconsequential matters as proper *ladies* are supposed to? I should sooner discuss the intensity of my most recent menstrual *flow*!"

And now Lizzie *was* shocked. Not only by the mention, from a virtual stranger, of a personal feminine matter best discussed between the closest of friends, but also by the fierceness with which Alison had spoken those last several words, as if the most natural of female occurrences was to her, in fact, abhorrent. Her green eyes were virtually blazing now, alarmingly so. For an instant, Lizzie suspected the woman would never have spoken so feverishly to anyone *but* a stranger lest a friend might consider her deranged. She decided she would make her apologies and leave. There was no telling *what* Alison Newbury might say, or do, next. And then, to her surprise, Alison's green eyes softened so that they resembled jade now more than they did sparkling emerald. Her mouth and her features softened, too, as though a terrible summer storm had passed in an instant, leaving behind it a cascade of sunlight that illuminated her exquisite face. She reached across the table as if to pat Lizzie's hand again. Instead, her fingers came to rest on Lizzie's arm. Her voice, when she spoke again, was low and apologetic, almost beseeching.

"I seek your friendship," she said.

"You shall have it," Lizzie said. "But surely, Alison . . ."

"Ah, then we *are* friends. That's the first time you've said my name."

"You *do* have a bad habit of interrupting, you know."

"So I've been told."

"And, really, if you assumed I might prefer idle chatter . . ."

"The thought crossed my mind," Alison said, and smiled. Her hand was still on Lizzie's arm.

"Wrongly, I'm sure. I do *not*, in fact, much care for it."

"I don't care for it at *all*," Alison said.

"Then why do you want to hear about a boy I've forgotten years ago?"

"Only if you care to tell me," Alison said, and took her hand from Lizzie's arm.

"And if I choose not to, you shall accuse me of being as empty-headed as my friend Felicity."

"The horns of a dilemma, to be sure," Alison said. She was no longer smiling.

"Your friendship may prove too costly," Lizzie said, and sighed.

"Most real friendships are," Alison said.

"What would you know, then?" Lizzie said.

"All, everything, all," Alison said, and suddenly clapped her hands together like a child. "Who was he, what was his name, how did you meet—*all*, Lizzie," and she leaned forward with great anticipation, clasping her hands in her satiny lap now, the long fingers intertwined, her green eyes wide, as though waiting for a cherished older sister or aunt to tell a fantastic story about witches and fairies and golden palaces.

"I shall disappoint you," Lizzie said. "It's a dreary tale."

"I'm certain it's not," Alison said.

"Very well," Lizzie said, and sighed again. "His name was Stephen Carmody . . . he was a student at Brown, visiting his aunt for the summer."

"How old were you?" Alison asked.

"Nineteen."

"A perfect age for a summer romance!"

"You haven't yet told me how old *you* are," Lizzie said.

"Oh, my!" Alison said, and burst out laughing. "And *I* was the one insisting on honesty!" Her laughter—bubbling from her mouth with such spontaneous mirth, such *self*-mockery this time—surprised Lizzie as much as had her earlier intensity; she had never met so mercurial a woman in her life.

"Well, *how* old then?" she insisted.

"Thirty-seven," Alison said.

"You seem much younger."

71

"My compliment returned. Bread upon the waters. Oh, would that I *were*, Lizzie! But you mustn't believe for an instant that this aged crone . . ."

"Crone, indeed!" Lizzie said.

". . . can so easily be sidetracked or hoodwinked. Oh, no, my dear. You were *about* to tell me of your beau . . ."

"Not precisely a beau . . ."

"Your young man, then . . ."

"Yes, young."

"How old?"

"My own age. Nineteen at the time. Well, about to be twenty. *He*, I mean. Stephen."

"Eleven years ago . . ."

"Yes."

"In the summertime . . ."

"And continuing into the fall."

"And did he love you madly?"

"So he said."

"Then he *was* a serious suitor."

"I believe so."

"Well, Lizzie, what *happened*? You could give Mr. Doyle lessons in suspense, truly!"

"He behaved badly. I was obliged to . . ."

"Behaved badly how?"

"Well . . ."

"A stolen kiss in the barn?"

"We do have a barn," Lizzie said. "But . . ."

"A *barn*, how delightful! And was it there that he behaved . . . *badly*?" she said, lowering her voice and narrowing her eyes.

"No. Alison, I shall call you to account each and every time I feel you're mocking me."

"Am I mocking you now?"

"A barn is surely not so uncommon a thing in England as to provoke . . ."

"But I've never *had* a barn!"

"Well, we do. Just behind the house."

"And I've certainly never had a young swain who behaved badly in one."

"I told you it *wasn't* in the barn."

"Then where was it? Some deserted pasture? Some idle country lane? An August moon shining above, the stars . . ."

"There's the mockery again. I realize Fall River isn't half so grand as London, but it *is* a city, you know, and not quite so rural as you'd have it!"

"How fierce, my Lizzie!"

"Yes!"

"How splendid in her anger!"

"I *am* angry, yes."

"Your very *hair* is on fire!" Alison said.

"It *has* been since birth!" Lizzie shouted, and both women burst out laughing. Neither of them could speak for several moments. Their laughter was the sort of spontaneous explosion Lizzie remembered from her girlhood, when the slightest comment could trigger an endless succession of irrepressible giggles between her and her sister. What was remarkable about the laughter now was that two grown women were overcome by it on a darkening afternoon in the city of London. The very *thought* of such an unimaginable happening caused a new burst of laughter from her and provoked a similar gust of mirth from Alison, who clutched her knees to her bosom and, gasping, said, "Tell me what this cad *did* to you!"

"*Un*did!" Lizzie said, and burst into fresh laughter. "My *corset*!" she managed to say, astonished to find herself laughing at what surely had been the most embarrassing event in her life. "Or *tried* to!" she said, and laughed till tears came to her eyes.

"Oh, the raging maniac!" Alison said, laughing.

"He couldn't get the *ties* undone!" Lizzie said. "I was wearing the shorter corset . . ."

"Yes!"

"Laced down the back, you know, and he kept fumbling about . . ."

"Mr. Fumblefingers!"

"Oh, my dear Lord!" Lizzie said, and brushed at her eyes with her handkerchief. "We struggled for what must have been a full ten minutes . . ."

"Under that bright August moon . . ."

"It was October, actually."

"He bobbing for apples, then . . ."

"Apples!" Lizzie echoed, exploding into laughter again.

"Or pears, more precisely. Or at *least* a pair!" Alison said, and threw her head back and let out the sort of bellow she'd earlier attributed to ill-mannered American girls. "Oh, Lizzie, I can just *visualize* it! There you were in the hay . . . your skirts above your head . . ."

"It was in a carriage," Lizzie said. Her cheeks were burning. She had never before this discussed the incident with anyone, so embarrassing had it been. And to be talking about it now, relating it in the manner of a . . . well, yes, a bawdy tale . . . hearing Alison compare her breasts to apples first and then to pears, and then *punning* on her own words, and to find it all so *hilarious*—she simply could not believe herself!

Both women were suddenly and surprisingly sober.

"In a carriage," Alison prompted.

"On the way home from a church social," Lizzie said.

"Oh, the *heathen*!" Alison said, and burst out laughing again.

"I was shocked speechless!"

"I can well imagine!"

"His *hands* were cold!" Lizzie said, and began laughing so hard she thought she would choke.

"Oh, dear," Alison said.

"Oh, my goodness," Lizzie said.

"Your goodness *assailed*!" Alison said. "So tell me what *happened*. How did you *rid* yourself of the bounder?"

"I was obliged to return his ring."

"Ah? That serious then, was it?"

"Not an engagement ring, no," Lizzie said. "Nothing of the sort. But he'd given me a simple gold ring he used to wear on his pinky, and which I wore on the third finger of my right hand. I gave back the ring, but it came again in the mail not three days later, together with a note apologizing for his . . ."

". . . beastly manners," Alison said, nodding.

"He didn't put it quite that way."

"How *did* he put it?"

"He said he couldn't understand what had come over him . . ."

"How original!"

". . . and he promised it would never happen again."

"Unless he first warmed his hands by the fire," Alison said. "And did you forgive him?"

74

"I never saw him again. Oh, around town, of course, whenever he was visiting his aunt. But not as a beau."

"Did you return the ring yet another time?"

"No."

"You certainly didn't throw it away, did you? Gold?"

"I gave it to my father," Lizzie said. "He still wears it."

"How clever of you," Alison said. "I must confess that the first time a strange man began fumbling with *my* stays I was less embarrassed than I was surprised. The very thought of a grown man actually desiring to fondle my meager treasures . . ."

"Hello?" Albert called. "Anyone home?"

"We're in here, darling," Alison said, rising and smoothing her apron. "Come say hello to Miss Borden."

He came into the drawing room, hatless this time, and dressed rather more somberly than he'd been on the train, wearing a black coat with a low, narrow, rolled velvet collar and trousers of the same cloth. He extended his hand, took Lizzie's in it and lowered his lips to it, brushing it lightly in the European manner.

"How nice to see you," he said. "Have you been having a pleasant chat? Is that clotted cream I spy?"

"Do help yourself, Albert," she said, "I'll ring for more hot tea." She turned to Lizzie and added, "My husband is a glutton."

"For punishment, if your tongue's any indication," Albert said, and smiled. "Has she been talking your ear off, Miss Borden?"

"Please call me Lizzie, won't you?"

"Lizzie then," he said. "But *not* Elizabeth."

"*Such* a keen memory," Alison said.

"We've had a lovely afternoon together," Lizzie said.

"Yes, haven't we?" Alison said.

"Interest rates will be going up from four to five percent," Albert said, and reached across the table for a scone.

4: FALL RIVER— 1892

Six witnesses were to be examined at the inquest on this Wednesday morning, August 10, and Lizzie Borden was to be the first of them. The clock on the wall read ten minutes to ten. Knowlton sat alone in the courtroom, a copy of the *Springfield Republican* open on the table before him. The editorial read:

All through the investigations carried on by the Fall River Police, a lack of ability has been shown seldom equalled, and causes they assign for connecting the daughter with the murder are on a par with their other exhibitions of lack of wisdom. Because someone, unknown to them and too smart for them to catch, butchered two people in the daytime on a principal street of the city, using brute force far in excess of that possessed by the girl, they conclude that there is probable reason to believe that she is the murderess. Because they found no one walking along the street with his hands and clothes reeking with blood, they conclude that it is probable, after swinging the ax with the precision and effect of a butcher, she washed the blood from her hands and clothes.

Well *that*, Knowlton thought. The fact that there had been no

76

visible blood on the girl when the police arrived. True enough. But was it actually so improbable that she *might* have had opportunity to cleanse herself after the gory acts? To hide, perhaps to destroy, the garments she'd been wearing? Beyond reasonable doubt, he reminded himself. What *might* have happened was nothing for him to ponder. He was here this morning to inquire again into what *had* happened, to ask Lizzie Borden again for a recital of the events as she had experienced them and perceived them on that fatal morning.

As for the police, he had no doubt but that they were performing their duties as diligently and as carefully as was within their power. Only yesterday afternoon, after it was reported that a paperhanger named Peleg Blightman had found a bloody hatchet hidden in a laborer's house on one of the Brayton Farms, close by one of the two farms Andrew Borden had owned in South Somerset, Marshal Hilliard had immediately dispatched Officer Harrington to the scene.

The policeman had arrived there at about four-thirty in the afternoon while Knowlton was still questioning Lizzie, and had talked first with a Portuguese woman who understood English only sparingly, and next to her husband, who was called in from the fields. The man said he knew nothing of such a hatchet, and when the officer searched the house, he found on the kitchen shelf only a hatchet without any blood stains. That very night, an order was adopted by the Fall River Board of Aldermen, stating, "Inasmuch as a terrible crime has been committed in this city, requiring an unusually large number of men to do police duty, it is hereby ordered that the City Marshal be—and he is hereby—directed to employ such extra constables as he may deem necessary for the detection of the criminals, the expenses to be charged to the appropriation of the police."

The police *were* doing their job; of that, Knowlton felt certain. He closed the newspaper and looked up at the clock. It was five minutes to ten. Professor Wood was still at the Borden house, he imagined, examining the premises again, after which he would go to the police station to receive a trunk from Dr. Dolan. The trunk would contain, among other things, the two axes and the claw-hammer hatchet that had been found in the cellar of the house. Knowlton wished he were already in possession of the results of the professor's examination, now, *before* he questioned

77

the witness again, but that was impossible. He glanced toward the door as Clerk Leonard shuffled into the courtroom. The men exchanged morning greetings. Annie White came in a few moments later, followed by City Marshal Hilliard. If Knowlton had come to know anything at all about Miss Lizzie Borden, it was that she would arrive promptly at the stroke of the hour.

"I shall have to ask you once more about that morning," he said. "I want you to tell me *just* where you found the people when you got down. That you *did* find there."

"I found Mrs. Borden in the dining room. I found my father in the sitting room."

"And Maggie?"

"Maggie was coming in the back door with her pail and brush."

"Tell me what talk you had with your mother at that time."

"She asked me how I felt. I said I felt better than I did Tuesday, but I didn't want any breakfast. She asked me what I wanted for dinner. I told her nothing. I told her I didn't want anything. She said she was going out, and would get the dinner. That's the last I saw her, or said anything to her."

"Where did you go then?"

"Into the kitchen."

"Where then?"

"Downcellar."

"Gone perhaps five minutes?"

"Perhaps. Not more than that. Possibly a little bit more."

"When you came back, did you see your mother?"

"I did not. I supposed she had gone out."

"She did not tell you where she was going?"

"No, sir."

"Now I call your attention to the fact that yesterday you told me, with some explicitness, that when your father came in you were just coming downstairs."

"No, I did not. I beg your pardon."

"That you were on the *stairs* at the time your father was let in, you said with some explicitness. Do you now say you did *not* say so?"

"I said I thought *first* I was on the stairs. Then I remembered I was in the kitchen when he came in."

"*First* you thought you were in the kitchen. *Afterwards*, you remembered you were on the stairs."

"I said I *thought* I was on the stairs. Then I said I *knew* I was in the kitchen. I still say that now. I was in the kitchen."

"Did you go into the front part of the house after your father came in?"

"After he came in from downstreet, I was in the sitting room with him."

"Did you go into the front hall afterwards?"

"No, sir."

"At no time?"

"No, sir."

"Excepting the two or three minutes you were downcellar, were you away from the house until your father came in?"

"No, sir."

"You were always in the kitchen or dining room, excepting when you went upstairs."

"I went upstairs before he went out."

"You mean you went up there to sew a button on."

"I basted a piece of tape on."

"Do you remember you didn't say that yesterday?"

"I don't think you asked me. I told you yesterday I went upstairs directly after I came up from downcellar, with the clean clothes."

"You *now* say—after your father went out—you didn't go upstairs at *all*."

"No, sir, I did not."

"When Maggie came in there washing the windows, you didn't appear from the front part of the house?"

"No, sir."

"When your father was let in, you didn't appear from upstairs?"

"No, sir. I was in the kitchen."

"After your father went out, you remained there either in the kitchen or dining room all the time."

"I went in the sitting room long enough to direct some paper wrappers."

"One of the three rooms."

"Yes, sir."

"So it would have been extremely difficult for anybody to

79

have gone through the kitchen, *and* dining room, *and* front hall without your seeing them."

"They could have gone from the kitchen into the sitting room while I was in the dining room. If there was anybody to go."

"Then into the front hall?"

"Yes, sir."

"You were in the dining room. Ironing."

"Yes, sir. Part of the time."

"You were in *all* of the three rooms."

"Yes, sir."

"A large portion of that time, the girl was out of doors."

"I don't know where she was. I didn't see her. I supposed she was out of doors. As she had the pail and brush."

"You know she was washing windows?"

"She told me she was going to. I didn't see her do it."

"For a large portion of the time, you didn't see the girl?"

"No, sir."

"So far as you know, you were alone in the lower part of the house a large portion of the time. After your father went away, and before he came back."

"My father didn't go away, I think, until somewhere about ten . . . as near as I can remember. He was with me downstairs."

"A large portion of the time, after your father went away and before he came back, so far as you know, you were alone in the house."

"Maggie had come in and gone upstairs."

"After he went out," Knowlton persisted doggedly, "and before he came back, a large portion of the time *after* your father went out, and *before* he came back, so far as you know, you were the only person in the house."

"So far as I know, I was."

"And during that time, so far as you know, the front door was locked."

"So far as I know."

"And never was unlocked at all."

"I don't think it was."

"Even *after* your father came home, it was locked up again."

"I don't know whether she locked it up again after that or not."

"It locks itself."

"The spring lock opens."

"It fastens it so it cannot be opened from the outside."

"Sometimes you can press it open."

"Have you any reason to suppose the spring lock was left so it could be pressed open from the outside?"

"I have no reason to suppose so."

"Nothing about the lock was changed before the people came."

"Nothing that I know of."

One of them was lying; either the servant girl or the woman who now sat watching him, her gray eyes unreadable. Bridget Sullivan had testified under oath that Lizzie had been upstairs when she'd let Andrew Borden into the house. Either in the entry or at the top of the stairs. She had specifically stated that she'd had difficulty unlocking the door, and had said "Oh, pshaw," and had heard Lizzie laughing, *upstairs*. Lizzie herself had yesterday claimed she'd been upstairs when her father came back to the house. She was now claiming she'd been in the kitchen. Why the lie, if indeed it was a lie? And if it was *not* a lie, he wanted all the details.

"What were you doing in the kitchen when your father came home?" he asked.

"I think I was eating a pear when he came in."

"What had you been doing before that?"

"Reading a magazine."

"Were you making preparations to iron again?"

"I'd sprinkled my clothes and was waiting for the flats. I sprinkled the clothes before he went out."

"Had you built up the fire again?"

"I put in a stick of wood. There were a few sparks. I put in a stick of wood to try to heat the flat."

"You had then started the fire?"

"Yes, sir."

"The fire was burning when he came in?"

"No, sir. But it was smoldering and smoking as though it would come up."

"*Did* it come up after he came in?"

"No, sir."

"How soon after your father came in before Maggie went upstairs?"

"I don't know. I didn't see her."

81

"Did you see her after your father came in?"

"Not after she let him in."

"How long was your father in the house before you found him killed?"

"I don't know exactly. Because I went out to the barn. I don't know what time he came home. I don't think he'd been home more than fifteen or twenty minutes. I'm not sure."

"When you went out to the barn, where did you leave your father?"

"He had laid down on the sitting-room lounge. Taken off his shoes and put on his slippers. And taken off his coat and put on the reefer. I asked him if he wanted the window left that way."

Now surely, she *knew* that her father had been wearing Congress *shoes* at the time of his murder, and *not* slippers, as she now claimed. But why lie about so inconsequential a matter as what the man had been wearing on his feet? Unless, of course, she was determined to weave reality and invention into a web that would totally obscure the truth. Meticulously relate detail after detail, some of them true, some of them false, until it would become impossible for him to distinguish fact from fancy.

"Where did you leave him?" he asked.

"On the sofa."

"Was he asleep?"

"No, sir."

"Was he reading?"

"No, sir."

"What was the last thing you said to him?"

"I asked him if he wanted the window left that way. Then I went into the kitchen. And from there to the barn."

"Whereabouts in the barn did you go?"

"Upstairs."

"To the second story of the barn?"

"Yes, sir."

"How long did you remain there?"

"I don't know. Fifteen or twenty minutes."

"What doing?"

"Trying to find lead for a sinker."

"What made you think there'd be lead for a sinker up there?"

"Because there *was* some there."

"Was there not some by the door?"

"Some *pieces* of lead by the open door. But there was a box full of old things upstairs."

"Did you bring any sinker back from the barn?"

"I found no sinker."

"Did you bring *any* sinker back from the barn?"

"Nothing but a piece of a chip I picked up on the floor."

"Where was that box you say you saw upstairs, containing lead?"

"There was a kind of a workbench."

"Is it there now?"

"I don't know, sir."

"How long since you've seen it there?"

"I haven't been out there since that day."

"Had you been in the barn before?"

"That day? No, sir."

"How long since you'd been in the barn before?"

"I don't think I'd been into it . . . I don't know as I had in three months."

And, of course, it was entirely possible that she *had* been to the barn, as she claimed, and that someone *had* stolen into the house to commit bloody murder while the servant girl lay on her bed in the attic room. In which case, the door . . .

"When you went out," he asked, "did you unfasten the screen door?"

"I unhooked it to get out."

"It was hooked until you went out?"

"Yes, sir."

"It had been left hooked by Bridget? If she was the last one in?"

"I suppose so. I don't know."

"Do you know when she *did* get through washing the outside?"

"I don't know."

"Did you know she washed the windows *inside*?"

"I don't know."

"Did you *see* her washing the windows inside?"

"I don't know."

"You don't *know* whether she washed the dining room and sitting room windows inside?"

83

"I didn't see her."

"*If* she did, would you *not* have seen her?"

"I don't know. She might be in one room and I in another."

"Do you think she might have gone to work, and washed all the windows in the dining room and sitting room, and you not know it?"

"I don't know. I'm sure, whether I *should* or not, I *might* have seen her, and not know it."

"Miss Borden, I am *trying* in good *faith* to get *all* the doings that morning of yourself and Miss Sullivan, and I have not succeeded in doing it. Do you desire to give me any information, or not?"

"I don't *know* it . . . I don't know what your *name* is!"

He was confused for a moment. Surely, she knew what his name was. And then he realized she was making reference to his barrage of questions, telling him, in effect, that he had her head in such a whirl she no longer could even remember his name. He debated for a moment whether he should soften his tone and his stance. He decided against it.

Flatly, deliberately, accusingly, he said. "It is certain beyond reasonable doubt she was engaged in washing the windows in the dining room or sitting room when your father came home. Do you mean to say you know nothing of either of those operations?"

"I knew she washed the windows outside—that is, she told me so. She didn't wash the windows in the kitchen, because I was *in* the kitchen most of the time."

"The *dining* room and the *sitting* room, I said."

"I don't know."

"Can you give me any information how it happened—at that particular time—you should go into the chamber of the barn to find a sinker to go to Marion with to fish the next Monday?"

"I was going to finish my ironing. My flats weren't hot. I said to myself, 'I'll go and try and find that sinker. Perhaps by the time I get back, the flats'll be hot.' That's the only reason."

"Had you got a fish line?"

"Not here. We had some at the farm."

"Had you got a fish hook?"

"No, sir."

"Had you got *any* apparatus for fishing at *all*?"

"Yes, over there."

"Had you any *sinkers* over there?"

"I think there were some. It's so long since I've been there. I think there were some."

"You had no reason to suppose you were *lacking* sinkers?"

"I don't think there were any on my lines."

"Where were your lines?"

"My fish lines were at the farm here."

"What made you think there were no *sinkers* at the farm? On your lines?"

"Because some time ago, when I was there, I had none."

"How long since you'd used the fish lines?"

"Five years, perhaps."

"You left them at the farm then?"

"Yes, sir."

"And you haven't seen them since?"

"Yes, sir."

"It occurred to you, after your father came in, it would be a good time to go to the barn after sinkers. And you had no reason to suppose there was not abundance of sinkers at the farm. *And* abundance of lines."

"The last time I was there, there were some lines."

"Did you not say before you presumed there were sinkers at the farm?"

"I don't think I said so."

"You did say so. Exactly. Do you now say you presume there were *no* sinkers at the farm?"

"I don't think there were any fish lines suitable to use at the farm. I don't think there were any sinkers on any line that had been mine."

"Do you remember telling me you presumed there were lines, and sinkers, and hooks at the farm?"

"I said there were *lines,* I thought. And perhaps *hooks.* I didn't say I thought there were *sinkers* on my lines. There was another box of lines over there beside mine."

"You thought there were *not* sinkers?"

"Not on *my* lines."

"Not sinkers at the farm?"

"I don't think there were any sinkers at the farm. I don't know whether there were or not."

"Did you then think there were *no* sinkers at the farm?"

"I thought there were no sinkers *anywhere*, or I shouldn't have been trying to *find* some."

"You thought there were no sinkers at the farm to be had."

"I thought there were no sinkers at the farm to be had."

"That is the reason you went into the second story of the barn. To look for a sinker."

"Yes, sir."

"You went straight to the upper story of the barn?"

"No. I went under the pear tree and got some pears first."

"Then went to the second story of the barn, to look for sinkers for lines you had at the farm, as you supposed, as you had seen them there five years before that time."

"I went up to get some *sinkers*, if I could find them. I didn't intend to go to the farm for *lines*. I was going to buy some lines *here*."

"You then had no intention of using your *own* line and hooks at the farm."

"No, sir."

"What was the use of telling me, a little while ago, you had no sinkers on your line at the farm?"

"I thought I made you understand that those lines at the farm were no good to use."

"Did you not mean for me to understand *one* of the reasons you were searching for sinkers was that the lines you had at the farm, as you remembered them, had no sinkers on them?"

"I said the lines at the farm had no sinkers."

"I did not ask you what you *said*. Did you not mean for me to understand that?"

"I meant for you to understand I wanted the *sinkers*. And was going to have *new* lines."

"You had not then bought your lines?"

"No, sir. I was going out Thursday noon."

"You had not bought *any* apparatus for fishing?"

"No hooks."

"Had bought nothing connected with your fishing trip?"

"No, sir."

"Was going to go fishing the next Monday, were you?"

"I don't know that we should go fishing Monday."

"Going to the *place* to go fishing Monday?"

86

"Yes, sir."

"This was Thursday, and you had no idea of using any fishing apparatus before the next Monday."

"No, sir."

"You had no fishing apparatus you were preparing to use the next Monday until then."

"No, sir. Not until I bought it."

"You had not bought anything."

"No, sir."

"Had not *started* to buy anything."

"No, sir."

"The *first* thing in preparation for your fishing trip the next Monday was to go to the *loft* of that barn to find some old *sinkers* to put on some hooks and lines that you had not then *bought*."

"I thought I would find out whether there were any sinkers before I bought the lines. And if there were, I shouldn't have to buy any sinkers. If there *were* some, I should only have to buy the lines and the hooks."

"You began the collection of your fishing apparatus by searching for sinkers in the barn."

"Yes, sir."

"Where did you look upstairs?"

"On that workbench, like."

"*In* anything?"

"Yes, it was a box. Sort of a box. And then some things lying right on the side that wasn't in the box."

"How large a box was it?"

"I couldn't tell you. It was probably covered up with lumber, I think."

"Give me the best idea of the size of the box you can."

"Well, I should say . . . I don't know . . . I haven't any idea."

"Give me the best idea you have."

"About that large," she said, and extended her gloved hands, measuring out the distance between the forefinger of each hand.

"That *long*?" Knowlton asked.

"Yes."

"How *wide*?"

"I don't know."

"Give me the best idea you have."

87

"Perhaps about as wide as it was long."

"How high?"

"It wasn't very high."

"*About* how high?"

Lizzie again extended her hands.

"About twice the length of your forefinger?" Knowlton said.

"I should think so. Not quite."

"What was in the box?"

"Nails . . . and some old locks . . . and I don't know but there was a doorknob."

"Anything else?"

"I don't remember anything else."

"Any lead?"

"Yes. Some pieces of lead, like."

"Foil? What we call tin foil? The same as you use on tea chests?"

"I don't remember seeing any tin foil. Not as thin as that."

"Tea-chest lead?"

"No, sir."

"What *did* you see in shape of lead?"

"Flat pieces of lead, a little bigger than that. Some of them were doubled together."

"How many."

"I couldn't tell you."

"Where else did you look? Beside in the box?"

"I didn't look anywhere of lead except on the workbench."

"When you got through looking for lead, did you come down?"

"No, sir. I went to the west window, over the hay. To the west window. And the curtain was slanted a little. I pulled it down."

"What else?"

"Nothing."

"That is all you did?"

"Yes, sir."

"That is the second story of the barn?"

"Yes, sir."

"Was the window open?"

"I think not."

"Hot?"

"*Very* hot."

"How long do you think you were up there?"

"Not more than fifteen or twenty minutes, I shouldn't think."

"Should you think what you've told me would occupy four minutes?"

"I ate some pears up there."

"I asked you to tell me *all* you did!"

"I *told* you all I did!"

"Do you mean to say you stopped your work, and then—*additional* to that—sat still and ate some pears?"

"While I was looking out of the window, yes, sir."

"Will you tell me *all* you did in the second story of the barn?"

"I think I told you all I did that I can remember."

"Is there anything else?"

"I told you I took some pears up from the ground when I went up. I stopped under the pear tree and took some pears up. When I went up."

"Have you *now* told me everything you did up in the second story of the barn?"

"Yes, sir."

"I now call your attention and ask you to say whether all you have told me—I don't suppose you stayed there any longer than necessary?"

"No, sir. Because it was close."

"I suppose that was the hottest place there was on the premises."

"I should think so."

"Can you give me any explanation why all you have told me would occupy more than three minutes?"

"Yes, it would take me more than three minutes."

"To look in that box—that you have described the size of—on the bench, and put down the curtain, and then get out as soon as you conveniently could—would you say you were occupied in that business *twenty* minutes?"

"I think so. Because I didn't look at the box when I first went up."

"What *did* you do?"

"I ate my pears."

"Stood there eating pears, doing nothing?"

"I was looking out of the window."

"Stood there looking out of the window, eating the pears."

"I should think so."

"How many did you eat?"

"Three, I think."

"You were feeling better than you did in the morning?"

"Better than I did the night before."

"That is *not* what I asked you. You were—*then,* when you were eating those three pears in that hot loft, looking out of that closed window—feeling better than you were in the morning? When you ate no breakfast?"

"I was feeling well enough to eat the pears."

"Were you feeling better than you were in the morning?"

"I don't think I felt very sick in the morning, only . . . yes, I don't know but I *did* feel better. As I say, I don't know whether I ate any breakfast or not. Or whether I ate a cookie."

"*Were* you then feeling better than you did in the morning?"

"I don't know how to answer you, because I told you I felt better in the morning, *anyway*!"

"Do you understand my question? My question is whether, when you were in the loft of that barn, you were feeling better than you were in the morning, when you got up?"

"No. I felt about the same."

"Were you feeling better than you were when you told your mother you didn't care for any dinner?"

"No, sir. I felt about the same."

"Well enough to eat pears, but not well enough to eat anything for dinner."

"She asked me if I wanted any meat."

The answer hardly seemed responsive, but he decided not to pursue the matter of her comparative health any further. The eating of the pears, he reasoned—and, he thought, correctly so—was simply an attempt on her part to explain what had taken her so long up there in the barn. Her trip to the barn, of course, *if* she was lying, had been invented to place her at some distance from the house where the murders had taken place. If she had not been in the house at the time, she could not have committed the murders. But why choose the barn? Why not the front walk? Or a neighbor's fence? Or indeed the shade of the pear tree? Knowlton walked back to his table, picked up a drawing of the house and yard, and carried it with him to the witness chair.

90

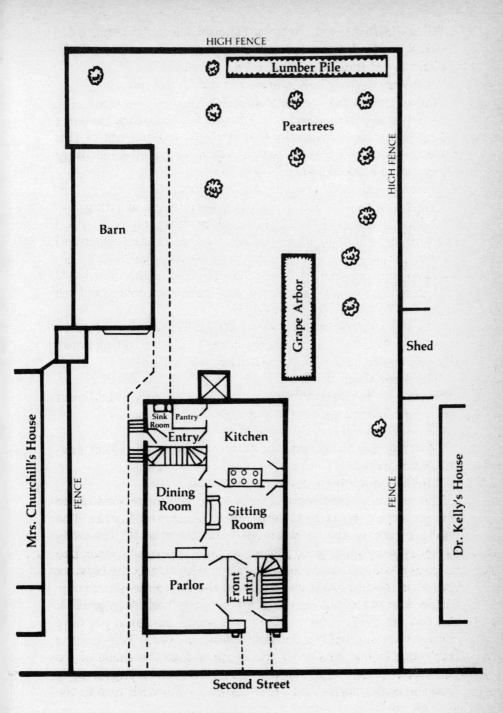

HIGH FENCE

Lumber Pile

Peartrees

HIGH FENCE

Barn

Grape Arbor

Shed

Mrs. Churchill's House

FENCE

Sink Room

Pantry

Entry

Kitchen

Dining Room

Sitting Room

Parlor

Front Entry

FENCE

Dr. Kelly's House

Second Street

"I ask you," he said, "why you should select *that* place, which was the only place which would put you out of sight of the house, to eat those three pears in?"

"I cannot tell you any reason."

"You observe that fact, do you not? You have put yourself in the *only* place, perhaps, where it would be impossible for you to see a person going into the house."

"Yes, sir, I should have seen them from the front window."

"From anywhere in the yard?"

"No, sir. Not unless from that end of the barn."

"Ordinarily, in the yard, you could have seen them. And in the kitchen, where you'd been, you could have seen them."

"I don't think I understand."

"When you were in the *kitchen*, you could see persons who came in at the back door."

"Yes, sir."

"When you were in the *yard*, unless you were around the corner of the house, you could see them come in at the back door."

"No, sir. Not unless I was at the corner of the barn. The minute I turned, I could not."

"What was there?"

"A little jog, like. The walk turns."

"I ask you again to explain to me why you took those pears from the pear tree."

"I didn't take them from the pear tree."

"From the ground, *wherever* you took them from, I thank you for correcting me. Going in the barn, going upstairs into the hottest place in the barn, in the rear of the barn, the hottest place, and there *standing* and *eating* those pears that morning."

"I beg your pardon. I was *not* in the rear of the barn. I was in the other end of the barn that faced the street."

"Where you could see anybody coming into the house?"

"Yes, sir."

"Did you not tell me you could *not*?"

"*Before* I went into the barn. At the jog on the outside."

"You now say . . . when you were eating the pears, you *could* see the back door?"

"Yes, sir."

"So nobody could come in at that time without your seeing them."

"I don't see how they could."

"After you got through eating your pears, you began your search."

"Yes, sir."

"*Then* you did *not* see into the house."

"No, sir. Because the bench is at the other end."

"Now. I've asked you over and over again, and will continue the inquiry, whether anything you did at the bench would occupy more than three minutes."

"Yes, I think it would. Because I pulled over quite a lot of boards in looking."

"To get at the box?"

"Yes, sir."

"Taking all that, what is the amount of time you *think* you occupied in looking for that piece of lead which you did not find?"

"Well . . . I should think perhaps I was ten minutes."

"Looking over those old things."

"Yes, sir. On the bench."

"Now can you explain why you were ten minutes doing it?"

"No. Only that I can't do *anything* in a minute."

Except perhaps commit murder, Knowlton thought, and sighed heavily. She was watching him, a somewhat smug expression on her face now, as though her previous answer had been irrefutably logical. How could *anyone* be expected to do anything in a minute, least of all a woman intent on finding sinkers for a fishing trip she was to take on the Monday following the murders?

"When you came down from the barn," he asked, "what did you do then?"

"Opened the sitting-room door, and went into the sitting room. Or *pushed* it open. It wasn't latched."

"What did you do then?"

"I found my father. And rushed to the foot of the stairs."

"What were you going into the sitting room for?"

"To go upstairs."

"What for?"

"To sit down."

93

"What had become of the ironing?"

"The fire had gone out."

"I thought you went out because the fire wasn't hot enough to heat the flats."

"I thought it would burn, but the fire hadn't caught from the few sparks."

"So you gave up the ironing and was going upstairs."

"Yes, sir. I thought I'd wait till Maggie got dinner, and heat the flats again."

"When you saw your father, where was he?"

"On the sofa."

"What was his position?"

"Lying down."

"Describe anything else you noticed at the time."

"I didn't notice anything else, I was so frightened and horrified. I ran to the foot of the stairs and called Maggie."

"Did you notice that he'd been cut?"

"Yes. That's what made me afraid."

"Did you notice that he was dead?"

"I didn't know whether he was or not."

"Did you make any search for your mother?"

"No, sir."

"Why not?"

"I thought she was out of the house. I thought she'd gone out. I called Maggie to go to Dr. Bowen's. When they came, I said, 'I don't know where Mrs. Borden is.' I thought she'd gone out."

"Did you tell Maggie you thought your mother had come in?"

"No, sir."

"That you thought you heard her come in?"

"No, sir."

"Did you say to anybody that you thought she was killed upstairs?"

"No, sir."

"To *anybody*?"

"No, sir."

"You made no effort to find your mother at all?"

"No, sir."

"Who did you send Maggie for?"

"Dr. Bowen. She came back and said Dr. Bowen wasn't there."

"What did you tell Maggie?"

94

"I told her he was hurt."

"When you *first* told her."

"I said, 'Go for Dr. Bowen as soon as you can. I think father is hurt.'"

"Did you then know that he was dead?"

"No, sir."

"You saw him . . ."

"Yes, sir."

". . . you went into the room . . ."

"No, sir."

"Looked in at the door?"

"I opened the door and rushed back."

"Saw his face?"

"No, I didn't see his face. Because he was all covered with blood."

"You saw where the face was bleeding?"

"Yes, sir."

"Did you see the blood on the floor?"

"No, sir."

"You saw his face covered with blood?"

"Yes, sir."

"Did you see his eyeball hanging out?"

"No, sir."

"See the gashes where his face was laid open?"

"No, sir."

"Nothing of that kind?"

"No, sir," she said, and covered her face with both gloved hands, as though trying to hide from her eyes the images he had conjured for her. She sat that way for what seemed an eternity, motionless, her hands covering her face. He thought she might be weeping behind those hands, but he heard no sound from her. He waited. At last, she lowered her hands. The gray eyes were dry. They met his own eyes unwaveringly.

"Do you know of any employment that would occupy your mother for the two hours between nine and eleven," he asked. "In the front room?"

"Not unless she was sewing."

"If she had been sewing you would have heard the machine."

"She didn't always use the machine."

95

"Did you see, or were there found, anything to indicate that she *was* sewing up there?"

"I don't know. She'd given me, a few weeks before, some pillowcases to make."

"My question is not that. *Did* you see, or *were* there found, anything to indicate that she had done any sewing in that room that morning?"

"I don't know. I wasn't allowed in that room. I didn't see it."

"Leaving out the sewing, do you know of anything *else* that would occupy her for two hours in that room?"

"No. Not if she'd made the bed up. And she said she had when I went down."

"Assuming the bed *was* made?"

"I don't know anything."

"Did she say she'd done her work?"

"She said she'd made the bed, and was going to put on the pillowcases. About nine o'clock."

"I ask you now again, remembering that . . ."

"I told you that yesterday."

"Never mind about *yesterday*. Tell me all the talk you had with your mother when you came down in the morning."

"She asked me how I felt. I said I felt better, but didn't want any breakfast. She said what kind of meat did I want for dinner. I said I didn't want *any*. She said she was going out, somebody was sick, and she would get the dinner, get the meat, order the meat. And . . . I think she said something about the weather being hotter, or something. And I don't remember that she said anything else. I said to her, 'Won't you change your dress before you go out?' She had on an old one. She said, 'No, this is good enough.' That's all I can remember."

"In this narrative, you have not again said anything about her having said that she'd made the bed."

"I *told* you that she said she'd made the bed!"

"In *this* time saying, you didn't put that in! I want that conversation that you had with her that morning. I beg your pardon again. In *this* time of telling me, you didn't say anything about her having received a note."

"I told you that before."

"Miss Borden, I want you now to tell me *all* the talk you had

96

with your mother when you came down, and *all* the talk she had with you. Please begin again."

The gray eyes flared. Her gloved hands tightened on the arms of the witness chair; for a moment, she seemed about to rise. He was suddenly aware of a thin sheen of perspiration on her upper lip. She took a deep breath. Her hands relaxed. Her eyes met his again. The anger was gone now. She stared directly into his face, and began speaking slowly, monotonously, almost hypnotically.

"She asked me how I felt. I told her. She asked me what I wanted for dinner. I told her not anything . . . what kind of *meat* I wanted for dinner. I told her not any. She said she'd been up and made the spare bed, and was going to take up some linen pillowcases for the small pillows at the foot, and then the room was done. She said, 'I've had a note from somebody that's sick, and I'm going out, and I'll get the dinner at the same time.' I think she said something about the weather, I don't know. She also asked me if I would direct some paper wrappers for her, which I did."

"She said she'd had a note?"

"Yes, sir."

"You told me yesterday you never saw the note."

"No, sir, I never did."

"You looked for it?"

"No, sir. But the rest have."

"Did you have an apron on Thursday?" Knowlton asked, abruptly shifting his line of questioning.

"Did I *what*?"

"Have an apron on Thursday?"

"No, sir, I don't think I did."

"Do you remember whether you did or not?"

"I don't remember sure, but I don't think I did."

"You had aprons, of course?"

"I had aprons, yes, sir."

"Will you try and think whether you did or not?"

"I don't think I did."

"Will you try and remember?"

"I had no occasion for an apron on that morning."

"If you can remember, I wish you would."

"I don't remember."

"That is all the answer you can give me about that?"

"Yes, sir."

Well, he thought, so much for any garment she might have been wearing over her dress to shield her from the almost certain torrent of blood caused by the butchering wounds. For surely, if an ax or a hatchet *had* been the murder weapon . . .

"Did you have any occasion to use the ax or hatchet?" he asked.

"No, sir."

"Did you know where they were?"

"I knew there was an old ax downcellar. That's all I knew."

"Did you know anything about a *hatchet* downcellar?"

"No, sir."

"Where was the old ax downcellar?"

"The last time I saw it, it was stuck in the old chopping block."

"Was that the only ax or hatchet downcellar?"

"It was all I knew about."

"When was the last you knew of it?"

"When our farmer came to chop wood."

"When was that?"

"I think a year ago last winter. I think there was so much wood on hand, he didn't come last winter."

"Do you know of anything that would occasion the use of an ax or hatchet?"

"No, sir."

"Do you know of anything that would occasion the getting of *blood* on an ax or hatchet downcellar?"

"No, sir."

"I don't *say* there was, but *assuming* an ax or hatchet was found downcellar with blood on it."

"No, sir."

"Do you know whether there *was* a hatchet down there before the murder?"

"I don't know."

"You aren't able to say your father *didn't* own a hatchet?"

"I don't know whether he did or not."

"Did you know there was found, at the foot of the stairs, a hatchet and ax?"

"No, sir, I did not."

"Assume that is so . . . can you give me any explanation of how they came there?"

"No, sir."

"Assume they had blood on them . . . can you give any occasion for there being blood on them?"

"No, sir."

"Can you tell of any killing of an animal, or any *other* operation, that would lead to their being cast there, with blood on them?"

"No, sir," Lizzie said, and hesitated. "He killed some pigeons in the barn last May or June."

"What with?"

"I don't know, but I thought he wrung their necks."

"What made you think so?"

"I think he said so."

"Did anything else make you think so?"

"All but three or four had their heads on. That is what made me think so."

"Did all of them come into the house?"

"I think so."

"Those that came into the house were all headless?"

"Two or three had them on."

"Were any with their heads off?"

"Yes, sir."

"*Cut* off? Or *twisted* off."

"I don't know which."

"How did they look?"

"I don't know. Their heads were gone, that's all."

"Did you tell anybody they looked as though they were twisted off?"

"I don't remember whether I did or not." A faraway look came into her gray eyes. When she spoke again, her voice was uncommonly low. "The skin was very tender. I said, 'Why are these heads off?'" She paused. The eyes snapped back into focus. "I think I remember telling somebody that he said they were twisted off."

"Did they look as if they were *cut* off?"

"I don't know. I didn't look at that particularly."

Did you look at your *stepmother* particularly? he wondered. Did you look at your *father* particularly? Did you wonder why *their* heads were off, or virtually off, after you butchered them to death with a sharp weapon, hatchet or ax, what*ever* you used? He realized all at once that he was sweating profusely. He took a handkerchief from his pocket and dabbed at his forehead.

"Is there anything else *besides* that," he asked, "that would lead in your opinion, so far as you can remember, to the finding of instruments in the cellar with blood on them?"

"I know of nothing else that was done."

Judge Blaisdell cleared his throat. "Was there any effort made by the witness," he asked, "to notify *Mrs.* Borden of the fact that *Mr.* Borden was found?"

"Did you make any effort to notify Mrs. Borden of your father being killed?" Knowlton asked.

"No, sir. When I found him, I rushed right to the foot of the stairs for Maggie. I supposed Mrs. Borden was out. I didn't think anything about her at the time, I was so—"

"At *any* time, did you say anything about her to anybody?"

"No, sir."

"To the effect that she was out?"

"I told father when he came in."

"*After* your father was killed."

"No, sir."

"Did you say you thought she was upstairs?"

"No, sir."

"Did you ask them to look upstairs?"

"No, sir."

"Did you suggest to anybody to search upstairs?"

"I said, 'I don't know where Mrs. Borden is.' That's all I said."

"You did not suggest that any search be made for her?"

"No, sir."

"You did not make any yourself?"

"No, sir."

"I want you to give me all that you did, by way of word or deed, to see whether your mother was dead or not. When you found your father was dead."

"I didn't do anything, except what I said to Mrs. Churchill. I said to her, 'I don't know where Mrs. Borden is. I think she's out, but I wish you'd look."

"You *did* ask her to look?"

"I said that to Mrs. Churchill."

100

"Where did you intend for her to look?"

"In Mrs. Borden's room."

She had told him yesterday that the last time she'd seen her stepmother alive was at about a quarter to nine in the morning when she'd come downstairs to find her dusting in the dining room. *Was* it conceivable that someone *had* somehow found his way into the house, killed Mrs. Borden, hidden himself somewhere on the inside, and then waited for Mr. Borden's return to kill him with the same weapon in the same manner?

"Will you give me the best judgment you can as to the time your father got back?" he asked. "If you haven't any, it's sufficient to say so."

"No, sir, I haven't any."

"Can you give me any judgment as to the length of time that elapsed *after* he came back and *before* you went to the barn?"

"I went right out to the barn."

"How soon after he came back?"

"I should think not less than five minutes. I saw him taking off his shoes and lying down. It only took him two or three minutes to do it. I went right out."

The shoes again. Why this idiotic insistence that the man had taken off his shoes, when for certain he was found *wearing* his shoes? Was her memory on this point simply faulty? Then why did it persist so strongly? Had he taken off his shoes, and then put them *on* again? Or was the remembered removal of his shoes only another attempt to account for lapsed time? *"It only took him two or three minutes to do it. I went right out."*

"When he came into the house," Knowlton said, "didn't he go into the dining room first?"

"I don't know."

"And there sit down?"

"I don't know."

"*Why* don't you know?"

"Because I was in the kitchen."

"It might have happened? And you not have known it?"

"Yes, sir."

"You heard the bell ring . . ."

"Yes, sir."

". . . and you knew when he came in . . ."

"Yes, sir."

101

"You didn't *see* him?"

"No, sir."

"When *did* you first see him?"

"I went into the sitting room, and he was there. I don't know whether he'd been in the dining room before or not."

"What made you go into the sitting room?"

"Because I wanted to ask him a question."

"What question?"

"Whether there was any mail for me."

"Did you not ask him that question in the dining room?"

"No, sir, I think not."

"Was he not in the dining room, sitting down?"

"I don't remember him being in the dining room sitting down."

A direct contradiction of Bridget Sullivan's sworn testimony. Knowlton decided to pursue it.

"At that time, wasn't Maggie washing the windows in the sitting room?"

"I thought I asked him for the mail in the sitting room. I'm not sure."

"Wasn't the reason he went *in* the dining room because *she* was in the sitting room, washing windows?"

"I don't know."

"Did he not go upstairs to his own room before he sat down in the sitting room?"

"I didn't see him go."

"He had the key to his room down there . . ."

"I don't know whether he had it. It was kept on the shelf."

"Don't you remember he took the key, and went into his own room, and then came back?"

"No, sir. He took some medicine. It wasn't doctor's medicine, it was what we gave him."

"What was it?"

"We gave him castor oil first, and then Garfield tea."

"When was that?"

"He took the castor oil sometime Wednesday, I think, some-time Wednesday noon. And I think the tea Wednesday night. Mrs. Borden gave it to him. She went over to see the doctor."

Again the welter of meaningless detail, as though she hoped

by sheer accumulation to bury the truth under an obfuscating mountain of trivial information.

"When did you first consult Mr. Jennings?" he asked.

"I can't tell you that. I think my sister sent for him. I don't know."

"Was it you or your sister?"

"My sister."

"*You* didn't send for him?"

"I didn't send for him. She said did we think we ought to have him. I said do as she thought best. I don't know when he came first."

Not fair, perhaps, he thought, to use an old lawyer's trick, leading the witness down the garden path, causing her to expect a line of questioning for which she would prepare her defense, and then going off on an entirely different tack, as he was about to do now.

"Now, tell me once more, if you please, the particulars of that trouble you had with your mother four or five years ago."

"Her father's house on Fourth Street was for sale . . ."

"*Whose* father's house?"

"Mrs. *Borden's* father's house. She had a stepmother and a half sister, Mrs. Borden did, and this house was left to the stepmother and a half sister, if I understood it right. And the house was for sale. The stepmother, Mrs. Oliver Gray, wanted to sell it, and my father bought out the Widow Gray's share. *She* didn't tell me, and *he* didn't tell me, but some outsiders said that he gave it to her. Put it in her name. I said if he gave that to *her*, he ought to give *us* something. Told Mrs. Borden so. She didn't care anything about the house herself. She wanted it so this half sister could have a home. Because she'd married a man that wasn't doing the best he could. And she thought her sister was having a very hard time, and wanted her to have a home. And we always thought she persuaded father to buy it. At any rate, he *did* buy it, and I'm quite *sure* she persuaded father to buy it. I said what he did for *her* people, he ought to do for his own *children*. So he gave us grandfather's house. That was all the trouble we ever had."

"You haven't stated *any* trouble between you and her."

"I said there was feeling four or five years ago, when I stopped calling her mother. I told you that yesterday."

103

"That's all there is to it, then?"

"Yes, sir."

"You had no words with your stepmother *then*?"

"I talked with her about it, and said what he did for her he ought to do for us. That's all the words we had."

"That's the occasion of his giving you the house that you sold back to him?"

"Yes, sir."

"Did your mother leave any property?"

"I don't know."

"Your *own* mother."

"No, sir. Not that I ever knew of."

Knowlton nodded and walked back to his table. Still standing at the table, hoping to surprise her with a sudden shift of questioning, he turned to her abruptly and asked, "Did you give to the officer the same skirt you had on the day of the tragedy?"

"Yes, sir."

"Do you know whether there was any blood on the skirt?"

"No, sir."

"Assume that there was . . . do you know how it came there?"

"No, sir."

"Have you any explanation of how it might come there?"

"No, sir."

"Assume that there was . . . can you give any explanation of how it came there? On the dress skirt?"

"No, sir."

"Assume that there was . . . can you suggest any reason how it came there?"

"No, sir."

"Have you offered any?"

"No, sir."

"Have you *ever* offered any?"

"No, sir."

He hesitated before asking his next question. In addition to the witness who—*if* she had committed murder—might not prove squeamish about discussing the loss of blood experienced during a woman's menstrual flow, there was nonetheless *another* woman in the courtroom, busily taking her stenographic notes, and he had no wish to offend her sensibilities. Nor had he any idea where or when the expression "having fleas" had originated as a euphemism for menstruation, but such it was, and the question had to be put because blood was a matter of some keen interest in this case.

"Have you said it came from flea bites?" he asked.

"On the petticoats, I said there was a flea bite. I said it *might* have been. You said you meant the dress skirt."

"I did. Have you offered any explanation how that came there?"

"I told those men that were at the house that I'd had fleas. That's all."

"Did you offer that as an explanation?"

"I said that was the only explanation that I knew of."

"Assuming that the blood came from the *outside* . . . can you give any explanation of how it came there?"

"No, sir."

"You cannot now?"

"No, sir."

"What shoes did you have on that day?"

"A pair of ties."

"What color?"

"Black."

"Will you give them to the officer?"

"Yes."

"Where are they?"

"At home."

"What stockings did you have on that day?"

"Black."

"Where are they?"

"At home."

"Have they been washed?"

"I don't know."

"Will you give *them* to the officer?"

"Yes, sir."

Judge Blaisdell suddenly asked, "Was this witness—on Thursday morning—in the front hall, or front stairs, or front chamber? Any part of the front of the house at all?"

"What do you say to that?" Knowlton asked.

"I had to come down the front stairs to get into the kitchen."

"When you came down first."

"Yes, sir."

"Were you *afterwards*?"

"No, sir."

"Not at all?"

"Except the few minutes I went up with the clean clothes, and I had to come back again."

"That, you now say, was before Mr. Borden went away."

"Yes, sir."

He was, in a way, grateful for the judge's interruption; he could think of nothing further to ask Lizzie Borden, could conceive of no ground they had not already covered. "Your Honor," he said, "there are other witnesses waiting to be heard, and I do not wish to overly tire Miss Borden. I have no further questions at this time, and I wonder if we might excuse her for the present, to recall her sometime tomorrow should the need arise."

"The witness is excused," Blaisdell said. "Mr. Leonard, would you call the next witness, please?"

And so, yesterday afternoon, after all the witnesses had been heard, Knowlton had issued a simple bulletin that stated only, "Inquest continued at ten today. Witnesses examined were Lizzie Borden, Dr. S. W. Bowen, Adelaide B. Churchill, Hiram C. Harrington, John V. Morse, and Emma Borden. Nothing developed for publication."

And earlier this afternoon, the eleventh day of August, he had questioned a drugstore clerk named Eli Bence, and several witnesses who had testified to the whereabouts of Andrew Borden on the morning he was killed, and lastly Bridget Sullivan again, who had left the Borden house to take up temporary residence at 95 Division Street, a mile from the courthouse. He considered it an oversight that a hack had not been sent for her and that she'd had to walk that distance in the interminably persistent August heat.

The heat did nothing to still the temper of the crowd outside. For two days now the officials had been promising an imminent verdict, but the bulletin boards outside the courthouse revealed no such definitive action. The crowd knew only that witnesses came and went; police officers were sent scurrying in every direction at the slightest rumor of a new clue; doctors and

106

professors secretly guarded their learned opinions, if indeed they had reached any opinions at all concerning the murders and the weapon or weapons presumably used. Knowlton knew that a decision, one way or the other, would have to be made today.

The Borden carriage, carrying the two Borden sisters and their friend Mrs. George Brigham had arrived not ten minutes ago, the driver cracking a whip to herd the milling crowd back. Knowlton had watched from the upstairs window of the courtroom, estimating the crowd to consist of at least two hundred men, women and children; remarkable the way they gathered so rapidly the moment the closed carriage came into view. One moment there would be only a handful of idlers in the street outside; the next moment a crowd would appear as if by magic, waiting for the decision that would either exonerate Lizzie Borden or cause her to be charged with the crime of murder.

He looked up at the clock.

It was getting late.

He sighed heavily.

"Is there anything you would like to correct in your previous testimony?" he asked.

"No, sir."

He nodded, went back to his table, picked up a slip of paper, consulted it and walked back to where she sat in the witness chair, watching his every move.

"Your attention has already been called," he said, "to the circumstance of going into the drugstore of Smith's . . ."

Her pale eyes narrowed warily.

". . . on the corner of Columbia and Main Streets—by some officer, has it not?—on the day before the tragedy."

"I don't know whether some officer has asked me. *Somebody* has spoken of it to me. I don't know who it was."

"Did that take place?"

"It did not."

"Do you know where the drugstore is?"

"I don't."

"Did you go into *any* drugstore and inquire for prussic acid?"

"I did not."

"Where *were* you on Wednesday morning, that you remember?"

"At home."

"All the time?"

"All day. Until Wednesday night."

"Did you go into the drugstore for any purpose whatever?"

"I did not."

Eli Bence, the drugstore clerk he'd examined earlier today, had positively identified her as the woman who'd come into the shop asking to buy prussic acid. Knowlton looked at her. She returned his steady gaze.

"Was the dress that was given to the officers the same dress that you wore Thursday morning?"

"Yes, sir."

"The India silk?"

"No, it's not an India silk. It's silk and linen. Some call it bengaline silk."

"Something like that dress there?" he said, and gestured toward Annie White, who was wearing a silk pongee with a knotty weave. The stenographer looked up from her pad, startled to find herself the sudden center of attention.

"No, it wasn't like that," Lizzie said.

"Did you give to the officer the same shoes and stockings that you wore?"

"I did, sir."

"Do you remember where you took them off?"

"I wore the shoes ever after that, all around the house Friday, and Saturday, until I put on my shoes for the street."

"That is to say, you wore them all that day, Thursday, until you took them off for the night?"

"Yes, sir."

He felt suddenly weary. He had asked all the questions there were to be asked; what further question remained? His future course of action seemed unavoidable, nay, inescapable. And yet, if only she would . . .

"Did you tell us yesterday *all* the errand that you had at the barn?"

"Yes, sir."

"You have nothing to add to what you said?"

"No, sir."

108

"You had no other errand than what you've spoken of?"

"No, sir."

Please, he thought. Won't you give me *something*? If you did not do this terrible thing, help me to believe you did not. Please.

"Miss Borden," he said, "of course you appreciate the anxiety that everybody has to find the author of this tragedy . . . ."

Lizzie nodded.

"And the questions that I put to you have been in that direction."

She nodded again.

"I now ask you if you can furnish any other fact, or give any other, even *suspicion*, that will assist the officers in any way in this matter."

Lizzie considered this for several moments. Then she said, "About two weeks ago . . . ."

"Were you going to tell the occurrence about that man who called at the house?"

"No, sir. It was after my sister went away. I came home from Miss Russell's one night, and as I came up—I always glanced toward the side door as I came along by the carriage way—I saw a shadow on the side steps. I didn't stop walking but I walked slower. Somebody ran down the steps, around the east end of the house. I thought it was a man, because I saw no skirts. And I was frightened, and of course I didn't go around to see. I hurried to the front door as fast as I could and locked it."

"What time of night was that?"

"I think about quarter of nine. It was not after nine o'clock, anyway."

"Do you remember what night that was?"

"No, sir, I don't." She hesitated, thinking, and then said, "I saw somebody run around the house once before. Last winter."

"One thing at a time," Knowlton said. "Do you recollect about how long ago that last occurrence was?"

"It was after my sister went away. She's been away two weeks today, so it must've been within two weeks."

"Two weeks *today*? Or two weeks at the time of the murder?"

"Isn't today Thursday?"

"Yes, but I thought you said she was gone two weeks the day of the murder."

"*Isn't* today Thursday?" Lizzie said again.

"Yes, but that would be *three* weeks. I thought you said the day your father was murdered she'd been away just two weeks."

"Yes, she had."

"Then it would be *three* weeks today. Your sister went away . . . a week has elapsed."

"Yes," she said, and again that faraway look came into her eyes, as though she were suddenly transported to some distant place he could not hope to reach. "I'd forgotten that a whole week has passed since the affair."

He watched her in silence for several seconds. He was suddenly aware of the ticking of the big clock on the courtroom wall.

"Different from that," he said, "you cannot state?"

"No, sir. I don't know what the date was."

"This . . . *form* . . . when you first saw it was on the steps of the back door?"

"Yes, sir."

"Went down the rear steps?"

"Went down toward the barn."

"Around the back side of the house?"

"Disappeared in the dark. I don't know where they went."

"Have you ever mentioned that before?"

"Yes, sir. I told Mr. Jennings."

"To any officer?"

"I don't think I have. Unless I told Mr. Hanscomb."

"What were you going to say about last winter?" he asked.

"Last winter, when I was coming home from church one Thursday evening, I saw somebody run around the house again. I told my father of that."

"Did you tell your father of this last one?"

"No, sir."

"Of course, you couldn't identify who it was *either* time."

"No, I couldn't identify who it was. But it wasn't a very *tall* person."

The clock on the wall ticked persistently. The courtroom was silent except for the ticking of the clock. Time was running out. Beyond this afternoon meeting, if he did not grant her time now, there would never again be opportunity for her to tell her side of the story; Jennings would never allow her to take the stand if this case came to trial. Now was the time, the one and only time. He granted her time.

"Have you sealskin sacks?" he asked.

"Yes, sir," Lizzie said.

"Where are they?"

"Hanging in a large white bag in the attic. Each one separate."

"Put away for the summer?"

"Yes, sir."

"Do you ever use prussic acid on your sacks?"

"Acid? No, sir, I don't use anything on them."

And again, he granted her time. Allowed her at least the small courtesy of time because there was little else he could offer her now. Desperately, recognizing the note of desperation in his voice even as the words left his mouth, he said, "Is there anything else that you can suggest that even amounts to *anything* whatever?"

"I know of nothing else. Except the man who came and father ordered him out. That's all I know."

"That you told about the other day?"

"I think I did, yes, sir."

"You haven't been able to find that man?"

"I haven't. I don't know whether anybody else has or not."

"Have you caused search to be made for him?"

"Yes, sir."

"When was the offer of reward made for the detection of the criminals?"

"I think it was made Friday."

"Who suggested that?"

"We suggested it ourselves, and asked Mr. Buck if he didn't think it was a good idea."

"Whose suggestion was it? Yours or Emma's?"

"I don't remember," Lizzie said. "I think it was mine."

In his mind the clock abruptly stopped ticking, though surely it had not.

"I have no further questions," he said.

Their eyes met.

"No further questions," he said again, and turned away from her steady gaze.

He found her later in the matron's room across from the

courtroom entry. She was sitting there with her sister, her friend Mrs. Brigham and her attorney. He asked Mrs. Brigham to leave. He turned to Marshal Hilliard, who had entered the room together with Detective Seaver. The marshal was holding a sheet of paper in his hand.

"I have here a warrant for your arrest," Hilliard said, "issued by the judge of the District Court. I shall read it to you if you desire, but you have the right to waive the reading of it."

She looked at Jennings.

"Waive the reading," Jennings advised.

Lizzie turned slightly in her chair. Her eyes met Knowlton's momentarily—he would never forget the glacial look in them—and then she turned stiffly to the marshal.

"You need not read it," she said.

5: LONDON—1890

On the morning after her tea with Alison, she wrote a thank-you note on hotel stationery, and asked the hall porter to mail it for her. He assured her that the postal service in London was without equal anywhere in the world, and that very few letters ever went astray.

"Our delivery is prompt, madam, *prompt*," he said. "We've between six to twelve deliveries each day, madam, six to *twelve* of them. Your letter should arrive there in a wink," he added, glancing at the address. "Kensington's but a stone's throw away."

"Thank you, sir," she said, and noticed the odd look he gave her. She had not yet learned that in London there was a vast difference between civility and servility. *Yes, sir* and *No, sir* were the verbal insignia of a servant, and a proper lady would not have addressed a hotel employee—however ancient he might have been, as was the hall porter—with the word *sir*. She would learn this later from Alison, who taught her the errors of her ways in Paris; for now, she felt only puzzled. Leaving her letter in what she felt certain were safe hands, walking away from the lobby desk, she wondered if the note had been too formal for the good fun she and Alison had shared yesterday afternoon. Never could she remember having laughed so heartily! Or at such patently bawdy humor! Exchanged by two *ladies*, no less—she blushed to think of it. Back in Fall River she might on occasion be passing a stable or a saloon and would overhear the men at their jokes or their sly innuendos, but she'd always hurry past, her ears flaming, before the peals of laughter burst forth from inside those dark and secret places where they congregated. To joke about that horrible event—she could still remember Stephen's cold hands fussing about under her clothing—and to accept his unfortunate groping and grasping as *humorous* in retrospect was something she could not have imagined herself doing a scant week ago.

Should she have made some allusion in her note to their giddiness? *I have never laughed so long or so hard?* But no, that would have seemed too plaintive, perhaps, a foreigner blatantly beseeching further invitation. Alison would have her letter sometime today; better to let her decide for herself, without prompting, whether she chose to extend any further courtesies. *I seek your friendship,* she had said. In which case she knew where to find it. For now, having followed what she was certain was proper etiquette, Lizzie stepped out of the hotel into a gloriously surprising balmy day, eager to explore the city further, this time unencumbered by Felicity's inane remarks, Anna's always imminent illness or even Rebecca's lively chatter.

Today, she wanted no chatter.

I do not much care for it, she'd told Alison, and she'd recognized in that moment that truly too *much* of her life was spent in conversations she did not enjoy. The other ladies (why did Alison use the words *lady* or *ladies* so sneeringly?) had asked her to accompany them to Madam Tussaud's, but Lizzie had politely refused, however famous that establishment might be. She preferred seeing *real* people rather than wax dummies, and was delighted to find Piccadilly bustling and alive even at so early an hour of the day.

She was almost to the corner of Old Bond Street, on her way toward Piccadilly Circus, guidebook in hand, when she heard a voice behind her shouting, "Miss Borden, mum, Miss Borden!" and turned to see one of the hotel pages in his gray livery trimmed with red at the collar pounding along toward her on the pavement. He was overweight for his thirteen or fourteen

114

years, with plump apple cheeks and sky-blue eyes, hatless now—she watched as he retraced his steps to pick up his cap where it had fallen to the pavement—and completely out of breath by the time he drew up beside her. "Miss Borden, mum, pardon me," he said, huffing and puffing, "but there's someone on the telephone for you, mum. Pardon me, mum, I didn't wish to interrupt your walk." He put on his little gray peakless cap with its red piping, and virtually bowed her back to the hotel, where he stood waiting while Lizzie rummaged in her purse for a twopence coin.

The hall porter whom she'd addressed as "sir" not a few moments earlier, came from behind his polished mahogany desk and said, "Ah, Miss Borden, ma'am! I thought it might be best to try catching you, the lady said it was urgent." He led her to a glass-enclosed booth round a corner in the hall, said, "You can just pick up, ma'am, she's on the line waiting," opened the door for her, and then eased it shut behind her.

Lizzie picked up the receiver. "Hello?" she said.

"Lizzie!" Alison said. "They were able to find you, were they? I do hope I haven't fetched you back at an awkward time."

"No, no, not at all," Lizzie said. "But what a coincidence! I've just this moment given the hall porter a thank-you note to mail."

"Ah, how sweet of you," Alison said. "With our beastly system here, it probably won't arrive till *next* Tuesday, when I'll be long gone. I must tell you why I'm calling," she said, somewhat breathlessly, Lizzie thought. "We'll be leaving for Paris tomorrow, as you know, which is a dreadful pity because I shan't be able to see you before then, what with tons of packing yet to do and getting the servants organized—they always seem to become as helpless as butterflies each time we make our summer move. I don't know how long we'll be there—Albert has some business to take care of, which may delay our leaving for Cannes—but I *did* want you to know where we'll be staying, on the off chance we'll still be there when you arrive. When did you say that might be, Lizzie?"

"The third, I believe. This coming Sunday."

"Oh my, you *will* travel on Sundays, won't you? In France, you'll be lucky to find a porter. It's always *some* sort of religious holiday there, and if it isn't, you'll find those surly frogs off to church, anyway, either praying or baptizing or else marrying a

115

plump little maiden who, within months, will have grown a handlebar mustache to rival her mama's. Do you have a pencil, Lizzie? I hear Moira shrieking at our gardener about something, and I'm afraid I'll have to run and set it straight, what*ever* the calamity may be this time." Lizzie could picture her rolling her green eyes heavenward. "Are you ready? I'm sorry, am I rushing you?"

Lizzie had picked up the stubby little pencil alongside the pad in the booth, and was waiting to write. "Yes, go ahead," she said.

"It's the Hotel Binda—do remember *not* to call it the Binda *Hotel* as there may be an utterly disreputable flophouse of the same name in Pigalle, if we're to learn anything at all from Albert's mistake. It's number eleven rue de l'Echelle, not a minute's walk from the rue de Rivoli and the Tuileries. We shall be there tomorrow sometime, and certainly through most of the week, unless Albert's business detains him—which, frankly, I hope it does. So that we may see each other again."

"How very kind of you," Lizzie said.

"Now tell me quickly where you and your friends will be staying. I do believe we have the Crimean War being fought all over again in the scullery."

"We'll be at the Anglo-Français," Lizzie said. "I'm sorry, I don't remember the address."

"Yes, I know it," Alison said. "It's in the rue Castiglione, not far from us, actually. Oh, I do so hope we'll still be there when you arrive! We'll have *such* fun, Lizzie!"

"I enjoyed yesterday enormously," Lizzie said.

"As did I. Look at me, won't you, I've almost forgotten! Please do say no to this if you find it awkward, Lizzie, won't you? But I *did* want to make your stay in our filthy city as comfortable as possible, and I should have seen to it in person had our own travel plans not been fixed so far in advance. I've taken the liberty of asking my brother to call upon you; he should be there at noon, if you find that agreeable. He's a Londoner to the marrow, and will do his utmost to show you some of the things you might otherwise miss."

"Well, really, Alison, that's . . ."

"And surely, you might enjoy lunching in something other than one of those dreary little places they've set aside for respectable *ladies* unaccompanied by the *stronger* sex. Geoffrey will see to it that you and your friends are escorted in style—he knows I shall behead him otherwise. And you must feel free to utilize him throughout your entire stay here. It will make it *so* much easier, Lizzie, truly. Do say yes, or I shall be cross with you."

"Well . . ."

"Done then," Alison said. "He'll be there at noon, his name is Geoffrey. Hastings, of course. Don't let his costume put you off; he's a gentleman through and through even if he does affect the style of a Piccadilly Johnnie—what we sometimes call a masher or a chappie. My God, I'm *sure* they're *breaking* things out there! Do let me go, Lizzie. Geoffrey Hastings, twelve noon, he's tall and green-eyed and devilishly handsome, and if you're lucky he won't be wearing stays. I shall hope and pray I see you in Paris, my dear. And *do* take full advantage of Geoff while you're here, though he's *such* a mash, really. I must run," she said, "ta."

Lizzie stared in astonishment at the telephone.

Geoffrey Hastings was quite as tall and as handsome as Alison had promised, a young man somewhere in his thirties, Lizzie surmised, standing some six feet two inches tall in his patent-leather buttoned boots with their suede uppers, and wearing besides a dress coat that looked rather like an Eton jacket, cut to show an immense amount of ruffled shirtfront. The coat fitted him tightly at the waist, and Lizzie was certain (as Alison had suggested) that he was corseted beneath it. He wore a gray top hat, which he swept from his head the moment Lizzie approached him in the lobby, revealing short blond hair parted in the center. His face was clean-shaven, and his eyes were a green so dark they bordered on black.

"My dear Miss Borden," he said, "how kind of you to make yourself available this afternoon." He spoke English rather the way American stage performers did when they were trying to *sound* British, his voice somewhat high and nasal, his words slurred so that they became a continual sort of hum. "I do hope you've been enjoying our unaccustomed sunshine," he said, and before Lizzie could reply, went on to say, "Allie told me you were up and about quite early this morning, and so I shan't bore

117

you with any more sightseeing till we've had a good lunch. I hope you're quite as famished as I am."

He took her for lunch (she felt hopelessly provincial thinking of it as *dinner* in her mind, the accepted word for it in Fall River) to a place called the Holborn Restaurant, where the glass and the brass and the marble columns were resplendently imposing, the room spacious, richly ornamented and attractively upholstered.

"I must tell you straight off," he said, as soon as they were seated, "that there are no restaurants in all of London which can in any way compare to Delmonico's or the Café Savarin in New York. Nor can you find here—at *any* price—a table d'hôte meal equal in quality or style of service to that furnished at Cambridge's on Fifth Avenue. Having made my national apologies, may I suggest that we start with the Whitstable oysters— our so-called native oysters—which are much my favorite, although many Americans find their flavor a trifle coppery and strong. The Chesapeake oysters, or the Great South Bay blue- points, might suit your palate better—*if* you like oysters at all, that is, and if they're indeed in season, which I suspect they're not. In any case, a bottle of Montrachet might be welcome, wouldn't you agree?"

The oysters were *not* in season, and so Geoffrey suggested she might like to try either the thick turtle soup, or the mulligatawny, both of which he'd sampled here and found excellent, unless she preferred the consommé with Italian paste—though surely she was traveling on to Italy, was she not? They both had the turtle soup, followed by the whitebait— which Geoffrey said was a British delicacy and not to be missed—and then Geoffrey ordered the calf's head and piquant sauce while she settled for the less exotic half roast spring chicken and ham, although he highly recommended the haricot oxtail.

"The wine isn't all that bad, is it?" he said, though she'd made no comment at all upon it, and in fact had not once brought her glass to her lips. "One must be terribly wary choosing wines in any London restaurant nowadays. Those tempted to drink bad wine generally pay the penalty in money and malaise. I truly feel that restaurateurs who label their bottles Château-this or Château-that should be penalized under the Adulteration Act.

Surely the adulteration of wine is no less a fraud than the adulteration of beer, wouldn't you agree? Now then, assuming we can finish off our meal with a really well-made cup of coffee, something not so easily procured in London, what would you like to see this afternoon?

"I must tell you, of course, that sightseeing in London falls into two categories: places that everyone *wishes* to see, but that few *can* see; and places that everyone *can* see, but that few have any *wish* to see. I should love taking you to see the interiors of the Queen's palaces, for example, but unfortunately I would first have to reckon with the Lord Chamberlain's Department, and I fear a mere idle curiosity would never suffice to gain his official permission, which in any case is rarely granted. On the other hand, Miss Borden, were we . . ."

"If I'm to call you *Geoff* . . ."

"May I then? Thank you so much, Lizzie. Were we to make polite application by letter, we *might* be granted permission to view the various spendid private art collections—the Duke of Westminster's in Grosvenor Street, the Duke of Wellington's at Apsley House, and so on. How long do you expect you'll be here?"

"We'll be leaving for Paris on the third."

"Scarcely time enough to get those titled gentlemen off their arses—you'll pardon me, Allie tells me you're easily shocked." Before she could protest, he said, "Dismissing the first category as unobtainable, then, and sliding past those places in the second category—the ones everyone *can* see, and which you and your friends will undoubtedly feel duty *bound* to see—may I suggest some alternatives for this afternoon and the several days ahead?"

"Yes, please do," Lizzie said.

"Well, then, do you like orchids?" he asked, and Lizzie suddenly remembered Alison's complimentary allusion. "Because if you do, the Chamberlain collection in Kew Gardens is possibly one of the very best on the face of the earth. I've seen it more than once, and it probably contains more rarities than any other amateur can boast of. If you favor roses, the finest collection in all England is at Waltham Cross, not a half-hour's journey by rail from the Liverpool Street terminus. Or have you had enough of rail travel? Unfortunately, you've already missed the

119

Rose Society's yearly exhibition at the Crystal Palace; it shut down almost two weeks ago. The same can be said of the Evening Floral Fête in Regent's Park. A pity you weren't here just a trifle earlier, Lizzie. I thought perhaps, for starters this afternoon, we might . . ."

He took her first to John Wesley's restored chapel in the City Road—something mentioned in none of her guidebooks, and certainly a place she might otherwise have missed—explaining that the chapel had only recently been reopened for public worship and asking what her religious persuasion might be, if indeed she was religious at all. She told him she was a member of the Central Congregational Church in Fall River, and that her religion, as such, was evangelical Protestant.

"And yours?" she asked.

"My sister and I both, I fear, are complete heathens, though our mother tried to raise us as proper Lutherans, against the Church of England wishes of my dear, departed pater."

"Am I to understand you do not go to church?" Lizzie asked.

"Only when I'm caught in a sudden downpour," Geoffrey said, "of which there are many in London. In that respect, one might say I'm an *avid* churchgoer."

"Then why have you taken me here?" she asked.

"Because I do so love this small house," he said. "Not for its historic significance, certainly not. After all, 1777—when Wesley laid the chapel's foundation stone—might be considered thoroughly modern, in terms of our lengthy, illustrious, and thoroughly blood-stained history," and here she detected a note of irony in his voice, so similar to Alison's. "But for its serenity. To wander these rooms, to see the man's study and conference chairs, his clock, his clothes and furniture—and in his tiny prayer room, the small table-desk and kneeler—these fill me with a sense of peace. Perhaps I *am* religious after all, Lizzie, though I shouldn't let my sister hear that."

In the spacious graveyard outside, as they stood by the tomb of the great founder of the Methodist church, Geoffrey—with a tone as mocking as his sister's—asked a caretaker, in what was an overly exaggerated awesome whisper, "Is this ground consecrated then?"

"Aye, sir, indeed it is," the caretaker replied.

"By what bishop?" Geoffrey asked at once.

"By none, sir," the caretaker replied. "Solely by depositing in it the body of that man of God, John Wesley."

In the hansom cab on the way to Westminster Hall where Geoffrey planned to show her St. Stephen's Crypt (which Alison had mentioned in passing yesterday) and the Jerusalem Chamber and Chapter House attached to the Abbey, he said, "The growth of our grubby little city continues to amaze me. Had you been here last year at this time, there'd have been twelve thousand fewer houses—do statistics interest you, Lizzie?"

"Well . . . yes. In moderation."

"I shall be moderate then, however contrary that may be to my nature. Be advised, then, that we shall be supplying somewhere near eight hundred thousand homes with running water this year—a commonplace in America, I'm sure, but quite remarkable for us."

Lizzie thought of her own house on Second Street in Fall River, where the toilet facilities were in the cellar, and where—although there was a well in the backyard, and a pump in the barn—the only running water was obtained either from a tap in the sink room off the kitchen pantry, or from the faucet over the washtub in the laundry room downstairs.

"It shall grow to be monstrous, I'm certain," Geoffrey said, "like Mary Shelley's awesome creation. At which time we shall all flee to the Riviera, as my wise sister is presently doing, and spend our entire *year* there with all those bloody unmannerly French. Gone will be the day when one can get about London without truly knowing the city; all you need do *now*, of course, is ask any cabman to take you where you want to go, and he'll find the tiniest little lane in the shabbiest little neighborhood." As if to fortify his point, he threw open the little trapdoor on the roof of the hansom, and called to the driver outside, "Isn't that so, cabbie?"

"Isn't what so, sir?" the cabman said, bending over from his erect perch on the platform behind them.

"That I might give you an address on the most obscure little street in all London, and you'd find it for me?"

"Did you not want Westminster Hall then, sir?" the cabbie asked.

"Ignore it," Geoffrey said. "The question was rhetorical."

121

"I beg your pardon then, sir," the cabbie said.

"Do you know what rhetorical means?" Geoffrey asked.

"Aye, sir, I do," the cabbie answered.

"And what might it mean?"

"It means unworthy of an answer, sir," the cabbie said, and stood erect again, and flicked his whip at the great black horse pulling them along.

Laughing, Geoffrey allowed the roof panel to fall loosely into place again. "There are fourteen thousand of these fellows in London," he said, "and all of them fancy themselves to be wits. They're absolutely right, of course—by *half*," he said, and laughed again. "They're supposed to charge you sixpence a mile, you know, but foreigners will often pay twice that to avoid any dispute; so do be wary, Lizzie, and firm as well. They rent these vehicles, and so I suppose they have to hustle a bit to earn a bob. A four-wheeler'll cost them ten bob a day, and a hansom like this one a pound."

"More like a guinea, sir," the cabbie said behind them, letting them know he'd overheard this last as well, and then slamming shut the trapdoor to advise them he cared to hear no more.

"We've even more policemen than we have cabbies, and if ever you should lose your way, don't hesitate to ask directions of them. They're well paid—your street-corner bobby will be earning something close to a quid and ten a week, with his sergeant getting closer to two quid—and they're only too delighted to assist in any way possible. You're not obliged to tip them for answering your enquiries, of course, but I've never yet known one to refuse a tanner in the palm. But then again, Lizzie, who in all *England* will not accept an offered tip? I haven't yet tipped the Lord of Buccleuch or the lord mayor, but I haven't yet *met* those honorable gentlemen," Geoffrey said, and laughed again.

How very much like Alison he is, Lizzie thought. The same fair hair and flawless complexion, the same somewhat petulant mouth with its cupid's-bow upper lip and pouting lower, the same green eyes, though very much darker than his sister's— almost too pretty to be a man. And, too, he was possessed of the same casually knowledgeable air, the same spontaneous wit, and—most especially—the identical biting tone of voice, as though anything that touched his mind or his eye was fair prey for his quicksilver derision. When he took her, just before tea-time, to the tropical department at Kew Gardens, she was re-minded again of Alison, and wondered if her comments the day before had had anything to do with Geoffrey's choice now. Had they discussed together the things she thought might interest Lizzie? Was this dazzling display of orchids meant as a subtle reminder of Alison's fanciful dissertation on American girls? But, oh, such a glorious array! And again how like his sister was Geoffrey, showing her through rows and rows of more orchids than Lizzie might have imagined in her wildest fantasies, as seemingly awestruck by their beauty as she herself was, and discoursing upon them (as Alison might have) in a manner that was at first informative and then—suddenly, unexpectedly—shocking.

"Aside from their extraordinary beauty," he said, and imme-diately interrupted himself to point out a violently red bloom, which he identified as *Ranthera* something or other, ". . . as scarlet as your own lovely hair," he said, and then, "*and* your flaming cheeks, I might add," for indeed his compliment had caused her to blush. "But aside from their extraordinary beauty," he went on, picking up where he'd left off, "they're not quite so useless as one might imagine. You know, of course, that vanilla is derived from the orchid . . ."

"No, I didn't know that," Lizzie said, still blushing.

"Oh, yes, the *Vanilla planifolia,* cultivated in Madagascar and the Seychelles and also the French West Indies, where yet *an-other* variety has yet another *use*—although a more plebian one. The bulbs there are boiled, dear Lizzie" (and this was the first time he used the affectionate adjective) "to abstract a liquid that is used for fish poisoning. Not to poison the fish *themselves,* you understand," he said, smiling, "but to cure the poison injected when one of those beastly undersea creatures of the tropics chooses to *bite* you. Throughout the world, various species of orchids are used in one way or another for medicinal purposes. The mucilage from one species is even supposed to heal broken bones, and in some Eastern tropics the tubers are eaten like potatoes. A pity our barbaric Irish haven't tumbled to *that* one, isn't it? In short—and you'll detect before long that I rarely address myself to *any* topic in brevity when greater length might suffice—the orchid, though so often compared to femi-

123

ninity by my dear sister, is not *quite* so uselessly ornamental as so many of our celebrated female beauties are these days."

Ah, then. Had Alison's little speech yesterday been a rehearsed and oft repeated one? Had she delivered it as a stage actress might, anticipating a response she knew would result the moment the words left her lips? Had it been, after all, flattery of the most blatant sort, and not the "honest praise" Alison had claimed it to be?

"The word *orchid* derives from the Greek, you know," Geoffrey said.

"Does it?" Lizzie said. She was still thinking of the extravagant compliments Alison had so lavishly dispensed yesterday. *There's something so fresh about you . . . You have such marvelous color, Lizzie, that wonderfully fiery hair, and those incredible gray eyes . . . How silly of me, you're quite beautiful enough without any artifice . . . Are there no looking glasses in all of Fall River then? . . . How prettily you blush . . .*

She felt suddenly gulled.

She felt suddenly foolish.

"From the word *orchis*," Geoffrey said.

"Indeed," Lizzie said.

"Which means testicle," Geoffrey said.

"Oh," Lizzie said, shocked beyond further speech.

"Because of the shape of some root tubers."

"Yes," she said, and turned away from him. "I do so love these tiny delicate ones," she said, knowing she was blushing again and unwilling to have him see her face or to comment upon it. She was quite beside herself, not wishing to reprimand a person Alison had described as "a gentleman through and through" (her *brother*, no less!) but at the same time reluctant to encourage any further discourse on the similarity of root tubers to portions of the male anatomy best left undiscussed in polite society. To her great surprise—and although he *surely* must have detected her diversionary tactic, such a great show of unbridled appreciation was she lavishing upon what was truly an insignificant if admittedly miniscule blossom—Geoffrey's next words were, "Sexually—and despite the Greek derivation of its name—the orchid is an uncommonly curious flower."

"Have we not seen enough of orchids?" Lizzie said politely. "I'm overwhelmed, truly"—which indeed she was, more by his

124

shocking language than by the riotous display everywhere around her—"but I'm not sure I can bear much more," and here she turned to face him squarely, her gray eyes meeting his, the set of her mouth clearly indicating (she hoped) that she did not appreciate such conversation and wished it would come to an immediate halt.

Apparently oblivious to her threatening glare or her compressed lips, blithely unaware of anything but the sound of his own voice and the certainty that he was disclosing something of enormous interest to her (or was he merely determined to shock, as had his sister been yesterday?), Geoffrey said, "The male and female sex organs, you see, are joined together in a single column. The stamens and the pistil, that is."

He then went on, surprising her further, to deliver a learned and not at all objectionable lecture on the various parts of the flower, using such botanical terms as *sepals* and *whorls* and *anthers* and *stigmas*, and quite bewildering Lizzie until, once again, he shocked her by saying, "In some species, the petals so closely resemble female insects, that male insects are lured into mating with them—or at least *trying* to—what is called *pseudo* copulation. In yet other species . . ."

"Geoffrey," she said, "I do believe . . ."

". . . a significant number of them, in fact, the orchid is self-pollinating, which I suppose isn't too surprising when one considers the proximity of the pollen tubes to the ovaries. I don't suppose one could consider it homosexual, though, since both sexes *are*, after all, represented. Well then," he said with a blithe smile, "we've had more than enough of orchids, I quite agree. Let me take you for tea at the Terrace, after which I shall deposit you at your hotel till eight this evening, at which time I shall stop by in a four-wheeler to collect you and your friends, assuming you will all do me the honor of joining me for dinner."

Lizzie did not know quite what to say.

"Done then," he said, echoing Alison.

He surprised her further at dinner that night—a sumptuous feast in the Grill Room at the Grand—first by his costume, and next by the gentlemanly attention and care he gave not only to the ladies' appetites, advising them about this or that item on the menu, instantly signaling to a waiter when a wine glass

125

needed replenishing (Rebecca and Felicity were drinking; Anna and Lizzie were not) but to their emotional needs as well, paying close mind to Rebecca's tedious recitation of all the tourist wonders the women had seen that afternoon, lending a sympathetic ear to the interminable list of Anna's fancied ailments, and responding with steadfast interest to Felicity's constant flirting.

He was dressed more conservatively, but nonetheless resplendently, than he had been this afternoon, wearing a dress coat with rolled, silk-faced lapels, open over a white dress shirt and collar, the collar somewhat higher (was this what Alison had called the "masher" style?) than Lizzie was accustomed to seeing in America, and adorned with a simple, rather thin, black bow tie. When Felicity, batting her lashes, asked if all men in England dressed for dinner, Geoffrey replied, "Some, I'm sure, go about stark naked," and glanced at Lizzie, causing her a moment of nervous apprehension until all the other women unexpectedly laughed, Felicity more heartily than any of the others, her face half-hidden behind her frantically fluttering fan.

"In all seriousness, though," Geoffrey said, "my tailor tells me it's not at all uncommon now for a fashionable man to array himself thrice daily. A tweed suit for his morning wear; a frock coat, smarter waistcoat and bigger tie for the afternoon; and, of course, evening dress for dinner."

"If only American men were so fashion conscious," Rebecca said, vying for his attention. "In Fall River, the men resemble undertakers more than anything else."

"A fine occupation," Geoffrey said, smiling, "in that they're never wanting for trade."

"What do *you* do, Mr. Hastings?" Anna asked, "if you do not consider the question impertinent."

"Not at all," Geoffrey said, "and please do call me *Geoff*, I implore you. The question is rather more pertinent than my vocation—or *avocation*, as I might more properly call it these days."

"And what might that be?" Felicity asked.

"Architecture."

"By *avocation*, do you mean—well, what *do* you mean?" Re-

126

becca asked. "Do you study architecture? Or teach it? Or are you a designer of buildings?"

"Alas, I'm an architect," Geoffrey said. "A designing one, I fear," he added, and glanced at Felicity who peered at him over her fan, her blue eyes fascinated. "For which, I might say in explanation, there is scant use in London where domiciles and places of business are springing up like toadstools and with as much reckless disregard for beauty or form."

"We find your city lovely," Anna said apologetically.

"I thank you," Geoffrey said, "but I can take no credit for it. The last building I had erected was in Birmingham, that foul mill town, and that more than a year ago. Were it not for a more than generous inheritance from my dear, departed father, I should be quite penniless, I'm sure."

"Oh, I'm *so* sorry," Rebecca said.

"I assure you, dear lady, we shall not have to scrub dishes tonight," Geoffrey said, smiling.

"I meant . . . about your father."

"Quite some time ago," Geoffrey said, "and after a long illness."

"The Lord was merciful then," Anna said.

"Quite," Geoffrey said, and glanced at Lizzie and smiled.

She sensed, all at once, that he seemed to believe they shared an awesome secret together, as though her inability to silence him effectively this afternoon had created between them an unspoken bond that was somehow illicit by its very tacitness. She kept waiting for him to say something openly provocative or outrageous, but aside from his coarse reference to male nudity and, just now, his sly affirmation (lost on the others) of his own Godlessness, he seemed content to reassure her silently and with sidelong glances and knowing smiles that the mortar binding them was stronger than the others could ever hope to guess, and this frankly confounded her.

Nor did he appear quite so daringly derisive here in the presence of the women and the other well-dressed, soft-spoken diners in this opulently carpeted, comfortably upholstered and resplendently tiled room, where the conversation was counterpointed by the occasional silvery laughter of the ladies all about or the discreet tinkling click of a ring against a crystal goblet. The food was magnificent, despite his protestations of English

127

culinary inadequacy, and Lizzie supposed it must be costing him a small fortune to feed them; she had no way of knowing since the menus presented to her and the other ladies had offered no hint of the tariff. Reflecting upon his generosity and his restraint, she began to think more kindly of him, certain now (as Alison had suggested) that outspokenness was simply a family trait that only occasionally erupted and was not to be taken seriously when it did.

When the ladies briefly excused themselves "to visit the facilities," as Felicity brainlessly put it, Geoffrey asked if they were well supplied with coppers, and then fished into his pocket for a handful of change, explaining that the lavoratory here at the Grand would cost each of them thrippence rather than the tuppence expected of hotel guests. Rebecca protested mightily, already fumbling at the purse stylishly fastened to a belt at her waist, but he waved her efforts airily aside and pressed the coins into Felicity's palm. Lizzie, thinking it impolite to leave him alone at the table, watched as the other women descended the opulent staircase leading below, its landing decorated with a marble fountain and Eastern rugs and fernery and Oriental lamps.

"Your friend," Geoffrey said, "is an outrageous flirt, isn't she?"

"I'm sure she's not," Lizzie said, knowing full well she was but attempting to end the conversation before it led to another outburst of the Hastings Curse.

"Don't misunderstand me, please," Geoffrey said, and reassuringly patted her hand. "I find it refreshing. The great charm of you American girls abroad is that you manage to combine the purity of the adolescent and the coquettishness of the young married woman. A young French or English girl, for example, would sit here in her modest, well-educated, and thoroughly simple way, maidenly eyes demurely lowered, exuding a soft, virtually saintly light that invites discreet observation, judgment and examination. You American girls, on the other hand, have something rather more flashing. You flit rather than walk. Your glances are like diamonds whose many facets force an onlooker to blink away from their blinding luster. Your hair is lightly and negligently knotted and not arranged to good form, giving you the *air chiffoné* of a pretty girl who may be admitted *into* the ballroom, but certainly not to the *ball* itself."

"You sound exactly like your sister," Lizzie said.

"I take that as a great compliment," Geoffrey said.

"But I'm not sure I enjoy the way both of you go on about American girls, as though we were a breed of horse to be compared to the Arabian or the . . ."

"A species of orchid, rather," Geoffrey said.

"Your sister again," Lizzie said, smiling.

"A species that needs more light and heat than any other," Geoffrey said softly.

"Such nonsense," Lizzie said, but she was still smiling.

"Well, surely, you *must* have observed for yourself the great difference between American women and our homegrown variety, nowhere more evident than in their behavior before and after marriage. Here, and *especially* in France, marriage is a license for flirtation of the most provocative sort strictly frowned upon *before* marriage. And, I might add, oftentimes leading to the fabled *quatre à cinq*—which is more than idle myth, believe me."

"And what on earth is a cat that sank?" Lizzie asked.

"Gentleman that I am," he said, smiling secretly again, "I shall leave that to my sister to explain."

"No, please do tell me."

"I shall offend your maidenly ears," Geoffrey said. "But having been *implored* so prettily to do so . . ."

"No, please don't," Lizzie said, rolling her eyes as Alison might have. "I regret having asked, truly," and they both laughed.

The ladies reappeared in that moment, exclaiming excitedly over the fairyland beauty of the lavatory, and the moment they were seated the *maître d'hôtel* arrived with the dessert cart, and there was much oohing and ahhing and much consultation and more advice from Geoffrey before pastries and fruits were chosen. All that while Geoffrey's sidelong glances continued to include Lizzie in a sort of—conspiracy, yes, that was the word for it. Oddly she now felt drawn into the secret she previously felt he alone had kept, and the thought of it was warming and curiously exciting.

When at last they all said goodnight outside the Albemarle,

she was delighted that he asked if he might call for them again early the next morning, "To show you," he said, and there was that trace of irony again, "whatever meager sights our paltry city has to offer."

The ladies laughed and protested, but Geoffrey was adamant. He would stop by in a carriage at ten sharp, he said, and then immediately corrected himself. "That might be a bit early," he said, and glanced in his sidelong way at Lizzie. "Shall we make it ten-oh-one?"

There was more laughter and handshaking all around, and when finally the ladies entered the hotel, and went to the separate rooms they shared, Lizzie felt a comfortable sense of well-being she could only attribute to Geoffrey's evening-long efforts to charm.

"Such a bright man," Rebecca said, slipping out of her dress. "Do help me undo my corset, Lizzie. So witty and quick, I *so* admire men blessed with a gift for language."

"Yes," Lizzie said, smiling, and thought again how very much like Alison he was.

And, oh, how the next four days flew past!

Geoffrey had advised them that there were several choices as concerned the possible routes from London to Paris but that far and away the best and shortest of these was the one via Folkestone to Boulogne. The only advantage of the Dover-Calais route, the second-best alternate, was that—owing to the depth of the water at Dover and Calais—the boats departed and arrived at fixed hours, whereas those plying between Folkestone and Boulogne were at the mercy of the tides.

On the other hand, the hours of departure by the tidal trains were far more convenient than those via Dover, and the Folkestone route was shorter by a full half hour. The time occupied in crossing the Channel from Folkestone to Boulogne, he went on (as he was wont to do, Lizzie thought with a smile), was some ten to fifteen minutes longer than from Dover to Calais. *But*—and this was an important *but*—Boulogne was three-quarters of an hour nearer Paris by rail than was Calais, and those few additional minutes on the Channel would be compensated for by the saving of the uninteresting railway journey from Calais to Boulogne. If the ladies would heed his advice, then, he would be only too willing to make all the necessary arrangements and to see to it that a four-wheeler (a "growler," he called it) got them to the railway station in time enough to catch the late Folkestone train on Saturday afternoon.

When Felicity complained that she had hoped to spend their last *full* night in London, Geoffrey explained that breaking their journey in Folkestone, where there were excellent hotels near the landings, would obviate the need of rising at an inconvenient hour on Sunday to take the early morning train, and would enable them besides to board the steamer *before* the arrival of the train passengers, thereby enabling them to secure the best positions and to make the necessary preparations for their trip without haste or confusion. Their luggage, he informed them, could be shipped directly to the Hotel Anglo-Français in Paris, to await their arrival there some eight hours later.

"If you so choose, then, I shall contact the . . ."

"Have you tired of our company so soon then?" Felicity asked, putting on a pouting, hurt expression.

"My dear lady, I assure you I should sooner tire of a glorious Venetian sunset," Geoffrey said. "I am thinking only of your comfort and convenience. Surely you will not wish to awaken at the crack of dawn, to be driven over our fog-enshrouded and deserted streets to the rail station? In addition, I feel I should warn you that the first Monday in August is what we fondly call a *bank holiday* and if you attempt to go out of London that Sunday, you will find the experience more curious than pleasing. Every railway is crowded with trains almost touching each other, each one jammed full of excursionists, what we call *trippers* here. You should be *most* uncomfortable, and I strongly suggest that you leave London at a convenient hour on Saturday afternoon."

"He no longer loves us," Felicity said, pouting.

"Ah, but indeed I do! Just wait and see what I've planned to fill our days and nights before your all too imminent departure!"

He took them wherever they wished to go, places Lizzie was certain he had seen a hundred times before — "Places that everyone *can* see," she recalled his having said, "but that few have any *wish* to see." Except tourists, of course, and he was determined that they should not leave London without having

131

viewed the houses of Parliament or the British Museum or the National Gallery or the Crystal Palace or Christ's Hospital, which he told them would soon no longer be seen in Newgate Street. He took them to all the parks, and pointed out the charming flower beds on the east side of Hyde Park by Grosvenor Gate, expressing concern that they would not be here on Sunday to hear the debates in Speaker's Corner, or indeed to visit the Zoological Society's Gardens on that day, when they would be closed to the public, but for which he might have got an order of admission from a Fellow of the Society. He took them to St. Paul's, of course, and to the Guildhall and the Clock Museum, and to the Silver Vaults and Dr. Johnson's house, and the Temple Church and the Nash Terraces, where afterwards they sat in the garden. He took them to the finest restaurants each night for dinner—Blanchard's in Beak Street, the Café Royal in Regent Street, Frascati's in Oxford Street—refusing to allow them to pay a farthing for their meals, explaining that they could extend their thanks to his dear, departed father.

On the evenings when they went to the theater (it was he who obtained tickets to the D'Oyly Carte and to *The Private Secretary* at the Prince of Wales) he took them to supper afterwards, and often they would walk homeward together in the deep London fog, Geoffrey explaining that he would not advise them to do this alone, even now that their beloved Jack no longer seemed to be afoot with his scalpel. They had heard of Jack the Ripper even in America, and Felicity plied him with questions about the infamous murders, causing Lizzie to shiver in the dark.

"I still shouldn't go wandering about in Whitechapel alone at night," Geoffrey said, "though Lord knows our Jack seems to have been quiet these past two years. His victims, of course, were 'ladies' of another sort, but even genuine ladies aren't quite immune to the rudeness of many of our so-called gentlemen (and here a rolling of his Alison-like eyes.) I'm sure you noticed that in the theater district it's *impossible* for ladies if they're alone, and even unpleasant if they're accompanied by a man. I should warn you, too, if ever you're afoot without me, to avoid Leicester Square and its adjoining streets, where there's a large foreign population and it's not usual for young women to go about alone; if you feel you absolutely *must* go, please do so in the mornings. Or better yet, wait for me to accompany you. The

132

same applies to the Strand, which in the late afternoon has a decidedly mixed class of—'passengers,' shall we say? As for the Burlington Arcade, admittedly full of luxurious little shops that might entice you, do avoid it in the late afternoon when women for whom you would not care to be mistaken begin their little walks there."

Everything then—all that any tourist might have wanted to see—he showed them. But he took them to other more surprising things as well. One night he walked them to the Westminster Bridge and asked them to gaze at the shimmering reflections in the Thames—the avenues of gaslights and rows of illuminated windows; the solitary electric lamp shining from the immense station at Charing Cross; the factories on the south side of the river, ablaze with light; the long straight line of lamps that stretched as far as the eye could see, above the bridge where Lambeth Hospital faced the houses of Parliament; the red, blue and green lamps on the railway bridge far away, and the long white plume of smoke drifting upward from an unseen locomotive, capturing the colors, reflecting them in a watery kaleidoscope. And one afternoon—she forgot which one, they all seemed to rush by so rapidly—he took them to see the annual review of the Metropolitan Fire Brigade on the football ground in Victoria Park, where fifteen steam fire engines and four manual engines and four hose vans and a hundred officers and men demonstrated their skills to a crowd of some fifty thousand spectators.

When he took them by the penny boat to Greenwich, he explained that the excursion was not in itself particularly attractive, but that it would give them an effective view of part of the waterfront "of our monstrous city; and besides, we shall be surrounded by a characteristic crowd of lower-class Londoners." One day he took them back to Westminster Abbey, where he paid an attendant sixpence and then led them up a steep winding stair above the Islip Chapel to show them a little room in which were eleven life-sized figures with wax faces, explaining that they were once carried at the funerals of the people they represented, and pointing out the effigy of Queen Elizabeth herself!

He saved the best—she would never forget it—for the Friday before their departure. He had warned them in advance that it would be a long day and that they would not be deposited at their hotel again until rather late that night, but he assured them they could sleep as late as they wished on the morrow, complete their packing without any sense of hurry, enjoy a leisurely lunch and then catch the late afternoon train to Folkestone, which would get them there in time for dinner at the hotel he'd already booked. He had also arranged with the Albemarle to make certain that their luggage (he would insist on calling it *luggage*) was labeled directly to the Anglo-Français in Paris and transported to the railway station sometime tomorrow. He advised them to keep out of their trunks whatever clothing they might need for today and the next two days, which they could easily pack into their overnight cases.

"I apologize in advance for the paucity of the spectacle you are about to witness," he said, "but the *Henley* Regatta takes place at the beginning of July, and anything following it is by comparison dull. I thought, however, that you might care to see to what use our citizens put the Thames in summertime, and perhaps you shall be pleasantly surprised. Besides, it always rains at Henley."

They were a bit dismayed when he took them to the railway station, apologizing again for the necessity of yet another rail journey when they would be taking one on the morrow, but explaining that the only attraction the Thames had to offer between London and Richmond was its muddy banks, and promising that the trip would be a short one. It was somewhat longer than they'd expected, and the cars were thronged with people taking early advantage of the long bank-holiday weekend, but his surprise was waiting at Richmond—a hired rowboat large enough to accommodate the entire party and two muscular young boatsmen as well.

The fields on either side of the river were rolling and green. The water lapped the sides of the boat. The sun was strong overhead. Felicity, more to capture the attention of the boatsmen than to make any pertinent comment, kept pointing out remarkable sights on the banks—a cow, a frolicking spotted dog, a man playing an accordian—objects of interest she seemed never to have seen before. The river was uncluttered and tranquil. On the grassy embankments, bees buzzed in the clover. And then, quite suddenly, the traffic became heavier, and a tiny

134

cat-and-mouse smile touched Geoffrey's lips for here was the *true* surprise he'd planned.

"We call it the Hampton Court and Dittons Aquatic Sports," he said, "which is in itself a mouthful. But if you like boats— well, ladies, you shall *have* boats indeed!"

There were more boats than Lizzie had ever seen in a single place before. They choked the river from shore to shore—sailing boats whose masts were covered with flowers, palms and exotic plants; rowboats decorated with flags and lanterns; canoes and steam launches, and dinghys and outriggers and houseboats; boats Geoffrey described as "dongolas" (had he twisted his tongue on *gondolas*?) and others he described as "sculls;" boats with brilliantly colored canopies and boats with striped awnings, boats poled by pairs and longer boats paddled by six or even eight—boats everywhere she looked! And all along the river bank were carriages and other vehicles, and gaily dressed people standing on the towpath under the hot summer sun, cheering or shouting or singing or simply watching the race—if indeed it *was* a race. But Geoffrey had made reference earlier to the Henley *Regatta,* hadn't he? And what was a regatta if not a race? Still, none of the people here on the river seemed frantically striving to *win* anything, seemed instead to be caught in some joyous exodus, their exuberant voices rising above the clatter of the paddles to join the buzz of voices on the embankments. A summertime spirit of—gaiety, she supposed—hung on the air, as palpable as the warm sunshine and the cool river breeze. She had never known such gaiety in her life.

And later, as dusk claimed the countryside, electric lights flashed on many of the pilings up and down the river, and on some of the boats as well. A houseboat named *Pitti-Sing* had hanging over its doorway two miniature canoes, each aglow with what Geoffrey called "fairy lights." The *Ione* had her name spelled out in similar lights—the candles of these, however, flickering in *red* glass containers—and yet another boat was decorated with a large gilt crown outlined in lights, its center ablaze with the letters *V.R.* A punt slipped past, the name *La Capa Negra* stitched in white on a red bunting that flew from a tall pole, and the three musicians in the boat spoke Italian to each other and wore black crepe masks and sang Italian songs (though Geoffrey assured her the men were English) and then

135

passed about a fishing net, soliciting money. In another boat there were men singing what Geoffrey called "nigger music," and in yet another a young girl sang to the accompaniment of a harp, her lilting voice floating out over the dark waters reflecting the glow of Chinese lanterns and illuminated stars in lamps draped with flags.

They sat on the embankment later, eating sandwiches Geoffrey purchased in a garden immediately opposite a bridge glowing with electric lights, watching the boats passing by in what Geoffrey called "our Venetian Fête." One of them was rigged as a Chinese pagoda, the children aboard dressed in Chinese costumes, a floating crimson palace lighted with an opal roof; another, smaller boat flickered with a myriad number of lanterns twinkling in a halo of greenery; yet another was startlingly decorated with a freshly cut tree festooned with lights on every bough. There was a boat with a large Japanese umbrella hung with small lanterns and fixed to its masthead. A punt decked out as a two-master floated past with lanterns hanging from the crosstrees of both masts. On one of the rowboats, a lantern caught fire, and one of the two men aboard seized a boathook and struck wildly at the flaming lantern, finally putting it out to the accompaniment of cheers from the crowd on the bank.

And then came the fireworks from the opposite bank, and the crowd held its breath as reds and blues and whites and greens exploded against the night. Lizzie's heart soared into the sky with each successive explosion, trailed to earth again in a shower of glowing sparks. And when at last the hour-long bombardment of rocket sticks had ended, and the lights of the boats dwindled on the distant river to be replaced by starshine on the black waters, Geoffrey got to his feet and extended his hand to her and said, "We must go, Lizzie. We'll be returning to Richmond by coach, and from there to London by train, but even so, the hour is late."

Lizzie rose, smoothing the back of her skirt, slightly damp from the grass. "I hate for it to end," she said, sighing. "You've made our stay here so wonderful. I can't imagine how we shall ever repay you."

"You've *just* repaid me more than adequately," he said. "Although it mightn't hurt," he added with a wink, "to mention to my dear sibling, should your paths chance to cross again, how devastatingly charming, thoughtful and witty was her brother. I know it will please her."

"You're so very alike," Lizzie said, as they walked up the embankment. "In so many ways."

"As well we should be," Geoffrey said.

"It's not *all* that usual, you know," Lizzie said. "Even in the closest of families, brothers and sisters . . ."

"Oh, but didn't she tell you?" Geoffrey said. "We're twins, you know."

And all at once Lizzie realized that having spent these past several glorious days with Geoffrey as her guide and constant companion had been the equivalent, virtually, of having *Alison* by her side all that time.

"We must hurry, you know," he said. "I shouldn't want to miss our coach. Ladies!" he called. "*Do* come! Felicity! Anna! Rebecca! Never mind your skirts, I shan't ogle your pretty ankles!" There was laughter behind them as the other women scurried up the bank, holding their skirts above their flashing legs.

"*Presto, signorine!*" he shouted in Italian, and winked at Lizzie and took her arm, and their smiles and their eyes met and joined in the star-drenched night.

6: NEW BEDFORD—1893

"**Be** good enough to lift your veil. What is your full name?"

"Anna H. Borden."

"You live in Fall River, Miss Borden, do you?"

"Yes, sir."

"And have all your life?"

"Yes, sir."

"You are, I believe, *not* a relative of the prisoner."

"No, sir."

"How long have you known her?"

"About five years."

"Did you at some time make a trip abroad with her?"

"I did."

"In what year?"

"1890."

"Did you occupy the same cabin in the steamship?"

"I did."

"On the outward and homeward voyages?"

"I did."

"When was your return voyage? What time did you arrive in New York, if you landed in New York?"

"I think it was the very first of November."

"And your voyage was about the preceding week? The week preceding the first of November?"

"Yes, sir. The last week of October, I think."

"During that voyage, did you have any talk—during the return trip, I am speaking of now—did you have any talk with the prisoner with respect to her home?"

"I object to that," Robinson said.

"*What* year?" Chief Justice Mason asked.

"1890," Moody said. "The week preceding the first of November in 1890. And this is simply a preliminary question. On the question of the admissibility of this testimony, I should like to say a word to Your Honors. I wish to call attention to the nature of the conversation in arguing upon its admissibility. Your Honors can very readily see that statements which indicate a *permanent* alienation may be of importance even though quite distant from the time under inquiry. In order to fully understand the nature of this testimony and its importance, I shall be obliged to state more fully about it. It is merely a preliminary question now."

"I object to the question on the threshold of the subject," Robinson said. "If there be any statement of substance, we will consider that subsequently."

"The witness may step down," Mason said. "The jury may retire with the officers and remain until sent for."

It was very hot for so early in June.

The shuttered windows on one side of the small courtroom were open wide to the street below, but there was scarcely a breeze and the glare beyond the glass panels seemed as bright as the burnished brass of the four gas-burning chandeliers that hung from the ceiling. The courtroom was situated on the second and uppermost floor of the old brick building that was New Bedford's Superior Court House, a structure graced with a roofed white porch and Corinthian columns but nonetheless eclipsed by the more pretentious residential dwellings in this remote section of the city. Outside the Court House, heavy strands of cable and telegraph wires had been strung from tall poles into the rear of the building and the old carriage sheds. Roughly improvised fences, constructed to keep back the curi-

139

ous crowds, lined the green sloping banks on either side of the concrete walk leading to the entrance.

This was the only courtroom in the building, and it was approached by a stairway leading upward from the ground level. The stairwell created an awkward opening in the courtroom floor, and the haphazard design was further cluttered by the witness box and the jury box to the left of the judges' high bench, the spectators' slat-backed wooden benches tiered at the back, the long tables and stools arranged near the court crier's box, and the hasty accommodations erected for the use of reporters. For several days now the newspaper representatives had been here in force, and each train still added to their swelling number.

Originally, a space in the courtroom beside the jury box had been set apart for them, and boards on sawhorses were set up as makeshift desks. But these could accommodate only twenty-five people and the space was promptly monopolized by the Bristol County and Boston papers. Yesterday, just before the prosecution began its opening statement to the jury, seats and desks were set up near the dock occupied by Lizzie and her attorneys. These were awarded to the reporters of the *Providence Journal*. The reporters from the New York dailies and the *Baltimore Sun*— and this pleased Lizzie because the description of her in the *Sun* still rankled—were left to take their chances finding places among the spectators, who had all been furnished tickets for their seats. Even before what properly might have been considered the first *true* day of the trial—when the jurors were being selected—the advance corps of newspaper artists had been on the spot, sitting on fences in the vicinity of the Court House, sketching everything immovable and even curious passersby. Lizzie had seen them roving around inside the House of Correction, and they were inside the courtroom now, drawing the interior of the place, making sketches of anyone and anything in sight.

On the day following the selection of jurors, she had been pleased to read an account in the *Providence Journal* that described her somewhat more flatteringly than had that in the *Sun*. She had, of course, been cautioned by her attorneys not to read *any* of the news stories written about the trial, lest they overly upset her and cause her to appear unlike her true self in

140

the courtroom, where all eyes were upon her, and where the artists' pencils scratched interminably at their pads. It was far easier to avoid the stories printed in the *New York Times* and the *Baltimore Sun*—and, oh, how she wished she *had*—but those in the *Journal* were available daily here in New Bedford.

"Lizzie Borden is still a marvel," the article had begun.

How many lines have been written descriptive of the immobility of her countenance, how many word portraits have been painted of her steady and unfailing nerve, of her remarkable self-possession, of her power of control and self-reliance. Yet at each apparent crisis in her career, the watchers have waited for an evidence of weakness, they have looked for a sign of what— for want of a better name—may be termed 'femininity,' they have waited for the first sight of nerve failure. And all in vain, for though these seekers are told that in the seclusion of her own forced retreat, when there is no one to gaze upon her every action, the woman is the same as other women: this person of the unflinching nerve and steadfast demeanor becomes the torn and tortured girl. Yet there is no weakening in public, and the curiosity mongers are still unsatisfied. And this, after all, is as it should be, for why should Lizzie Borden expose to the world her sorrow and her pain?

Her face expressionless now, she watched as Moody approached the judges' bench to argue this question of the admissibility of Anna Borden's testimony.

From where George Dexter Robinson sat at the defense table, attorney Jennings on his left, attorney Adams on his right, he had an unobstructed view of the bench as opposing counsel approached it.

"Your Honors," Moody said, "the evidence which we offer is substantially this. That upon the return voyage, after this witness and the prisoner had spent the summer in various parts of Europe in travel, there was this conversation which I am about to state, which was several times repeated. It was, in substance, that she—the prisoner—regretted the necessity of returning home after she had had such a *happy* summer, because the home that she was about to return to was such an *unhappy* home.

"This conversation, as I say, was repeated several times, and

141

we submit that it would be competent. I should agree that if at that time there had been any characterization of Mr. and Mrs. Borden such as might come from a *passing* feeling of resentment, that the distance of time of the conversation would be such as in Your Honors' discretion would well warrant, if not *compel*, the exclusion of the testimony offered. But there is no language that can be stronger than the language used to express a *permanent* condition of things in that household."

William H. Moody was a good lawyer, and Robinson *still* regretted the day the district attorney had asked him to join in the prosecution. Together, Knowlton and Moody would be a formidable pair. Dark-haired and dark-eyed, Moody wore a mustache under his prominent nose and was a stocky, muscular, rather short man, the descendant of a Welsh ironworker who'd settled here in the colonies with his wife and son. A *cum laude* graduate of Harvard College, he'd been admitted to the bar in 1878, and early on in his career—or so courthouse rumor maintained—had formulated the rule that had since governed his practice of the law: "The power of clear statement is the greatest power at the bar."

As yet Robinson had seen no evidence of this guiding precept; yesterday Moody's opening statement for the government had been turgid at best, nor had his just begun argument on Anna Borden's now disputed and pending testimony been anything but convoluted. Somewhere in his notes Robinson had jotted down the words, "Moody fond of horseback riding and literature." His task now was to make certain Moody did not ride roughshod over the three judges, however *un*literary his argument might be.

"The word *home* means a great deal in everybody's mind and everybody's mouth," Moody said, "and I submit that where a person states that he has an unhappy home, states it *deliberately*, states it *more* than once, it expresses such a continued and existing state of feeling that it is competent, even though it occurred two years *before* the homicide into which we are inquiring. This is a case *not* of the expression of feeling toward persons who are brought casually together, but it is the expression of a feeling by one member of a family in respect to the *whole* family. And *continuously* a member, because—according to this testimony—there was no absence except this absence in Europe.

"And, of course, *after* she returned home, she continued always to live in the family up to the time of this homicide. It is to be taken into account, also, with what we know of the feelings of persons who have been absent from home, unless their feeling about the home is firmly hostile and firmly *fixed* as a hostile feeling, we would hardly expect such a statement as we offer to show was made in this case. I think I have made the ground upon which we offer this clear to Your Honors. Perhaps I have not expressed it so fully or so well as I might do, but I think Your Honors understand precisely what I mean."

"Mr. Robinson?" Mason said.

Moody took a seat again beside his co-counsel, and watched Robinson closely as he rose and approached the bench. For all his fifty-nine years, the chief counsel for the defense looked exceedingly fit, a tall, deep-chested, clean-shaven man with pale blue eyes and gray hair turning white. His ancestors—like Moody's own—went back for generations in Massachusetts history, had, in fact, fought in the Revolutionary War battles of Concord and Lexington. It was near Lexington that Robinson had lived as a boy, working on his father's farm, attending the district school for only three or four months each year. Like Moody, he was also a Harvard graduate, living on a pittance while a student there. That this man—springing from such mean roots and coming to the practice of the law when he was already thirty-two years of age—had come so far so fast was a testament to his determination and an ominous gauge of the sort of opponent he would be in this trial. Moody was not pleased that Robinson had been governor of the state until a scant six years ago; nor did it please him that many *still* called the man "Governor."

In a familiar tone, almost as though he were addressing friends and colleagues (as indeed two of them had been and still were, Moody thought) in his own sitting room rather than arguing to the three men who would rule on this matter of law now before them, Robinson said, "Now, of course, we stand upon this statement: that it is altogether too remote. I cannot see how it can *possibly* fall within the line of the cases permitting such statements to be made. The witness had been abroad, we

143

understand, in Europe, traveling in Europe during the summer. Two ladies together, perhaps more, I am not informed. And as they are coming across upon the ship, this conversation occurs. Now there is nothing in it that anyone would think of offering an objection to, except that her home was an unhappy one. However much we all want to get home after we've been abroad a long time, those who've had an opportunity to go—a great many have not—but however much we think of that, I presume there's not a party that has ever gone on a journey that doesn't say, 'Well, we've had so good a time I really wish I wasn't going back.' That's about all there is of it.

"Suppose she had said, abroad in 1890, 'My home is unhappy'? Suppose she had said it two or three times with no reference to anybody in person? Is that significant of a state of mind that was operative down through till the fourth of August, 1892? Within the lines of the distinctions made in the case of Commonwealth versus Abbott—which Your Honors must be quite familiar with—it is properly held to be too remote. I do not need to enlarge on this," Robinson said. "It seems to me it lies right close up to our experience all around."

The three judges who now conferred all appeared much older than they actually were, perhaps because each of them had white hair and a white beard, perhaps because the heat had caused them all to wilt prematurely on this sweltering June day. The chief justice, Albert Mason, was only fifty-seven years old, a veteran of the Civil War and a former member of the Massachusetts state legislature where he'd worked in committee with the then-senator from Plymouth County—Robinson himself. Although his expression was a somewhat mournful one, his pale eyes were alert. Robinson knew that he had three daughters whose ages were close to Lizzie Borden's.

Caleb Blodgett of Boston was the senior of the two associate justices sitting with Mason. A graduate of Dartmouth, he had been an expert in bankruptcy law before his appointment to the Superior Court bench eleven years earlier. The unfortunate possessor of a lantern jaw exaggerated by the further thrust of his beard, he rather resembled a belligerent bulldog draped in judicial robes. But for all his fierce demeanor, Robinson knew him to be a genial, unaffected man.

The junior associate justice, a man named Justin Dewey,

flanked Mason on the side opposite Blodgett. Dewey was strikingly handsome in a leonine way, with a full head of white hair and a white beard trimmed rather more closely than was Mason's. He was a graduate of Williams College, a former member of the state legislature, a former state senator, and had been a Superior Court justice for the past seven years now, ever since his appointment in 1886. Robinson knew him well. In fact, it was Robinson who—while serving as governor of the state of Massachusetts—had appointed Dewey to his present position, a lifetime post.

"The Court are of the opinion," Chief Justice Mason said, "that the character of the testimony offered, the expressions used, are too ambiguous, so that—*aside* from its remoteness—the evidence is not competent.

"If the expression were distinct of personal ill will to either the father or the stepmother, it might not be too remote.

"We think the evidence should be excluded."

It had taken a remarkably short time to settle upon the twelve men who would weigh the evidence and deliver the verdict, especially when one considered that virtually all of them examined had formed a prior opinion about the case, and many of the candidates were opposed to capital punishment. On the first day of the trial, Chief Justice Mason had put the identical questions to each of the prospective jurors:

"Are you related to the prisoner, or to Andrew J. or Abby D. Borden?"

"Have you formed or expressed an opinion in relation to this case?"

"Are you sensible of any bias or prejudice in it?"

"Have you formed any opinion that would preclude you from finding the defendant guilty of an offense punishable by death?"

Each side had been allowed twenty-two challenges. The prosecution had exhausted fourteen of them and the defense twenty-two by the time the last juror was selected at three in the afternoon. That first day of the trial had been uncomfortably hot, and the atmosphere inside the courtroom oppressive at best. Lizzie, sweltering in a black brocade dress and black lace hat, had sighed in relief when the twelfth man took his seat in the jury box.

She watched them now as they came back into the courtroom.

Most of them were farmers; one of them was a blacksmith. Three of them had similar last names: Wilbar, Wilber and Wilbur. All of them were wearing either mustaches or beards. Her fate, it appeared, would be decided by twelve hirsute jurors and three equally hirsute judges. Somehow she was grateful that Governor Robinson was clean-shaven and that Mr. Jennings's mustache was somewhat less flamboyant than that of Melvin Ohio Adams, her third attorney, whose name she found almost as preposterous as the adornment over his upper lip.

She had fainted yesterday.

She had fainted after Moody's opening statement to the jury. The reporter for the *Times* had written:

> The prisoner sat behind the Deputy Sheriff and listened to Mr. Moody's careful address with the closest attention, as calm and as unmoved as ever. Her eyes looked straight toward the speaker. Indeed, the spectators seemed as much interested in the prosecutor's words as did Miss Borden, and but for the uniformed being sitting beside her, she might have been taken by a stranger for one of those who had come to the courtroom with no greater interest than that of curiosity. It was a great surprise, therefore, to everybody when just as Mr. Moody finished speaking Miss Borden fell back in her chair in a faint.

As if the swoon had been something entirely within her power to control, and not an honest reaction to Moody's grisly recitation of the Government's case against her.

> As the District Attorney ceased speaking, the prisoner—who, with her face covered by the fan, had sat motionless for the last hour—suddenly succumbed to the strain that had been put upon her nervous system and lost consciousness. The Reverend Mr. Jubb, sitting directly in front of her and separated only by the dock rail, turned to her assistance, and Mr. Jennings, the attorney, hurried to the place from his position. Smelling salts and water were brought into immediate requisition, and soon entire consciousness returned. In the meanwhile, the jury had retired to enjoy a brief recess, and when

146

they returned Miss Borden again resumed her old position of interest, though marks of agitation were still plainly visible.

That same reporter was undoubtedly in the courtroom now, she surmised, somewhere among the spectators; his story had not been signed. Neither had the one in the *Sun*, which *still* annoyed her because it had described her so unfairly:

> Her forehead is low but shapely, and her eyes are large and clear. She has pretty ears, small and delicate and held closely to her head. Her nose is straight . . .

All well and good up to that point.

> . . . and if it might be disassociated from the heavy jaws, the wide mouth, and the thick, long and somewhat protruding lips beneath it, it could be called sensitive.

And now it began in earnest:

> That which makes Lizzie Borden's face a coarse face and all that leaves it possible for her to have committed this crime are the lower features—the mouth, the cheeks and the chin. Here her face is wide and full. It seems to possess little mobility and it indicates the possession of a sort of masculine strength that one does not like to observe in the face of a woman.

Well, she had never thought of herself as beautiful. And yet . . .

> But looked at anywhere else, she is seen to advantage. Her attitudes are entirely graceful and womanly and her movements always easy and refined . . .

Thank God for small favors.

> She sits for long periods motionless, with her eyes closed and her head resting lightly on the fan which she holds at her chin. Her dress, dark, plain and ordinary, is rather more in the mode than one is apt to see in a New England town . . .

147

Tailored by a dressmaker!

Her hat, too, was made by someone who understood the milliner's art. She wears her hair in the old French twist, which, however suggestive of an antiquated fashion-plate . . .

Antiquated!

. . . nevertheless becomes her. It is well-brushed hair and greatly aids in rendering her appearance neat and ladylike . . .

Ah, how kind of you, sir.

This effect is heightened by the shapeliness of her arms, so far as the present style allows them to be seen below the elbows, and by her long, slender, well-gloved hands. Nobody would pick out Lizzie Borden for the fiend incarnate she must be if the indictment at issue here is credible.

She had thought while reading the article that the reporter had appointed himself as judge and jury both, deciding from the cut of her clothes, the configuration of her arms and hands, the style in which she wore her hair, the sensitivity of her *nose*, and the *grossness* of her mouth, cheeks and chin whether or not she could possibly be a fiend incarnate.

His words bothered her still.

Today, for the first time since the trial began, she had taken a seat closer to her attorneys, to the left and slightly behind them, within the bar enclosure and removed from the prisoner's dock where she had previously sat alongside the deputy sheriff. She had come into the courtroom today bearing a small cluster of pansies, the petals of which she now idly touched, perhaps because she was determined to express only attitudes the reporters observing her would consider "entirely graceful and womanly."

There seemed to be more women among the spectators today than there had been previously. She was not certain how she felt about this. Neither was she certain how she felt about the jury being composed entirely of men, most of them beyond middle age. Aware that she was being studied by reporters, artists, spectators and jury alike, she watched now as the next witness was called, fully cognizant of the fact that her very life was hanging in the balance here in this swelteringly hot courtroom in this small New England town.

"What is your full name, madam?"

"Mrs. Hannah H. Gifford."

"You live in Fall River, do you?"

"Yes, sir."

"What is your occupation there?"

"I make ladies' outside garments."

"That is, by 'outside' you mean cloaks? Outside of the dresses?"

"Yes, sir."

"Had you made cloaks of the ladies of the Borden family?"

"Yes, sir."

"For how long?"

"Seven or eight years, more or less."

"Did you do some work for Miss Lizzie Borden in the spring of 1892?"

"Yes, sir, I did."

"What did you make for her then?"

"A garment. A sack."

"Did you at any time have any talk with her about Mrs. Borden, the stepmother?"

"I object to that," Robinson said.

"She may answer," Mason said.

"Now, Mrs. Gifford, will you state the talk? What *you* said, and what *she* said?"

"I was speaking to her of a garment I had made for Mrs. Borden, and instead of saying 'Mrs. Borden,' I said 'Mother.' And she says, 'Don't say that to me, for she is a mean, good-for-nothing thing.' I said, 'Oh, Lizzie, you don't mean that.' And she said, 'Yes, I don't have much to do with her. I stay in my room most of the time.' And I said, 'You come down to your meals, don't you?' And she said, 'Yes, but we don't eat with them if we can help it.' And that is all that was said."

My name is Nathaniel Hathaway, and I reside in New Bedford. I'm an analytical chemist. I was educated as such at the

149

School of Mines in New York. Columbia University. I've been practicing my profession since 1879, and I've often had occasion to be called as a witness in matters involving it.

I am acquainted with the nature and uses of drugs, and I am acquainted with the drug called hydrocyanic or prussic acid in its diluted form. What is called the two-percent solution. What is known as prussic acid in commerce. When we're speaking of commercial prussic acid, I can only say it's quite volatile, very volatile. I can't give any ratio or degree of volatility. In that volatile form, if distributed in the air upon a person in the vicinity of it, it would cause headache and nausea. It passes off in the air, you see, like a number of other liquids. Ammonia, for one. Hydrochloric acid for another, a strong acid, sometimes called muriatic acid. And benzine.

I'm a family man, I have a house, but I've never used benzine for cleansing purposes, except for taking out spots or removing grease. Benzine would be destructive to small animal life, bugs, flies, moths, all those things would go. They'd either emigrate or die. Ether would probably cause death to insects, too. All those creatures. The same is true of chloroform and naptha. They're all volatile. Their volatility renders them unsuitable for such use, and yet they're used that way right along in everyday life. All of those articles.

As another example, arsenic is an ingredient of the common article known as Rough on Rats. Something that's very commonly used in households to dispose of rats. Well, I would rather have the rats than have such stuff about my house. I think we're all going wrong in using those poisons that'll kill rats. Because somebody may get it by accident into his own stomach, or find a chance to use it criminally. It's a dangerous commodity to have in the house, arsenic.

As for prussic acid, what is known as the two-percent solution, you could mix it with water or mix it with alcohol, you could dilute it a hundred times more, until it contained two *hundredths* of a percent. But as to whether or not that would kill a piece of animal life on a fur, it would be impossible for me to say without experimenting on it. I *have* used the two-percent solution, tried its effects on insects. It'll promptly kill them. But whether any greater dilution would accomplish the result, I don't know.

150

I tested the effect of prussic acid upon insect life between last night and this morning, took the common prussic acid used in commerce, the two-percent solution, and tried that. On ants. No difficulty about killing them and various nondescript bugs. Unfortunately, I'm not a naturalist—I can't tell what the various small insects I used were. I remember some spiders.

But to my knowledge, prussic acid in *any* form is not used for the purpose of cleaning furs.

In my opinion, it's unsuitable in connection with furs.

It has no suitability or adaptability for use in cleaning furs.

"What is your full name?"

"My name is Eli Bence."

"Do you live in Fall River?"

"I do."

"What is your occupation?"

"I'm a drug clerk."

"For whom do you work?"

"For D. R. Smith."

"Where is Mr. Smith's shop?"

"On the corner of South Main and Columbia Streets, in Fall River."

"How long have you been connected with that business?"

"Something between thirteen and fourteen years."

"How long have you been employed by Mr. Smith?"

"Something over four years now."

"And always at the same place?"

"For Mr. Smith, yes, sir."

Robinson leaped to his feet.

"May it please Your Honors," he said, "there's a question here that we consider of vital importance, and I believe the Commonwealth also recognizes it as of that character. This inquiry, I suggest, ought to stop here, and the question be discussed with the Court alone."

"There are certain preliminary things and characteristics," Moody said, "that are to be considered, that we want to prove. Perhaps, however, if it would suit the convenience of the other side, we could state what we expected to prove upon that subject better."

"I'm speaking of *this* evidence," Robinson said, "when there's any question about it. It's deemed important to both sides, and it's important for the Court to consider and pass upon it."

"That's entirely in the hands of the Court," Moody said. "We wanted to prove, however, one or two preliminary things, not at all turning in the direction of the prisoner."

"I *understand* what the question is," Robinson said, "and I say that it isn't quite the statement that should be made—because it really involves and touches this case somewhat."

"I'm entirely content to state it," Moody said.

"I think you'd better *not* state it now," Robinson said.

"No, I understand. I'm entirely content to state it upon the *argument* to Your Honors."

"It's nothing that ought to be stated now," Robinson insisted.

Chief Justice Mason looked at both men.

"The jury may retire with the officer and remain until sent for," he said. "The witness may return downstairs."

Lizzie sat in the airless courtroom and watched Bence and the jurors filing out. Was it only her imagination that Bence tossed a look at her over his shoulder as he departed? She recalled suddenly the words Knowlton had put to her in Fall River last year, recalled her own answers as vividly as if the exchange were taking place here and now:

"Your attention has already been called to the circumstance of going into the drugstore of Smith's on the corner of Columbia and Main Streets—by some officer, has it not?—on the day before the tragedy."

"I don't know whether some officer has asked me. Somebody has spoken of it to me. I don't know who it was."

"Did that take place?"

"It did not."

"Do you know where the drugstore is?"

"I don't."

"Did you go into any drugstore and inquire for prussic acid?"

"I did not."

Her own attorneys had asked her these same questions over and again. She had repeatedly told them that she had not gone to any drugstore in Fall River or anyplace else and had made no attempts to buy prussic acid or any other sort of poison on the day before the murders. Her attorneys knew the government had witnesses who claimed they could identify her as the woman who'd made the inquiries for prussic acid. In the end

152

Robinson had felt it best—considering the danger such patently mistaken identification might present—to argue for exclusion of the testimony once the matter came up in court.

It had come up now.

It was fully upon them now.

She leaned forward intently as Moody began speaking.

"I perhaps ought to state what the testimony is that we offer," he said. "We offer to show that prussic acid is *not* an article in commercial use, that it is an article which is *not* sold except upon the prescription of a physician and as a part—a *minute* part—of a prescription. That this witness during his experience as a drug clerk, up to the third of August, 1892, *never* had a call for prussic acid. That it is *not* used for the purpose of cleaning capes—sealskin capes, or capes of any *other* sort—and has *no* adaptability to such use.

"We now offer to show that upon the third day of August, sometime in the forenoon, the time of which isn't material, the prisoner came to this shop in which the man was employed and asked for ten cents' worth of prussic acid, stating that she wished it for the purpose of cleaning capes—either sealskin capes, or capes, I'm not sure which—and that she failed to procure the poison for which she asked. Perhaps I ought to state it with some accuracy," Moody said, and went to the defense table where his co-counsel sat. Knowlton immediately handed him the document he was seeking, and Moody approached the bench again.

"These are Mr. Bence's exact words," he said, and began reading from the typewritten sheet of paper in his hands. "This party came in there, and inquired if I kept prussic acid. I informed her that we did. She asked me if she could buy ten cents' worth of me. I informed her that we did not sell prussic acid unless by a physician's prescription. She then said that she had bought this several times, I think. I think she said several times before. I says, 'Well, my good lady, it's something we don't sell unless by prescription from the doctor, as it's a very dangerous thing to handle.' I understood her to say she wanted it to put on the edge of a sealskin cape, if I remember rightly. She left without buying anything, no drug at all, no medicine."

Moody looked up from the typewritten sheet.

"Then follows merely the identification of the prisoner by Mr.

153

Bence," he said. "I don't know in what way Your Honors desire to hear the discussion."

"Perhaps we'd better hear the objection," Mason said.

Robinson, sitting at the defense table with his co-counsels, did not rise for a moment. Lizzie looked at him expectantly, wondering why on earth he didn't immediately spring up. Jennings, on his left, who had been her father's attorney at the time of the murders, and who had been called into the case from virtually the very beginning, handed Robinson a sheet of paper, which he glanced at and then nodded.

Sitting on Robinson's right, Melvin Ohio Adams leaned over to whisper something in his ear. Adams might have been considered handsome, Lizzie thought, were it not for his ridiculous waxed mustache. He was forty-two years old, a graduate of Dartmouth College who'd met Jennings at Boston University while both men were studying law there. A resident of Boston, Adams had been district attorney for that city until seven years ago, and both her other attorneys had assured her he would be a valuable asset in their cause.

He seemed to whisper for an eternity. Robinson listened, nodded again and—still not rising from his chair—turned to Moody and said, "I understand that the offer doesn't include facts to show that there was any *sale*."

"No, sir," Moody said.

"And—we perhaps may anticipate—but I believe it may be fair to ask whether there *is* any evidence of any sale to this defendant?"

"No, sir."

"In any other place?"

"No, sir. It *would* be fair to say we have evidence to show some attempt to purchase prussic acid in another place, with the same negative result."

"You propose to bring evidence upon attempts, but no success."

"Yes, sir."

"Well," Robinson said, and rose at last to approach the bench. "It appears that the stomachs of the deceased persons showed no traces of any poison whatever. *Certainly* not any prussic acid. So there is shown no connection as assailing the lives of those two persons. Lizzie Borden is charged in the indictment with

154

slaying or killing those two people with a sharp instrument; committing the murder with an ax, for instance. Nothing else. Now here, if it has any force at all, suppose it were carried away up to its legitimate result? It is an attempt to charge her with an act causing death by a wholly *different* means—for which, of course, she is not now on trial. It must be shown, I maintain, that any act which is to be put in evidence on the part of this defendant must have some natural tendency to show that she has committed the act for which she stands on trial.

"To my mind, it does not show that. It is an attempt to buy an article which is used for other purposes. It is said that it is an article that is not used in the arts, but it *is* an article which a person may legitimately buy. Its sale is provided for under the statute, and it is not to be said that because a person may wrongfully use, in a distinct transaction, an article which he purchases, therefore its purchase has a tendency to show that he has committed some *other* crime for which he is indicted. Does it have any tendency at *all* to show that this defendant killed those two persons with an *ax*? I maintain it does not. I must say I have said all the Court desires to hear, and I have made my meaning, I trust, plain."

"Mr. Moody," Mason said, "the Court desires to have restated the limitations or purpose for which the testimony is offered."

"There is no purpose of offering this testimony for any other use than as bearing upon the state of mind of the defendant *prior* to the homicide—the intent, the deliberation, and preparation. And for that, or any part of it which Your Honors may suggest it has a natural tendency to prove . . . we offer it."

"We will withdraw for consultation," Mason said.

Robinson smiled.

Lizzie saw the smile and read it to mean that her attorney felt confident about the judges' eventual ruling; Eli Bence, the druggist, would not be allowed to continue with his testimony.

Idly she plucked a withering pansy from the cluster she held in her lap.

Her face showed no expression whatever.

My name is Alice M. Russell, and I live in Fall River. I don't know how long I've lived here. A good many years. I'm unmarried, used to live in the house now occupied by Dr. Kelly, lived

155

there just eleven years. During all that time, the Bordens occupied the house just north. I was well acquainted with all of the family—Mr. Borden, Mrs. Borden, Miss Emma Borden and Miss Lizzie Borden. I occasionally had calls from Lizzie, and I went to her house as well. Whenever I called at her house, she received me upstairs, in what's called the guest room, used it for a sitting room while I was there.

On Wednesday night, August third, of last year, Lizzie Borden came to visit me. I'm not sure what time it was, I think about seven. Sometime in the evening. She came alone, as far as I saw, stayed with me until nine, or five minutes after, as near as I know. We talked together about various subjects. I think when she came in she said, "I've taken your advice, and I've written to Marion that I'll come." I don't know what came in between, I don't know as this followed that, but I said, "I'm glad you're going," as I'd urged her to go before . . .

"Be kind enough to speak a little louder, if you can," Robinson said.

"Shall I repeat that?"

"If you please. Because I didn't hear it."

. . . I said, "I'm glad you're going." I'd urged her before to go, and I didn't know she'd decided to go. I said, "I'm glad you're going." And I don't know just what followed, but I said something about her having a good time, and she said, "Well, I don't know, I feel depressed. I feel as if something was hanging over me that I can't throw off, and it comes over me at times, no matter where I am." And she said, "When I was at the table the other day, when I was at Marion, the girls were laughing and talking and having a good time, and this feeling came over me, and one of them spoke and said, 'Lizzie, why don't you talk?'"

I don't remember of any more conversation about Marion. Whether there was or not, I don't remember. The conversation went on, I suppose it followed right on after that. When she spoke again, she said, "I don't know, father has so much trouble." Oh, wait, I'm a little ahead of the story. She said, "Mr. and Mrs. Borden were awfully sick last night."

And I said, "Why? What's the matter? Something they've eaten?"

She said, "We were *all* sick. All but Maggie."

"Something you think you've eaten?"

156

"We don't know. We had some baker's bread, and all ate of it but Maggie, and Maggie wasn't sick."

"Well, it couldn't have been the bread," I said. "If it had been baker's bread, and all ate of it but Maggie, and Maggie wasn't sick. If it had been baker's bread, I should suppose *other* people would be sick, and I haven't heard of anybody."

And she said, "That's so." And she said, "Sometimes I think our milk might be poisoned."

"Well," I said, "how do you get your milk? How could it be poisoned?"

"We have the milk come in a can," she said, "and set on the step. And we have an empty can. They put out the empty can overnight, and the next morning when they bring the milk, they take the empty can."

"Well, if they put anything in the can," I said, "the farmer would see it. What time does the milk come?"

"About four o'clock."

"Well, it's light at four. I shouldn't think anybody would *dare* to come then and tamper with the cans. For fear somebody would see them."

"I shouldn't think so," she said. "They were awfully sick, and I wasn't sick, I didn't vomit. But I heard them vomiting and stepped to the door and asked if I could do anything, and they said no."

I think she told me they were better in the morning, and that Mrs. Borden thought they'd been poisoned, and went over to Dr. Bowen's—said she was *going* over to Dr. Bowen's. And . . . I can't recall anything else just now. Of course she talked about something else, because she was there two hours, but I can't think about it. Well, about trouble with tenants, yes.

She said, "I don't know, I feel afraid sometimes that father's got an enemy. He has so much trouble with his men that come to see him." And she told me of a man that came to see him, and she heard him say—she didn't *see* him, but heard her father say—"I don't care to let my property for such business." And she said the man answered sneeringly, "I shouldn't think you'd care *what* you let your property for." And she said her father was mad and ordered him out of the house.

She told me of seeing a man run around the house one night

when she went home, I've forgotten where she'd been. "And you know the barn's been broken into twice," she said.

And I said, "Oh, well, you know that was somebody after pigeons. There's nothing in there for them to *go* after but pigeons."

"Well," she said, "they've broken into the house in broad daylight, with Emma and Maggie and me there."

"I never heard of that before," I said.

"Father forbade our telling it," she said.

So I asked her about it, and she said it was in Mrs. Borden's room, what she called her dressing room. She said her things were ransacked, and they took a watch and chain and money and car tickets, and something else, I can't remember. And there was a nail left in the keyhole, she didn't know why that was left. I asked her if her father did anything about it, and she said he gave it to the police but they didn't find out anything. And she said her father expected they would catch the thief by the tickets, "Just as if anybody would *use* those tickets," she said.

"I feel as if I want to sleep with my eyes half-open," she said. "With one eye open half the time. For fear they'll burn the house down over us. I'm afraid somebody will do something. I don't know but what somebody *will* do something," she said. "I think sometimes, I'm afraid sometimes, that somebody will do something to him, he's so discourteous to people. Mrs. Borden told him she was going over to Dr. Bowen's, and father said, 'Well, *my* money shan't pay for it.' She went over to Dr. Bowen's, and Dr. Bowen told her—she told him she was afraid they were poisoned—and Dr. Bowen laughed and said No, there wasn't any poison. And she came back, and Dr. Bowen came over. I was so ashamed, the way father treated Dr. Bowen. I was so mortified."

That's all I can remember about our talk on the night before the murders.

My name is Martha Chagnon, I live on Third Street. My yard's right in the rear of the Borden yard. There's a fence between my yard and the Borden house, and a corner there where there's a doghouse. On the night preceding the Borden murders, I heard a noise . . .

158

"Can you fix the time a little better?"

"It was about eleven o'clock at night."

"Won't you tell what you heard," Jennings said. "What the noise sounded like?"

"Wait a minute," Knowlton said. "I pray Your Honors' judgment about that."

"She may describe the noise," Mason said.

"Please describe the noise," Jennings said. "Tell us about it as well as you can."

"Well, I couldn't *describe* the noise, because I didn't see it."

"Well, you don't often *see* a noise, do you?"

"Why, no, sir."

"How it sounded to you," Jennings said.

"Wait a minute, I object to that," Knowlton said.

"That's a proper question," Mason said. "It calls for a description of how it sounded."

. . . Well, the noise sounded like pounding. Like pounding on wood. On the fence. Or a board. It came from the direction of the Borden fence, somewhere along the line of the fence. It continued for about four or five minutes. I didn't go outdoors to see what it was. I didn't do anything to investigate the cause of the noise. I was in the sitting room downstairs, on the south side of the house. There's a room between that and where the noise appeared to be. The dining room. The dining room was between me and where the noise appeared to be. My stepmother was with me when I heard the noise. I don't remember whether she looked to see what had occasioned it. We couldn't see out from where we were to the back part of the yard. It was too dark, and the curtains were down.

I'd been away all that day, went off at eight o'clock in the morning, to Providence. I got home at about six o'clock. My stepmother hadn't gone with me, but she was in the room when I heard the noise. Her name is Marienne. Marienne Chagnon. She was in the room at the same time I was. The windows in that room were all shut. There are three of them in that room, and one of them faces east, onto the piazza. The other two face south. I can't tell how I knew the direction from which the sound came. It was nothing more than an impression. I couldn't say positively that the sound came from over the fence, but in that direction. I didn't go out of the room, and I didn't look out

159

the window, either. I simply heard a noise, and it sounded to me as if it had come from that way.

There's an icehouse, the next house but one to ours. But the sound didn't come from the icehouse direction, it wasn't from the icehouse, it wasn't in that direction. There was a dog on the premises. On the piazza. He didn't leave the piazza at any time when that noise was going on.

My name is Marienne Chagnon, and I live on Third Street in Fall River. My house is in the rear of the Borden house. On the evening before the murders, I was home, and something attract my attention. About eleven o'clock. Some noise. I would describe it as the sound of steps on wood. On a wood sidewalk. Or on a fence. There is a fence between our yard and the Borden yard. And a doghouse there at the corner. At the time I heard the noise, I was on the sofa in the sitting room, on the south side of the house.

I heard the noise coming from the back yard. Near the window of the dining room. We heard the noise and we thought that noise would be—I don't speak very well—would be the same on the fence as on a wood sidewalk. There's a short fence between Mr. Borden's yard and our house. I heard the noise like it was a step on the fence. It lasted about five minutes, with space between the noise. We heard some noise, and after—we wait, and we heard noise again. There was a space of two or three minutes between the noises. I tell to my daughter, because I don't wonder that she was afraid, I didn't think it was the sound of a dog. The dogs sometimes come into our yard, I have seen them. I have an ash barrel in the yard, and it sometimes contains bones. And sometimes dogs come to that ash barrel. But . . .

"Did the noise sound to you like pounding?" Knowlton asked.

"What is it?" Mrs. Chagnon said.

"Did the noise sound to you like pounding?"

"Like?"

"Pounding."

"I don't understand that expression."

"Pounding?"

"No, sir."

160

"Don't you understand what pounding is?"

"Pounding?"

"Yes."

"No, sir."

"*What?*"

"No, I don't understand it."

"Don't know that word?"

"No, sir, pounding."

"All right, I can't put the question," Knowlton said. "You don't understand the word *pounding?*"

"No, sir."

"To pound," Knowlton said.

"Pounding?"

"Yes."

"No."

"All right. Do you remember of seeing the dogs there at the ash barrel at anytime afterwards?"

"We have since seen some dogs sometimes taking some bones in the barrels."

"And do you remember of your husband pounding that dog one time . . . excuse me . . . *moving* that ash barrel at one time?"

"I don't understand."

"What?"

"I don't understand."

"Do you remember of Mr. Harrington, the officer, being there one day?"

"Yes, sir."

"And your husband made a noise with that barrel?"

"Yes, sir."

"And didn't you say that it sounded like the noise you'd heard?"

"Yes, sir, but . . ."

. . . It wasn't in the same direction. It was the same noise but I tell to my husband it isn't in the same direction. It was *nearly* the noise. But that night the ash barrel was in the barn. In the back yard. It was in the barn that time. The noise of the ash barrel was about that noise, but it was not in the same direction. To make that noise with the ash barrel, my husband strike the barrel near the . . . the little barn, and he said, "Is it not that noise you heard?" I tell, "Yes, perhaps it is so, but it seems to me

161

it was not in this same direction." He strike the barrel with his hand. And when he strike the barrel with his hand, it seems like the same noise that I heard.

Because it sounds on the wood like that.

My name's Charles N. Gifford. I work at C. E. Macomber and Company, the clothing store, and I live at 29 Third Street. That's the house next north of the Chagnons. Uriah Kirby lives there, too. I was there at the house about eleven o'clock on the night before the murders.

I saw a man on the steps, the steps leading into the yard, right there on the side steps. The man, I should judge, weighed between a hundred and eighty to ninety pounds, and he sat there on the steps, apparently asleep, with a straw hat pulled over his face. I took hold of his arm and shook him, and in shaking him his hat fell off onto the sidewalk. I lit a match and held it up in front of his face to see if I knew who it was, and found that I didn't. I know most of the people living in that vicinity, I've lived there—with the exception of twelve years— about thirty-one years. In that same house, my father's house. I didn't smell any liquor about him, got no response from him whatever, don't know what became of the man. I went into the house and left the hat on the sidewalk. A few minutes afterward, Mr. Kirby came by . . .

My name is Uriah Kirby, I live in Fall River, on Third Street. The house next north of the Chagnons. I was living there on the third day of August last year. When I went home that night about eleven o'clock, there was a man sitting on the steps, four stone steps leading from the sidewalk which reached up into the yard.

I spoke to him, hollered out to him, spoke loud. No reply. Sat there dormant, as it were, in about the middle of the step, I should think, either the second or third. There was four steps in all, and he was back in this form, laid back against the side of a little fence that ran there, with his hat pulled down nearly over his eyes, and sitting there very quietly. Didn't seem to move at all, paid no attention to my voice. I put my hand on his hat, on top of his head, and shook him in this form, and spoke again to him. No reply.

162

I didn't take hold of him on any other portion of the body except the hat. It was a dark hat. Didn't smell any signs of liquor on him. He said nothing, did nothing, couldn't seem to arouse him. These steps are some fifteen to seventeen feet from the Chagnon driveway, just south of the steps there. I left him there, and went into my house. Mr. Gifford had already retired.

That's all that took place that night.

7: PARIS—1890

A dozen red roses waiting in the room!
And a handwritten note from Alison!

Bienvenue, Chérie!
Albert's beastly business will detain us here for the better part of a week. For once, I am grateful to his financial machinations. Do telephone me the moment you're comfortably settled. I have made delicious plans for us!
          A.

She was tempted to telephone the Hotel Binda at once, but the porters were arriving with their baggage, and again there was the nuisance of figuring what to tip them, complicated this time by the strange French currency—*just* when she was getting accustomed to the British coins. The two hulking men in their blue smocks struggled the trunks and valises into the room, and stood blinking in stupefied amazement as Felicity did a series of pirouettes in the vast chamber and then threw herself full length on the only bed in the room, a massive, four-postered and canopied antique against the wall opposite the inner door. The men continued to gape as Felicity began squealing and giggling, raising her knees and pumping her feet against the air as though she were riding a bicycle, skirts flying, her childish abandon exposing her petticoats and her black stockings and all but her underdrawers.

"Felicity!" Lizzie shouted, and she at once brought her knees down and lay as stiff as a board, legs together, eyes closed, arms crossed over her ample bosom as if she'd suddenly been struck dead by an unseen hand. She began giggling again as Lizzie paid the porters, sorting out the coins, remembering that Geoffrey had told her the franc—for all practical purposes—could be estimated at tenpence in English, or twenty cents in United States money.

Felicity was off the bed again as the porters bowed themselves out of the room, scruffy gray caps clenched in their hands, mumbling, *"Merci, madame, mademoiselle,* (a nod at Felicity) and then closing the inner door behind them. She scurried to the windows, drew open the curtains, threw open the shutters, and then, opening her arms wide, shouted to the courtyard below and the Parisian afternoon in general, "Hello, Paris!" and then, in surely inaccurate and positively atrocious French, "Adoo, Paree, adoo! We're here!"

"Felicity, *do* be still," Lizzie warned. "There may be people napping!"

"In *Paris*? Don't be silly, Lizzie!" She rushed across the room to her, threw her arms about her, hugged her fiercely and said, "Oh, I'm *so* excited! Aren't you excited?"

"I am, yes, but *Felicity*, you shall crush my *ribs*!"

"Adoo, Paree, adoo!" she squealed again, and, giggling, began dancing and prancing about the room as though she had completely lost her wits, touching the upholstery on the chairs, fingering the silk brocade coverlet on the large bed, dancing away again, passing her hands over the wallpaper, flicking the electric lamps on and off, on and off, going to the windows again, shouting "Napoleon, we are here!" and finally collapsing onto the bed again, where she continued to giggle uncontrollably, quite affirming the surmise that she had lost her mind.

Lizzie herself, though not as exuberantly overcome, was nonetheless impressed by the size of the room and the luxurious furnishings in it. They had arranged—in order to be relieved of having to figure their daily cost at so much for the room, so much for breakfast, so much for luncheon and dinner, so much for service and the use of electricity—to pay an all-inclusive (even as concerned wine) tariff of fifteen francs per day, which came to exactly three dollars a person and which, considering the generous size and fine appointments of the room and the reputed excellence of the hotel's table and cellar, was really an uncommonly low rate.

She might have preferred two beds in the room, as had been the case in London, but only because she herself was a restless sleeper (though she'd slept like the very dead in that city) and had been told by girl friends with whom she'd shared beds on her trips to Boston or New York or nearby Marion that sleeping with her was akin to sleeping with a squirrel, so jerky and continuous were her nocturnal fidgets. But the bed seemed spacious enough for even her reputed acrobatics, and she had been assured by Rebecca that Felicity definitely did not snore, a hazard that might have contributed to even more fitful sleep. The danger now, in fact, seemed to be that her lunatic friend might *giggle* the night away.

Monsieur Foubrier—the proprietor of the hotel and a gentleman of decidedly courteous and pleasant manners, who having lived in England for twenty years was as perfectly at home in English as he was in his native French—had informed them that "the five o'clock" (as he referred to the British custom of late afternoon tea) would be served shortly, if perhaps the ladies should care to freshen themselves first. Lizzie herself was famished and would have gone down without bothering to bathe or change first, but Felicity leaped suddenly off the bed, declared that she could not live another moment without a hot tub, dashed into the bathroom even as she was unlacing her corset and shouted over the roar of the running water, "Lizzie, could you *possibly* lay out a change of clothing for me? I'm totally encrusted with *filth!*"

"What did you plan on wearing?" Lizzie shouted.

"What?" Felicity shouted back.

"What did you . . ."

Felicity opened the bathroom door and said, "The water's scalding hot, *what* did you say?"

"What do you want to wear?" Lizzie asked.

"You're such a dear," Felicity said, squirming out of her chemise and petticoat. "Just the things I set aside in the overnight case—oh, my *Lord*, we're about to have a flood!" She dashed back into the bathroom, giggling, turned off the faucets, undressed herself completely and climbed into the tub. Splashing water, she began singing at the top of her lungs—"Oh, *les enfants de la pa-tree-ee-yuh,* dah-dah-dee-dah, da-da-dee-*dum,*" over and over again, "Oh, *les enfants de la pa-tree-ee-yuh* . . ."

The telephone rang.

"If it's Napoleon," Felicity shouted, "tell him I'm indisposed at the moment! Oh, *les enfants de la* . . ."

"Hello?" Lizzie said into the mouthpiece.

"Lizzie, is that *you*?" Alison said. "How lovely to hear your voice!"

". . . *pa-tree-ee-yuh,*" Felicity bawled, "dah-dah-dee-dah, dah-dah . . ."

"What on earth is that horrendous squawling?" Alison asked.

"Felicity, I can't hear a *word*!" Lizzie shouted, and in the bathroom Felicity fell comparatively silent, humming softly to herself now as she soaped and splashed about.

"Has someone been beheaded in your room?" Alison asked. "I shouldn't put it past the French."

"It's Felicity in the tub," Lizzie said.

"Advise her not to seek an operatic career, won't you?" Alison said. "My dear, how *are* you? Did my great lummox of a brother treat you grandly in my absence? If not, say the word and I'll have him shot at dawn."

"He was most attentive," Lizzie said. "And gentlemanly. And thoroughly charming. You didn't tell me you were twins. I was so surprised when he . . ."

"Ah, didn't I? An oversight. He likes to think he's by far the prettiest of us, and so I tend to downplay the unfortunate fact that we were once wombmates."

Despite herself, Lizzie found she was smiling.

"That's a pun, dear," Alison said.

"Yes, I know," Lizzie said.

"And *your* roommate, has she drowned?" Alison asked. "I can't hear her delightful aria any longer, thank God."

"She's still bathing," Lizzie said.

167

"Have you bathed as well? Are you ready to come do the town?"

"Why, no, I . . ."

"Well, *surely*! Your first night in Paris? Or have you made other plans?"

"None. Except to go down for tea in a bit."

"Nonsense," Alison said. "You won't enjoy tea at *all* here in France. Zee fife o'clock," she said, falling into a broad French accent, "is so much *plein, n'est-ce pas,* of zee cream poofs, and zee *marrons glacés*, and zee *Madeleines*, it is to throw up, *ma chérie, non, non, non.* And besides," she said in her normal voice, "it will only spoil your dinner. We've made marvelous plans for tonight, and I'm hoping . . ."

"Meals are included in our hotel rate," Lizzie said. "And, Alison, we couldn't *possibly* allow you to entertain us again. I tried to argue against it in London, but Geoff . . ."

"As well he should have. Don't talk drivel, my dear. And don't even *mention* dining at your hotel when there are so *many* restaurants here."

"I don't know what the others . . ."

"Well, rescue buxom Felicity from the waters, and ask her to put on some clothes. And alert your other friends. I shall hear no more of it. Albert and I will be by to collect the lot and parcel of you at seven-thirty sharp." She hesitated, and then said, "Well, that may be a bit too early. Shall we say seven-thirty-one?"

Suddenly reminded of Geoffrey, Lizzie said, "What's a cat that sank?"

"A cat that *sank*? I have no idea. Is it a riddle? I *love* riddles."

"It has something to do with the French ladies," Lizzie said. "Geoffrey told me . . ."

"A cat that . . . oh, the scoundrel! Has he been corrupting my dear Lizzie?"

"What on earth *is* it?"

"I shall tell you later, I love to see you blush. Seven-thirty then, in the lobby. Ta, Lizzie, I'm *so* delighted you're here!" she said, and—before Lizzie could thank her for the roses— abruptly broke the connection.

"I must tell you straight off," Alison said, again reminding

168

Lizzie of her brother, "that the art of cookery is in a terrible state of decadence in Paris."

"As is everything *else*," Albert added.

"But the *Café Anglais* is the best of the lot, or we shouldn't have taken you here. Lizzie? Felicity? May either of us help you with these indecipherable French menus?"

They were, the four of them, sitting on a velvet-covered banquette in the brightly lighted dining room, deprived of the company of Rebecca and Anna because both of them, as they'd protested, were too exhausted to move from the hotel. Anna, especially, was still feeling queasy after the rough channel crossing that morning, a two-hour journey that had unsettled *all* of the women a bit. Lizzie had eaten nothing for lunch in Boulogne and, at Alison's suggestion, had forsaken tea this afternoon. The aromas in the dining room now, the sight of steaming meals wheeling past on trolleys, of silver covers lifted by maitres d'hôtel beaming in anticipation, of carving knives flashing in waiters' hands, made her almost giddy with hunger.

"If you've a hearty appetite," Albert said, "may I suggest the beefsteak for two?"

"No ordinary beefsteak, this one," Alison said. "It's the Chateaubriand, a kernel of meat cut from the very heart of the filet."

"Or the Rouen duck, perhaps," Albert said.

"For that matter, the sole—with *any* of the sauces—is truly divine."

"I think I might go for that, in fact," Albert said. "With the sauce *à l'Orly*. Ladies, might you care for some soup to start? I shouldn't recommend what the French consider to be *oysters*, although I'm told the *marennes vertes* are at least edible."

"But undoubtedly out of season," Alison said.

"Undoubtedly," Albert said. "Ladies? Some bisque? The *consommé de volaille*? Or would you prefer the escargots?"

"What's that?" Felicity asked.

"Snails," Alison said.

"Oh, my goodness!" Felicity said.

The maitre d'hôtel advised them that the *specialité* tonight was *matelotte d'anguilles*, which Felicity learned—to her greater horror—was something like stewed eels. He was recommending the bouillabaisse as well, when Albert interrupted (rudely,

169

Lizzie thought) to say, "Not a'tall, not a'tall! It isn't the genuine article, Felicity. The proper fish elements are wanting because they can't bear transportation from the seaside."

"If *mademoiselle* will be journeying to Marseilles," the maitre d'hôtel said graciously, "she would indeed be well advised to wait. Shall I give you several more moments to decide? Please do not feel at all hurried."

With the man still within earshot, Albert said, "The French claim to have artesian wells here in Paris, which are said to be quite safe. But in general the water has a bad name, and you had best drink the St. Galmier."

"Is that a wine?" Felicity asked.

"No indeed, my dear," Albert said, laughing. "It is, in fact, mineral water. But I *shall* be ordering wine, of course. Let me do that now," he said, "so we'll have a bottle on hand while we order." He looked around the room, snapped his fingers, called "*Garçon!*" and looked pleased when a man across the room snapped to attention and came running to the table. "*La carte des vins, s'il vous plait,*" he said, and Lizzie detected at once that his French was nowhere near as good as Alison's, sounding more, in fact, like Felicity's absurd attempts when they'd entered their hotel room that afternoon. She was surprised, nonetheless, when Alison somewhat sharply said, "The wine butler is addressed as *sommelier*, Albert, not *garçon*. He's inferior to the waiter in the hierarchy of table service, and should *never* be elevated to the level of *garçon*."

"I shall try to remember that . . . *madame*," Albert said drily. "Now then, ladies, what do you think might suit your fancy?"

He seemed intent on annoying Alison all through dinner, insisting on talking first—though this was prompted by Felicity's questions—about the notorious Jack the Ripper, who only two years earlier had terrorized the prostitutes near the Whitechapel district of London's East End, dispatching seven of them to their reward and allegedly mailing to the police half a kidney removed from one of his victims (this while Felicity was slicing her Chateaubriand), and next discussing at length the various diversions that had been available to a London gentleman before the new laws—he seemed to blame these on Victoria's late prince consort, whom he called the Teutonic Prince—made them illegal. Among these (and he described with great relish

170

the many he had seen during his boyhood and, in fact, till the time he was twenty) were the public hangings at Newgate—

"Oh, my *goodness!*" Felicity said.

—abolished in 1868, and two pastimes that were enjoying a heyday before he was born, but which his father had described in detail and which he himself wished were still permitted. These, he explained, were cockfighting and ratting. The ratting had apparently taken place in a gaslit room, usually a cellar someplace, where gentlemen would stand about a pit in which a dog attempted to kill as many rats as he could within a given period of time, the men wagering on his speed and efficiency. At this point Felicity put her napkin to her mouth and asked where she might find the ladies' lounge. Albert rose at once, solicitously put his arm about her waist and said he would lead her there at once.

"He *will* behave like a swine at times," Alison said, smiling thinly.

"He's being perfectly charming," Lizzie said politely.

"Is he then? An odd notion of charm, you Americans must have."

"We're enjoying ourselves *so* much," Lizzie said. "Truly. And I *must* thank you again for putting Geoffrey at our disposal in London—which reminds me. He was absolutely firm about paying for *everything*—but *everything*—whenever we were with him, which was virtually all of the time. I objected, of course, but he'd hear none of it, and I didn't think it my place to argue violently with a man. But, Alison, we're both women . . ."

"We are indeed," Alison said.

". . . and I feel I can be more forthright with you than I was with him. I absolutely *insist*, if we are to spend any time at all together in Paris, that we be allowed to pay our own . . ."

"Nonsense," Allison said. "Albert has more money than he knows what to do with, millions to squander on smaller pleasures than these, believe me. Besides, he rather enjoys patting and pinching Felicity's bottom, have you noticed?"

Lizzie hadn't noticed. She cleared her throat and looked about at the other diners, hoping Alison had not been overheard. In an attempt to change the subject and never once suspecting what lay in wait, she asked, "Now what's this about a cat that sank? Geoffrey seemed certain I'd be shocked. Is it some sport

171

similar to ratting? Are cats drowned in some horrible manner? I did, by the way, see men selling *cat* meat on the streets of London. Do the English *really* eat cat meat?"

"Pussy on a stick," Alison said, nodding. "To suit the more discerning palate."

"And a cat that sank? What's that?"

"A *quatre à cinq*, Lizzie," Alison said. "It's French. *Quatre à cinq*. It means a 'four-to-five.'"

"And what's a four-to-five?"

"The hour when many *petites femmes*—perhaps that's too strong—the hour when many Parisian *ladies* manage to slip away from their coachmen to sidle up the back stairs. *L'heure de femme*, as it's called."

"I don't understand," Lizzie said.

"An hour to be with their lovers," Alison said.

"Oh," Lizzie said.

"Between four and five," Alison said.

"Yes, I . . ."

"Between the sheets," Alison said.

She looked steadily at Lizzie.

"I've shocked you again," she said.

"No, you haven't," Lizzie said.

"Good. Then perhaps we're making progress."

She was not, in fact, shocked again until later that night, when they took her and Felicity to a Parisian "theater and dance hall" (as Albert described it) which had opened only the year before and which was (again according to Albert) *"le rendezvous du high life."*

As their carriage came up the hill on the boulevard de Clichy, the horse plodding upward along the long dark avenue, Lizzie was first aware of a lurid glare in the distance and realized that it was coming from the furthermost end of a modest square. As they came closer, she saw that the facade of the building dominating the square was ablaze with white and golden electrified globes and high above these she saw a great windmill slowly turning, its wings decorated with thousands of red electric lamps. There was the sound of music and laughter from within, and as she climbed down from the carriage, accepting Albert's proffered hand, she saw—to her relief—that several respectable-looking American ladies were being led by their gentlemen escorts through the open entrance doors.

The interior was spacious and illuminated by the same dazzling electrical display as had adorned the facade. She found herself in a huge garden at one end of which was a stage, beside which stood a hollow elephant some forty feet high and forty feet long. "During the winter, they use the elephant as a café," Alison shouted into her ear, as well she might have since the din in the place was unimaginable. A five-piece band—piano, drums, trumpet and two trombones—were positioned around the small stage, mercilessly blaring what sounded like Offenbach. Several women were dancing on the stage. Lizzie was certain she saw their underdrawers, and looked quickly away. There were a great many tables all about the grounds, and as they settled themselves around a small one close to the stage, a rather garishly dressed woman approached Albert and brazenly said, "*Avez-vous une cigarette, monsieur?*"

"No, no, move along," Albert said, but he was smiling.

"*Ah, oui,*" she said, her painted mouth widening into a grin. Lapsing into heavily accented English, she said with seeming delight, "All-rai-tee, you are Eeen-glesh! You buy me *une bière Anglaise*, yes?"

"No, no," Albert said, and patted Felicity's hand.

The woman tapped him on the cheek, poutingly said, "*Vous êtes très méchant, monsieur,*" and sidled off to the next table.

The band had begun another song now, no less spirited or loud than the one preceding it. There were monkeys scurrying about the room, frightening Lizzie until she realized they were all on long chains. Backing away from a particularly frisky one who came dangerously close to their table, she turned unwittingly toward the stage again, where four rather fleshy young women were grouped in a loose semicircle, immodestly shaking their ample bosoms in time to the pounding of the big bass drum and the clashing of the cymbals. Their breasts, billowing in the tops of gowns slashed in wide Vs from shoulders to waist, seemed powdered with flour, and their mouths were exaggerated by the smears of wet glossy paint that decorated their lips. As she watched, unable to believe her eyes, the girls lifted their skirts and kicked out their black-stockinged legs—a flash of lacy underclothes, a glimpse of pale white thighs, she

173

turned away. The women (she could not see them now) began shrieking and making odd little whistling sounds. Lizzie was certain she was blushing bright. She felt Alison's reassuring hand on her arm.

At the table next to them, she saw three young French officers, their long swords trailing onto the floor. Behind them, there were school-feast flags hung all about the mirrored garden, draped from the balconies and galleries that surrounded a small dance floor. A great many men sat alone at the tables, but they were not long without company, she noticed, since women circulated incessantly about the vast room, shamelessly displaying themselves, imploring the men—as they had Albert earlier—to buy them a beer or a glass of wine, to share with them a cigarette or a dance. A woman dressed entirely in black boldly approached a table of young men and raucously bellowed, "*Et alors, vous n'avez jamais vu une vraie femme?*" and then, taking in their blank and somewhat stupefied stares, translated, "'Ave you nevaire see a real womans, eh?" and suddenly kicked one leg straight up toward the chandelier, her skirts billowing in a swirl of frothy lace. Her underclothes were trimmed with delicate pink ribbons, her black silk stockings fastened above the knee by diamond-studded garters. Her powdered thighs quivered as her slippered foot made a small circle on the air. A laugh exploded from her mouth.

"They're Russian," Alison explained. "The boys. But *that*, they understood, I'm sure."

Felicity stared wide-eyed as another woman approached from the opposite end of the room, passing the stage where the dancers still cavorted, swinging past the hollow elephant, her leghorn hat decorated with a spray of yellow plumes, her otherwise blond hair streaked with a startling swath of midnight black, her white dress brocaded with flowers, a violent display of diamonds glistening about her throat and falling into the wide V of her bodice to nestle in her full (and almost fully exposed) breasts. As the other woman had just done, she kicked one leg up toward the ceiling, knocking the hat clear off the head of a bald man who sat not four tables away.

And now there was more shrieking and whistling from the women on the stage, and the band rose as if on signal, and began filing out into what Lizzie saw was an adjoining room of

174

equal size, the trumpeter and trombonists blaring their horns, the drummer pounding the bass drum as though he were in a marching band, the pianist waving his arms and imploring the crowd to follow them. "*La quadrille!*" one of the painted women shouted, "*Suivez-nous!*" and there was a general rush out of the room. Lizzie felt Alison's hand tighten on her own, heard her voice over the bedlam shouting, "Come!"

"It's midnight!" Albert shouted to Felicity, and took her hand and hurried her along into the other room, where the women of the place—many more of them now—were taking up positions, four by four, and the crowd was jostling for seats in the low balconies surrounding the dance floor. The piano player seated himself behind an upright piano identical to the one in the garden except that it was decorated with posters depicting women Lizzie was sure she recognized as those roaming among the tables, struck a few chords, and waited while the drummer seated himself behind his duplicate set of drums. A hush fell over the room, as though the vast place had suddenly become a cathedral. The piano player struck yet another chord, and the music began.

Facing each other, the dancers executed the first few figures of a quadrille, and then advanced toward the center of their loosely formed square, kicking their legs above each other's heads, and holding this position, their heels impossibly high in the air, bejeweled hands shaking their skirts, flashing their petticoats and underdrawers and thighs. They lowered their legs at last, and turned their backs this way and that to the audience, knees and legs pressed together now, and—bowing over from the waist—threw their skirts up over gartered stockings and beribboned underwear, exposing the fullness of their buttocks in the loose-fitting garments. They stood upright again, and turned to face the audience, and kicked again, seemingly higher this time, and then collapsed to the floor as though they were puppets whose strings had broken, their limbs spread in opposite directions. A wild cheer went up from the audience.

A man dressed as a toreador came magically from behind a red velvet curtain, and there was a woman sitting upon his shoulders, her arms about his neck, her black silken shiny knees thrust forward, skirts back, his hands clutching her an-

175

kles as together they cavorted among the other wildly kicking dancers. The woman, her hair a red as flaming as Lizzie's, her mouth painted a deeper scarlet, suddenly—and again as if by magic—reversed her perch on the man's shoulders so that now she faced him, her midnight knees pressed against the sides of his neck, her ankles locked on his back, and hurled herself backward and away from him, arms akimbo, tufted red hair showing in her armpits, the small of her back caught in his hands as upside down he twirled her about the floor, her head hovering above his knees someplace, the garish inverted smile, her red hair sweeping the floor.

The other dancers assumed even more immodest positions, sitting on the floor and spreading their legs wide, whistling and shrieking in an exhibition of rank indecency that provoked more shouting and cheers from the audience. Another man was on the dance floor now—Lizzie could not tell whether he was employed here or was merely a customer who'd succumbed to the frenzy of the moment—waggling his legs in their loose trousers, wriggling about like a snake. One of the women reached for the front of his trousers and he darted away in mock outrage, to be pursued by several of the other dancers who, when they had him surrounded, kicked their legs up over his head repeatedly until, seemingly overcome by the sight of their flashing gartered limbs and the open revelation of their lacy underthings, he fell to the floor in a dead swoon.

Giggling, the dancers stepped over him and, legs akimbo over his prostrate form, flounced their skirts above him until his eyes flickered open and rolled about in his head as though the perfume emanating from between their powdered thighs had revived him. He slithered along the floor on his back, his eyes popping open wide now (surely he was one of the performers) and leaped to his feet again, spanning a dancer's waist with his huge hands, lifting her high above his head, and parading her about the room while she opened her legs as wide as seemed humanly possible.

Hardly a man was seated now. They packed round the dance floor four and five deep, applauding whenever one of the women assumed another attitude of shameless immodesty, shouting for drinks, thronging onto the floor to dance with female companions who'd been circulating in the balconies throughout the course of the riotous display. There were more raucous calls, cries in French and English and languages Lizzie could not identify, until finally the floor was cleared again for the final quadrille, during which the cavorting women seemed to abandon whatever shred of modesty had previously restrained their contortions. When at last they left the place ("It's called the Moulin Rouge," Alison said to her on the street outside), Lizzie felt shaken to the core. Her hand was trembling on Albert's arm as she accepted his assistance into the carriage.

"So now," he said in his dry English way, "you've seen the *demi-monde* of Paris."

8: NEW
BEDFORD—1893

"**What** is your full name?"

"Bridget Sullivan."

"And were you in the Borden household sometimes called Maggie?"

"Yes, sir."

"By whom were you called Maggie? By the whole family?"

"No, sir."

"By whom?"

"By Lizzie and Emma."

"By Miss Emma and Miss Lizzie?"

"Yes, sir."

"But that was not unpleasant to you?"

"No, sir, it was not."

"Not at all offensive?"

"No, sir."

"Did not cause any ill feeling or trouble?"

"No, sir."

"Did Mr. and Mrs. Borden call you by some other name?"

"Yes, sir. Called me by my own, right name."

"Won't you be kind enough to tell us how old you are, Miss Sullivan?"

"Twenty-six years old."

"I believe you've never been married."

"No, sir."

"How long have you been in this country?"

"Six years last May . . . *seven* years last May."

"And where were you born?"

"In Ireland."

"And came here seven years ago?"

"Yes, sir."

"Came to what part of this country?"

"I came to Newport."

"Newport, Rhode Island?"

"Yes, sir."

"Did you have any folks here when you came here?"

"No, sir."

"Father, mother, brother or sisters?"

"No, sir."

"And have you any here now?"

"No, sir. I ain't got no folks here, no more than relations."

"When you went to Newport, did you stay there quite a while?"

"Twelve months."

"And from Newport, where did you go?"

"I went out to South Bethlehem."

"That was in Pennsylvania?"

"Yes, sir."

"When did you come to Fall River?"

"I came there four years—I was two years out when I came to Fall River. Two years in America, when I came to Fall River."

"Did you go to the Bordens the first place in Fall River?"

"No, sir, I went to Mrs. Reed."

"When did you go to work for Mr. Borden?"

. . . I was there two years and nine months at the time of his death. There wasn't any other domestic servant there while I was there. There was a man on the farm who used to come there and do chores, and go back again. His first name was Alfred. I don't know his last name, I never asked him. My general duties in the household were washing, ironing and cooking, with sweeping. I had no care of any of the chambers except my own. I slept in the third story of the house, right over

179

Mr. Borden's room, which is right over the kitchen. I don't know who did the chamber work in Mr. Borden's room and Mrs. Borden's room. Themselves did it. I don't know which of them. I didn't do it, and neither of the daughters did it.

I don't know who took charge of the room in the front part of the house, either. When Miss Emma was home, she done it. When Mr. Morse was there, and when Mrs. Borden had any of her friends there, I guess she done it, or helped do it. That is, as far as I can remember. The rooms belonging to the daughters, themselves took care of them, as far as I know. I didn't have anything to do with the rooms, nothing of any kind to do with any bedroom.

I never had any trouble there in the family. I liked the place. As far as I know, they liked me, too. I never saw anything out of the way. Never saw any conflict in the family. Never saw any quarreling or anything of that kind. Miss Lizzie always spoke to Mrs. Borden when Mrs. Borden talked to her. There was not, so far as I know, any trouble that morning of the fourth. I did not see any trouble with the family.

I felt kind of a dull headache as I got up that morning. I got up at a quarter past six. I have a timepiece in my room, a clock, one of them little round clocks. I didn't look at the clock in my room, but I looked when I came down to the kitchen. There's a clock there. It was a quarter past six when I came down. I went downcellar then, and brought up some wood to start my fire, went down and got some coal. Brought that up in the coal hod. Then I unlocked the door, and took in the milk can, and put a pan out for the iceman and a pitcher with some water in it. The locks were just the same way as I'd left them the night before. After I'd taken in my milk and put out my pan for the iceman, I hooked the screen door, left the panel door open.

Before anyone came downstairs, I started my work around the kitchen, getting ready for breakfast. I had clothes on the clotheshorse, I suppose I took them down, as I generally did. Mrs. Borden was the first one appeared on that Thursday morning. I was in the kitchen, and she came through the back entry, downstairs from her bedroom. After she came down, she gave me directions for breakfast. Might have been twenty minutes of seven, or half past six. I can't tell the time, for I never noticed it. Mr. Borden came downstairs, down the back stairway from his bedroom, no more than five minutes later, I don't think. He went into the sitting room and put a key on the shelf there. The key of his bedroom door. He ordinarily kept that in the sitting room, on the shelf. Then he came out into the kitchen, put a dressing coat on, as far as I think, and went outdoors. Took his slop pail outdoors. He emptied the slop pail and unlocked the barn, and went into the barn. Then he went to the yard where the pear tree was, and brought in a basket of pears that he picked off the ground. I can't say whether he hooked the screen door or not. He washed up in the kitchen and got ready for breakfast. Up to that time, I hadn't seen anyone but Mr. and Mrs. Borden. Not until I put the breakfast on the table and Mr. Morse sat down to breakfast.

There was some mutton for breakfast that morning. And some broth and johnnycakes, coffee and cookies. The broth was made of mutton. It might have been a quarter past seven when they sat down to breakfast, I can't exactly tell the time. While breakfast was going on, I was around the kitchen cleaning up things. I don't know exactly what I was doing. I'd finished my ironing the day before, and put away the clothes. I guess they must have gone in the sitting room after breakfast. The bell from the table rang, and when I went in there was nobody in the dining room. So I sat down and had *my* breakfast. Then I took the dishes off out of the dining room and brought them out in the kitchen and began washing them. The next I remember to see was Mr. Borden and Mr. Morse going out the back entry, the back door. Mr. Morse went out, but Mr. Borden returned. He came to the sink, and he cleaned his teeth in the sink, and after that he took a bowl, a big bowl, and filled it with water, and took it up to his room. He had the key in his hand as he went up with the pitcher, took it off the shelf in the sitting room.

I was washing the dishes at the sink when Miss Lizzie came through. It was no more than five minutes later, I think. I don't remember how the time was. She came from the sitting room, and through the kitchen, and she left down the slop pail, and I asked her what did she want for breakfast. She said she didn't know as she wanted any breakfast, but she guessed she would have something, she would have some coffee and cookies. She got some coffee, got her cup and saucer and got some coffee. And I went out in the backyard, and she was getting her own

181

breakfast. Mr. Borden hadn't come back down again. The screen door was hooked, and of course I unhooked it when I went out.

I went out because I had a sick headache and I was sick to my stomach. I went out to vomit. In the back yard. I can't tell how long I was out there. Maybe ten minutes, maybe fifteen. I didn't see Mr. Borden again after he went up to his room with the water. I don't know where he'd gone in the meantime. When I got back in the kitchen, I completed washing my dishes. Some of them was washed, but all of them wasn't, and I finished them and took them in the dining room, and I got them completed, and Mrs. Borden was there as I was fixing my dining-room table, and she asked me if I had anything to do this morning. I said no, not particular, if she had anything to do for me. She said she wanted the windows washed. I asked her how, and she said, "Inside and out both. They're awful dirty." She was dusting, had a feather duster in her hand, dusting between the sitting room and dining room, the door.

I didn't see Miss Lizzie anywhere at that time. I don't remember to see her. I can't exactly tell the time, but I think it was about nine o'clock . . .

My full name is Adelaide B. Churchill. I'm unmarried at the present time, I'm a widow. I've been a resident of Fall River for forty-three years and some months. With the exception of about six months, I've lived at my present residence all my life, forty-three years and some months, the house I was born in. It's called the Mayor Buffinton house, after my father, Edward P. Buffinton. It's the house next north of the Borden house. I occupy the whole house, live there with my mother, sister, son, niece and the man that works for us.

I've known the Borden family for the past twenty years. Been on terms of social relations with them, calling backwards and forwards. I can perhaps best describe Mr. Borden as tall and straight . . . a tall, straight man. Mrs. Borden was very fleshy, I can't think she was as tall as I am, not any taller, A short, heavy woman.

On the morning of August fourth, 1892, I first saw Mr. Borden at about nine o'clock or so, somewhere along there, I can't tell just exactly. I saw him from my kitchen. He was standing by the steps. Not *on* the steps, but on the walk by the steps. He wasn't in motion, he was just standing. On the side of the house toward the barn.

"Can you tell me, Miss Sullivan, what you did after you received this direction from Mrs. Borden? Where did you go and what did you begin to do?"

"I was out in the kitchen."

"What were you doing in the kitchen?"

"Oh, I was cleaning off my stove and putting things in their places and so forth. And when I got ready, I went in the dining room and sitting room and . . ."

. . . left down the windows which I was going to wash and went downcellar and got a pail for to take some water. The windows was up, and left down the windows. There was no curtains there. The shutters was open at the bottom, I remember. I didn't see anybody there when I went in the dining room and sitting room to close the windows. I got a wooden pail downcellar, came upstairs, and in the kitchen closet I found a brush which was to wash the windows with. I filled my pail with water in the sink and took it outdoors. As I was outside the back door, Lizzie Borden appeared in the back entry and said, "Maggie, are you going to wash the windows?"

I said, "Yes. You needn't lock the door, I'll be out around here. But you can lock it if you want to. I can get the water in the barn." She made no reply to that, but she didn't hook the door. I don't know where she went then. *I* went to the barn to get the handle for the brush. It was in the barn, right in one of the stalls. On the first floor of the barn. Before I started to wash the windows, as I had the water and brush, Mrs. Kelly's girl appeared, and I was talking to her at the fence . . .

My name is Abraham G. Hart. I am treasurer of the Union Savings Bank in Fall River. The bank is situated in what is sometimes called Market Square, North Main Street, a few rods from the City Hall. Upon the east side of North Main Street, just north of City Hall.

Mr. Borden was president of the bank for four or five years before he died. I was acquainted with him for forty years or more. On the morning of the homicides, Mr. Borden came into the bank as was his usual custom in the morning, about half-

183

past nine. It wouldn't vary but a few minutes from that time, I think, though I don't think I looked at any timepiece. To my sight that morning, Mr. Borden did not seem in the usual health. I think he was under the weather, as we say. He did not look as well as usual. He remained there about five minutes, no more than seven. There's another bank in the same building. The National Union Bank, a separate organization from the savings bank.

My name is John T. Burrill, my occupation is cashier of the National Union Bank, in the same building as the Union Savings Bank. Mr. Borden was a stockholder and depositor at my bank. On the morning of August fourth, I saw him in the bank, in front of the counter where I work. I saw him in conversation with Mr. Hart and a colored man who was there in regard to a loan. That is Mr. Abraham Hart, the last witness. I think it must have been between quarter-past nine and quarter-to ten.

My name is Everett Cook, I'm cashier of the First National Bank of Fall River. The bank is situated on North Main Street, between the Union Savings Bank and the Mellen House, on the other side of the street from the Union Savings Bank. The Trust Company is in the same building, behind the same counter. Mr. Borden was a director of the Trust Company, and Miss Lizzie A. Borden had an account there at the time. On August fourth, 1892, her balance was $172.75.

I transacted some business with Mr. Borden that morning. He came into the bank at about a quarter of ten. There was a clock, and I should say about that time I had the right of way on the counter, that morning, and I glanced at the clock, and I should fix the time about quarter of ten.

"It is agreed, if Your Honors please," Knowlton said, "to save calling a number of witnesses . . ."

"I'll state what we agreed to," Robinson said. "For the purposes of this trial, Your Honors, the defendant having no knowledge in regard to a will or otherwise—so far as is now ascertained—it is agreed that the deceased was intestate. Also, without any further inquiries, that the amount of the property in the name of Andrew J. Borden at the time of his death may be taken to be from two hundred and fifty to three hundred thousand dollars."

"That is agreeable to us," Knowlton said. "That saves calling a number of witnesses."

My name is Delia S. Manley, I live in Fall River. At 203 Second Street. Lived there for four years, and am familiar with the premises about the Borden House, though I did not know Mr. Borden while he was alive. But I do know where he lived. And I know the Kelly house, too. My sister-in-law occupies that house at this time. I happened to pass by the Borden house on the morning of the murders. This was either at a quarter of ten, or ten minutes of ten.

A man was standing in the north gateway, dressed in light clothes. I should say he was a young man. I didn't look at him sufficient to describe his features at all. He was standing in the gateway, leaning his left arm on the gatepost. The man was not Andrew J. Borden. Nor was it John Morse, who I saw in the District Court below. It was not as old a man as that. I'd never seen this man before. He was standing there, seeming to be looking at us, and taking in what we were talking about, I should judge. By us, I mean, Mrs. Hart of Tiverton, she was with me. We were both going down the street together. We stopped there to see some pond lilies that a young fellow had in a carriage. The carriage had stopped between the two houses— between the Borden house and the Churchill house. A little nearer the Borden house than the Churchill house.

I first noticed the man when I was coming from the street back onto the sidewalk. The team stopped, and I went back of the team to see those pond lilies, and as I was coming back on the sidewalk, that was when I saw this man. Standing in this gateway, resting his arm upon this gatepost. And of course, as I stepped back from the carriage onto the sidewalk, I came nearly face to face with him, not exactly.

I couldn't say how long the man stood there, for all I saw of him was just—I stepped onto the sidewalk and saw him, and I went right away. The first I saw of him, he was standing there. And the last I saw of him, he was standing there. Quietly. In full view of everybody. And looking right toward me. I didn't know who he was. I should say he was a man about thirty, as

185

near as I could judge. I noticed nothing out of the way about him. He had nothing in his hand that I noticed.

My name is Sarah R. Hart, I live in Tiverton, near Adamsville. Live on a farm there, but I used to live in Fall River, ten years ago. I lived there for fifteen or twenty years. On Second Street most of the time, so that I'm very familiar with Second Street. I knew Andrew J. Borden by sight when he was alive, but I wasn't particularly acquainted with him.

I was on Second Street the day of the murders.

I passed by the Borden house near ten o'clock. I think somewhere near ten minutes to ten. I was with my sister, Mrs. Delia Manley. We had occasion to stop near the gate of the Borden house, the north gate. I stopped to speak to my nephew, who was in a carriage. I stepped from the sidewalk to the back of the carriage to get some pond lilies. The pond lilies were in a tub in the back of the carriage. I noticed someone in the gateway, I should judge he was somewhere near thirty years of age. He was not Mr. Borden. He was standing, resting his head on his left elbow, and his elbow on the south post of the gateway. He was looking at me, as I thought, and then turned and looked at the street as though he were uneasy trying to pry into my business. I was there five minutes, and he was there when I went away, down toward Borden Street. From there onto Main, in time to catch the ten o'clock car for the north. It comes down Main Street and stops there by the City Hall. It left City Hall as the clock was striking ten. I can fix the time as of ten minutes of ten when I saw him because I took the horsecar at ten o'clock.

My name is George A. Pettee. I've lived in Fall River for fifty-four years. I knew Andrew Borden since I was a young boy. I used to live in the Borden house. Twenty-two years ago last March. Lived in the upper part. I was the tenant, or one of the tenants, preceding Mr. Borden.

On the morning of the fourth of August last year, I was passing the house sometime, I should think, about ten o'clock. Bridget Sullivan stood in front of the house, nearly opposite the front door. She had a pail and dipper and brush with her. I thought she had been washing windows.

* * *

186

My full name is Jonathan Clegg. My business is hatter and gents' furnishings. On August fourth, 1892, my place of business was at Number 6 North Main Street. With reference to the Union Savings Bank, it might have been fifty yards, the opposite side of the street. I saw Mr. Borden on the opposite side of the street that morning, and called him into the store. I wished to see him that morning. I was wanting to see him specially that morning.

I was having some dealings with him with reference to hiring another store. I had already hired it. I wanted to see him to make arrangements. I had gone to Mr. Borden's house to visit him with reference to this store. Twice. On Tuesday, the second of August, and on the following day, Wednesday. I was there the two days preceding the homicide. Mr. Borden let me in the first time. Bridget let me in the second time. I remained in the house with him, well, about ten minutes. The subject of our conversation was hiring the store.

On the morning of August fourth, Mr. Borden left my shop at exactly twenty-nine minutes past ten. Just as he left me, I looked at the City Hall clock.

I never saw him alive again.

My name is Benjamin J. Handy. I'm a physician in Fall River, been practicing there nearly the whole of twenty years. I know where the Andrew J. Borden house is, and I remember the day of the murders. I went by that house on the morning of the murders. At about half-past ten, a little after probably.

At that time, I saw a person in the vicinity of the house. I didn't know who he was. A medium-sized man of very pale complexion, with his eyes fixed upon the sidewalk, passing slowly toward the south. In reference to the Borden house, as near I can tell, he was opposite a space between the Kelly house and Mr. Wade's store. What attracted my attention to him in the first place, he was a very pale individual, paler than common. And he was acting strangely.

I turned in my carriage to watch him as I drove by, to look at him. I had a faint idea that I'd seen him on Second Street some days before. It was not Thomas Bowles that works for Mrs. Churchill and used to work for me. Nor was it George L. Douglass that used to keep the stable on Second Street, just above Spring. I know him well, and it wasn't he. This man was dressed in a light suit of clothes. He was well dressed, collar and necktie. He seemed to be agitated about something or other. Seemed to be moving, swaying—rolling possibly—a little. Not staggering, but I thought it more than ordinary movement.

I think I'd seen him before that day. I wouldn't state it as a fact, but I think I may have seen him before, on some other day, on the same street. On *that* day, I hadn't seen him before. That was the only time I saw him on that day. Somewhere between twenty minutes past ten and twenty minutes of eleven.

My name is Joseph Shortsleeves, I'm a carpenter by trade. On the fourth of August, 1892, I saw Mr. Borden coming from the direction of the shop Mr. Clegg then occupied, toward where we was working on the new store Mr. Clegg had hired. We were making changes in the front windows, lowering them down. He came into the front door, went to the back part of the store, picked up a lock that had been on the front store door. It was all broken to pieces. He looked at it, laid it down again, went upstairs, then went from the back part of the shop up to the front part of the shop upstairs over our head. He was there a few moments, and came down again and picked the lock up and walked out. In the course of all this, we exchanged no words.

He went toward the west across the road, partways across Main Street. Then he came back, then turned around and looked at us. Says I, "Good morning, Mr. Borden," and says he, "Good morning to you." As near as I can remember, this was between half-past ten and quarter to eleven. I had a watch in my pocket, and I had the City Hall to look at, but I had no occasion to look at a timepiece. My testimony as to the time is an estimate. Mr. Mather was at work with me that day. James Mather.

On the fourth day of August, 1892, I was working up in Jonathan Clegg's store, fixing it for him, the store he was going to occupy. I was working with Mr. Shortsleeves, the last witness who came in here. We were going to drop the front windows down lower, near that sidewalk. Working on the outside, pretty near all the time. The City Hall clock was in my view while we were working.

Mr. Borden went inside the store and picked up a lock, and then went out again. He turned in the direction of Spring Street. I was on the outside, so I could see him. He went away at about twenty minutes of eleven. I looked at the City Hall clock.

My name is Caroline Kelly. I'm married, the wife of Dr. Kelly of Fall River. We live in the next house to the south of the Borden house, and were living there on August fourth of last year. It was a very warm day, a pleasant day. I was about the house that morning, attending to ordinary household duties, and had an engagement to go downtown, to the dentist's. Before I started downtown, I consulted the kitchen clock, and then went right out. The kitchen clock showed about twenty-eight minutes of eleven.

When I got out on the street, I turned to the right and north, downhill. And in going down the hill, I had to pass by Mr. Borden's house. I know Mr. Borden to speak to as well as by sight. He was on the inside of his yard, coming round the house. From the back of the house, east, I think. He went inside the fence to the front door, and stooped down as though putting a key in the door. He had a little white parcel in his hand, I think.

I didn't speak to him, and he didn't speak to me. I don't think he saw me. This was when I was going out to the dentist. Immediately after I'd looked at my clock. It's an old-fashioned clock, a square wooden clock with weights. It's been in the family for years, I've only had it for two years in my house. In August of last year, it wasn't a good timekeeper, nor could it be depended upon for accurate time. It doesn't run at all now, it's broken.

. . . When I completed the rinsing of the windows, I put the handle of the brush away in the barn, and brought the pail and dipper in, and put the dipper behind, and I got the handbasin and went into the sitting room to wash the sitting-room windows. Up to that time, I hadn't seen Miss Lizzie since I saw her at the screen door.

I had the upper part of the window down, in the sitting room, when I heard something. Like a person at the door was trying to unlock the door and push it, but couldn't. I'd heard no

189

ringing of any bell. I went to open the door, caught it by the knob—the spring lock, as usual—and it was locked. I unbolted it, and it was locked with a key. As I unlocked it, I said, "Oh, pshaw," and Miss Lizzie laughed, upstairs. Her father was out there on the doorstep, she was upstairs. Either in the entry or in the top of the stairs, I can't tell which. Not a word passed between me and Mr. Borden as he came to the door. I let him in, and went back to washing my windows, into the sitting room again. And he came into the sitting room and went into the dining room. He had a little parcel in his hand, same as a paper or a book.

He sat down in the chair at the head of the lounge. I was washing my windows. I went out into the kitchen after something, I see the man sitting on the lounge, and the chair at the head of the lounge. Miss Lizzie came downstairs, probably five minutes later. She came down through the entry, the front entry, into the dining room, I suppose to her father. I heard her ask her father if he had any mail, and they had some talk between them which I didn't understand or pay any attention to, but I heard her tell her father that Mrs. Borden had a note and had gone out.

The next thing I remember, Mr. Borden went out in the kitchen and come in the kitchen door, come from the kitchen into the sitting room and took a key off the mantelpiece and went upstairs to his room. Up the back stairs. When Mr. Borden come back downstairs again, I was completed in the sitting room, and taking my water and taking the handbasin and stepladder into the dining room. As I got in there, he pulled a rocking chair, and sat down in the rocking chair near the window, and let down the window as I'd left it up when I got through. I was washing the dining-room windows when Miss Lizzie appeared.

She came into the dining room, went out in the kitchen and took an ironing board, and placed it on the dining-room table and commenced to iron. Meantime, I was washing the last window in the dining room.

She said, "Maggie, are you going out this afternoon?"

I said, "I don't know. I might and I might not. I don't feel very well."

She said, "If you go out, be sure and lock the door, for Mrs. Borden has gone out on a sick call, and I might go out, too."

"Who's sick?" I said.

"I don't know," Miss Lizzie said. "She had a note this morning. It must be in town."

She was ironing handkerchiefs. Her flats she was ironing with were in the stove, in the kitchen. When I finished my windows, I went into the kitchen, washed out the cloths that I had washing the windows, and hung them behind the stove. As I got through, Miss Lizzie came out and said, "There's a cheap sale of dress goods at Sargent's this afternoon, at eight cents a yard." I don't know that she said "this afternoon," but "today." And I said, "*I'm* going to have one," and went upstairs to my room . . .

My name is Mark P. Chase. I'm a hostler, formerly a patrolman on the police force. My place of business is right opposite Dr. Kelly's, on Second Street. The New York and Boston Express barn. I have charge of it, right opposite the Kelly house. I was at the barn all morning on the day Andrew J. Borden was murdered.

At about eleven o'clock, I saw a carriage standing right by a tree, right front of Mr. Borden's fence. An open buggy, a box buggy. It was a high top seat, high back. A man with a brown hat and black coat was in it. Sitting in the carriage, back to me. I should say this was about five to ten minutes of eleven. I'd never seen such a buggy as that around there before. Never saw that man around there before. I could see the man from his shoulders up to the top of his head. The side of his face. I didn't recognize him as anybody I knew.

. . . When I got up in the bedroom, I laid down in the bed. I heard the bells outdoors ring, the City Hall bell, as I suppose it was, and I looked at my clock, and it was eleven o'clock.

My name Hymon Lubinsky.

I peddle ice cream. Ice-cream peddler. I work for Mr. Wilkinson. I peddle by team. I keep my team on Second Street. Charley Gardner's stable. Near the corner of Second and Rodman Street. Near Morgan Street, too. Between Rodman and

191

Morgan. Up a little from the Borden house. That morning, I get my team from the stable and drive toward Second Street, by the Borden house. It was after eleven, a few minutes after eleven.

I saw a lady come out the way from the barn right to the stairs back of the house—the northside stairs, from the back of the house. She had on a dark-color dress, I can't tell what kind of color it was, nothing on her head. She was walking very slow, toward the steps. I don't know if she went in the house, I couldn't tell this, I was in the team. I didn't stop the team, I just trotted a little, not fast.

The woman I saw was not the servant. I have delivered ice cream to the servant, oh, two or three weeks before the murder. The woman I saw the day of the murder was not the same woman as the servant.

I am sure about that.

. . . I was lying in the bed, I know I wasn't drowsing or sleeping, and up to that time, I heard no noise, heard no sound of anybody, heard no opening or closing of the screen door. If anybody goes in or out and is careless and slams the door, I can hear it in my room.

The next thing that occurred, Miss Lizzie hollered, "Maggie, come down!"

I said, "What's the matter?"

"Come down quick!" she said. "Father's dead! Somebody came in and killed him!"

This was ten or fifteen minutes after the clock struck eleven, about as far as I can judge. I ran downstairs. I had not changed any of my clothing or taken off any clothing at all. When I came downstairs, the first person I saw was Miss Lizzie. She was standing at the back door, standing at the door that was leading in, a wooden door. The door was open. She was inside the threshhold, standing with her back to the screen door. I went around to go right in the sitting room, and she said, "Oh, Maggie, don't go in! I've got to get a doctor quick! Go over! I've got to have the doctor!"

I went over to Dr. Bowen's right away. I guess I ran, I don't know whether I did or not. But I guess I went as fast as I could. His wife came to the door, and I told her that Mr. Borden was dead. I think that's what I told her. And she said the doctor wasn't in, but she expected him along any time, and she would send him over . . .

"Mrs. Churchill, you testified earlier that on the morning of August fourth, 1892, at about nine o'clock, you saw Mr. Borden standing on the walk by the steps. On the side of his house toward the barn, is that so?"

"That's so, yes."

"At any time on that morning, did you leave your house and go upon some errand?"

"Yes, sir."

"About what time did you leave the house?"

"I don't know. Somewhere near eleven o'clock, I should think."

"Where did you go to?"

"I went to M. T. Hudner's market."

"On what street is that?"

"South Main Street."

"How far from your house?"

"Just a little ways. Nearly opposite our house, only a little north."

"Nearly opposite your house on a parallel street?"

"Yes, sir."

"Did you do any business there?"

"Yes, sir."

"What was the general nature of it?"

"I got three articles for dinner. Something for dinner."

"Did you delay in the shop there after you bought the articles?"

"I asked my brother, who worked there, to send a telephone message for a woman who was at our house."

"Had some brief conversation?"

"Yes."

"Then what did you do?"

"I went right home."

"When you reached the neighborhood of your house, did you notice anything?"

"Bridget Sullivan was going across the street from Dr. Bowen's house to the Borden house. She looked very white, and I thought someone was sick. She was going fast."

*   *   *

. . . When I came back to the house, I said, "Miss Lizzie, where were *you*? Didn't I leave the screen door hooked?"

"I was out in the back yard," she said. "And heard a groan. And came in, and the screen door was wide open."

She wanted to know if I knew where Alice Russell lived, and I said I did.

"Go and get her," she said. "I can't be alone in the house."

So I stepped inside the entry and got a hat and shawl that was hanging inside the entry and went down to Miss Russell.

At that time, no outcry or alarm had been given to any of the neighbors . . .

"You saw Bridget Sullivan going from Dr. Bowen's house back to the Borden house . . ."

"Yes, sir."

"Then what did you do, Mrs. Churchill?"

I went right in the north side of our house, in the back door, passed through the dining room into the kitchen, and laid my bundles on a long bench. And I looked out the window, and I saw Miss Lizzie at the inside of the screen door. She looked as if she was leaning up against the east casing of the door, and she seemed excited or agitated to me, as if something had happened, and I stepped to the other window—the other kitchen window, the east window—and I opened the window and said, "Lizzie, what's the matter?"

She said, "Oh, Mrs. Churchill, do come over! Someone has killed father!"

I shut down the window, passed right through the kitchen and dining room into the front hall, and went right out the front door over to Mr. Borden's. I didn't see Bridget there when I arrived. I stepped inside the screen door and Miss Lizzie was sitting on the second stair, at the right of the door. I put my right hand on her arm and said, "Lizzie, where *is* your father?"

"In the sitting room," she said.

And I said, "Where were you when it happened?"

"I went to the barn to get a piece of iron," she said.

"Where's your mother?" I asked.

"I don't know. She'd got a note to go see someone who's sick. I don't know but *she's* killed, too, for I thought I heard her come in. Father must have an enemy," she said. "We've all been sick,

194

and we think the milk's been poisoned. Dr. Bowen's not at home," she said, "I *must* have a doctor!"

"Lizzie," I said, "shall *I* go and try to get someone to get a doctor?"

"Yes," she said, and I went out.

My full name is A. J. Cunningham. The *J* stands for John. I'm a newsdealer in Fall River. On the morning of August fourth, as I was going up Second Street, what attracted my attention was Mrs. Churchill running across the street. She started from the Borden residence and she run triangular across the street to an office there of Mr. Hall's, the place that's called Hall's Stable. I was opposite Hall's Stable. I went up as far as Varney Wale's store where my business there was collecting money for newspapers. The weekly payment was twelve cents. I was there a few seconds, and then I went on the opposite side of the street to Mr. Gray's paint shop—on the corner of Spring and Second. To collect the same amount there. I was there about the same time, and before I reached Hall's Stable again, I see Mrs. Churchill standing on the sidewalk, talking to two or three gentlemen that was in front of Mr. Hall's office. When I got there, I learned from another party that there was some trouble in the Borden house.

There's a paint shop on the corner of Borden and Second Streets, that's Mr. Gorman's paint shop. I went in there and asked for the use of his telephone. To telephone to the Central Police Station.

I know the city marshal's voice, it was the marshal himself who answered the phone.

My name is Rufus B. Hilliard. I'm the city marshal of Fall River, been connected with the police force there for a little over fourteen years, been city marshal a little over seven years. Prior to that time, I was assistant city marshal.

On the fourth of August last year, my attention was first called to the trouble at the Borden house by a telephone message. The person who telephoned was John Cunningham, the news dealer. The guardroom adjoins to the southward the room in which the telephone is. I left the telephone and went into the guardroom to talk to Officer George W. Allen.

*　*　*

At a quarter past eleven, the marshal came to me and said, "Officer Allen, there's a row up on Second Street." Came from his office in the Central Police Station and addressed me where I was sitting at the guardroom door. Right in front of his office, at the side. I looked at the clock to see if I had time to commit my prisoners at half-past eleven. I was a committing officer at that time, and my duty was conveying those who'd been committed by the District Court at Fall River to the place of confinement. Had a regular time for that duty each day. At half-past eleven and at a quarter past three. It was a quarter past eleven when Marshal Hilliard gave me this direction.

My name is Seabury W. Bowen. I'm a physician and surgeon practicing in Fall River, lived and practiced my profession there for twenty-six years. During a large part of that time—twenty-one years—I've lived at my present residence, diagonally opposite from the Borden house, to the northwest. I've been the family physician for, I should say, a dozen years, probably.

On the morning of August fourth, I returned to my house sometime after eleven and before half-past eleven. I had no occasion at the time to note the time of day. As I came up to the house, Mrs. Bowen came to the door looking for me. As a consequence of that, I went across the street into the house of Mr. Borden. Through the side door. Miss Lizzie Borden and Mrs. Churchill were there when I arrived. They were in either—at the end of the hall, side hall, or close to the kitchen door. That is, just at the end of the back hall. There was no other living person there at that time.

It is pretty hard work for me to recall how Lizzie was dressed that morning. Probably, if I could see a dress something like it, I could guess. But I could not describe it. It was a sort of drab, not much color to it to attract my attention. A sort of morning calico, I should judge. An ordinary, unattractive, common dress that I did not notice specially. There are many shades of drab to a woman's dress, I should judge.

As soon as I entered the house, I said, "Lizzie, what's the matter?"

Her reply was "Father's been killed." Or stabbed. Stabbed or killed, I couldn't say which it was. I asked the question, "Where is your father?"

196

"In the sitting room," she said.

I went directly into the dining room, and from there into the sitting room. As I came into the sitting room, I saw the form of Mr. Borden lying on the sofa, or lounge, at the left of the sitting-room door. Upon an inspection, I found that his face was very badly cut with apparently a sharp instrument, and there was blood over his face, his face was covered with blood. I felt of his pulse and satisfied myself at once that he was dead. And I took a glance about the room and saw there was nothing disturbed at all. He was lying with his face toward the south, on his right side, apparently at ease. As anyone would if they were lying asleep.

I should hardly say his face was to be recognized by anyone who knew him.

. . . When I first run to get Miss Russell, I went in the corner house, the corner of Second and Borden Street. I said I was Bridget Sullivan, and I learned that Miss Russell wasn't there, and I went out and on the corner I met a man which Mrs. Churchill had sent looking for a doctor, and learned where Miss Russell lived. On Borden Street, in the little cottage house next the baker shop. I can't tell how far I went, or how long it was, before I found her. She was at the screen door as I came to the door. She appeared at the door, and I told her. And after some conversation with her, I went back home. To the house where I left. Mrs. Churchill was in, and Dr. Bowen. And Miss Lizzie. I think Miss Lizzie was in the kitchen with Mrs. Churchill, and Mrs. Churchill and I went into the dining room, and Dr. Bowen came out from the sitting room and said, "He is murdered, he is murdered."

Then I turned to Mrs. Churchill and said, "Addie, come in and see Mr. Borden."

She said, "Oh, no, doctor, I don't want to see him. I saw him this morning. I don't want to see him."

I asked Miss Lizzie some questions.

The first question I asked was if she had seen anyone.

The reply was, "I have not."

The second question was, "Where have you been?"

The second reply was, "In the barn, looking for some irons."

* * *

My name is Charles S. Sawyer. I'm a painter. Ornamental, fancy painter. The first I heard of the trouble, I heard there was a man stabbed by the name of Borden. I was in Mr. A. E. Rich's shop, number 81 Second Street, near the Borden premises, on the same side of the street that the Dr. Bowen house is.

After I heard of the stabbing, I went out and went down over the steps, and I saw Mr. Hall, the man that keeps the stable connected with the building that I was in. I asked him what he'd heard. Then I saw Miss Russell going up on the other side of the street, and I crossed over to see if she knew any particulars. Had a talk with her and walked along with her toward the Borden house. When I got to the gate, I said I guessed I wouldn't go in. I turned around and came away, started back.

I saw Officer Allen about that time. He was about . . . well, he was just north of Mrs. Churchill's, the house that Mrs. Churchill lives in. The first that I saw him I was right there at Mrs. Churchill's gate, I should say . . .

"Miss Russell, what were you doing when Bridget Sullivan came to you?"

"I was at my work."

"In consequence of what Bridget told you, did you go somewhere?"

"Yes, sir. I went upstairs to change my dress."

"What did you do then?"

"I went over to Mr. Borden's."

"Speak up, please."

"I went over to the Borden house."

"When you got to the Borden house, do you recall who was there?"

"I only remember Lizzie."

"Where was she when you got there?"

"I'm not positive."

"Was she upstairs or downstairs?"

"Downstairs."

"Did you have any talk with her, or did she say anything to you?"

"Yes, sir."

"Well, go on and tell us what it was."

"I cannot tell it in order, for it's very disconnected. I remember very little of it. I think she was standing in the door—leaning against the doorframe—as I went in, and I asked her to sit down in the rocking chair, which she did. There was somebody came around, I don't know who they were. There were people there, came in; either they were there or came right in or something. I don't know what followed . . ."

"Now Dr. Bowen, after she replied that she had been in the barn looking for some irons . . ."

"Or iron."

". . . was there any other conversation in that connection?"

"She then said that she was afraid her father had had trouble with the tenants, that she had overheard loud conversation several times recently. That was the extent of the conversation in the dining room."

"Then what was done?"

"Then I asked for a sheet to cover up Mr. Borden."

"To whom did you address that request?"

"I addressed that to Mrs. Churchill and to Miss Lizzie Borden at the same time. They were both in the same room. And to Miss Russell, who was there by then."

"What was done in consequence of your request? Describe everything that was done."

"Bridget Sullivan said, 'I guess the sheets are up in Mrs. Borden's room, Mrs. Borden's desk where she keeps the bed-clothes . . .'"

. . . and I asked Dr. Bowen if he would get the keys off the shelf in the sitting room. And he did so, and Mrs. Churchill said she would do anything to help me. She went in and unlocked the door and got two sheets, I guess . . .

. . . when the sheets were brought back, I covered the body, and Miss Lizzie Borden asked me if I would telegraph to her sister Emma. Directly after I took the address, I asked, "Where is *Mrs.* Borden?" The answer was that Mrs. Borden had received a note that morning to visit a sick friend. I wished to notify the officers, and as I was going out, Officer Allen—I didn't know him at the time, a short, thickset man—came in, and I satisfied

199

myself that the officers knew of the affair. I met him in the kitchen. As I was going out, he was in . . .

I went in the sitting room where Mr. Borden was. He was lying on the sofa side of the door that opens from the dining room to the kitchen. I went to the front door, the front halls, and looked at the door. The door was locked with a night lock and also with a bolt. I looked behind the door to see if anyone was standing there, and then I came out and I told the doctor I'd go down and get some officers to investigate the case. When I went out, I saw a closet there, and I thought I'd look into the closet. Then I looked in a clothes press there, nigh the stove, in the kitchen. I made no other investigation before I left the house. I told Mr. Sawyer to stay there until I came back . . .

After Mr. Allen left me there, the other persons, I don't know whether they were ministering to her some way, they seemed to be fanning her. Rubbing her hands or face, seemed to be. I couldn't tell exactly what they were doing, but they appeared to be . . . I don't know but that they were rubbing her hands. At one time I was within three feet of her, I should judge. Stood there quite a while. In fact, she wasn't more than three or four feet from the door that led from the entry.
She was sitting in a rocking chair . . . well, not quite in the *middle* of the room but quite near the door to the back entry. She was sitting there and appeared to be somewhat distressed, I thought from her appearance. I didn't see any signs of blood upon her hands, her hair, or her dress. I couldn't tell you the color of the dress, or whether it was light or dark. I think the people there were Mrs. Churchill, Bridget and Miss Russell . . .

I started to unloosen her dress, thinking that she was faint, and she said, "I'm not faint, Alice." Her dress was loose here, where I started to unloosen it. It was loose here, so it pulled out. I think I fanned her. I don't remember whether I bathed her face. I don't think I bathed her face in there. I did not see any blood on her clothing. Not a speck of it. Nor upon her hands. Or her face. I don't think her hair was disturbed. I think I should have noticed it if it was disordered. I can't give any description of the dress she had on that morning. None whatever . . .

* * *

200

My name is Phoebe B. M. Bowen. I live right across the street from Mr. Borden's, lived there nearly all my life. I'm Dr. Bowen's wife. When I got to the house on the morning of the murder, Mr. Sawyer was at the door, and Mrs. Churchill, Miss Russell and Miss Lizzie were in the kitchen. Miss Lizzie was sitting in a chair, and Miss Russell was sitting in a chair beside Miss Lizzie. Mrs. Churchill was standing in front of her, fanning her. She was reclining in a chair, with her head resting against Miss Russell.

I thought she had fainted, she was so white, until I saw her lip or chin quiver, and then I knew she hadn't fainted. I stood directly in front of her. Miss Russell asked me to wet a towel to bathe her face and hands, and Lizzie shook her head no. Her hands were very white as they laid against her dark dress, in her lap. The dress had a blouse waist, with a white design on it. A dark dress. Her hair was arranged as it usually was. I did not see any blood on her hands, or face, or any part of her . . .

. . . after I brought the sheets to Dr. Bowen, after him and the officer left, I said, "Miss Lizzie, if I knew where Mrs. Whitehead's was, I'd go and see if Mrs. Borden is there." Mrs. Whitehead is Mrs. Borden's sister that lives in Fall River.

And she said, "Maggie, I'm almost positive I heard her coming in. I'm sure she's upstairs."

And I said, "I'm not going up again."

Mrs. Churchill said she would go with me.

I went from the dining room into the sitting room and upstairs.

The door to the spare room was open as I came up the stairway.

As I went upstairs, I saw the body under the bed.

Right between the bed and the wall . . . the bed was high enough to see. I went right into the room and stood at the foot of the bed. I don't recall anything about the curtains or shutters in that room at that time, I couldn't tell how they were. I couldn't tell anything about how light it was in that room at that time. I didn't stay long enough to notice anything, didn't stop to make any examination of Mrs. Borden to see what was the matter with her.

Mrs. Churchill was behind me.

* * *

Bridget was leading the way, and as we went upstairs, I turned my head to the left. And as I got up so that my eyes were on the level with the front hall, I could see across the front hall and across the floor of the spare room. At the far side of the north side of the room, I saw something that looked like the form of a person. I turned and went back down, into the dining room, and made some noise. Miss Russell said, "Is there another?"

I said, "Yes, she's up there."

My name is John J. Manning, I'm a reporter. I was a reporter last August when I heard of the Borden murder. Mr. O'Neal, city editor of the *Globe*, told me to go up to Second Street, a stabbing affray had taken place there. I received the information between twenty-five minutes and half-past eleven. I ran the greater portion of the way. On the way to the house, near the entrance to Hall's Stable, I saw Mr. Cunningham, Mr. Bowles and one or two other persons whom I don't recall at this time. I crossed the road—they didn't care to say much about what had happened—I crossed the road and went into the yard. I tried to open the door, and Mr. Sawyer was inside. It was a screen door. I was not allowed to go in. I sat back on the steps, waited for some person to come, with whom I could go in. I had been there some two or three minutes, and Dr. Bowen came in. I bade him good morning. He passed in, and I wasn't allowed to go in with him.

On my return from the telegraph office, I met Mrs. Churchill at about the same place in the entry or hallway—the kitchen hallway—at the same point. She said, "They've found Mrs. Borden."

"Where?" I said.

"Upstairs in the front room," she said. "You'd better go up and see."

I went directly through the dining room and the corner of the sitting room into the front hall, up the stairs, front stairs, and stopped a moment at the door of the front chamber . . . guest chamber . . . front bedroom. At that point, I looked over the bed and saw the prostrate form of Mrs. Borden. I was standing directly in the door of the room. My first thought, when I was standing in the doorway and saw the form . . . my first thought

was that she had fainted. I went around the back of the bed—
that is, the foot of the bed—and between the form and the bed,
and placed my hand on her head. It was a little dark in the
room, somewhat dark, not very light. The shutters on the north
side were partly closed. The shutters toward Mrs. Churchill's
house. The inside shutters, the board shutters. I placed my hand
on her head and found there were wounds in the head. Then I
placed my . . . felt of her pulse . . . that is, felt of the wrist, and
found she was dead.

9: PARIS—1890

The peculiar thing about Lizzie's illness was that it came without warning. In the hectic days that followed their visit to the Moulin Rouge, there wasn't the slightest hint that her energy was waning; indeed, when finally she was stricken, it seemed that Anna's predictions of ill health befalling one or all of them had been heeded by a vengeful God—and a capricious one at that, else He would most certainly have chosen Anna *herself* as the victim.

As had been the case with Geoffrey in London, Alison had immediately put herself at their disposal, taking them to tourist attractions she had surely tired of long ago, a favor for which Lizzie was enormously grateful, having discovered early on that Rebecca's much vaunted French was as much a figment of her imagination as were Anna's dire predictions of ill health. At the Louvre, where a French guide promised "I show you much in *Anglais* beautiful," Alison answered him in fluent French (not a word of which Lizzie understood) that caused the man virtually to cower away from them, and then went on to lead them familiarly to all the treasures she felt they "absolutely must see." Their heads were spinning when at last they came out into bright sunshine at the noon hour.

"You must on no account loiter under the arcade across the street in late afternoon," she said, "for you shall certainly be mistaken for ladies of quite another sort," but then proceeded anyway to lead them across the rue de Rivoli and to show them, in the various shop windows, the photographs of actresses "and other conspicuous people" (as she called them), many of them depicted in *toilettes* that recalled that of the Young Lady of Crete.

"But we must not stand about gazing and admiring," she warned, "as it is incomprehensible to the French mind that *nice* girls should do so." Whereupon she promptly hailed a pair of victorias, as the larger of the Parisian cabs were called, and gave the driver of the lead vehicle (carrying only herself and Lizzie) the address of a restaurant suitable for *ladies*—again the stress on the word—to frequent alone.

"Were that wretch Albert not occupied with business the livelong day," she said in the cab, "we might lunch in style. As it is, we shall have to settle for one of the Bouillons Duval, where the company may not be terribly exciting, but at least it will be *respectable*. A woman must be even more careful here than in London," she said, "making certain she dresses quietly and behaves with reserve and discretion. A *married* woman, of course, may go anywhere her husband chooses to take her, and read any book he doesn't specifically forbid. But single women do not, as a rule, read French novels—it would be unthinkable for them to even *glance* at a single page of Maupassant's *Bel Ami* or Daudet's *Sappho*—far too wicked, my dear. Nor would an unmarried woman dare to go to the theater alone, unless the offered piece is entirely unobjectionable.

"Had you any desire to see Ibsen's *Ghosts*, I should suppress it, were I you. *Verboten*, dear Lizzie, to lapse into my sainted mother's language. But I'm sure something 'harmless' will be showing at the Théâtre Français or the Odéon—I've already asked Albert to see to getting us tickets, in fact. We *ladies* shall have to sit in the orchestra stalls, of course, though we shan't be allowed in the first three rows. And *sans chapeaux, naturellement*. Women are not permitted to wear hats in many of the theaters here, a rule prompted by necessity—oh, the towering absurdities some of them are wearing these days!

"On the whole, Lizzie, because so many American girls have begun studying and living here now, a young lady roving about alone won't attract as much attention as she might have formerly. But I should nonetheless avoid walking on the boulevards in late afternoon, and never—I repeat *never*—look at any man, however well dressed and gentlemanly he might appear. But, oh how silly! I shall be with you every moment, and shall see to it that no harm befalls you."

She was as true to her promise as Geoffrey had been in London, taking them to all the places they had planned to see, anyway—the Cathedral of Notre Dame, of course, and the Eiffel Tower, built only the year before for the great Paris Exposition; Sacré-Coeur and the Place des Vosges; the Luxembourg Gardens and the Conciergerie; Sainte-Chapelle . . . and St. Séverin . . . and St. Pierre . . . and St. Julien-le-Pauvre . . . and . . . *all* of it, everything she knew would delight their tourist eyes.

But she took them as well (as Geoffrey had in London) to places they might otherwise have missed. In the rue de Prony, she escorted them to the studio of a talented French painter who had died only six years earlier and whose journal had only recently been published in English and French. Here, the concierge led them up a dim, narrow staircase and into the gloomy studio itself, where she cranked a handle that caused a metal panel to slide back off the roof. Sunlight streamed in to fall upon the dead girl's portrait—palette on thumb, an alert Parisian face ("She was twenty-four when she died," Alison said), a somewhat disdainful, determined and inquisitive look about the painting's eyes.

All around the room, there were charcoal studies and other paintings; the concierge indicated a large canvas standing apart from the others, and spoke to Alison in French. "It's the one Miss Bashkirtseff was working on when she died," Alison whispered in English. The painting showed a scene on the boulevards, men and women sitting on a bench, one or two of the heads and figures almost finished.

The concierge was speaking again.

"Her work killed her," Alison translated. "She caught cold from sketching too much in the open air."

Marie Bashkirtseff's things were everywhere about the room: a pair of guitars with flaccid strings; a square, turntable bookcase with only a book of poetry upon it; a chiffonier with a glass

206

front behind which were piled her shoes and slippers and a pair of boots with her initials worked into the front.

The concierge whispered something in French.

"Those are the boots she wore whilst shooting in Russia," Alison said, and then, with sudden poignancy, "Oh, how sad!"

On one of their nighttime excursions, and of course in Albert's company, she took them to a place called Le Rat Noir (which even Rebecca was able to translate as The Black Rat), a room with a large quantity of heavy black oak and a high Jacobean fireplace, a massive, highly ornamented bar, and long low beams—"Reminds me of the old Cock," Albert said, "as it used to look by Temple Bar"—at the farthest end of which was an inner chamber from which they could hear laughter and loud voices and the sound of piano, cello and fiddle.

The man behind the bar told them that the theater in the room above opened at precisely nine-thirty, and then sold them tickets at five francs each. They went up a narrow flight of stairs (a painted board halfway up read *Passant, sois moderne*) and into the theater itself, where there were a good many women present—but all of them French, Lizzie decided, since the place seemed hardly the sort any lady might come to, even accompanied by a gentleman. "*Mesdames et messieurs,*" the proprietor said to the gathered audience, "*bienvenue aux Ombres Chinoises,*" which Rebecca instantly translated as "Welcome to the Chinese Shadows," mysterious enough until Alison explained they were about to see a series of shadow plays, quite popular in France at the moment.

The effect, she said (while the proprietor rattled on in French), was achieved by puppeteers manipulating cutouts between a bright light and the screen before which they now sat. Even as she spoke (the proprietor had stopped his prologue now, and bowed toward the screen), the lights lowered, and the first of the little plays began. The proprietor marched up and down the middle aisle, hoarsely describing in French the story of the silhouetted action they were viewing. Alison was hard put to keep up with a translation; laughing at one point, she said that the proprietor was really quite witty. The shadows on the screen caused Rebecca to blush and Anna to cough uncontrollably. Felicity watched in rapt but uncharacteristically silent fascination; Lizzie noticed that Albert's arm was around the back of her chair.

Between each of the shadow plays, a poet or a singer came out to perform one of his original compositions. "They all look like broken-down French masters in a fourth-rate English school," Albert commented, but Alison explained that they were for the most part students in ardent revolt against the reputations of the day, and that their compositions were *moderne* in every sense. The proprietor, realizing that they were speaking English, deferred to his foreign guests and announced, in a heavily accented voice, "I should like now to introduce my comrade, the good poet Henri Chaulet, who will recite one of his small poems. Do not laugh, please, at his Languedoc accent; it is his only defect."

He repeated the same introduction in French, and a young man in a tight and seedy frock coat came up to stand by the piano. Fixing his soulful eyes on the ceiling, he began a long and seemingly endless poem which Alison could not possibly translate simultaneously without distracting others in the audience. When at last he concluded, she said merely, "It was all about joy and life and seizing the flying hours," and Albert snorted and said, "Nothing very modern in all that, is there, Felicity?" and patted her knee.

The last of the shadow plays was, in Lizzie's estimation, the best—and least objectionable—of the lot. It was called *La Marche à L'Etoile* (which Rebecca translated as *The Walk of the Star*) and it depicted, surprisingly enough, the progress of the star of Bethlehem across the sky to its position above the holy manger. A ringing tenor voice accompanied the graceful silhouettes. She sat transfixed.

On the way out of the theater, Alison said drily, "The French have a strange mania at present for sacred subjects. The exhibition of the Champ de Mars is full of them—do you think you might enjoy seeing it tomorrow?"

But more than anything else, Lizzie enjoyed the single afternoon she and Alison spent alone together. The women were eager to have clothes made in Paris, and sought Alison's advice as to which of the dressmakers they should visit. She promptly popped them into two victorias and had them driven to an area she described as "a neutral ground which French politeness abandons to its guests," somewhere near the center of the city, where she led them through a courtyard lined with Doric columns, and up a private staircase into an ebony-walled anteroom, and from there into a larger room walled with mirrors and paneled with Gobelin tapestries.

A receptionist showed the ladies to one of the mirror-lined galleries at the farther end, where they sat on brocaded seats in palm-enshrouded nooks. The air was redolent of a subtle perfume. The lighting was soft and unobtrusive. Beneath a cloud-filled sky-ceiling painted by Mademoiselle Abbema (or so they were informed in charmingly accented English), the models of the house glided past in exquisite gowns, languidly, imperturbably—and somewhat somnolently, it seemed to Lizzie. She had every intention of buying couturier clothes in Paris, and had indeed left space in her bags for new acquisitions. But she found as the showings progressed that she was feeling—not *quite* ill, but somehow uneasy with her own body. And before long she was surprised to find herself becoming a trifle headachey. In fact, all at once, she seemed to ache all over, and her throat felt suddenly sore. Alison, forever alert to her comfort, detected this at once, and suggested that she might like to step outside for a bit of fresh air, an invitation Lizzie pounced upon as though her very life depended upon it.

Making certain the ladies were in good hands, giving Rebecca the cards of several other couturiers should they not find anything to their liking here, Alison rehearsed again the fares they should expect to pay for hiring a victoria, asked repeatedly if they were sure they could find their way back to the hotel without assistance ("You take a cab with either a red or a green glass in its lantern—not the blue or the yellow, as *their* stables will be in other quarters of the city") and, finally convinced that her charges could manage without her, led Lizzie out into the street again.

Arm in arm, they walked.

It was Friday, and a so-called bargain day at the Bon Marché in the rue du Bac. Hordes of determined women marched in and out of the doors, discouraging Lizzie and Alison from even *entertaining* the thought of shopping. As they passed the glittery shop windows with their array of merchandise, Alison said, "There's a perhaps apocryphal story I've heard," and placed her

209

hand on Lizzie's arm and leaned closer to her. "About the young American girl who, when asked what she had most admired in the Louvre, replied that on the whole she had preferred the *gloves* there to those at the Bon Marché." She laughed, and then said, "There *is* a store called the Magasin du Louvre, you know, so perhaps her error was genuine—*if* the story has any merit at all."

In a charcuterie on a small and twisting side street away from the roar of the boulevards, they bought a cold roast chicken, and from another shop nearby a bottle of *vin ordinaire*. They wandered down to the Seine then, and sat on the embankment where men and women alike fished beneath signs that read *Ustensile de pêche*, and in the distance on the river they could see the floating baths side by side, with laundries for the poor. There, under an intensely blue and cloudless sky, they removed their gloves and tore apart the chicken with almost savage intensity. They ate in ravenous silence for several moments. Alison lifted the wine bottle to her lips, drank and then offered the bottle to Lizzie.

"I don't drink alcohol," Lizzie said.

"Don't be ridiculous," Alison said. "Wine?"

"It would be against my principles?"

"Principles? A mild white wine?"

"I belong to the WCTU."

"Ah, yes, *that* sober lot. I'm afraid we English, when thirsty, drink wine, beer or something stronger. Have you not been drinking all along? How unobservant of me. But you shall choke on your chicken, Lizzie. Do have at least a swallow."

"I couldn't."

"You're on *holiday*, for heaven's sake!"

"I should feel guilty."

"There's scarcely enough alcohol in this entire *bottle* to . . ."

"Please, Alison."

"A sip?"

Lizzie shook her head.

"I shan't tell a soul," Alison said, narrowing her eyes conspiratorially.

"It isn't that."

"Then what is it?"

"It would be wrong to value a precept, and then practice the exact opposite of that . . ."

"Practice, yes! *Precisely* what you need! Now take this bottle at once, or I shall become cross with you. The very idea! Wine? There's wine in the Bible, is there not? No one is advocating that you lurch down the street in drunken disarray, but Lizzie, my dear, a teeny, tiny sip of wine will neither disorganize your senses nor compromise your beliefs. For God's sake, *take* it, or I shall pour it all over your head!"

Lizzie took the bottle.

"Now, drink. Not too much mind you, for we wouldn't want you falling down in the gutter."

Lizzie took a sip, grimaced and handed the bottle back to Alison, who put it to her mouth and drank a great draught.

"Ladies *quite*," Alison said, and to her surprise, Lizzie found herself laughing.

Afterwards, they bought a cheapback book from one of the stalls along the river (*"Demandez le plan de Paris!"* a street hawker shouted. *"Les vues de Versailles! C'est pour rien, mesdames, vingt sous!"*) and tore out the pages and used them as makeshift napkins to rid their hands of the chicken's lingering grease ("Though I would much prefer to *lick* it off," Alison said, and rolled her eyes) only to discover that their hands were now stained with ink and looked as black as any chimney sweep's. They were obliged, at last, to stop into one of the Bouillons Duval where—to the proprietor's obvious annoyance when they told him they wished only to use the lavatory—they washed their hands, and Alison, for the first time since they'd been together, actually allowed Lizzie to pay for something: the services of the old woman in attendance, who offered them towels and accepted four sous in return, with a wide toothless grin and a cheery *"Merci beaucoup, mesdames."*

"De rien, madame," Alison replied and when they were again on the street outside, told Lizzie that whereas in England, proper ladies and gentlemen only said "sir" or "madam" to persons of the blood royal, once across the Channel one could scarcely be too generous with this trifling compliment, and its frequent omission by the English had given rise to a long-standing French grudge. Remembering the hall porter's look when she had addressed him as "sir," Lizzie flushed, and Ali-

son—detecting this at once—asked her what she'd said *now* to shock her. When Lizzie told the story, she hugged her close and said, "Oh, my dear Lizzie, be sure *never* to do that again!"

In the Café Procope on the Left Bank, they sat at an outdoor table, and Alison ordered thimblesful of Madeira, which Lizzie found sweeter and more to her liking than had been the wine she'd tasted at lunch. Still, she drank it sparingly, and not without feelings of guilt. The proprietor came to their table, introduced himself, commented on the lovely weather and then told them that this would be his last summer here, his large soulful eyes moisting with tears when he explained that this historic place would soon close its doors forever. He pointed out to them the table at which Voltaire used to sit to write his letters to the king of Prussia. He showed them through the smoke-stained rooms, where hung portraits of Rousseau, d'Alembert, Crébillon and Mirabeau. He led them back to their outside table again, and asked them to linger as long as they chose, for soon there would be no lingering here at all.

They drank more Madeira; they sat in silence and watched Paris go by. A bareheaded boy with the face of an angel offered matches for sale—"*Des alumettes, mesdames, pas chèr*—" and then drifted off to the next café. A man stopped at the table, pulled a pair of opera glasses from under his coat, said, "*Une vraie occasion, mesdames, vous ne trouverez pas de deux,*" and though Alison assured him in French that she had no need of opera glasses, *merci*, he insisted persuasively, and did not move on until she rudely turned her back to him. No sooner was he gone than a young woman approached, piping in a high childlike voice, "*De jolies fleurs, de belles violettes, de jolies fleurs, de belles violettes.*" Alison bought a nosegay and handed it to Lizzie. They sipped more wine in the golden lazy sunshine.

There was a man offering little terriers and green parakeets for sale. A confectioner's boy came by, wearing a white apron and carrying glacéed apples on a stick. A young woman, carrying a baby in one arm, offered long-stalked roses for sale. There was a man selling canes, and another selling plaster figurines. An artist with long gray hair covered by a tam-o'-shanter, wearing gymnasium shoes and carrying a large oil painting under each arm, stopped at their table and explained in flawless English that owing to a momentary want of money, he wished

212

to dispose of his work to a connoisseur in whose home it might be properly displayed.

And suddenly, inexplicably, it was four o'clock, the hour of the newspaper, and the boulevards burst into a fever of activity. All up and down the avenues, parcels of newspapers smelling of fresh ink were piled up before the iron kiosks, the carriers running along the sidewalks, the vendors folding the sheets and displaying one of them on a long pole, forbidden to cry out the news as was done in London, Alison explained, for fear they might excite the populace or become the mouthpieces of revolutionaries. Lizzie could well understand the law; the purchasers forced their way to the kiosks, using elbows—and fists, in some instances—seeming in a rage to get at the latest news.

They walked slowly back to her hotel.

They kissed each other's cheeks before they parted, and Alison reminded her that she and Albert would be by at seven sharp.

"Well, make it seven-oh-one," she said, and grinned and said, "Ta, Lizzie!" and walked swiftly and gracefully toward a waiting coupé.

The moment Lizzie entered the room upstairs, her headache returned. And all at once, without warning, she felt desperately ill. She took off her dress and hung it on one of the satin-covered hangers in the chifforobe. She was unlacing her corset when she became suddenly dizzy and blamed it at once on the wine. She took off her shoes and lay down on the bed. Felicity came into the room not a moment later and found her lying there that way—in her petticoat and chemise, her underdrawers and black cotton stockings, her corset only partially unlaced, her eyes glazed. When Felicity touched her forehead, it felt blazing hot to her hand.

She immediately telephoned Alison at the Binda and left a message with the concierge, asking him to have her phone back the moment she arrived. Alison returned the call not five minutes later; by that time, Felicity had removed Lizzie's corset and stockings and had bathed her feverish brow with a cold, damp cloth.

"What's the matter?" Alison asked at once.

"Lizzie's burning with fever," Felicity said. "I think we shall

213

need a doctor. Should I call downstairs and ask them to fetch one?"

"You will do nothing of the sort," Alison said. "Monsieur Foubrier is a dear man, and he operates his hotel beautifully, but I should sooner trust my health to a wild boar as to a French physician. You must immediately ring St. George's Nursing Association in the rue de la Boche. They have English-speaking nurses there, and they will put you in touch with an English-speaking doctor. The last thing you want is some Frenchman putting his ear to Lizzie's chest and muttering imponderables in a language they cherish as though sacred. I shall be there immediately; I should walk if the hour weren't so late, but I'll engage the nearest coupé, and hope the driver doesn't become hopelessly snarled in traffic. Make your telephone call at once, Felicity."

Alison was there some ten minutes later; the doctor had not yet arrived. She touched Lizzie's forehead, said, "Oh, dear," and then immediately unbuttoned her chemise. "Open some windows," she said, "the child is burning alive. We shall need cold cloths; I'll ring down for some ice."

The doctor, when he arrived, looked as if he had just been shaken out of a deep sleep, though it wasn't quite yet five o'clock. (Alison later suggested that perhaps they had interrupted his *quatre à cinq*.) He seemed to be just this side of fifty, a tall and rumpled Englishman who introduced himself as Dr. Charles Fawcett and then immediately set to work, further unbuttoning Lizzie's chemise, spreading the lace-trimmed muslin open over her naked breasts, and then putting his stethoscope to her chest, causing her to let out a startled little gasp when the metal touched her flesh. He listened for what seemed an inordinately long time, and then said only, "Mm."

Wiping a clinical thermometer with a swab of cotton he wet from a small vial of alcohol, he put it into Lizzie's mouth and then asked, while her lips were closed about it and it was impossible for her to speak, "Have you been experiencing muscular pains, madam?"

Lizzie nodded.

"Headaches?"

She nodded again.

"Aches in the joints? Sore throat?"

214

Again she nodded. He took the thermometer from her mouth, studied it, said, "Mm" again, wiped the thermometer with the same cotton swab, put it back into its case, put stethoscope, thermometer and vial of alcohol back into his bag, and then said to Alison, whom he had undoubtedly singled out as being in charge here, "I frankly thought we'd seen the end of this—if indeed it's what I *think* it is."

"The end of what?" Alison asked.

"Influenza," Fawcett said. "We had our first case of it last December, and it was rather prevalent during January and February. Did it not reach England as well, madam?"

"Indeed," Alison said.

"Yes," he said, nodding. "But, as I say, I thought it had long ago left Paris. Always seems to start in Russia, doesn't it? Their beastly climate. Moves westward through all of Europe, always has, always will, I suppose. Probably depends more on easterly and northeasterly winds than it does on human intercourse. At any rate, it does seem your friend has come down with it."

"With influenza?" Lizzie said, suddenly feeling sicker than she had before.

"Yes, indeed," Fawcett said, "but I shouldn't worry too much about it were I you. The course of the disease is a short one— four to six days, sometimes as many as ten days—and unless there are complications . . ."

"Complications?" Lizzie said.

"Well, don't fret about those now," he said, and smiled.

"*What* complications?" Alison asked.

"Bronchitis," Fawcett said. "Pneumonia. But normally . . ."

"Pneu . . ." Lizzie started to say, but Fawcett's voice continued on over hers.

". . . *normally* , you needn't worry about a grosser infection. I shall prescribe a proper laxative to cleanse the bowels, and the local chemist will let you have mustard for hot footbaths. You should drink plenty of liquids and fruit juices and unless the fever reaches alarming heights . . ."

"Alarming?" Alison said.

"It's not uncommon for the temperature to fluctuate somewhere between the hundred-and-one, hundred-and-three range. It may fall one day, only to rise again the next. But, as I say, that's all quite normal, and to be expected. Should the

215

temperature rise *higher* than that, I should recommend sponging her down with alcohol. And if she *still* seems exceedingly hot to the touch, you should not hesitate to fill a tub with cold water and lower her into it. I suggest you see a chemist at once to buy a clinical thermometer and, of course, the mustard and alcohol. Do not hesitate to ring me should an exceedingly high fever persist. Were you planning on leaving Paris soon?" he asked Lizzie.

"Next Tuesday," she said.

"I ask only because the disease sometimes has a lingering debilitating effect, and I would not advise serious traveling for at *least* a week after the symptoms have disappeared. As for those," he said, "I fear you will experience chills accompanying the high fever, and you will feel extremely weak, depressed and listless. There will also be all manner of bodily aches that will cause you to wish you were dead—but you won't die, I shall see to that. There will be some dry coughing and rapid breathing, and your nose will be quite stuffed up, and your eyes will turn as red as your hair, and there may be a thin, watery discharge from them as well. All quite normal, however—if one can consider the routine course of *any* disease 'normal.'"

"Ohhhhh," Lizzie moaned, and closed her eyes.

"Tut-tut," Fawcett said, "you will be healthy again in no time at all. I shall write you my bill," he said to Alison, "and . . ."

"*I'll* take the bill," Lizzie said, and attempted to sit up.

"You will stay exactly where you are," Alison said.

"I don't believe you'll need a prescription either for the mustard or the alcohol, but I shall write one out anyway," Fawcett said. "Some of the chemists here in Paris are extremely sticky about dispensing medicines—*especially* to foreigners, whom they suspect of being raging opium eaters or worse. I shall write out one for aspirin as well, which will help bring the fever down. When the fever *does* start to break, incidentally, you'll want to begin drinking hot lemonade to encourage further perspiration. Now then," he said, to Alison, handing her a sheet of paper, "my normal fee for a hotel visit is twenty francs, which I should prefer having in cash since these odious French make cashing checks a virtual impossibility for foreigners. If you find yourself short, however . . ."

"I have the francs," Alison said.

216

"Ah, excellent," Fawcett said as she went for her purse. "Now then, here are the prescriptions. There's a chemist not far from here—just down the street, in fact—and I'm sure the concierge will be happy to send someone round there for you. Ah, thank you," he said, as Alison handed him the gold louis. "They still call this a Napoleon, you know, the French," he said idly, looking at the coin, "even though the head of the Republic—such as it is—has adorned it for the past thirty years. Ah well, the French," he said. "It's a pity such a beautiful country is wasted on them, is it not?"

He pocketed the coin, snapped his bag shut, said, "You have my telephone number, do not hesitate to use it." He turned to the bed then and said, "Cheer up, you'll soon be up and around again. Did I mention absolute bed rest? Oh, yes, *that* is a *must*, I fear. Except for when you must relieve yourself, I don't want you stirring from this bed. *Au revoir*, madam," he said in French that sounded like Albert's, and then turned, bowed stiffly to Alison and Felicity, said, *"Au revoir"* again and let himself out of the room.

The moment he was gone, Lizzie said, "I shall die, I know it. Just like that Marie what's-her-name."

"Nonsense, you will *not*!" Alison said sharply.

Monsieur Foubrier, for all his joviality and perfect English, was none too thrilled to learn that there was a sick American on the third floor of his fine hotel. His distress reached monumental proportions when he discovered that her illness had been diagnosed as the dread *grippe*. He paid an impromptu visit to the room (necessitating a hasty covering of Lizzie's naked body before he bounded in after a single knock) and demanded at once that all the windows be closed lest the disease be transported through them and thence carried across the courtyard to the rooms on the other side. And whereas he was prompt to assure Lizzie that she might have as many changes of sheets as were required by her excessive perspiration (he did not have the English word for this; he used the more delicate French word—*transpiration*), he felt it necessary to inform her, nonetheless, that he could not provide the additional linen without adding a small surcharge to the bill; and should his chambermaids be required to make and remake the bed at frequent

217

intervals, he would have to charge additionally for that as well. Lizzie's friends were concerned only that she be as comfortable as possible while the disease ran its course; they would have paid Foubrier *twice* what he asked for, which knowledge—had only he possessed it—would have caused him many a sleepless night.

Her illness caused an immediate problem in that the women had planned to leave on the next leg of their journey on the coming Tuesday, and whereas Lizzie hoped she would be well by then (the doctor had said four to six days, hadn't he?), she was mindful of the fact that he had recommended a convalescent period of at *least* a week before she might consider traveling again. On Saturday, her temperature surprisingly dropped to a shade above ninety-nine, which Fawcett assured her on the telephone was virtually normal. But the very next day, it shot up to a hundred and three again, and it became apparent to her that she would not be able to accompany the other women when they left on the twelfth—if indeed they decided to leave.

Anna, as was to be expected, never once ventured into the room, so fearful of contracting the disease was she. To Felicity's credit, it was she who spent all night Friday, Saturday and Sunday lying half-awake beside Lizzie on sheets that became damp again almost the moment they were changed, escorting her to the toilet and back again, taking her temperature whenever she felt inordinately hot to the touch. But although she and Rebecca protested that they wouldn't *dream* of leaving Lizzie behind while they voyaged further, Lizzie detected that they were *all* eager to get on their way, and that her illness was an inconvenience that posed a serious threat to their plans. Surely they were not supposed to linger here, were they, during the convalescent period as well? Assuming, of course, that the disease ran the minimum number of predicted days and not the maximum. ("And assuming," Anna said pessimistically—as later reported by Rebecca—"that there are *no* complications.")

By Monday, the eleventh, it became apparent that a decision simply had to be made. Lizzie's fever showed no signs of breaking; it hovered at the hundred-and-three mark, and she required constant alcohol baths to keep her from burning to an absolute crisp. It was Alison who, during the daytime, ministered to her every need, relieving Felicity of her nursing chores and making certain that she caught up on the sleep she'd lost at night, though Felicity would much have preferred to accompany the other two women on their sightseeing jaunts around the city.

Albert had concluded whatever business had delayed the couple here, and when he came to see Lizzie that Monday, he seemed eager to get down to their villa on the Riviera. He came bearing roses and chocolates for the patient—who could not smell the roses and who would have vomited up the chocolates—and he sat beside the bed and patted her hand, which rested on the sheet dampened by her naked body beneath it.

"Now, dear lady," he said, "you must get well soon, do you hear? We simply won't have you lying about this way."

Lizzie, her eyes and her nose running, her brow beaded with sweat, nodded weakly.

"It has been *such* a pleasure knowing you," he said, and his words had an ominous ring of finality to them.

But Alison showed no indication of wanting to leave Paris before Lizzie was entirely well again. It was she who suggested to the others, quite firmly and in Lizzie's presence, that they leave as scheduled on the morrow. She would personally see to it that Lizzie was well taken care of until she was able to catch them up later. If necessary, she would ask Geoffrey to come over from London when Lizzie was well enough to travel again, and he would accompany her to wherever the ladies might then be, avoiding any risk of misinterpretation that might result from the sight of a woman traveling alone. The ladies protested (but not overly, Lizzie felt) and finally were persuaded to pack their bags in preparation for their departure in the morning.

On Tuesday, the twelfth, the ladies left for the Loire valley and Albert left for Cannes. Alison had her things moved from the Binda, surprising Monsieur Foubrier when she announced that she was moving into the room he felt contained the decaying body of a plague victim. Day and night it was Alison now who regularly took her temperature; Alison who changed the sheets when the chambermaids were too slow to respond to the summons of the bedside button; Alison who soaked rags with alcohol and bathed Lizzie's trembling body from head to toe; Alison who slept beside her each night, alert to every moan or sigh.

219

The fever lingered, though on the Friday after the others had left—a full week after she'd taken ill—it dropped again to below a hundred ("Ah, splendid!" Fawcett said on the telephone. "I'm sure we're seeing the last of it.") Then, on Saturday, it soared to a hundred and four, which Alison considered to be in the alarming range they'd been warned about.

When she first saw the reading on the thermometer, she thought it was surely a mistake. Something had gone wrong with the instrument; the mercury wasn't properly recording Lizzie's temperature. Or perhaps she wasn't properly translating centigrade to Fahrenheit. She shook down the thermometer, stuck it once again into Lizzie's mouth, timed a full five minutes by the ornate gilded clock hanging on the wall opposite the bed and then studied it again.

A hundred and four—in fact, a trifle over that!

She went immediately into the bathroom, soaked a cloth with alcohol, came back into the bedroom to lower the sheet covering Lizzie, and began bathing her hot and naked body, soaking the cloth again and again, moving it over Lizzie's brow and neck and shoulders and breasts and belly and thighs. Lizzie recoiled each time the cloth touched her flesh. Alison murmured soft, encouraging words, "Yes, dear, I know, dear, yes, yes," her hands moving, her eyes darting to the clock again and again. She took the wet top sheet off the bed, and replaced it with the last cool, dry one in the room. When she took Lizzie's temperature again a half hour later, it had risen to a hundred and five.

Truly frightened now, she went immediately to the telephone and asked the concierge to ring Dr. Fawcett for her. A woman speaking with a clipped English accent told her that doctor was out on a call and would telephone her as soon as he returned. She told the woman it was urgent and went to the bed again and put her hand on Lizzie's forehead. It was scalding to the touch, and now she had begun trembling violently. Alison looked up at the wall clock. Then she went into the bathroom and began running cold water into the tub.

She was struggling to lift Lizzie from the bed when a knock sounded at the door.

"*Entrez!*" she shouted, and the chambermaid she had summoned to change the sheets an hour earlier opened the inner door and peered into the room.

"Avez-vous sonné, madame?" she asked.

Alison had one arm under Lizzie's knees, and was attempting to get a firm hold across her back and under her arms.

"Yes!" she shouted in English, without turning toward the door. "Lend me a hand here!" And then immediately, in French, *"Aidez-moi! Madame est en danger! Vite!"*

The chambermaid, terrified by the stories she had heard of the gravely ill woman in room 305, hesitated in the doorframe.

Alison turned to look at her. Her green eyes flashed. "Come help me!" she said in English, and then immediately in French, *"Je vous ferai couper la tête, espèce de salope! Je vous ordonne de venir ici immédiatement!"*

The chambermaid rushed to the bed, her eyes wide. Together they lifted Lizzie and carried her into the bathroom. "Be careful with her now," Alison said in English, and then in French, *"Attention, doucement, doucement,"* and they lowered Lizzie into the tub. Her back arched when the cold water touched her naked buttocks. For a moment Alison thought she might go into convulsion and feared she was doing exactly the *wrong* thing—but wasn't it what the doctor had advised? Or wasn't a hundred and five alarming enough to warrant such emergency action? And then, as they lowered her still further into the tub, as the water covered her knees and her belly (the sleeves of their garments soaked to the elbows) and then her breasts (the nipples puckering from the shock) and her shoulders, submerging her to the neck, Alison's supporting hand behind her head now, she seemed suddenly to relax. A great sigh escaped her body on a shiver that rushed through it like a fleeting wind. Where an instant earlier she had been trembling, her body now became still—so still that it frightened Alison again. Her eyes fluttered open. She gazed up into Alison's face, and then closed her eyes again, and again sighed deeply.

The chambermaid said, *"Je crois que ça va mieux maintenant."*

They lifted her out of the tub. The chambermaid supported her limp body while Alison toweled her dry, and then they carried her to the sofa, and Alison sat on the edge of it, holding Lizzie's hand while the chambermaid put fresh, clean sheets on the bed. Together they carried her back to the bed again, and Alison said to the chambermaid, *"Merci, madame, vous m'avez*

221

rendu un grand service," and the chambermaid answered, *"Mon plaisir, madame,"* and left the room as quickly as she could.

Lying on the bed, Lizzie was vaguely aware of Alison standing beside it. She opened her eyes. Alison was staring down at her. She closed her eyes again a moment before Alison raised the top sheet over her naked body.

She could later remember very little about her immersion in that tub of icy cold water, except that, oddly and contradictorily, the first touch of it had felt scaldingly *hot* to her. She confided to Alison, too, that she had imagined she was being abducted by a pair of swarthy French bandits who were intent on drowning her, this until she looked up into Alison's face and saw her green eyes wide in alarm as great as her own had been. But, as little as she could recall, she knew for certain that somehow, as the waters closed about her naked body, she felt the fever magically breaking, and she had sighed in relief with the knowledge that the worst of her illness was behind her.

She became now an undemanding convalescent who gratefully accepted Alison's mother-hen fussing. Alison was with her constantly—fluffing up a pillow, smoothing a sheet, feeding her (though she wasn't yet quite up to eating anything much), helping her to change her nightdress, reading to her from the English-language books she found in the stalls along the Seine, taking her temperature at regular intervals to make certain the recovery was not an illusion—and Lizzie was beginning to realize that she had never had such a friend in her life and possibly might never have again.

In the evenings, after their meal had been served and Alison had changed into her own nightdress, they sat listening to the sounds of the Parisian night flooding through the open court-yard windows, and they talked together—talked as Lizzie had never before spoken to another woman, indeed to any other human being. She was surprised to learn that she was not alone in the mixed feelings she felt about her stepmother, with whom her relationship was cordial, but not what she would have termed "loving." Alison's *own* mother—the German woman who had so influenced her early years—had died when she was barely fifteen, admittedly much older than Lizzie had been when she'd lost her mother, but her father's subsequent remar-

222

riage had had the same profound effect upon her. Lizzie was quick to point out that she had never, before this moment, given much thought to her relationship with Abby, as her stepmother was called—

"Is that short for Abigail?" Alison asked.

"No, it's Abby," Lizzie said. "That's the whole of it."

"What odd names you Americans have," Alison said.

—and that she would hardly call her father's remarriage an event that had had a "profound effect" upon her, since she could, in all honesty, not remember her true mother at all. Of course, her sister Emma remembered her well, and often told stories of their childhood, but as for any personal knowledge—

"And yet, you call her your 'true' mother," Alison said.

"Well, she is," Lizzie said. "Or, rather, *was*."

"And what do you mean by *loving*?" Alison asked.

"Abby's not a particularly demonstrative or affectionate woman," Lizzie said, "Not that I would particularly *want* her to be."

"Are you?"

"Affectionate, yes . . . I suppose. I'm very fond of my sister, and I can't begin to tell you how much I appreciate all *you've* done for me."

"Ah, but appreciation isn't quite affection, is it?"

"One who denies a compliment only seeks the same compliment twice," Lizzie quoted, smiling.

"How quickly my dear Lizzie learns," Alison said, and burst into laughter. "But demonstrative? Do you consider yourself demonstrative?"

"Well, I don't go about hugging and kissing total *strangers*," Lizzie said, "but, yes, I should say I'm affectionate and demonstrative with people I know, good friends, yes. I should think it strange, wouldn't you, if we failed to embrace in greeting? Or when saying good-bye?"

"I should think so, yes," Alison said.

Lizzie found herself talking of Fall River then, the city as it was now and the city as her father recalled it when he was growing up there. She explained that the town stood at the head of what was called Mount Hope Bay, on both sides of the Quequechan River, which was the Indian word for—

223

"I keep forgetting you still have Indians in America," Alison said.

"Yes, but not in Fall River."

"But you said . . ."

"There *were* Indians there, yes, but very long ago. Quequechan is the Indian word for Fall River . . ."

. . . from which the town had taken its name, and from which it derived the power that drove its mills and factories. She described in glowing terms the rapid waters of the river, the fish that could still be seen leaping over the falls, the two big lakes—

"Well, we call them ponds," Lizzie said, "but actually they're lakes. North Watuppa and South Watuppa . . ."

"Indian names as well?"

"Yes, but I don't know what they mean. They're quite pretty, actually, the ponds. And, of course, the town is surrounded by beautiful hills and valleys, and at certain times of the year—the spring and fall—it can all be very lovely."

But she spoke far less generously of the cotton mills, and the rolling and slitting mills, and the nail factory and the ironworks and the oil manufactory, and the granite quarries, and all the various other commercial enterprises that had turned what had been a peaceful village in her father's youth to what was now a bustling port of entry concerned only with business. She rather imagined it had all changed after the Great Fire of '43, which had consumed the town and necessitated its reconstruction.

Her father (and she smiled now with the memory) had told her stories of what it had been like to be a boy back then, walking the dusty sidewalks of the village, listening for the sound of the fire-alarm bell—fire was always a hazard in a town constructed almost entirely of wood, as it was then—rushing out into the streets, barefooted more often than not, to race after the horse-drawn engines. Back then, all of the engines—even those still drawn by hand—had names as well as numbers, mysterious names that conjured all sorts of derring-do for Lizzie when her father repeated them, names like Hydraulion Number Two and Cataract Number Four and Torrent Number Two and—her favorite because she always visualized an Indian lashing the horses—Mazeppa Number Seven.

Whenever her father heard the cry "Fire!" he would rush through the streets echoing it, "Fire!" Fire!", hoping to be the first to reach the bell rope and ring the alarm bell, the hero who would save the town from destruction. He could vividly recall—and recreated for Lizzie as she did now for Alison—the two men who drove horse-drawn wagons in the performance of street-work for the city. Whenever the fire bell rang, those two would leap down from their high seats, unhook the whiffletrees, leave the wagons wherever they stood and drive their horses bareback—the horizontal wooden crossbars clattering behind them—to the nearest station, there to harness them to engines and race off to the conflagration. Her father—

"You love him very much, don't you?" Alison said softly.

"Yes, I do," Lizzie said.

"And Fall River? Do you miss it terribly now?"

"Not in the slightest," Lizzie said. "Why? Do I sound nostalgic?"

"Not in the slightest," Alison said, and smiled.

And when later each night, they crawled into bed and turned out the bedside lamps and lay together in their nightdresses side by side in the darkness, they still talked, though with lowered voices now lest the sound carry across the courtyard to awaken other guests. Lizzie wanted to know what it felt like to be a twin, and Alison told her she had once heard twinship described as "a gang in miniature," which wasn't too far from the truth.

"You have no idea how uncomfortable it is for anyone to be with Geoff and me when we're rattling on together. It's as though we were some sort of two-headed monster controlled by a common brain. Our speech overlaps, we will make the same gestures, the same grimaces; it's as if we speak with a single tongue and with no real awareness of each other except as an echo of sorts. I'm told we drive people to distraction. You're fortunate, truly, in not having had to put up with us *à la fois*. But he's such a darling, and I truly love him to death. And when it comes to hugging and kissing, oh my, you have *never* witnessed such affection or demonstration! Were we not brother and sister, I'm sure we should have been arrested and imprisoned ages ago! I *must* telegraph him soon, you know, to arrange for your escort through the wilderness."

225

As the days stretched into a week and Lizzie's strength gradually returned, she knew she could no longer postpone the journey that would reunite her with her friends. Moreover the virtually daily telephone calls from the south of France made it apparent that Albert was not enjoying the overseeing of a household full of servants and would most earnestly welcome Alison's presence in as near the future as she could manage. When he asked to speak to Lizzie on the telephone one day, he brusquely asked, "Well, then, Lizzie, how much longer do you suppose it'll be till you've fully regained your health?" When Lizzie reported this to Alison afterwards, she said, "Oh, the rude *bastard*!" thoroughly shocking Lizzie, who had never heard profanity from the lips of *any* woman, whatever her social class.

But still they procrastinated.

They consulted Lizzie's itinerary and figured it would be so much easier to catch the other women at *such* and such a place rather than at *such* and such, and then revised their estimate when they realized that this or that train would take seven or eight or nine hours as opposed to this or that which would take only six should she decide to meet them *here* rather than *there*. Alison kept promising Albert on the telephone that she would be there momentarily, and then asked to speak to Moira, and the gardener, and the coachman and the cook, giving them long-distance instructions on how to maintain the equilibrium of the household in her absence. She sent a tin of Russian caviar to Albert as well as a box of expensive cigars.

When she suggested one night—as though the idea had suddenly occurred to her, an inspiration purely out of the blue— that Lizzie accompany her to Cannes to complete her recuperation there at the villa, Lizzie was too astonished to speak for a moment.

"Well?" Alison said.

"But I'm *already* fully recuperated," Lizzie said.

"Nonsense!" Alison said. "I'm sure you'll suffer an immediate relapse on these abominable French trains—unless your friends are *already* in Italy, whose rail system is even *more* wretched. Where are they now, *anyway*? I have such a difficult time keeping up with them, and truly I don't care *where* they are!"

The bedside light snapped on. Alison sat up abruptly. She

was wearing a white linen nightdress with lace tucking and pink ribbon ties, its yoke neck cut low over her breasts. Her hair was tied back with a ribbon that matched those on the nightdress, and her eyes were flashing with the familiar intensity Lizzie now associated with anger or resolve or both.

"Now listen to me," she said. "I have no desire to spoil your first trip abroad or to deprive you of the obviously enchanting company of sour-faced Anna, voluptuous Felicity-Twit, or Rebecca and her exquisite *German*, which she tells me is even superior to her *French*, God help us! Nor am I suggesting for a moment that you miss the splendors of Italy—I should be a cruel and unfeeling friend if such a thought ever *once* crossed my mind. But, surely, Lizzie, you can spend a fortnight with us on the Riviera, can you not? In a sun-washed villa on a promontory overlooking the sea, with rooms enough to house the entire royal family, and gardens so lush they are virtually *edible*? I have rooms and rooms full of orchids, too, my pride and joy, unless that idiot gardener has allowed them to wither and die in my absence. Oh, Lizzie, do you wish *me* to wither and die in *your* absence? How shall I face each morning without my dearest child to greet me with those pale gray eyes in her round pale face—you *must* have sunshine, Lizzie, or you will perish! I promise I shall telegraph Geoffrey the instant you weary of our hospitality, and he will lead you to your sheeplike companions—*do* forgive me, I know they are dear to you—wherever they may be grazing at the time, be it Florence, Venice, Berlin, Siberia, *wherever*! You *must* grant me this single wish or I shall fill the tub with water again and drown myself in it, even as those swarthy French bandits might have drowned you. Say yes or I shall open the faucets at once!"

Her chest was heaving, a faint flush running across it just above the yoke neck of her nightdress and spreading upward toward her shoulder bones. Her cheeks were flushed as well, a stray strand of blond hair falling loose from the pink ribbon to cascade across one of them, as though lending rebellious support to the ardor of her speech and the flaming intensity of her eyes.

"*Well*, then?" she demanded.

"Well . . . *yes*, then," Lizzie said, and Alison clutched her fiercely, and showered kisses upon her cheeks and her hair, and said, "Oh my, perhaps there *is* a God after all."

227

10: NEW BEDFORD—1893

It often seemed to Lizzie, sitting in this courtroom, listening to the witnesses and the contending attorneys, that she was as much a prisoner of a relentlessly unwinding fate as she was of the Commonwealth of Massachusetts. This crowded, humid, cramped and swelteringly hot room had become a battlefield upon which both sides fought unremittingly, one hoping to condemn her, the other to exonerate her, but both—it seemed to her—oddly removed from the reality of her predicament.

In the way that soldiers had no true vocation until a war was declared, so had the attorneys here—and she included her own among them—been without meaningful occupation till they'd responded to a battle cry they might have heeded regardless of the cause. She sometimes felt that none of them recognized the fact that they were here neither to defend nor attack some lofty ideal, but instead to persuade a jury of twelve men that they should vote in favor of or against the hanging of a human being.

The newspaper reports maintained that she was not an adventuress. Yet this was surely the greatest adventure in her life, a life more dear to her than to any of the warriors who daily fought over it, a life that in the welter of claim and counterclaim

228

had become increasingly more cherishable. She had lived that life, the newspapers wrote, without making any other history than that which came to the ordinary New England girl who lived in the home of her parents and busied herself from morning till night to add to its comforts. But yet another history was being made in this time, in this place, an intensely *personal* history that could end abruptly with a verdict of guilty. For the attorneys the history was only of the moment. The warlike outbursts from each side would undoubtedly culminate in handshakes and accolades of "Well done, comrade, well fought," once the verdict was in. The field of battle would be cleared, and the only true casualty—if history went against her—would be she herself.

The newspaper reports claimed she was not handsome nor did she look particularly refined, little realizing what pain those words caused even when the criticism was tempered with the observation that there was a certain old-fashioned simplicity in her countenance and an absence of anything that implied the ferocity, at once calm and audacious, that must have moved her if the prosecution's story was to be believed.

The prosecution's *story*.

Ah, yes.

And the defense's *story*.

The relating of events in what must appear but a fanciful fiction to those twelve solemn jurors, an entertainment contrived for the pleasure of men with nothing to do but while away time on a hot June day.

It was all very real and immediate to her.

Every bit of it.

But here were the generals in command again, and here again came the parade of foot soldiers to tell of their derring-do, lost in their memories of events long past, mindless of how great a loss *she* might suffer, depending on whether their tales were believed or not.

It is my *life* we are quarreling over in this room, she thought fiercely.

Mine!

My name's Everett Brown, I'm eleven years old.

I live at 117 Third Street in Fall River. I was in Fall River on the day of the Borden murder, down there at the Borden house. Went down with Thomas Barlow. Walked down Third Street from my house, over Morgan, and down Second. I don't know whether it was before eleven or after eleven when I left. I couldn't say if it was nearer eleven or twelve that I left the house, because I didn't notice the time. When I went down Second Street, I saw Officer Doherty come out of the yard, run across the street and down Spring Street.

So I went in the Borden yard.

Went into the side gate and went up along the path to the door, tried to get into the house, and Charlie Sawyer wouldn't let us in. I asked him to let us in, but he wouldn't. So the party that was with me, Thomas Barlow, said, "Come on in the barn, there might be somebody there." We thought we would go up and find the murderer. I didn't open the door, Thomas Barlow did. I don't know if the pin was in the hasp. I didn't open the door. We stood a minute to see who'd go up first. Who would go upstairs first. He said he wouldn't go up, somebody might drop an ax on him.

So we went upstairs and looked out of the window on the west side, and went from there over to the hay, and was up in the barn about five minutes. Upstairs.

My name is Thomas Barlow, I'm twelve years old.

I work for Mr. Shannon, the poolroom on the corner of Pleasant and Second streets. Clean up around there and set the balls up. On the day of the murder, I wasn't working then. I wasn't doing anything then. I've been working there now about a month.

I got to Everett Brown's house about eleven o'clock. He lives at number 117 Third Street, a little ways up from my house, it ain't very far apart. He'd had his dinner when I got there. We left about eight minutes past eleven. I know because I looked at his clock when we left his house.

"What time is it now?" Knowlton said. "Don't look at the clock."

"I can't say."

"What time was it when you came up here to testify?"

"I don't know."

"Have you noticed the time today at all?"

230

"No, sir."

"And yet you *did* look at the clock just when you were going out?"

"Yes, sir."

"And remember it was eight minutes past eleven?"

"Yes, sir."

"Did you go right down to the Borden house?"

"We took our time."

"How far was it down to the Borden house?"

"I can't say. I never measured it."

"Well, how many squares is it?"

"About three, I should say."

"You walked three squares?"

"Yes, sir."

"You didn't stop?"

"Oh, we stopped, Fooling along, going down."

"What do you mean by 'fooling along'?"

"Playing. Going down."

"What do you mean by 'playing'?"

"He was pushing me off the sidewalk, and I was pushing him off."

"How long do you think it took pushing him off the sidewalk, and he you?"

"About ten or fifteen minutes, I should say."

"How do you fix that time?"

"I don't fix it. I say it was about between ten and fifteen."

"Wasn't it twenty?"

"No, sir."

"When you arrived near the Borden house, did you see any person leave the yard?"

"Yes, sir."

"Who was it?"

"Officer Doherty."

"Do you know what part of the yard he came out of?"

"I should say the front gate."

"Where did he go to?"

"Across the road, over toward Spring Street."

"What did you do then?"

"We went in the side gate."

"You say 'we.' Who?"

231

"Me and Brownie."

"Well, tell us what you did now."

"We went up to Mr. Sawyer, he was on the back steps, and asked him to let us go in the house, and he wouldn't let us in, so we went in the barn and went right up to the hay loft."

Lizzie understood exactly what Knowlton was attempting.

She had been warned by her attorneys that the testimony she'd given at the inquest in Fall River could—in the hands of the skillful Government team—be turned against her if the transcript was admitted in evidence. Part of that testimony detailed what she had told Knowlton about her visit to the barn. She'd said she had gone there shortly after her father returned to the house. She'd said she had remained upstairs in the barn loft for twenty minutes.

She did not need her attorneys to tell her now that Knowlton's interest was exceedingly keen as concerned who—if anyone—had visited that barn loft before *and* after the murders. He had spent a great deal of time on the barn when he'd repeatedly battered her with questions last August. He seemed prepared to use the same tactics now—on a twelve-year-old boy.

She listened intently.

"How did you go into the barn?"

"Through the door."

"Did you open the door?"

"Yes, sir."

"Was it locked?"

"It was . . . kind of a thing. Pin like."

"Was it fastened?"

"Yes, sir."

"What made you go into the barn?"

"Why, to see if anybody was in there."

"Did you go anywhere else except up into the barn loft?"

"No, sir."

"Did you look around downstairs in the barn?"

"No, sir."

"The place you went up to was up in the barn loft."

"Yes, sir, on the south side of the house. I went over to the front window on the west side and looked out the window. Then we went and looked in under the hay."

232

"How was the heat up in the barn compared with it out in the sun?"

"It was cooler up in the barn than it was outdoors."

"What do you suppose made that so much cooler than the rest of the country?"

"I couldn't say. It's always warmer in the house, I should say, than outdoors."

"And you should think the barn loft was cooler than any place you found that day?"

"Yes, sir."

"You mean that, do you?"

"Yes, sir."

"Has anybody told you to say that?"

"No, sir."

"And you went up there to see if you could see a man up there?"

"Yes, sir."

"Walked around up there?"

"Yes, sir."

"Because it was cool?"

"No. We went up to see if anybody was in there."

"Did you look for anybody after you got there?"

"Yes, sir."

"Thought perhaps the man might be hidden in the hay?"

"Yes, sir."

"Weren't afraid of him?"

"No, sir."

"Was there any officer there at the side gate when you went in?"

"No, sir."

"Any on the walk?"

"No, sir."

"Any on the steps?"

"No, sir."

"Do you know Officer Medley?"

"No, sir."

Officer Medley, she thought.

Whose testimony—when it came, and if it were believed by the jury—would make what she'd said at the inquest seem untruthful. Her mind circled back to the inquest testimony. Her

233

attorneys were fearful of its admission and were proceeding under the assumption that it *might* be admitted. In which case they were carefully preparing the ground for all she'd said about her visit to the barn. The ground Officer Medley could overturn as if with a shovel—*if* he were believed by the jury.

When Medley took the stand and when either Knowlton or Moody put him through his carefully rehearsed paces, would it matter *who* had seen *what* at the barn or who had gone into the loft *before* Medley? Whether it had been she alone, or half a hundred men, would it matter? If the jury believed him, would any of this matter to the hangman adjusting her noose?

Nervously, she waited.

My name is Walter P. Stevens. I was a reporter for the *Daily News* at Fall River at the time of the Borden murder. I arrived there with Officer Mullaly. There were several people in front of the house. I didn't see Officer Medley when I arrived. I went around the front of the house and yard between the Kelly yard and Borden house. Looked out through the grass and along the fence. Then I went to the rear fence and looked over it into the Chagnon yard, along the length of the fence, following it to the corner. I didn't spend very much time in the yard before I entered the house. I was standing in the side entryway when Mr. Medley passed me. Going in. Very shortly after he came in, I went out to the back of the house again, and went back as far as the fence. I think I looked over the fence again. Then I went into the barn.

When I went into the barn there was nobody downstairs. While I was in there, I heard somebody go upstairs. I think I heard at least three people going upstairs. I heard them going upstairs, and they had disappeared when I turned.

This couldn't have been many minutes after I saw Mr. Medley in the house.

"Your name is William H. Medley?"
"Yes, sir."
"You are at present doing special work on the Fall River police force?"
"Yes, sir."
"Under the title of what is called inspector?"

234

"Inspector."

"And last year you were a patrolman?"

"Patrolman."

"Did you act in any special capacity last year?"

"From the fourth day of August afterwards. I've not returned to patrol duty since."

"Upon the fourth day of August, did you obtain any knowledge of a homicide at the Borden house?"

"Yes, sir."

"Where were you when you obtained it?"

"Near the North Police Station—or rather *in* the North Police Station."

"From whom did you obtain the information?"

"The city marshal. By telephone."

"What time was it at that time?"

"About twenty-five minutes after eleven o'clock."

I stopped a team that was going by the police station and rode in the team to the city marshal's office. A sort of grocery-order wagon with a cover on it. I couldn't say as to the gait of the horse, but it was quite fast, as fast as I could get the man to urge the horse. It took six or seven minutes to get to the city marshal's office. I delayed there long enough to get a message from Marshal Hilliard, and then I walked to 92 Second Street, arriving there at about twenty or nineteen minutes to twelve.

The first person I saw when I got to the Borden house was Mr. Sawyer, a man at the door. I inquired for Mr. Fleet, but he did not get there until a minute or two later. After Mr. Fleet came, I went round the house, and walked round part of the way to the back door, and tried a cellar door. The cellar door was fast. I went in the rear of the house and saw Mr. Fleet again, and Mr. Mullaly, and Miss Russell, and Mrs. Churchill, and one or two doctors, and Miss Lizzie Borden. I asked her if she had any idea as to who committed the crimes, and she didn't have the remotest idea. I asked her where Bridget had been, and she told me that Bridget had been upstairs in her room.

"Where were you?" I asked.

"Upstairs in the barn," she said. Or "up in the barn." I'm not positive as to the "stairs" part. She said she was up in the barn. I talked with her only that one time. She was upstairs in her room, at the head of the front hallway stairs.

235

There were quite a number of officers there—seemed to come very rapidly—and they were searching everywhere. And I came downstairs from there and went through the room where Mr. Borden lay, and went out of the house. Mr. Sawyer was outside of the door, outside of the house, standing on the step, as I recollect it. There were quite a number outside in the yard, one or two officers, Mr. Sawyer, and Mr. Wixon and someone else. I couldn't recall them all. I went to the barn. The barn door was fast with a hasp over a staple and an iron pin in it. By a hasp, I mean a piece of metal that goes over the staple and is held in place by a pin.

I went upstairs until I reached about three or four steps from the top, and while there, part of my body was above the floor—above the level of the floor—and I looked around the barn to see if there was any evidence of anything having been disturbed, and I didn't notice that anything had or seemed to have been disturbed.

I stooped down low to see if I could discern any marks on the floor of the barn having been made there.

I did that by stooping down and looking across the bottom of the barn floor.

I didn't see any.

I reached out my hand to see if I could make an impression on the floor of the barn, by putting my hand down so, and found that I made an impression on the barn floor. I could see the marks that I made quite distinctly when I looked for them in the accumulated dust.

I stepped up on the top.

It was hot in the loft of the barn, very hot. You know it was a hot day.

There's a little door on the side of the barn upstairs—I think it was on the south side of the barn—which they used for putting in hay. There was two windows, one on each side of the barn. The door and the windows were closed.

I took four or five steps on the outer edge of the barn floor, the edge nearest the stairs that came up, to see if I could discern those—and I did.

I discerned those footprints that I'd made by stooping and casting my eye on a level with the barn floor.

And could see them plainly.

236

I saw no other footsteps in that dust than those which I'd made myself.

Lizzie looked at the jury box.
The faces of the twelve jurors were impassive.

My name is Michael Mullaly, I've been a Fall River police officer for something over fourteen years. On August fourth, last year, I first went to the Borden house when Officer Allen went back there. It was he who gave me the news at the patrol-wagon house on the corner of Rock and Franklin Streets. I went from there to the station house and then to the Borden house. Officer Allen and I went in the door on the north side of the house. There was quite a number of people around the house, out at the gate, outside the fence. I didn't notice anyone inside the fence.

I told Mrs. Churchill that I'd come there for a report, and she told me that I would have to see Miss Lizzie Borden. I went to Miss Borden and told her that the marshal had sent me there to get a report of all that had happened to her father, that is, he who laid dead on the sofa at the time. She told me that she was out in the yard, and when she came in she found him dead on the sofa. I then inquired of her if she knew what kind of property her father had on his person, and she told me that her father had a silver watch and chain, a pocketbook with money in it, and a gold ring on his little finger. About that time, Officer Doherty came back in . . .

"Now Mr. Doherty, when you returned to the house the second time, did you see anybody you hadn't seen before?"
"Yes, sir. Mrs. Churchill and Miss Russell and Miss Borden."
"Where did you see her?"
"In the kitchen, I think."
"Can you give any description—and if so, do it the best you can—of the dress that she had on when she was downstairs in the kitchen?"
"I thought she had a light blue dress with a bosom in the waist, or something like a bosom. I have a faint recollection; that is all I can say about it."
"Any figure on it? Do you remember any figure?"

"I thought there was a small figure on the dress, a little spot like."

"What color was the figure?"

"Something . . . I can't tell exactly."

"Did you have any talk with her at that time?"

"Yes, sir."

"Will you be kind enough to state what that was?"

Miss Borden told me that Bridget would show us where the axes were. When we started to go downstairs, I told Bridget what I wanted to find, that we were going for axes and hatchets in the cellar. Bridget led the way for me and Officer Mullaly. We went into two or three dark places, wood or coal rooms or something. We separated. I got over near the sink and I noticed a pail and some towels . . .

"Pass from those," Knowlton said quickly. He had no desire to have the thrust of Doherty's testimony detoured by any talk of the menstrual towels in the pail under the sink.

"Mr. Mullaly was looking at something," Doherty said. "I came and looked over his shoulder. He had a hatchet in his hands."

My name is William A. Dolan. I'm a physician, been in practice eleven years at the Fall River Hospital. I was educated at the University of Pennsylvania, Medical Department. I've been engaged in general practice, including surgery as well as the practice of medicine, more surgery than anything else. I'm also the medical examiner for the county of Bristol, have held that office for two years next month. I was in office for a year when this thing happened.

I first went to the Borden house that day at about a quarter to twelve. I happened to be passing by the house, and I fix the time because I was in there about ten to fifteen minutes when I heard the City Hall bell strike twelve. The first person I saw was Charles Sawyer. He was at the door. And the next person I saw, I think, was Dr. Bowen, who met me at the kitchen door. I saw also, I think—in the kitchen—Bridget Sullivan and Mr. Morse. I'm not sure about Mr. Morse, but I think so. Mrs. Churchill and Alice Russell were in the dining room.

I went in the sitting room and saw the form lying upon the sofa. The sofa was placed against the north wall of the room, running east and west with the head toward the parlor—that is, toward the east—and the feet toward the west, the kitchen. The end of the sofa was flush with the jam of the dining-room door. The body was covered with a sheet. Dr. Bowen was with me when I looked at the body.

I took hold of the hand of the body and found it was warm. The head was resting upon a small sofa cushion that had a little white tidy on it. The cushion in turn, I think, rested on his coat—his Prince Albert coat—which had been doubled up and put under there, and that, I think, rested upon an afghan, or sofa cover . . . a knitted affair. The lowest of the three was the afghan, then came the coat, and then the sofa cushion.

The blood was of a bright red color and still oozing from the head. At the head, it was dripping on the carpet underneath, between the woodwork, the head of the sofa and the sofa body. It was not coagulated. The blood that was on the carpet had been soaked in. There was no blood, really, on top of the carpet. I should think there were two spots soaked with blood. I should judge eight inches in diameter. Right under the head of the sofa. That is, practically underneath where the head of the sofa joins the body of the sofa. I made an examination and found that there were from eight to ten wounds—I wasn't positive at that time—on his face.

I observed the position of the body, and the clothing he had on. On the outside, he had on a cardigan jacket—that is, a woolen jacket—black vest and black trousers, and a pair of Congress shoes. He had a watch and pocketbook. I examined the pocketbook and found some money in bills and some in specie. I couldn't tell the exact figure, I have it here in my notes—he had $81.65.

I think that's all that was in the pocketbook, possibly some specie in his pocket. The largest portion of that was bills. The sixty-five cents was in change. I didn't find anything else in his pocketbook. The watch and chain were in his upper vest pocket, the watch. He had a ring on his left hand—I'm not quite positive as to that, I forget really. A gold ring, if I remember correctly.

Upstairs, Mrs. Borden was lying between the dressing case, which was on the north side of the building, and the bed. She was lying with her back exposed, and also the right back of the head exposed, and her hands were something in this position. That is, just around the head. Her head was not resting on them. Her hands didn't touch. They came very near to each other, but they didn't touch. The face was resting in such a position that the right back of the head was exposed. Turned to the left. Probably a more convenient way to express it would be to say that she was lying on the left side of her face. That is, the left side of her nose and eye were resting upon the floor. Her clothing was bloody—the *back* of her clothing, that is. The upper part of it. Her waist.

I felt the body with my hand, touched her head and her hand, and found it was warm. I could not say the temperature, but a warm body. I had a clinical thermometer with me, but I didn't use it. When I use the word *warm*, I don't quite mean the warmth of life. I'm referring to the warmth as distinguished between the warmth of life and the coldness of death. I'm using it in the medical sense, the word warmth. The body was much colder than that of Mr. Borden. Her blood was coagulated and of a dark color. The blood on her head was matted and practically dry. There was no oozing from it as in Mr. Borden's. I counted the wounds, and lifted the body with Dr. Bowen's assistance, in order to get at the wounds more quickly.

Then, in consequence of what had been told me, I collected a sample of that morning's milk, and a sample of the milk of the previous day. Bridget Sullivan gave me those samples. I sealed them up hermetically, put them in separate jars, and marked them according to the day on which the milk was sampled. I think I put something like this: "Sample of milk of August 4th" . . . "Sample of milk of August 3rd." Then I put them in charge of a policeman to keep, and sent them later to Professor Wood.

I went with the officer then, through the lower floor and through the cellar. In the cellar, we saw some axes and hatchets that were there. I think there were two axes and two hatchets. I made no examination at the time, other than just to look at them. I used no glass or anything of that sort. But I noticed that one of them—the heavy claw-hammer hatchet—looked as if it had been scraped. When I went again to look at Mr. Borden a second time, Mr. Fleet was just coming in . . .

I should say I got the information about twenty-five minutes

240

to twelve. A driver for Mr. Stone, stablekeeper in Fall River, brought it. I was at my residence, number 13 Park Street. I put on my coat and hat, or cap, and went to 92 Second Street.

I was then, as I am at present, assistant city marshal of Fall River.

I went there in a police-department buggy, arrived there at about fifteen minutes to twelve, I should say. As I approached the house, I first saw Mr. Manning, reporter for the *Fall River Globe*. I saw Officer Medley outside of the house, had some words with him and then went into the house. Mr. Morse and Bridget Sullivan were in the kitchen, and I think Mrs. Churchill. I went through the kitchen to the sitting room, and saw Dr. Dolan standing or leaning over the body of Mr. Borden. Andrew J. Borden. I found that the blood was on his face and ran down onto his shirt, his clothing, and also went through the head of the lounge and on the floor or carpet. There was quite a little pool of blood there.

I then went upstairs to the front bedroom—or spare bedroom, so-called—and saw Mrs. Borden laid dead between the bed and the dressing case, face downward, with her head all broke in or cut. She was covered with blood, and there was considerable blood under her head, and the blood was congealed and black. That is, of a dark color. The blood about Mr. Borden's head was of a reddish color, and much thinner.

I came out the head of the stairs, and then went into the room where Miss Lizzie Borden was, sitting down on a lounge—or sofa—with Reverend Mr. Buck, Miss Russell being in the room.

I told Miss Borden who I was, made known who I was—I was then in citizens' clothes, as I am now—and I asked her if she knew anything about the murders. She said that she did not. All she knew was that Mr. Borden—her father, as she put it— came home about half-past ten or quarter to eleven, went into the sitting room, sat down in the large chair, took out some papers and looked at them. She was ironing some handkerchiefs in the dining room, as she stated. She saw that her father was feeble, and she went to him and advised him and assisted him to lay down upon the sofa.

She then went into the dining room to her ironing, but left after her father was laid down and went out into the yard and up in the barn. I asked her how long she remained in the barn. She

241

said she remained in the barn about a half hour. I then asked her what she meant by "up in the barn." She said, "I mean *up* in the barn. *Upstairs, sir.*" She said after she had been there about half an hour, she came down again, went into the house, and found her father on the lounge, in the position in which she had left him.

But killed.

Or dead.

"Who was in the house this morning or last night?" I asked her.

"No one but my father, Mrs. Borden, Bridget, Mr. Morse and myself," she said.

"Who's this Mr. Morse?" I asked.

"He's my uncle," she said. "He came here yesterday, and slept in the room where Mrs. Borden was found dead."

"Do you think Mr. Morse had anything to do with the killing of your parents?" I asked.

She said no, she didn't think he had, because Mr. Morse left the house this morning before nine o'clock, and didn't return until after the murder. I asked her if she thought Bridget could have done this, and she said she didn't think that she could or *did.*

I should say here that I didn't use the word *Bridget* at that time, because she'd given me the name as Maggie; I *should* say Maggie.

I asked her if she thought Maggie had anything to do with the killing of these. She said no, that Maggie had gone upstairs previous to her father's lying down on the lounge, and when she came from the barn she called Maggie downstairs.

I then asked her if she had any idea who could have killed her father and mother.

"She's not my *mother,* sir," she said. "She's my *step*mother. My *mother* died when I was a child."

That's about all the conversation I had with her at that time.

I then went downstairs in the cellar and found Officers Mullaly and Devine down there. When I got there, Officer Mullaly had two axes and two hatchets on the cellar floor. I looked around in the cellar to see if we could find any other instrument that might have been used for the purpose of killing, but failed to find anything. The two hatchets and axes were left there that day.

The largest hatchet, the claw-hammer hatchet—with the rust stain on it, and the red spot upon the handle that apparently had been washed or wiped—was placed behind some boxes in the cellar adjoining the wash cellar. I put it there, separating it from the other hatchet. I went out in the yard then, and instructed some of the men—who'd been sent by the marshal to me—to cover the different highways and depots, and then I went upstairs, the front hallway upstairs.

I went to Lizzie's door and rapped on it.

Dr. Bowen came to it, holding open the door—*opening* the door, I should say—about six or eight inches, and asked what was wanted. I told him that we had come there as officers to search this room and search the building. He then turned around to Miss Borden and told me to wait a moment, and closed the door. He then opened the door again and said that Lizzie wanted to know if it was absolutely necessary for us to search that room. I told him as officers, murders having been committed, it was our duty to do so, and we wanted to get in there. He closed the door again, and said something to Miss Borden, and finally opened the door and admitted us.

We proceeded to search, looking through some drawers, and the closet and bedroom. While the search was still going on, I said to Lizzie, "You said that you were up in the barn for half an hour. Do you say that now?"

She said, "I don't say half an hour. I say twenty minutes to half an hour."

"Well, we'll call it twenty minutes then," I said.

"I say from twenty minutes *to* half an hour, sir," she said.

I then asked her when was the last time that she saw her stepmother—when and where. She said that the last time she saw her was about nine o'clock and she was then in the room where she was found dead, and was making the bed.

That is to say, at nine o'clock she was making the bed in the room where she was found dead.

She then said that someone brought a letter or note to Mrs. Borden and she thought she had gone out and had not known of her return.

As we continued to search Lizzie Borden's room, she said she

243

hoped we should get through with this quick, that she was getting tired, or words to that effect—it was making her tired— and we told her we should get through as soon as we possibly could. It was an unpleasant duty—that is, considering that her father and stepmother were dead. We searched that room, and then we went to the room where Mrs. Borden was found dead.

I saw a door there which would lead into Lizzie Borden's room and on Lizzie Borden's side was a bookcase and, I think, desk combined. This was situated directly in front of the door, or in back of the door leading from where Mrs. Borden was found dead. The door was locked. I'm not sure on which side, but I think upon Lizzie Borden's side.

I searched a clothespress that was in the room directly in front of Lizzie's room, and then I searched Mr. Borden's room, and went up to the attics and searched Bridget's room, and the closet, together with the room adjoining the other rooms, and the west end of the attics. Then I came downstairs, went down in the cellar again, saw Dr. Dolan, saw Officer Mullaly, and asked where he got the axes and the hatchets, and he showed me.

I found—in a box in the middle cellar, on a shelf or a jog of an old-fashioned chimney—the *head* of a hatchet.

"Is this the hatchet you found?" Moody asked.

"This looks like the hatchet that I found there. Pretty sure that that's the one. This piece of wood was in the head of the hatchet, broken off close."

"Broken off close to the hatchet?"

"Very close to the hatchet."

"Mr. Fleet, will you describe everything in respect to the appearance of that hatchet, if you can?"

"Don't want anything but just what the hatchet was at *that* time," Robinson said. "Don't want any inferences."

"I think he'll be careful," Moody said. "Any appearances that you noticed about the hatchet, you may describe."

"Yes, sir, I don't want to do anything else, Mr. Attorneys. The hatchet was covered with a heavy dust or ashes."

"Describe the ashes as well as you can."

"It was covered with white ashes, I should say, upon the blade of the hatchet. Not upon one side, but upon both."

"Could you tell anything about whether there were ashes upon the head of the hatchet?"

"I don't think you should make any suggestions," Robinson said. "I object to that style of question."

"Well," Moody said, "describe further."

"I should say that upon this hatchet was dust, or ashes as though the head . . .

"Wait a moment!" Robinson said. "I object to that!"

"Describe on what parts of the hatchet," Moody said.

"On both the faces and all over, the hatchet was covered with dust or ashes."

"Was that fine dust . . . ?"

"Wait a moment," Robinson said. "The witness didn't say *fine* dust. We object to that."

"Describe the dust there," Moody said.

"The dust, in my opinion, was ashes."

"According to your observation, what did it look like?"

"I object to it," Robinson said.

"Describe it," Mason said. "Whether he recognized it as ashes or any particular substance, he may say."

"I recognized it as ashes."

"Can you tell me how fine or coarse the ashes were?"

"They were fine."

"Did you notice anything with reference to the *other* tools in the box at the time?"

"Yes, sir. There was dust upon them."

"The same as upon this?"

"No, sir."

"What difference was there, if any?"

"The dust on the other tools was lighter and finer than the dust upon that hatchet."

"At that time, Mr. Fleet, did you observe anything with reference to the point of breaking of the hatchet?"

"The only thing I recognized at the time was that this was apparently a new break."

"I object to that answer," Robinson said. "That this was a *new* break."

"At that time," Moody said, "did you observe anything, with reference to the ashes, upon the point of the break upon the handle, upon the wood where it was broken?"

245

"There seemed to be ashes there like the other."

"Now Mr. Mullaly," Robinson asked, "when did *you* see the one that has no handle?"

"When Mr. Fleet called my attention to it."

"Well, how was that? What was the condition of that?"

"That had ashes, what I call ashes, on each side of it. The handle was broken and it looked fresh, fresh broken."

"I haven't asked you about that just now. I am asking you about the *hatchet* part, the *metal*. How did that look as compared to today?"

"It looked different."

"How?"

"That is, it was covered with ashes."

"And those have been removed since that time?"

"There is none on there now that I can see."

"And do you know where that has been since?"

"I do not."

"And that piece of the handle—which is now out of the eye of the hatchet—you think does not look so new as it did at that time?"

"It don't to me, not now."

"Did you afterwards look in the box?"

"I did not. As I remember of, I didn't look in it."

"Do you know anything of what became of the box?"

"No, sir."

"Nothing else was taken out of it while you were there?"

"Nothing but the hatchet and parts of the handle."

"Well . . . *parts*? That piece?"

"That piece, yes."

"Well, that was in the eye, wasn't it?"

"Yes. Then there was another piece."

"Another piece of *what*?"

"Handle."

From where Lizzie sat, she saw Robinson's back stiffen, as though he were a hunting dog catching the scent of an elusive quarry. In the same instant the jury became suddenly alert, the bearded and mustached faces seeming to come alive all at once. From the spectators' benches at the back of the courtroom, she heard a murmur like a single exhalation of breath, and then all

246

was silent again. At the prosecutors' table, both Moody and Knowlton were frowning.

"Where is it?" Robinson asked.

"I don't know," Mullaly said.

"Don't you know where it is?"

"No, sir."

"Was it a piece of that *same* handle?"

"It was a piece that corresponded with that."

"The *rest* of the handle?"

"It was a piece with a fresh break in it."

"The other piece?"

"Yes, sir."

"Well, where *is* it?"

"I don't know."

"Did you see it after that?"

"I did not."

"Was it a handle to a *hatchet*?"

"It was what I call a hatchet handle."

There was the same murmur at the back of the courtroom. One of the justices, looking annoyed, glared toward the spectators' benches. The twelve jurors, to a man, were leaning forward, listening intently now. Lizzie searched their faces, and then turned her attention back to Robinson.

"I want to know how long it was," he said.

"Well, I couldn't tell you how long it was. I didn't measure it."

"Well, did you take it out of the box?"

"I did not."

"Do you know where Mr. Fleet is now, this minute?"

"I do not."

"Is he below?"

"I don't know."

"Have you seen him since this morning?"

"I saw him downstairs."

"You mean before the adjournment?"

"Yes, sir."

"I would like to have Mr. Fleet come in," Robinson said. "I would like to have him sent for."

She welcomed the respite.

The day, which had begun so uncomfortably hot and humid,

had turned considerably milder. Aware of the spectators' eyes upon her, she walked nonetheless to one of the open windows, the deputy sheriff at her side like a shadow, and glanced down at the grass growing on the courthouse lawn. She took in a deep breath. Giant elms arched their branches over the walk below, their leaves moving gently in the new breeze. Sparrows sang in the capitals of the great Grecian columns. The flowers in the little plots on the lawn and in the big boxes on the courthouse portico bloomed red, white and yellow. She longed to be there in the warm sunshine, free for a moment from the strain of this confined room and the tensions it contained.

There were crowds outside even now.

This morning, as she'd made her way up the path to the Court House entrance, escorted by the deputy sheriff, the crowds had jostled and shoved beyond the erected fences, and many of the women had called out taunts and jeers to her. She could not understand why her own sex had turned against her, but their enmity was so positive and manifest that even in the courtroom the female spectators looked disappointed whenever a witness said anything to her advantage. She suddenly wondered, and this was a prospect she had never before considered, what her life would be like if and when the jury found her innocent. Would she ever again be able to enjoy in peace and privacy the harmless beauty of a June morning?

Someone in the crowd below had spied her at the open window.

She turned abruptly away.

Fleet was being led back into the courtroom.

"Mr. Fleet, returning to the subject we had under discussion this morning, about what you found in that box downstairs."

"Yes, sir."

"Will you state again what you found there at the time you looked in?"

"I found a hatchet head, the handle broken off, together with some other tools in there and the iron that was inside there. I don't know just what it was."

"Was this what you found?" Robinson asked, and showed him the hatchet head.

"Yes, sir."

"Did you find anything else? Except old tools?"

"No, sir."

"Sure about that?"

"Yes, sir."

"Who was with you at that time?"

"Michael Mullaly."

"Anybody else?"

"Not that I recall."

"Did you take this out of the box yourself?"

"Yes, sir."

"Mullaly didn't?"

"No, I don't think he did."

"Now, if I understand you," Robinson said, showing him the small section of wood, "this piece was in the eye of the hatchet."

"Yes, sir."

"That has been driven out since."

"By somebody."

"Yes, not by you. And taking those two together, that was *all* you found in the box, except some old tools which you did not take out at all. Is that right?"

"That is all we found in connection with that hatchet."

"You did not find the *handle*? The *broken* piece? Not at *all*?"

"No, sir."

"You didn't *see* it, did you?"

"No, sir."

"Did Mr. Mullaly take it out of the box?"

"Not that I know of."

"It was not there?"

"Not that I know of."

"You looked in so that you could have seen it if it was in there."

"Yes, sir."

"You have no doubt about that, have you at all?"

"What?"

"That you did *not* find the other piece of the handle that fitted on there?"

"No, sir."

"You would have seen it if it had been, wouldn't you?"

"Yes, sir, it seems to me I should."

"There was no hatchet handle belonging to that picked up right there?"

"No, sir."

"Or anywhere around there?"

"No, sir."

"Or any piece of wood—beside that—that had any fresh break in it?"

"Not that came from that hatchet."

"Or in that box, anyway?"

"No, sir, not in the box."

"Or round there anywhere?"

"No, sir, not that I am aware of. I did not see any of it."

"What did you do with the hatchet head, Mr. Fleet?"

"I put it back in the box."

My name is Philip Harrington. I've been on the Fall River police force ten years last March. My rank is captain. My position in August of last year was patrolman. I was at dinner, had just finishd dinner when my attention was called to the trouble on Second Street. I immediately put on my coat and hat and took a horse car. I got to the house between fifteen and twenty minutes past twelve. That's my judgment, I did not consult a timepiece. I was led to think so by the time the car arrived at City Hall. It was what was known as the "quarter-past-twelve" car.

I went in the front gate, walked along the yard front of the house to the north side, along the north side to the north door on the side. Mr. Sawyer was at the north door. I went into the house and saw Officer Devine on the ground floor. Miss Lizzie Borden was not there. I saw several ladies there, I didn't know who they were. I asked a question or two, and I was directed to Miss Borden's room. In that room, I saw Miss Borden and Miss Russell. Miss Lizzie Borden, I mean, of course.

I stepped into the room, and taking the door in my right hand, I passed it back. Miss Russell stood on my left, and she received the door and closed it. There was no one except Miss Russell and Miss Borden there at the time, not outside of myself. Miss Russell stood in front of a chair which was at the north side of the door which I entered. Miss Lizzie Borden stood at the foot of the bed, which ran diagonally across the room.

250

The dress she had on was a house wrap, a striped house wrap, with a pink and light stripe alternating, the pink the most prominent color. On the light ground stripe was a diamond figure formed by narrow stripes, some of which ran diagonally or bias to the stripe, and others parallel with it. The sides were tailored, fitting—or fitted—to the form. The front from the waist to the neck was loose and in folds. The collar was standing, plaited on the sides and closely shirred in front. On either side, directly over the hips, was caught a narrow, bright red ribbon, perhaps three-fourths of an inch—or an inch—in width. This was brought around front, tied in a bow, and allowed to drop, with the ends hanging a little below the bow. It was cut in semitrain or bell skirt, which the ladies were wearing that season . . .

"Don't go quite so fast. Cut in *what*?" Robinson said.

"A bell skirt."

"Bell skirt?"

"Yes, sir."

"You usually called that kind of a dress a bell skirt, did you?"

"The *cut* of the dress. Not that *kind* of a dress."

"That was your description of it? As you spoke in conversation about it?"

"Yes, sir."

"Nobody told you that?"

"No, sir."

"What has been your business before you became a policeman?"

"I was in the painting business."

"What before that?"

"I was in the book business before that."

"Prior to that?"

"Wood business."

"Were you ever in the dressmaking business?"

"No, sir."

"Were you ever in the dry-goods business?"

"No, sir."

"Did you ever have anything to do with colors except as a painter?"

"Nothing any more than to admire them."

"You admire them. But did you admire a red ribbon on a pink wrapper?"

"Well, I am not speaking of my taste, sir."

"Go on, then."

I told Miss Lizzie I would like to have her tell me all she knew about this matter.

She said, "I can tell you nothing about it."

I asked her when she last saw her father.

She said, "When he returned from the post office with a small package in his hand and some mail. I asked him if he had any for me, and he said no. He then sat down to read the paper, and I went out in the barn. I remained there twenty minutes. I returned and found him dead."

"When going to or coming from the barn," I said, "did you see anybody in or around the yard? Or anybody going up or down the street?"

"No, sir," she said.

"Not even the opening or closing of a screen door?" I said. "Why not? You were but a short distance, and you would have heard the noise if any was made."

"I was up in the loft," she said.

I was silent a moment, and then I said, "What motive?"

"I don't know," she said.

"Was it robbery?"

"I think not, for everything appears all right, even to the watch in his pocket and the ring on his finger."

I then asked her if she had any reason to suspect anybody, no matter how slight. "No matter how insignificant it may be," I said, "it may be of great moment to the police, and be of much assistance to them in ferreting out the criminal."

"No," she said. "I . . . have not."

"Why hesitate?" I asked.

"Well," she said, "a few weeks ago father had angry words with a man about something."

"What was it?"

"I don't know, but they were very angry at the time, and the stranger went away."

"Did you see him at all?"

"No, sir, they were in another room. But from the tone of their voices, I knew everything wasn't pleasant between them."

252

"Did you hear your father say anything about him?"

"No, sir."

About here, I cautioned her of what she might say at the present time. "Owing to the atrociousness of this crime," I said, "perhaps you are not in a mental condition to give as clear a statement of the facts as you will be on tomorrow. By that time you may recollect more about the man. You may remember of having heard his name, or of having seen him, and thereby be enabled to give a description of him. You may recollect of having heard your father say something about him or his visit. By that time you may be in a better condition to relate what you know of the circumstances."

To this, she made a stiff curtsy, shaking her head, and she said, "No, I can tell you all I know now, just as well as any other time."

"Mr. Harrington," Moody said, "without characterizing, can you describe her appearance and manner during the conversation?"

"Wait a moment," Robinson said. "What she *did* and what she *said*."

"If the witness observes the question carefully," Mason said, "he may answer it."

"Your Honor very properly says *if* he discriminates carefully, he may answer properly," Robinson said. "The difficulty is he may give his judgment upon her state of *mind* from what he *saw*. That's the difficulty with it."

"The question doesn't call for it," Mason said, "and the witness appears intelligent. Having his attention called to it—that he is to do nothing but to answer the question—he may answer it."

"I'll ask a preliminary question," Moody said. "Do you understand the distinction that I intend to draw?"

"Well, I would like to have the question read."

"Without characterizing," the stenographer read, "can you describe her appearance and manner during the conversation?"

"She was cool—"

"Wait!" Robinson said, leaping to his feet.

"Well, that's the difficulty," Moody said.

"Well," Harrington said, "it's rather a difficult thing to get *at*, sir."

"By leading a little," Moody said, "perhaps I can get at it."

"It should be stricken out," Robinson said. "It's not a completed answer."

"It's not completed because you *stopped* him," Knowlton said. "I suppose what he said—'She was cool'—is an answer strictly within the rule."

"If you're content to have the answer stop there, it may stand," Mason said.

"I'm content to have it stop there," Moody said.

"I'm content if it stays there," Robinson said.

"During any part of the interview, was she in tears?" Moody asked.

"No, sir."

"Did she sit or stand during the talk with you?"

"She stood."

"Was there any breaking of the voice, or was it steady?"

"Steady."

"Now will you state anything more that was said while you were there?"

. . . I then spoke to her again about the time that she was in the barn. She said twenty minutes. I asked her wasn't it difficult to be so accurate about fixing the time, to fix the time so accurately. "May you not have been there half an hour or perhaps fifteen minutes?" I said.

She said, "No, sir, I was there twenty minutes."

I went out the door, downstairs, through the front hall, and passed through the sitting room into the kitchen. There were quite a number of people there, among whom I noticed—or recognized—Dr. Bowen and Medical Examiner Dolan, Assistant Marshal Fleet and the servant girl, whose name at the time, I did not know.

Just as I went to pass by Dr. Bowen, between him and the stove, I saw some scraps of notepaper in his hand. He was standing a little west of the door that led into the rear hall or entryway. I asked him what they were, referring to the pieces of paper, and he said, "Oh, I guess it's nothing."

So he started to arrange them so as to determine what was on them, or to learn their contents. They were very small, and it was rather difficult. But on one piece, on the upper lefthand corner, was the word *Emma*. And that was written in lead pencil, as well as other pieces I saw. I asked him again what they contained, and he said, "Oh, I think it's nothing. It's something, I think, about my daughter going through somewhere." He then turned slightly to his left and took the lid from the stove and threw the papers in—or the pieces in.

I then noticed the firebox.

The fire was very near extinguished. On the south end there was a small fire which I judged was a coal fire. The embers were about dying. It was about as large as the palm of my hand. There had been some paper burned there before, which was rolled up and still held a cylindrical form. I should say it was about that long. Twelve inches, I should say, and not over two inches in diameter . . .

"Had you paid any attention to that stove before?" Robinson asked.

"No, sir. Any more than to see it as I passed by."

"And then Dr. Bowen took off the cover in the ordinary way?"

"Yes, sir."

"And put those papers in?"

"Yes, sir."

"Did he take off the cover over the little spot of coal you said was there?"

"No, sir."

"Took it off at the other end?"

"At the other end."

"So he threw it right down in where there wasn't any fire?"

"Yes, sir."

"And upon some embers of burnt paper?"

"No, sir. It went down between that burnt paper and the front part of the firebox."

"That is, that was a piece of burnt paper?"

"Yes, sir."

"Rolled up?"

"Completely carbonized."

"About a foot long?"

"Yes, sir."

"And I think you said about an inch or two inches."

"I thought about two."

"Lying there all charred and burned?"

"Yes, sir."

* * *

"Dr. Bowen, did you subsequently see Miss Borden in her room upstairs?"

"Miss Lizzie? Yes, sir. Sometime between one and two o'clock. At that time, I gave her a preparation called bromo caffeine. For quieting nervous excitement and headache."

"Did you give any directions as to how frequently that medicine should be given?"

"I left a second dose to be repeated in an hour."

And here, again, Lizzie understood exactly how carefully her attorneys were preparing the ground for the possible admission of her inquest testimony. The government would without question attempt to introduce into the record all that she'd told Knowlton in Fall River last August. Her own attorneys had asked her repeatedly why her testimony had sounded so confused and contradictory, and she had told them it had naturally been a shocking time, a bewildering time—and then she had remembered that Dr. Bowen had prescribed drugs for her. Robinson had seized upon this immediately.

"The poor girl was drugged!" he'd said to Jennings.

This, now, was the first mention of any medication given by Dr. Bowen in the days immediately preceding the inquest. She knew there would be more. Whatever might be said of Robinson's sometimes bombastic courtroom tactics, she knew he was a fastidious man who would layer in—as meticulously as an expert mason spreading mortar between bricks—a solid precautionary defense against the possible admission of the inquest testimony.

"Edward S. Wood is your name?"

"Edward S. Wood."

"You live in Boston?"

"Yes, sir."

"At present, what is your occupation?"

"I am a physician and chemist—professor of chemistry in the Harvard Medical School."

"How long have you held that position?"

"As an assistant professor of chemistry from 1871 to 1876, and professor of chemistry since 1876."

"Have you given special attention to any particular branch of science?"

256

"To medical chemistry."

"Does that also include what is also called physiological chemistry?"

"Yes, sir."

"Have you had experience in that sort of work? In medical or physiological chemistry?"

"Yes, sir."

"To what extent?"

"To a very great extent in medicolegal cases, poison and bloodstain cases."

"Have you been called upon as to that branch of science in the trial of cases?"

"Yes, sir."

"To what extent?"

"I don't know, sir. Several hundred, I should think."

"Large number of capital cases?"

"Yes, sir."

"When was your attention, professor, first called to this matter?"

On the fifth of August last year, I received by express a box which was unopened. I opened the box and found in it four preserve jars, one of which was labeled Milk of August 3rd, 1892; the other, the second, was labeled Milk of August 4th, 1892; the third tag was labeled Stomach of Andrew J. Borden; the fourth was labeled Stomach of Mrs. Andrew J. Borden. These tags were tied closely about the neck of the bottles, with strings, the strings being sealed. I opened the jars simply by cutting the strings, leaving the seals intact.

I first examined the jar marked Stomach of Mrs. Andrew J. Borden. The jar was opened and the stomach removed. I found what was apparently a stomach—so far as the external appearance was concerned—of perfectly normal appearance. And it was unopened, a ligature, or string, a cord being tied about the upper and lower end of the stomach. Surgically unopened, I mean. I cut the ligatures and opened the stomach myself while it was fresh, shortly after I received it, and removed the contents into a separate vessel and thoroughly examined the inner surface of the stomach which I found to be, so far as I could determine, perfectly healthy in appearance. There was no evidence of the action of any irritant whatever.

257

The contents of the stomach were then examined and their quantity noted to be about eleven ounces. It was of semisolid consistency, consisting of at least four-fifths solid food and not more than one-fifth—I should say probably not more than one-*tenth*—of liquid, of water. And upon examination of those contents of the stomach, I found them to consist of partially digested starch, like wheat starch such as would be found in bread or cake or any other food in the making of which wheat flour is used.

There was also a large quantity of partially digested meat—muscular fiber—with the food and a considerable quantity of oil and some pieces of bread and cake. Some of the pieces of meat were quite sizable pieces—as large, for instance, as a whole pea. And one or two pieces were larger than that—as large as the end of my forefinger—so that their nature was very readily determined.

In addition to this, there was a large number of vegetable pulp cells which resembled those of some fruit, or a pulpy vegetable such as boiled potato. Or an apple or pear. And there was also an undigested skin of a vegetable or of a fruit, one piece of which I have here. It looks like the red skin of an apple or pear.

So far as anything could be determined from the appearance of the food, it was undergoing the normal stomach digestion. And from the quantity of the food in the stomach, it would—if the digestion had progressed normally in the individual before death—indicate a period of approximately somewhere from two to three hours of digestion from the last meal taken, possibly a little longer than that.

That was the stomach of Mrs. Borden.

The character of the food found in the stomach of *Mr.* Borden differed from that in the stomach of Mrs. Borden in that there was very much less of it, and that it consisted mostly of water and contained only a very small quantity of solid food. This would indicate that the digestion—had it gone on normally, at the normal rate—in the stomach of Mr. Borden was much further advanced than that in the case of Mrs. Borden, since nearly all of the solid food had been expelled from the stomach into the intestine. It would make it, therefore, somewhere in the neighborhood of four hours, say from three—anywhere from three and a half to four and a half hours, the digestion.

Both of those contents of the stomachs were immediately tested for prussic acid. Because prussic acid—it being a volatile acid, it is necessary to make an immediate test for it as it would escape very shortly after its exposure to the air, and escape detection therefore. Therefore, those were both tested for prussic acid, with negative results. Afterwards they were analyzed in the regular way for the irritant poisons, with also a negative result.

I found no evidence of poison of any kind.

Both jars of milk were also tested in the same way, and without obtaining any evidence of poison in either the milk of August third or the milk of August fourth.

Assuming that the two persons whose stomachs I had under examination ate breakfast at the same table and time and partook of the same breakfast substantially, the difference in the time of their deaths—assuming the digestion to have gone on naturally in both cases—the difference would be somewhere in the neighborhood of an hour and a half, more or less.

Digestion stops at death. It stops so far as the expulsion of food from the stomach is concerned. There is a sort of digestion that goes on *after* death in which the stomach wall itself is partially digested. Taking all the facts as I've heard them and also the examinations that I made myself, taking all those circumstances that I regard as important—the difference in the period of digestion, both stomach and intestinal, the drying of the blood and the temperature of the body—I should think that one corroborated the other, that they all tended to the same conclusion as to the difference in time of death of the two people.

And that conclusion is an hour and a half, more or less.

11: CANNES—1890

They left for the Riviera on August 26, a Wednesday, and although they arrived at the rail station a full hour before the scheduled departure of the express, there were nonetheless great crowds milling about, and the consequent confusion Alison claimed was to be expected at *any* French terminus.

"These people cannot *bear* to see any member of the family departing without arranging a bon voyage gathering of monstrous proportions," she said as they waited in line to purchase their tickets. "One witnesses what appears to be a general exodus caused by a revolution or a plague, only to discover that but a sole member of the family is leaving, and the rest are here en masse only to wave the pilgrim tearfully on his way."

They nonetheless managed to have their luggage weighed and tagged, and were walking leisurely toward their *wagon-lit* by a quarter of eleven, fifteen minutes before the scheduled departure. "During the season, of course, one can take a train direct from *London*," Alison said, "but I assure you this is by far the best time of the year to enjoy the pleasures the Riviera has to offer." The journey to Marseilles, she said, would occupy the better part of fifteen hours, and from thence to Cannes yet another four. If all went well, they should arrive at the villa sometime before lunch tomorrow, "A tiring enough trip, but *imagine*, dear Lizzie, what it was like for us *before* they put on sleeping cars only seven years ago!"

They entered the car at one end of it, stepping into an enclosed vestibule and then walking past the ladies' dressing room, its door open to reveal a water closet and a lavatory over which was hanging a mirror that reflected yet another mirror on the wall opposite. There were four divided compartments opening off the corridor, two of them containing single berths, the remaining two fitted with seats that converted into double berths at night. Their own double compartment was at the far end of the corridor, near the gentlemen's lavatory and water closet. It was not quite so commodious as Lizzie's shipboard accommodations had been, but it was nonetheless carpeted and richly appointed, its plush-upholstered seats comfortably enclosed by wood-paneled walls, its large windows affording a splendid view of the French countryside.

Some three miles outside of Paris, they passed Charenton ("Where the loonies are kept," Alison remarked drily) and did not stop for the first time—and then for only five minutes—until they reached Melun, some twenty-eight miles further on. The train rolled into the valley of the Seine, lushly verdant in the bright August sunshine. They took their lunch, and later their dinner, in the elaborately decorated restaurant car. Night had fallen upon the countryside. Outside there were only the lights in the farmhouses now, and then not even those. They were both ready to retire long before their train pulled into Tonnere.

An attendant miraculously transformed their seats into the bed upon which they would sleep that night, rotating the seats a full 180 degrees upon their axes so that they formed a berth at right angles to the route of travel, the bedclothes already upon it and enclosed in a stout oiled silk that prevented them from slipping to the floor. As the attendant made up their bed, first Alison and then Lizzie—both wearing their daytime garments, and reluctant to traipse down the corridor in nightdresses and robes—separately went to the ladies' dressing room. When Lizzie returned to the compartment, Alison was lying naked on the bed.

261

She closed the door quickly behind her, realizing with a start that she had never seen her friend completely disrobed before this moment; in the Paris hotel, there had been the vast *salle de bain*, and Alison had always retreated there when performing her nighttime and morning toilettes. She was rather more beautiful nude than Lizzie could have guessed. The only light in the compartment came from an electrified lamp over the bed, diffused by a translucent rose-colored shade. Her blond hair was spread loose on the pillow under her head. Her eyes were closed, her exquisite face utterly serene. She lay in repose with her arms at her sides, her slender body softly illuminated, her breasts rather larger than she had demeaningly described them, the aureoles and nipples a pale pink softened by the rosy glow of the overhead lamp. The hair at the joining of her long legs seemed extravagantly lush, a wild golden garden—Lizzie looked away, and turned to lock the door behind her.

"Forgive me," she said.

"Whatever on earth for?" Alison asked.

"I didn't mean to . . . waken you."

"I wasn't asleep."

Lizzie had still not turned from the door.

"Are you having trouble with that dicey lock?" Alison asked.

"No, it seems to be secure now."

"Then hurry to bed," Alison said, "or we shall have precious little sleep before the thunder and bellow of Marseilles. You'll find it a trifle stuffy in here, I don't think you shall need a nightdress. We might do best, in fact, to sleep without a cover."

Lizzie turned from the door. Without so much as glancing again at Alison, she clicked off the lamp over the bed, undressed in the dark, and then—despite Alison's suggestion—pulled a nightdress over her head.

She felt quite warm and flushed lying beside Alison in the dark, the wheels of the train clattering beneath them, but she did not remove the nightdress. When the train roared into the Marseilles station sometime in the empty hours of the night, she was drenched in perspiration, and wondered if she might be suffering a relapse.

They had telegraphed ahead from Paris, but the Newbury coachman was not waiting at the Cannes railroad station for

262

them and Alison was beside herself with anger. She engaged a porter to carry their luggage to a waiting carriage, snapping her fingers imperiously, shouting instructions in rapid French, and then settling back beside Lizzie and sighing deeply as the carriage got under way.

"I can never stay agitated for long in this delightful spot," she said. "The telegram must have gone astray, wouldn't you say? I shouldn't put it past the French. Either that, or there was some sort of domestic crisis which that financial *wizard* was unable to resolve." She was referring, of course, to Albert. Lizzie wondered, suddenly, if she spoke of him in this fashion to all her *other* friends.

"You shall find the town utterly deserted," Alison said. "Even the cheaper hotels and pensions here near the railway station are abandoned during the summertime." The carriage was passing a garden-enclosed establishment with a sign advising that it was the Pension Mon Plaisir. "'My *Pleasure*,' indeed," Alison said. "It's probably crawling with vermin and lice. You'll find your better hotels fronting the beach east and west of the town center, although some visitors prefer the ones inland, which are less conducive to wakefulness—did you sleep well last night, Lizzie?"

"Restlessly," Lizzie said.

"Ah, yes, the compartment *was* close, wasn't it? Beachfront or hillside, you shall find them *all* moribund at this time of year. The moment there are lilacs in England, don't you know, it's simply *time* to go home. Never mind the fact that London often has *snow* in May. And the *instant* the British depart, of course, the links and the tennis courts and the casino and most of the restaurants shut down tighter than crypts. Which is exactly how I prefer them. I *love* it here during the summertime!"

The air was indeed balmy at this late hour of the morning, and the scent of oranges wafted in through the open carriage windows as they made their way slowly through the town center and then began moving steadily inland on a gradually sloping road, leaving the broad blue stripe of the Mediterranean behind them. Higher and higher they climbed. "Their villas are scattered all about town," Alison said. "The Duke of Albany's, who died six years ago, the Villa Edelweiss, owned by Mr. Saville and visited by the queen—when was it? 1887? Well, quite

263

recently at any rate. The Rothschild villa, and Lord Brougham's—we passed his statue on the Allées de la Liberté, did you notice it? Between the Hôtel de Ville and the Splendide? He died two years ago, but he's the acknowledged founder of modern-day Cannes. Before him the place was an insignificant little fishing village—oh, would that it were again! That was back in 1834, dear Lizzie, long before either you or I were born. We're almost there, be patient, I know the ride is bumpy."

It seemed at first that they were only moving further inland, yet more distant from the sea. The woods through which the road wound were white with myrtle, scattered here and there with the vibrant red of geraniums. They passed through a stand of pines, and then a copse of tropical growth that ended abruptly against an escarpment of vine-covered rock. The carriage turned a bend around the boulders, and Lizzie caught a glimpse of the cobalt sea again, glistening with pinpoint pricks of sunlight, framed with a dense and fragrant white floral growth that began again on the southern side of the rock formation. The carriage rounded another turn in the road, the horse struggling with the steep incline, and suddenly she saw the house.

Where Alison's home in London had seemed a pile of structured gray granite softened only somewhat by the Grecian-style columns supporting the entrance portico, Lizzie saw now a low and sprawling array of interconnected stucco buildings, painted a white that blindingly reflected the rays of the sun. Tropical plants grew low against the walls, vines climbed toward the sun, the exotic fragrance of alien blooms wafted through the open carriage windows and mingled with the aroma of dust to create an oddly heady scent.

"Kensington is Albert's," Alison murmured beside her. "*This is mine.*"

The cabman stepped down and opened the carriage doors on either side for them. The thick entrance doors to the villa were set back in a shadowed arch and fashioned of a pale wood diagonally joined, studded with great black iron bolts and strapped with massive black hinges. The doors were wide open, and through them Lizzie could see a tiled interior court with a tiled center fountain and surrounding beds of flowers, small blooming trees in tubs and tiled columns supporting a gallery that ran clear around the upper story. A vagrant breeze idled through the courtyard as they entered, carrying on it the unmistakably salty aroma of the sea.

And now came Moira, dressed quite differently here in the south of France than she had been in London, wearing a full white skirt and petticoats, a lace-edged blouse and an apron embroidered in reds and blues and yellows that echoed the blooms everywhere in the courtyard.

"Miz Newbury, mum," she said, beaming, "welcome! We've missed you," and curtsied, and shouted "George! Come see to the luggage! Welcome, Miss Borden," she said, and curtsied again, and then picked up her skirts and went clattering over the tiled floor, disappearing through an arched doorway, shouting "George!" as she went.

"Come," Alison said proudly. "Let me show you."

More arched doorways at the far end of the courtyard opened onto a terrace floored with orange tiles, and beyond that was the most luxuriant garden Lizzie had ever seen, blooming with jasmine and sunflowers, fuchsias and nasturtiums, chrysanthemums and dahlias, zinnias, asters and other flowers that were entirely strange to her but that spread a fragrant scent on the air. The garden sloped off onto a vast grassy lawn which the Newbury gardener, wearing a French workman's blue smock, was watering down with a hose. Beyond the garden and the lawn, far below, was the pristine sea. The sky above it was a paler cloudless blue. The air was balmy; it kissed her face and caused a smile to appear on her mouth.

"Ah, there's my husband," Alison said, and called, "Albert! No welcome? After all your fussing, I should have expected a band, at least."

He was sitting in a wicker chair in the sun, reading an English-language newspaper, wearing white trousers and shirt, white shoes and a straw hat with an overly large brim. "Well, well," he said, putting down the newspaper and rising. "Better late than never, eh?"

"*Never* might have been more appropriate as regards George," Alison said. "Where was he? Didn't you receive my telegram?"

"George has sprained his ankle," Albert said, coming to where they were standing. "More than likely in pursuit of these comely Cannois virgins. You'll be fortunate if he can struggle your luggage into the house." He kissed his wife perfunctorily on the cheek, took Lizzie's hand, lowered his lips to it and said, "Was your journey a pleasant one?" Without waiting for a reply, he said, "You look terribly pale, Lizzie, we shall have to set you out in the sun. Cook has been gone all morning," he said to Alison, "haggling with these French brigands over tonight's meal. Her French leaves something to be desired, to say the least. You must inform her that there is no such thing as a neuter article in this beastly language, and that the locals take offense at her casual intermingling of the 'le' and 'la.' So then, have you had lunch? I know cook has prepared a cold tray, and I'm famished myself, having spent an energetic morning reading this sorry excuse for a newspaper. Shall I ask Moira to set it out while you both change into something more suitable to the climate? You shall suffocate in those heavy garments. Breathe in deeply of the sea air, Lizzie. I'm told it does wonders for all the cripples and invalids who make their permanent residence here. Will you show Lizzie to her room? I know Moira spent all morning tidying it. There should be fresh lemonade in a carafe on the bedstand, though I fear ice is a virtual impossibility here—as it is in England as well. I know how terribly fond of ice you Americans are. Well, do get hopping, both of you, or I shall die of starvation."

"Oh, how *forceful* you are!" Alison said, rolling her eyes. "Come, Lizzie, before he gets *truly* cross. He's a bear when he's hungry."

They came through the courtyard again—she noticed for the first time that several of the tubbed trees were lemon trees—and climbed a curving flight of tiled steps to the gallery above. There were orchids hanging in clay pots everywhere, and Alison stopped at several of them, examining the blooms, nodding in apparent approval of the gardener's care. On the western end of the gallery, overlooking the gardens and the lawn and the sea far below, she led Lizzie first into the master bedroom and then opened a connecting door in an archway, and showed Lizzie the room she would be occupying.

As promised, a carafe of lemonade stood on the bedstand, its pale yellow echoing the color of the spread on the bed and the cushions on the chairs. The windows were wide open to the air outside. A tiny spider tirelessly spun a glistening web in the branches of the orange tree just outside the window. There was the overpowering scent of the oranges themselves and the muskier fragrance of the flowers in the garden, and saturating all, the omnipresent aroma of the sea.

"We shall be right next door to each other," Alison said, "should you need anything. Please feel free to wander wherever you choose. The house isn't quite so cavernous as the one in London, and you won't get lost, I'm certain. The idea, of course, was to keep it spacious and airy, and I think Geoffrey has succeeded admirably, don't you?"

"Did *he* design it?" Lizzie asked, surprised.

"Down to the last nail," Alison said.

"And the furnishings and decorations?"

"I take full responsibility for those. Had I left it to Albert, we should have had a replica of our London mausoleum, as so many people here do. I took the matter into my own . . ."

"I thought the London house was beautiful," Lizzie said.

"Well, thank you, you must be sure to tell Albert. I wanted something more fanciful here though—bright and cheerful and gay. Why does one *come* to the Riviera, after all, if not for the sun and the sense of freedom it allows? On Sundays, when the lot of them are gone, you'll find me lying shamelessly naked on the lawn. We're quite protected from prying eyes here, and with the servants away, who is there to comment on the pagan manners of the mistress? You *must* feel free to dress however casually you wish during your stay here. I myself favor white with a touch of embroidery here and there—you saw Moira's apron? Undoubtedly purchased from a shrewd French peasant who charged the sky for it. You need not worry about petticoats or frills or even *shoes*, for that matter. I wander about barefoot more often than not—but *do* be careful of bees in the clover! And you must be careful as well to wear something long sleeved at dusk, lest the mosquitoes devour you alive. They're dreadful here, the size of falcons and as bloodthirsty as vampires. In town, of course, we shall have to appear the proper *ladies*, but here at the villa we may set aside any notions of convention or formality or custom or even time. I'm inviting you, in short, to abandon yourself completely to the sun and the sea and the fragrant air and to feel, dear Lizzie, as perfectly at home here as I myself am."

267

"Thank you," Lizzie said softly. "I don't think I've gone about barefoot since I was a little girl."

"Exactly the point, my dear. Barefooted, bare-arsed, however you wish—and please don't blush."

"I'm long past blushing at *anything* you say," Lizzie said, and smiled.

"Good. Let's change our clothes and hurry down to lunch before Albert eats the tablecloth. If you haven't packed anything suitably hedonistic, just give a shout, and I shall try to fit you out. You won't have time for a proper bath, but there should be hot water in the basin there, if Moira's properly prepared the room. We shall have good French wine with our lunch, so I'd ignore the tepid lemonade, were I you. You can find your way down to the terrace, can't you? I shall meet you there. Lizzie," she said, and hesitated. "I'm so happy you're here."

"And I," Lizzie said.

In the evening they sat on the terrace in a circle of illumination provided by the oil lamps, and listened to the chatter of the insects in the grass and in the surrounding woods. The oil had been liberally laced with citronella, and its scent hovered on the air, though Lizzie wasn't certain it was having much effect on the mosquitoes. She had been bitten twice since dinner time, once on the ankle and another time—*through* her skirt—on the thigh. Albert avuncularly warned her not to scratch the bites as that would only irritate them further. He himself seemed immune to attack. "My meat's too sour for them," he explained. "They prefer the sweeter stuff. Besides, I'm English."

"He's complimenting you, I believe," Alison said.

"I am," Albert said, and filled their glasses with wine again.

It had grown colder than she expected it would. The afternoon sun had been so deliciously hot, but now she felt the slightest bit chilled in the night air, even though she had thrown a shawl over her shoulders. Alison, on the other hand, showed not the slightest sign of discomfort, though she was wearing only a wide peasant skirt and embroidered blouse; for all her warnings about the fearsome mosquitoes, she was barefooted, and the blouse was sleeveless.

"We've been invited to lunch at the Ashtons on Sunday," Albert said.

"I hope you declined," Alison said.

"I certainly did *not*," Albert said. "I rather fancy Mildred. Besides, it'll be my last day here."

"Your last day? What on earth do you mean?"

"I'm off to Berlin on Monday."

"You will have to go alone then," Alison said.

"I hadn't *expected* you to attend a business . . ."

"I meant to the Ashtons. Lizzie and I shall be taking the sun. I refuse to give up my one day of solitude for the sake of listening to Mildred blather on about the latest Parisian fashions."

"I've already begged off for you *twice*," Albert said, "awaiting your . . ."

"You will simply have to beg off for me *again* then, won't you?" Alison said. "You can explain that I'm caring for a convalescent friend. Benjamin should quite understand convalescence. He's been convalescing from asthma for as long as I've known him."

"There'll be some Russians, I'm told."

"I can do without Russians as well," Alison said. "Did you want to meet some Russians, Lizzie?"

"Well, I . . ."

"I'm sure you wouldn't enjoy *that* sober lot, nattering on in *dreadful* English. I should sooner listen to the drone of the mosquitoes."

"They *do* seem out in force tonight," Albert said. "Are you being eaten, Lizzie?"

"Not at the moment," Lizzie said.

"Good, perhaps the bloody citronella's working. I have no faith in it myself. So what shall I tell them?"

"I've already *told* you what to tell them."

"They'll want to meet her. They *swarm* about Americans, you know."

"Not *this* American," Alison said. "Unless, of course . . . how rude of me, Lizzie. Do you think you *might* enjoy lunch with the Ashtons? They're just down the road; you saw the roof of their villa on the approach. It's grandly called La Villa Bella, in the Italian fashion—I believe there *is* some Italian in her, isn't there, Albert? Away back somewhere? Lord knows she speaks it as an Indian elephant might, but I'm sure I heard that her grandfather

269

or her great-*great*-grandfather—well, who *cares*, really? Lizzie, forgive me, of *course* we shall lunch with the Ashtons this Sunday. And Albert, we must show her the town tomorrow, and perhaps take her to Monte Carlo on Saturday night—have you ever gambled, Lizzie?"

"No, never."

"It can be fun," Alison said.

"Only if you win," Albert said.

"Even if you lose," Alison said. "When did you say you were leaving for Germany?"

"On the first. This coming Monday."

"How thoughtless of you! You *know* we shall be needing an escort. How long will you be gone this time?"

"Through most of September."

"My, my, there must be *millions* involved."

"I wish," Albert said.

"Well, dear, do make scads and scads of money," Alison said.

"I think I'll go up to bed now," Albert said. "Will you be coming along soon?"

"In a bit."

"Excuse me then," he said, rising. "I hope your bites stop annoying you," he said to Lizzie. "We have some sort of salve, don't we, Allie? You might let her have some before she retires."

"I don't know of any salve," Alison said.

"Ask cook, she'll know," Albert said. "Good night, Lizzie. You'll enjoy the Ashtons, they're . . ."

"He can be *so* persuasive," Alison said, and rolled her eyes.

"They're not a bad lot, actually," he said, and sighed. "Well then, good night. You'll do with a blanket, Lizzie. It'll get even more chilly during the night." He hesitated, seemed about to say something more, and then simply left the terrace and walked into the courtyard. She could hear his footsteps on the stairway leading to the courtyard gallery.

"I shall be glad to see him gone," Alison said.

Despite Alison's promises of a largely deserted out-of-season resort, Lizzie had expected the town to be somewhat more bustling than she found it to be. Even the flower market was a disappointment, although Albert grudgingly admitted that the variety offered here was more extensive than was to be found at

Nice's similar market—"Although Nice is a great deal livelier on the whole, which may be why the Prince of Wales much prefers it."

"Perhaps the prince finds the Niçoises *cocottes* more to his liking," Alison said, and glanced sidelong at him.

"Well, you'll find the *demi-mondaine* here as well, I'm sure," Albert said.

"Though not in such overwhelming numbers," Alison said.

"Well, wherever there are men on the loose . . ." Albert said, and let the sentence trail.

They were walking in brilliant sunshine through the Old Town now, heading for the breakwater and the port. Everywhere about them, there were Frenchmen in shirtsleeves, sitting in the sunshine and sipping beer at gaily painted tables. Lizzie had expected the women to be wearing traditional Provençal costumes, but again she was disappointed. In the Fall River Library, she had thumbed through volume after volume with full-color drawings of women in chintz skirts stitched with intricate geometric or floral designs, women in needle-quilted cretonne, women wearing printed shawls and black hats and white aprons. Here, instead, the women scurried along in cheap models of fashionable Parisian dresses, wearing artificial silk stockings and high heels, bangled like gypsies and sporting pearls Lizzie was certain were fake. As though reading her mind, Alison said, "Gone is the *costume du pays*, more's the pity."

"I hate this place in the summertime," Albert said. "In fact, I don't much care for it at *any* time. To be perfectly honest, France itself—*all* of France—leaves me decidedly cold."

"He much prefers Germany," Alison said, with a smile. "Don't you, Albert?"

"With the Germans one always knows where one stands," Albert said. "The French are a devious lot."

"How fortunate, then, that you'll be leaving for Germany on Monday," Alison said, and again glanced sidelong at him.

"Yes," he said drily.

They came past the casino, closed now, on the east end of the Old Town, and strolled onto the Promenade de la Croisette, palms and plantains everywhere about, and—wafted on the brisk sea air—the scent of a white flower Alison described as a

271

tuberose, native to Mexico, but thriving here in the genial climate. There was the scent of jasmine as well, mysteriously lingering, suffusing the air, the combined aromas as exotic and as lulling as the somnolent town itself. The generous beach behind the casino was dotted with a handful of gaily colored umbrellas, and children in bathing costumes built sand castles and challenged the mild surge of the sea. They walked along the shore to the Restaurant de la Réserve, also closed, and there hired a carriage and pair for which Albert paid the *cocher* twenty francs after haggling him down from the twenty-five he demanded; this was, after all, the summertime.

"Not all of them speak English, you know," Albert said, obviously proud of his bargaining in the native tongue.

"How happy that some of them understand *l'idiome britannique*," Alison said.

"Yes, some of our countrymen *do* fracture the language," Albert answered, blithely unaware of her sarcasm—or perhaps simply ignoring it. Lizzie felt, all at once, that Albert was—for all his exterior bluffness—a very sad man. The thought saddened her as well, and she sat in silence as the carriage made its way along the coastal road to the Golfe Juan, and then up the valley to Vallauris, some two hundred fifty feet above the sea.

The gentle hills were covered with heather.

"Reminds me of home," Albert said, and again Lizzie felt this sense of ineffable sadness about him.

There was mimosa everywhere, growing along the roadside ditches. On foot they crossed a bridge just a little below Massier's pottery and then ascended a broad dusty road to the Observatoire, where they looked out over the Alps and the country about Bordighera toward the coast. There were few visitors beside themselves.

They ate *omelettes aux pommes de terre frites* in a small restaurant in the town itself, forsaking the heavier fare offered at the Observatoire, and although Lizzie was enormously attracted to the flawless quality of the pottery being offered everywhere for sale, she wisely decided that buying any would be risking certain damage on the long journey ahead. She still had no real concept of when she would be rejoining her friends, but surely it would be within a week or so. Alison, after all, had only extended her invitation for a fortnight.

They returned to Cannes via the Corniche, down onto the Boulevard de Californie, and thence to the villa itself. Oddly, for the day had been a leisurely paced and tranquil one, she felt exhausted.

The Russians had been to Monte Carlo the day before.

There were two of them at the Ashton villa that Sunday afternoon. Both of them were titled—one a count, the other a baron. Both were wearing beards and mustaches and white uniforms hung with medals. They both owned villas in Nice, but they had never before visited the Riviera during the summertime. The overseeing of extensive renovations to the count's villa was the cause of their presence here now, at such a "not so gay time," as he put it in his heavily accented English. The count's name was Popov. Lizzie found this amusing, but she managed to hide her mirth behind her fan. He was much more at home in French than he was in English, but in deference to his hostess and the other guests—all of them English, with the exception of Lizzie—he struggled with their language, "so full of too many vords," he said.

The baron's last name was unpronounceable. He suggested to Lizzie that she simply use his given name, Yakovlevich, which she found equally difficult. His English was only a trifle better than Popov's, and he frequently lapsed into French when describing their excursion to Monte Carlo in the "uff sizzon," as he called it.

"There vas so few pipple at *les tables,* you know? Why they are remain open at all is *le grand mystère, n'est-ce pas?* You know?" He had spent a pleasant hour or two shooting pigeons in the company of some Englishmen on the green beneath the casino terrace, and then had returned to the roulette table, where a young woman was in distress over what had just happened to her. "I am sure they have *chitt* her, you know?" he said. "She have lost all but twenty francs. *Elle lui jette les vingt francs* . . . she is throw the money to *le croupier*, and she say, 'Le numéro quatre,' the number four, you know? *Lui, feignant de ne pas entendre* . . . He pretends not to hear, you know? He places her bet instead on *le zéro. La bille venait justement de partir*. The ball has already start to go, yes? The lady says she does not understand. *Le croupier, avec un geste de mauvaise humeur* . . . he is in a bad temper now, the *croupier*, and so he push the piece *au numéro quatre*, to the number four, as she wishes. *Au même instant, son collègue* . . . in the same time, his colleague announces *le zéro*, where the ball has stop."

"Why, they were trying to *help* her, not *cheat* her!" Albert said, fascinated by the tale.

"You believe so?" the baron said.

"Well, certainly," Albert said. "Everyone *knows* the wheels are manipulated. They have a gadget of some sort under the table, and they have absolute control over the ball."

"It is what I say, no?" the baron said. "They have chitt her. I much prefer *le trente et quarante*, but vhere vas there pipple to play? *Abandonné, monsieur, complètement abandonné.*"

The terrace upon which they sat was the least cluttered spot in the Ashton villa. One would have thought that every stick of furniture, every painting, every piece of bric-a-brac in the brimming drawing room, as Mildred Ashton insisted on calling it, had been transported directly from their London home. Whereas Lizzie had found the jumble in Alison's Kensington house somehow—well, cozy wasn't the proper word . . . enclosing? comforting?—such a decorative scheme seemed entirely out of place here on the Riviera. Equally unsuitable was the fashionable clothing all of the guests wore; Lizzie was beginning to appreciate the more casual costumes, sometimes resembling little more than a petticoat and chemise, Alison wore in her own home. There was a sense of artificiality here, of conversation too polite, of manners too carefully rehearsed, all out of keeping with the brilliance of the sunshine, the distant murmur of the sea, the fragrance of blossoms on the salt-laden air.

Popov was explaining that a countrywoman of his had lived in Nice for a long time, had indeed begun her recently published journal there when she was but a child and "madly in luff" with the Duke of Hamilton. Lizzie realized all at once that he was talking about Marie Bashkirtseff, whose studio Alison had taken her to in Paris. (That incisive face, the disdainful, determined and inquisitive look about the eyes.) Popov was quoting from the published diary now, telling of how Miss Bashkirtseff had once hurled a plate of pasta to the floor and then set fire to a chair, "perhaps vun or *two* chairs," because an expected invitation to a ball had not arrived. "She vas a little bit *dérangée*, I

274

tink," Popov said. "She writes one time . . . wrote? . . . about she runs to throw a clock in the sea. *Fou, sans aucun doute, n'est-ce pas?* But, oh, how she luffs this Nice! She says, 'Nice is my country. Nice made me to grow. Nice gaves to me the health and the beautiful *couleur. C'est magnifique, Nice.'"*

After lunch, which had been served rather late, the men retired to a room of the villa Mildred had set aside for her husband's "enjoyment of cigars," and the ladies sat alone on the terrace and asked Lizzie innumerable questions about America and about her recent visit to Paris, and seemed charmed by every word she uttered. They were properly sympathetic when they learned of her bout with influenza ("A horrid disease," Mildred said) and agreed that a little time in the sun here would do wonders for her.

"But you're so *fair*, Miss Borden," one of the ladies said. "Won't you burn to a crisp? With your complexion and that red hair? She has beautiful hair, hasn't she, Alison?"

"Yes," Alison said.

She had been oddly quiet throughout the afternoon, offering little by way of comment, her usual garrulity strangely checked, her spirited sarcasm entirely and mysteriously absent.

"Your American friends are *always* so lovely and charming," Mildred said, and Lizzie at once thought extravagant praise was surely a British trait, and then wondered how *many* American friends Alison had, and how many of them had been brought here for luncheon at the Ashtons.

The men returned from their port and cigars, the afternoon lingered, the sunset over the sea was spectacular. It was not until they returned to the villa that Lizzie realized she had been bored witless by the Ashtons and all their guests, including the Russians in their dairymen uniforms and their dime-store medals.

12: NEW
BEDFORD—1893

"**Your** name?"

"James E. Winwood."

"You are an undertaker?"

"Yes, sir."

"Did you have charge of the funeral of Andrew J. Borden and his wife?"

"I did."

"While you were preparing Mr. Borden's body for the grave, did you observe whether or not he had any ring upon his finger?"

"I cannot remember positively now. I cannot remember positively."

"Did you see him have any ring upon his finger while you were having anything to do with him?"

"I cannot remember so long ago."

Ah, but Lizzie could remember longer ago than that, could recall in vivid detail that summer of 1890 when in Alison's beautifully cluttered drawing room they had taken tea and laughed away the lengthening shadows of dusk. She had told her about the ring then, how she had returned it to her beau, and how it had come back in the mail not three days later.

"Did you return the ring yet another time?" Alison had asked.

"No."

"You certainly didn't throw it away, did you? Gold?"

"I gave it to my father. He still wears it."

"Dr. Bowen, I wish to know if—after you had given Miss Borden the bromo caffeine on Thursday—you had occasion to prescribe for her on account of mental distress and nervous excitement?"

"Yes, sir."

"When was it?"

"Friday."

"The next day?"

"Friday night. At bedtime."

"Was the prescription of medicine the same as the other?"

"It was different."

"What was it?"

"Sulfate of morphine."

"Well, what is commonly called morphine?"

"Yes, sir."

"You directed morphine to be taken?"

"Yes, sir."

"In what doses?"

"One-eighth of a gram."

Lizzie watched as Marianna Holmes entered the witness box and was sworn in. She had known the woman for the better part of her life, and had gone to the same school as her daughters. At the Central Congregational Church, she and Mrs. Holmes were both members of the Christian Endeavor Society, and though they were not engaged together in many church activities—Mrs. Holmes was a member of the Sunday school Bible class, whereas Lizzie taught in the Chinese department—they nonetheless served on the same board at Fall River's Good Samaritan Hospital. She was fond of the older woman, and seeing her now recalled for Lizzie a happier, less complicated time. Mrs. Holmes took her hand from the Bible, sat and then turned her attention to Jennings, who asked the preliminary questions that identified her to the jury.

277

"Now, tell us, Mrs. Holmes," he said, "anything you can about Lizzie's conduct at the funeral, more particularly in relation to the dead body of her father."

"I pray Your Honors' judgment," Knowlton said.

"I will withdraw the question," Jennings said. "Mrs. Holmes, were you there on the day of the funeral?"

"I was."

"What day was it?"

"On Saturday, August the sixth."

"Forenoon or afternoon?"

"Forenoon."

"About what time?"

"Eleven, I think."

"Before the funeral began, did Miss Lizzie go down to see her father's remains?"

"Wait a minute," Knowlton said. "I pray Your Honors' judgment."

"Assuming the question to be preliminary only," Mason said, "it may be answered."

"Please state your question again."

"Before the funeral began, did Miss Lizzie go down to see her father's remains?"

"She did."

"Where were they?"

"In the sitting room."

"Were they in the casket?"

"They were."

"Prepared for burial?"

"They were."

"Both bodies in the same room?"

"They were."

"What did Miss Lizzie do after she went down into the room?"

"Pray Your Honors' judgment," Knowlton said.

"Exclude the question," Mason said.

"Now, Mrs. Holmes," Jennings said, "just pay attention to the question which I ask you, and do not attempt to answer anything else except that particular question. On the Saturday morning two days after the murder, did Lizzie Borden come

278

downstairs into the room where her father's body was lying prepared for burial?"

"She did."

"And did she go to the casket?"

"She did."

"In your presence?"

"Yes, sir."

"When she was viewing her father, did she shed tears?"

"She did."

"Did she *kiss* her father?"

"She did."

On Saturday, I doubled the dose of sulfate of morphine to one-quarter of a gram . . .

"Miss Russell, how long did you remain at the Borden house after the day of the murder—homicide?"

"I went there when I was called, and I came away the next Monday morning. I occupied what was Mr. and Mrs. Borden's room Thursday and Friday nights. Saturday and Sunday nights, I occupied Miss Emma's room."

"Were you there on Saturday, August sixth, when the officers went all over that house, over and over again?"

"Yes, sir."

"Was there any part of it they didn't examine?"

"I don't know. I didn't go round with the officers."

"How long were they there on that business?"

"They were to come at three. I don't know what time they got through."

"Didn't they come just as soon as the funeral party went from the house?"

"There were some came."

"What hour was the funeral?"

"I don't remember."

"Wasn't the funeral in the forenoon?"

"Yes, I think so."

"Eleven o'clock or so?"

"I think so. I'm not sure. Eleven or twelve."

"You know the location of the cemetery where Mr. and Mrs. Borden were buried?"

"Yes, sir."

"About how far is that from the house?"

"I don't know."

"Did you go to the cemetery?"

"No, sir."

"You remained in the house?"

"Yes, sir."

"Who else remained there?"

"Well, I think the undertaker's assistants and Mrs. Holmes."

"Miss Lizzie went to the cemetery?"

"Yes, sir."

"Now, didn't the officers come right into the house as quick as the funeral party went, and search everything about the house in her absence?"

"No, sir."

"*Didn't* they come in during that time?"

"Yes, sir."

"And they made searches."

"They made a search, but they didn't search *everywhere*. They went into her room, I think one of the officers took the keys that lay on the bureau after Miss Lizzie had left, and unlocked one or two drawers in her bureau, and didn't search any further there. I think they opened what she called her toilet room, pulled the portiere to one side, just looked there a little. I don't know how much they searched. I don't think very much. And they went into Miss Emma's room and looked around, and opened the cupboard door in her room, and I remember one of the officers pressing against a bundle after he shut it, some pillow or blanket, something of that kind. And the bed was taken to pieces. That's all that I saw."

And now, Lizzie knew, they would go on and on about her dresses. Trying to determine which dress she was wearing on the morning of August 4, when all was confusion following the murders. Trying to determine whether or not there had been blood on any of the clothing in her possession. Whether, too, there had been paint stains on one of those dresses.

The paint stains were important.

She watched as Assistant Marshal Fleet came to the stand again, dressed in civilian clothing as he'd been last August, he

280

of the sloping brow and sparse hair, narrow eyes that appeared on the verge of tears, though certainly they were not, an unkempt shaggy mustache that hid his mouth almost entirely, a high collar and simple dark neck scarf. Robinson had once mentioned to her that a good lawyer never asked a question to which he did not already know the answer—though he himself had been surprised earlier by Officer Mullaly's testimony about yet another part of the disputed hatchet handle. She herself did not expect any surprises from Fleet now. Her mind wandered as he testified that he'd arrived at the house on that Saturday, August 6, just after the funeral procession had left . . .

The two hearses and eleven hacks made their way slowly toward the Oak Grove cemetery, an ivy wreath on her father's bier, a bouquet of white roses and fern leaves bound with a white satin ribbon on her stepmother's. Inside the house, they had lain within their caskets as if entirely at peace, the mutilated portions of their heads turned so that the cuts could not be noticed.

"Did you examine all the dresses that you found there?"

"We looked at them, yes, sir."

Immense crowds of people lined the streets. As the procession moved slowly along North Main in the hot August sun, Lizzie—sitting with her sister in the first hack behind the hearses—saw many of her father's friends and associates raising their hats in respect.

"Did you see, either in that closet or in any other closet in the house, or *anywhere* in the house, a dress with marks of paint upon it?"

"No, sir."

Several hundred people stood about the cemetery grounds, awaiting the burial. A dozen policemen kept the crowds back. No one in the funeral party left the carriages during the ceremonies save for the pallbearers, her Uncle John and the officiating clergy.

"Did you find any blood upon any dress? Did you find anything that looked like blood or any discoloration of any kind?"

"No, sir."

Fleet rose ponderously and stepped down from the witness box. She heard State Police Officer Seaver called. She watched him approaching the stand. She watched him as he placed his hand on the Bible.

At the cemetery, Reverend Buck opened his Bible and began reading.

"'I am the resurrection and the life; he who believes in me, though he die, yet shall he live, and whoever lives and believes in me shall never die. Do you believe this?' She said to him, 'Yes, Lord, I believe that you are the Christ, the Son of God, he who is coming into the world.'"

"I commenced on the hooks and took each dress," Seaver was saying, "with the exception of two or three in the corner, and passed them to Captain Fleet—he being near the window—and he examined them as well as myself, he more thoroughly than myself."

". . . went and called her sister Mary, saying quietly, 'The Teacher is here and is calling for you.' And when she heard it, she rose quickly and went to him . . ."

"I did not discover anything upon any of those dresses."

"When Jesus saw her weeping, and the Jews who came with her also weeping, he was deeply moved in spirit and troubled; and he said, 'Where have you laid him?'"

"I did not see a light blue dress, diamond spots upon it, and paint around the bottom of the dress and on its front."

And now Captain Desmond was on the stand, telling of his part in the search of the house that Saturday, and in her mind's eye she saw the Reverend Dr. Adams standing beside the graves and praying for the spiritual guidance of all, and the inclination of all to submit to divine control, praying that justice would overtake the wrong that had been done and that those who were seeking to serve the ends of justice might be delivered from mistake, be helped to possess all mercifulness, as well as all righteousness, and praying at last that all might be delivered from the dominion of evil.

"Did you see anything that attracted your attention with reference to any dress?"

"No, sir," Desmond answered.

"Did you see any dress that was soiled with paint or with spots of any sort?"

"No, sir."

On that day of the funeral a telegram from Boston informed the police that they should not allow the bodies to be buried. Following instructions they returned both caskets to the hearses and then moved them into a receiving tomb.

Her sister Emma was dressed entirely in black.

282

There was a buzz of excitement in the courtroom as she walked toward the witness box, took off her glove and placed her hand on the extended Bible. Her face appeared tranquil, her pale white complexion only faintly tinged with a pink blush as she took the oath in a low, firm voice, and then replaced the glove on her left hand. There was a look of sadness, almost resignation, Lizzie thought, in her large brown eyes.

That her sister would stand by her, she had not the slightest doubt. Watching her she felt an all but irresistible urge to cross to where she was sitting, take her in her arms and hold her close, comfort her as she herself had been comforted by Emma after the death of their mother all those years ago. It was Emma who'd told her that on her deathbed, their mother had extracted a promise that she would always watch over Baby Lizzie, as she'd called her. Emma, as part of that obligation, had insisted on paying half the costs of the trial, a heavy burden she need not have assumed.

She was saying now that she was Emma L. Borden, that she was the sister of Miss Lizzie Borden. She was saying she had lived at the house on Second Street for twenty-one years at the time of the murders. She and her sister had always lived there with their father and Mrs. Borden. She told how she had been in Fairhaven when she received Dr. Bowen's telegram, and had come home, of course, as soon as she could, arriving on that Thursday of the murders at about five o'clock.

She said that she had made a search for the note her step-mother was said to have received that day.

"I looked in a little bag that she carried downstreet with her sometimes, and in her little workbasket," she said. "I didn't find it."

She told how she had caused a search to be made for the supposed writer of the note.

"I think there was an advertisement put into the paper by my authority. In the *News*. The *News* is a newspaper of large circulation in Fall River. It was there for some time, I think several days, perhaps. It requested the one that carried it," she said. "I think it referred to the messenger. I don't know. I didn't see the advertisement."

And then Jennings asked her about the ring.

"My father wore a ring upon his finger," she said. "It was the only article of jewelry he ever wore. He received the ring from my sister Lizzie . . . I should think ten or fifteen years before his death, I can't tell you accurately."

Their eyes met. Emma's brown and appearing moist now. Lizzie's gray and blinking to hold back tears.

"Previous to his wearing it, she had worn it," Emma said. "After it was given to him, he wore it always." She paused. "It was upon his finger at the time he was buried."

The courtroom was utterly still.

"Have you an inventory, Miss Emma," Jennings asked, "of the clothes that were in the clothes closet on Saturday afternoon, the time of the search?"

"I have of the dresses."

"Of the dresses, very well," Jennings said. "You *were* there on the afternoon of the search?"

"I was."

"Did you or Miss Lizzie at any time during that search Saturday afternoon, furnish any assistance to the officers?"

"We both together went to the attic to assist them about opening a trunk."

"Did you or Miss Lizzie, so far as you know, at any time make any objection whatever to the searching of any part of that house?"

"Not the slightest."

"Or of anything in it?"

"Not the slightest objection."

"Did you assist them in any way you could?"

"By telling them to come as often as they pleased and search as thorough as they could."

"Now, then, Miss Emma, do you know how many dresses were in there that afternoon?"

"I do. Somewhere about eighteen or nineteen."

"And whose were those dresses?"

"All of them belonged to my sister and I except one that belonged to Mrs. Borden."

"How many of those dresses were blue dresses or dresses in which blue was a marked color?"

"Ten."

"To whom did these belong?"

"Two of them to me and eight to my sister."

284

"Now, without telling me what I said, did I communicate to you or to your sister, Miss Lizzie, what Marshal Hilliard said in regard to the search of the upper portions of the house, as to whether it was completed or not?"

"You did, Mr. Jennings."

"And when was that?"

"Saturday afternoon."

"Then I will ask you to state what it was I said to Miss Lizzie and yourself about the completeness of the search in the upper part of the house."

"You said everything had been examined, every box and bag."

"Was any exception made?"

"No, sir."

"Was that *after* Marshal Hilliard had taken the dress away or had been given the dress?"

"Yes, sir."

I had asked Mr. Jennings where the dress was that Lizzie Borden wore that day, the day of the homicide. I was then in the room where Mrs. Borden was found upstairs. He went out into the hallway and came back into the room with a dress. I saw the prisoner soon after that in what is called Miss Emma's room, just inside the door, standing and talking with somebody else. By that time I had passed the dress to Dr. Dolan after it was handed to me—the dress, skirt and waist which were presented to me by Mr. Jennings.

The dress was rolled up, and the white skirt was rolled up. I rolled up the dress skirt, underskirt and dress waist with what I call a lounge cover that was taken from the dining room. A green-striped cover. I rolled them up, rolled them in a paper, and tied them up, and Mr. Jennings brought them down onto Main Street. I met him at the corner of the Granite Block, and he passed them over to me. The same bundle I gave to him. After I got possession again, I carried them to my office and passed them over to Dr. Dolan.

"Professor Wood, what was the next thing that you had to do with this matter?"

I received at the police station in Fall River, from Dr. Dolan, a trunk containing a large number of substances—including the white skirt, which is there, and the blue dress skirt and blue dress waist. I later received in Boston from City Marshal Hilliard a box which I have here. It contained this pair of low shoes or ties, and this pair of black stockings.

The bottom of the shoe has certain stains which, so far as you could see from inspection, *might* have been blood stains. But they proved not to be.

And the stockings had no suspicious stains, either.

The blue dress skirt has near the pocket, if I can get it—yes, I have it here, that inner pocket here—a brownish smooch with a part of it I have cut out, and underneath which I have placed a pin in order to note the position of it. It is situated about three inches from the corner of the top of the pocket. In color, that simply resembled or might have been blood.

But upon holding the cloth up to the light it could easily be seen that it did not clog the meshes of the cloth in any way, and probably was not therefore a bloodstain.

But, to be sure, the portion was removed and thoroughly tested and soaked out in order to remove any blood pigment, and found not to be blood.

There was another spot similar to that lower down in the skirt. That was also tested and no blood was detected on it whatever.

Those were the only possible suspicious stains on the whole skirt. I did not determine what those stains were. I simply tested them for blood and found that they were not blood, and went no further. The dress waist was thoroughly examined, and there is not even a suspicion of a blood stain on it.

The white skirt, this one, contains a small blood spot on a line—it is sixteen inches to the left of this line from the placket hole to the bottom of the skirt, and six inches from the bottom of the skirt.

It is this stain here, a portion of which I have cut out, but I have left there about one-quarter or one-third of the complete stain, and it can only be seen by careful inspection. I had to make a larger hole in the cloth in order to avoid removing the whole of the blood spot, it was so small.

This blood spot was about one-sixteenth of an inch in diameter, about the size of the diameter of the head of a small pin—

not a large pin nor a medium-size pin, but a small pin—and it appeared to me to be a little bit more extensive and plainer on the outside of the skirt than on the inside. I don't know as that could be detected now because it has been rubbed so much, but at that time it was perceptible, when the stain was whole.

I examined that, and found it to be a bloodstain.

And the blood corpuscles when examined with a high power of the microscope averaged in measurement 1/3243 of an inch. That is the average measurement within the limits of human blood, and it is therefore consistent with its being a human bloodstain.

"Professor Wood . . . assuming that the placket hole of the skirt had been worn behind, where would that bring the spot of blood?"

"A little to the left of the back."

"When you saw it, it was dried blood?"

"Yes, sir."

"And is the examination of the corpuscle of dried blood satisfactory in determining whether it is human blood or the blood of some other animal?"

"If it is satisfactory at all, it is."

"Yes, if it is satisfactory at all. Are you able to say that this was *not* a spot of blood which might have gotten on from the menstrual flow of the woman?"

"No, sir, I am not."

"It would be entirely consistent with that, would it?"

"Yes, sir, it may have been menstrual blood, or may not, so far as I can determine."

"But it may be consistent with that?"

"Yes, sir."

My full name is John W. Coughlin. I am a physician and surgeon in Fall River. In 1892 I was the mayor of that city, as I am now. On the Saturday evening following the homicide I went to the Borden house with City Marshal Hilliard. As we approached, I saw a large number of people congregated about the house. The sidewalk on the east side some little distance down, both north and to the south, was crowded with people. The middle of the street—there were a large number of people gathered there, and, in fact, it was with great difficulty that we

287

were able to drive through without running some of them down. I notified the marshal that they should be removed. We drove to a police box, he got out of the carriage, and pulled in the box, calling the officers. After coming back from the corner of Fourth and Rodman Streets, we went into the house.

The first person that I saw was Miss Emma Borden. I later talked to Miss Lizzie, Miss Emma, and Mr. Morse in the parlor. Upon taking my seat, as near as I can recall, I said to the family, "I have a request to make of the family, and that is that you remain in the house for a few days, and I believe it would be better for all concerned if you did so."

There was a question arose—I think Miss Lizzie, to the best of my recollection, Miss Lizzie asked me, "Why? Is there anybody in this house suspected?"

"Spoke up earnestly and promptly, did she?" Jennings asked.

"She made that statement," Coughlin said.

"Will you answer my question?"

"He may answer," Mason said.

"She spoke up somewhat excitedly, I should say."

"She did?"

"Yes, sir."

"What was the next thing?"

"Lizzie said, 'I want to know the truth.'"

"Lizzie said so?"

"Yes, sir. And she repeated it, if I remember rightly."

"Before you answered?"

"Yes, sir."

"What did you say?"

"I said, 'I regret, Miss Borden, but I must answer yes, you are suspected.'"

"What did she say?"

"She said, as I now recall it, 'I am ready to go now.'"

"'Or *any* time,' didn't she?"

"I cannot recall that. She may have said it."

"Spoke up earnestly and promptly then, didn't she?"

"It would depend altogether by what you mean 'earnestly and promptly.'"

"I mean what the words mean."

"She replied in a manner you can call earnestly and promptly. There was no hesitation about it."

"That *is* promptly—no hesitation, isn't it? You understand that, don't you?"

"I do, yes, sir."

"Now did she speak earnestly?"

"Well, I would not say she *didn't* speak earnestly."

"What's that?"

"I should say I would *not* say she *didn't* speak earnestly."

"I know you say so. *Did* she speak earnestly?"

"Well, I should say yes. She spoke earnestly so far as the promptness of the question goes."

"Do you know any difference between promptness and earnestness?"

"There is a difference between promptness and earnestness."

"Keeping that distinction in mind, you say she answered you, did she—earnestly?"

"She did, as far as I—"

"What's that?"

"As far as I would be able to determine by her action, she was earnest."

"That's what I asked you—prompt and earnest. What was then said?"

"Miss Emma Borden said, 'Well, we've tried to keep it from her as long as we could.' I then asked Miss Lizzie where she went after leaving her father. She said that she went to the barn for some lead for sinkers. I asked her how long she remained in the barn. She said about twenty minutes. I believe I then said that if the people annoyed them in any way, that they should notify the officer in the yard and instruct him to tell the marshal. On leaving, I think Miss Emma Borden made the statement, 'We want to do everything we can in this matter.' And on leaving, I stated that I would return on Sunday, but I did not, on account of my mother being taken ill. She was out at Stone Bridge, and I was summoned to see her very early in the morning, and didn't get back till late that night."

Sitting there listening as the next witness testified, Lizzie suddenly wondered how the jury could possibly keep track of all this, how these simple country people could possibly hope to understand where all of it was leading.

In the past several hours they had heard more testimony

289

about dresses than any but a dressmaker's assistant had any right to hear, the search for the dresses themselves, the search for blood or paint stains on the dresses, the expert testimony that there had been discovered only a minuscule drop of blood on any of the garments, and *that* possibly menstrual blood—her ears had burned when she'd heard Professor Wood's testimony in so public a place as this. Yet what of all this was the jury retaining?

When it came time for them to deliberate, would they wonder why they had listened, as they did now, to a man named John W. Grouard, who said he was a housepainter, and who further said he had painted the house of Andrew J. Borden at 92 Second Street in May of last year, three months before the murders? Would these twelve men be able to remember the significance of the fact that she herself had been about the premises where the paint was, had indeed supervised the mixing of the paint, looking on to see that it was done properly? Or that she had been standing there beside him when he tried a color sample on the corner of the house near the back steps?

Would these farmers know and understand why John W. Grouard the housepainter had been called by her attorneys to testify?

"I painted the steps and everything connected with the house," he said. "The well house and fence, everything."

My name is Mary A. Raymond. I am a dressmaker. I live at 31 Franklin Street, in Fall River. I have done dressmaking for Miss Lizzie Borden for a number of years. Ten years at the house, and before that at my own home. I also worked for Mrs. Borden—not for Miss Emma—for Mrs. Borden during that time. I worked for her in the same room that I did Miss Lizzie's dresses. At the same time. Both of them were in there at the same time.

A year ago this spring I made some dresses for Miss Lizzie. This was the first week in May. I was there three weeks. One of the dresses was a Bedford cord. I made that the first one. She needed it, needed it to wear, and had it made first. I couldn't tell how long it took to make it, couldn't tell the exact time, but I should think three days.

The dress was a light blue with a dark figure. Quite a light blue. I can't remember the shape of the figure. It was a dark figure, I can't say how large. The dress was made with a blouse waist, and a full skirt, straight widths. The sleeves were full sleeves, large sleeves. The length was longer than she usually had them, I should certainly say a finger longer, two inches longer. I also made a pink wrapper for her at that time. I should think the Bedford cord was longer than the pink wrapper.

"Now what was the material of which this Bedford cord was made?"

"Why, it was a Bedford cord! That was the name of the material."

"Well, I meant as to whether it was cotton or woolen or cheap goods."

"It was cotton, a cheap cotton dress."

"Was it trimmed at all?"

"Trimmed with a ruffle around the bottom."

"A ruffle of what?"

"Of the same."

"Do you know whether or not, at that time you were there, they were painting the house or did paint the house?"

"They did paint the house at the time, yes, sir."

"Do you know anything about whether at that time there was any paint got upon the dress?"

"There was."

"How soon after it was made did Miss Lizzie begin to wear it?"

"Just as soon as it was finished."

"And how soon was it after that, as you recollect, that she got the paint upon it?"

"I can't tell you that. I don't remember."

"Was it while you were there?"

"Oh, yes, sir."

"Was anything said about it by you at the time? To her?"

"Yes, sir."

"Where was the paint, if you recollect?"

"It was on the front of the dress and around the bottom of the dress. Around the ruffle. On the underneath part of the hem."

"Did she wear the dress most or all the time you were there?"

"Yes, sir."

"Do you remember anything about the wearing of it?"

"Well, it either faded or the color wore off, I can't tell you which. It changed color."

"At that time, did she have an *old* wrapper which this was being made to take the place of?"

"Yes, sir."

"Do you remember what she did with the old wrapper?"

"Yes, sir."

"What did she do with it?"

"Wait a minute!" Moody said. "*If* she knows of her own knowledge. I object anyhow."

"The witness is only asked with reference to her own knowledge," Mason said.

"My objection, however, is general. I meant to have put it so."

"She may answer," Mason said.

"Do you know what she did with the old wrapper that this took the place of?"

"She cut some pieces out of it and said she should burn the rest."

Was it beginning to fall into place for them? Lizzie wondered. Was all this testimony about dresses and dressmakers, painters and paint stains, beginning to assume a decipherable form reasoned out by her attorneys well in advance and presented now in a progression of facts so precise that even the dullest farmer might understand them? Or would it all have to wait until the events of that Sunday morning, August the seventh, were related in detail?

Her sister now, her sister again.

"Now, then, Miss Emma, I will ask you if you know of a Bedford cord dress which your sister had at that time."

"I do."

"Won't you describe the dress, tell what kind of a dress it was?"

"It was a blue cotton Bedford cord, very light blue ground with a darker figure about an inch long and, I think, about three-quarters of an inch wide."

"And do you know when she had that dress made?"

"She had it made the first week in May."

"Who made it?"

"Mrs. Raymond, the dressmaker."

292

"Now where was that dress, if you know, on Saturday, August sixth, the day of the search?"

"I saw it hanging in the clothespress over the front entry."

"At what time?"

"I don't know exactly. I think about nine o'clock in the evening. After Mayor Coughlin and Marshal Hilliard had left."

"How came you to see it at that time?"

"I went in to hang up the dress that I had been wearing during the day, and there was no vacant nail, and I searched round to find a nail, and I noticed the dress."

"Did you say anything to your sister about that dress in consequence of your not finding a nail to hang your dress on?"

"I said, 'You haven't destroyed that old dress yet? Why don't you?'"

"Did she say anything in reply?"

"I don't remember."

"What was the condition of that dress at that time?"

"It was very dirty, very much soiled, and badly faded."

"Were you with her Friday and Saturday when she had it on?"

"Almost constantly."

"When did you *next* see that Bedford cord dress?"

"Sunday morning, I think. About nine o'clock."

Jennings nodded. The nod was almost imperceptible, certainly lost on the jury whose attention was focused entirely on Emma. But it was not lost on Lizzie. The nod told her that all the careful preparation would now come to fruition, the mystery of the dresses revealed as if by a magician pulling a paint-stained rabbit out of a torn top hat.

She almost smiled.

"Now will you tell the Court and the jury all that you saw or heard that Sunday morning, August the seventh, in the kitchen?"

"I was washing dishes," Emma said, "and I heard my sister's voice, and I turned round and saw she was standing at the foot of the stove, between the foot of the stove and the dining-room door. This dress was hanging on her arm, and she said, 'I think I shall burn this old dress up.' Do you wish me to go on?"

"Go right along."

"I said, 'Why don't you?' or 'You had better,' or 'I would if I were you,' or something like that—I can't tell the exact words, but it meant 'Do it.' And I turned back and continued washing the dishes, and did not see her burn it, and did not pay any more attention to her at that time."

"Had you been to breakfast before this happened?"

"Yes, sir."

"Who was there at breakfast?"

"Mr. Morse, Miss Russell, my sister and I."

"Do you know where Mr. Morse was at that time?"

"I do not."

"Was Miss Russell there?"

"Yes, sir."

"Do you remember the breakfast on Sunday morning, Miss Russell?"

"No, I do not."

"Who got the breakfast Sunday morning?"

"I got the breakfast."

"After the breakfast had been got and the dishes had been cleared away, did you leave the lower part of the house at all?"

"Yes, sir."

"Afterwards, did you return?"

"Yes, sir."

"About what time in the morning was it when you returned?"

"I don't know."

"Was it before noon?"

"Yes, sir."

"Will you state what you saw after you returned?"

I went into the kitchen, and I saw Miss Lizzie at the other end of the stove. I saw Miss Emma at the sink. Miss Lizzie was at the stove, and she had a skirt in her hand, and her sister turned and said, "What are you going to do?"

"I'm going to burn this old thing up," Lizzie said. "It's covered with paint."

I don't know whether she said "covered *in* paint" or "covered *with* paint." The dress was a cheap cotton Bedford cord. Light blue ground with a dark figure—small figure. I'm not sure when she got it. In the early spring, I think, that same year. The first time I saw it, she told me that she had got her Bedford cord, and she had a dressmaker there, and I went there one evening, and she had it on, in the very early part of the dressmaker's

294

visit, and she called my attention to it, and I said, "Oh, you have got your new Bedford cord."

"Is that what we call a calico?" Jennings asked.

"No, sir."

"Quite different from a calico?"

"Yes, sir."

"And is it a cambric?"

"No, sir."

"So it is neither a calico *nor* a cambric."

"No, sir."

"Very different material, isn't it?"

"Yes, sir."

"You are certain about that. Neither a calico nor a cambric. No doubt about it, is there?"

"I didn't take hold of it to see and I didn't examine it."

"But you know what it was."

"I know I suppose it was that same dress that I have reference to her having made in the spring."

"And that was the Bedford cord."

"Yes, sir."

"No doubt about that. And any woman knows or ought to know the difference between the two, doesn't she?"

"I don't know as they do."

"Well, *you* do. Did you see any blood on that dress?"

"No, sir."

"Not a drop?"

"No, sir."

"Did you see that it was a soiled dress?"

"The edge of it was soiled as she held it up. The edge she held toward me, like this, was soiled."

"As she stood there holding it, you could see the soil on the dress, could you?"

"Yes, sir."

"Did you actually see it put into the stove?"

"No, sir. I'm quite sure I left the room. When I came into the room again, Miss Lizzie was standing at the cupboard door. The cupboard door was open, and she appeared to be either ripping something down or tearing part of this garment. I don't know what part for sure. It was a small part. I said to her, 'I wouldn't let anybody see me do that, Lizzie.'"

"Did she do anything when you said that?"

"She stepped just one step farther back up toward the cupboard door."

"Now, Miss Emma," Knowlton said, "do you recall the first thing you said when Miss Lizzie was standing by the stove with the dress?"

"Yes, sir. I said, 'You might as well,' or 'Why don't you', something like that. That is what it meant. I can't tell you the exact words."

"Wasn't 'Lizzie, what are you going to do with that dress?' the first thing said by anybody?"

"No, sir, I don't remember it so."

"Do you understand Miss Russell to so testify?"

"I think she did."

"Do you remember whether that was so or not?"

"It doesn't seem so to me. I don't remember it so."

"Why doesn't it seem so to you, if I may ask you?"

"Why, because the first I knew about it, my *sister* spoke to me."

"That's what I thought you'd say. Now, you don't recall that the *first* thing you said to her, the first thing that was said by *anybody* was, 'What are you going to do with that dress, Lizzie?'"

"No, sir. I don't remember saying it."

"Do you remember that you did *not* say it?"

"I am *sure* I did not."

"You swear that you didn't say so?"

"I swear that I didn't say it."

"Did you see your sister burn the dress?"

"I did not."

"Did you see Miss Russell come back again the second time?"

"I don't remember. I think she was wiping the dishes and came back and forth, and I didn't pay attention."

"Did you hear Miss Russell say to her, 'I wouldn't let anybody see me do that, Lizzie?'"

"I did not."

"And did you notice that for any reason your sister Lizzie stepped away after something was said by Miss Russell?"

"I didn't see my sister at all after she left the stove."

"Miss Russell," Moody said, "you testified before the inquest, did you?"

"Yes, sir."

"You testified at the preliminary hearing?"

"Yes, sir."

"And you testified once and then again before the grand jury?"

"Yes, sir."

"At either of the three previous times—at the inquest, at the preliminary, or at the first testimony before the grand jury—did you say anything about the burning of the dress?"

"No, sir."

"Wait a moment," Robinson said. "I don't see how that's at all material. The government isn't trying to *fortify* this witness, I hope."

"Well, I won't press it," Moody said. "If you don't want it, I don't care to put it in."

"Oh, it's not what *I* want," Robinson said. "*You're* trying the Government's case. *I'm* objecting."

"I waive the question," Moody said.

"I think it should be stricken out," Robinson said.

"I agree that it may be stricken out," Moody said.

"Miss Emma . . . who was Mr. Hanscomb?"

"A detective of the Pinkerton Agency in Boston."

"Employed by whom?"

"By us."

"'Us' means whom?"

"Why, my sister and I."

"Miss Russell, do you know Mr. Hanscomb?"

"Yes, sir."

"Did you see him at the Borden house on Monday morning, August the eighth?"

"Yes, sir."

"I do not ask what he said to you or you to him, but did you have some conversation with him?"

"Yes, sir."

"In what room?"

"The parlor."

"In consequence of that conversation, what did you do? What did you do after the conversation with Mr. Hanscomb? Did you see anyone after that conversation?"

"I saw Miss Lizzie and Miss Emma."

Miss Russell came to us in the dining room and said Mr. Hanscomb had asked her if all the dresses were there that had been there on the day of the tragedy, and she'd told him yes. "And of course, Emma," she said, "that was a false . . ."

No, I'm ahead of my story.

She came and said she had told Mr. Hanscomb a falsehood. And I asked her what there was to tell a falsehood about.

And *then* she said that Mr. Hanscomb had asked her if all the dresses were there that had been there on the day of the tragedy, and she had told him yes.

There was other conversation, but I don't know what it was. That frightened me so thoroughly, I cannot recall it.

I know the carriage was waiting for her to go on some errand, and when she came back we had some conversation with her, and it was decided to have her go and *tell* Mr. Hanscomb that she had told a falsehood. She went into the parlor and told him, and in a few minutes she returned from the parlor and said she had told him.

We asked why she had told the falsehood to begin with, and she said, "The burning of the dress was the worst thing Lizzie could have done."

And my sister said to her, "Why didn't you tell me? Why did you let me do it?"

"Dr. Bowen," Robinson said, "I asked you about the morphine that you were giving Miss Lizzie, and you told me on Friday you gave one-eighth of a grain—which is the ordinary dose, I understand, mild dose—and on Saturday you doubled it, gave it, sent it. Did you continue the dose on Sunday?"

"Yes, sir."

"Did you continue it Monday?"

"Yes, sir."

"Did she also have it on Tuesday, August ninth?"

"She continued to have it."

"She had been given for several days this double dose of morphine?"

"Yes, sir."

"I suppose physicians well understand the effect of morphine on the mind and on the recollection, don't they?"

"Supposed to, yes, sir."

"Is there any question about it?"

"No, sir."

"Do you know whether she had ever had occasion before to have morphine prescribed for her, as far as you know?"

"I don't remember that she had."

"Does not morphine given in double doses somewhat affect the memory, and change and alter the view of things, and give people hallucinations?"

"Yes, sir."

As Annie White took the stand, Lizzie recalled again the inquest in Fall River last August. Knowlton waiting to question her in the near-empty courtroom. The crowds outside as she approached in the hack, the driver cracking his whip to clear a path through the spectators. She had been aware of Knowlton standing at the upstairs window, looking down into the street as she got out of the carriage, but she had not so much as glanced up at him.

All the while they talked, Annie White took stenographic notes.

Annie White was now the Government's prelude to admission of the inquest testimony.

Lizzie leaned forward.

In front of her, and slightly to her right, she saw Robinson lean forward as well, as though coiled to spring.

"What is your full name?" Moody asked.

"Annie M. White."

"You are the official stenographer for Bristol County, are you?"

"Yes, sir."

"Were you present at a proceeding at Fall River sometime in August of last year?"

"Yes."

"Do you recall the date of it?"

299

"The inquest was August ninth."

"Did you see Lizzie Borden? I am referring now to Tuesday, August the ninth."

"I did."

"And Mr. Knowlton, the district attorney?"

"Yes."

"In what room were you present?"

"In the District Courtroom in Fall River."

"Who was there beside those whom you have named?"

"Judge Blaisdell and Mr. Leonard, the clerk of the court. And Dr. Dolan. And Mr. Seaver was there part of the time. And Marshal Hilliard was there all of the time. And there was one or two persons came in there I didn't know. Strangers."

"Did they stay, or come in and go out?"

"No, I think they were there only one forenoon. One gentlemen, or two, that I was not acquainted with."

"Now was there some conversation between Mr. Knowlton and Miss Borden at that time?"

"Yes."

"Wait right there," Robinson said, rising. "This, may it please Your Honors, brings us to an important consideration which must be addressed to the Court, and I take it that Your Honors will desire to hear us in the absence of the jury, as is usual in matters of this importance. Now the Court, I have no doubt, have anticipated this question, which was likely to arise. It cannot have been otherwise. I am perfectly willing to make my statement but I wish to do it with some care. I ask that the further hearing of this witness be suspended at this point."

13: CANNES—1890

On Monday morning, the first day of September, Albert departed for Germany, and the villa settled into what Lizzie would come to realize was its normal summertime routine. Early that morning (Lord knew *what* time Albert had left) she and Alison were served their breakfasts of bacon and eggs with a side platter of cold meat and game in their respective bedrooms, the connecting door closed since Alison professed she was unfit company for man or beast when first she greeted the day. Alison always drank tea with her breakfast; in deference to the American guest, a pot of lukewarm coffee had been prepared for Lizzie by the cook—whose name, she discovered, was Isabel, but whom Alison addressed simply as Cook.

After breakfast, they bathed and dressed, and then took a brisk walk into town, where Lizzie purchased a bathing costume and slippers for Alison's vaguely promised outing to the sea "sometime later this week." Lizzie was accustomed to a rather more substantial midday meal than was served that noon on the terrace, and was frankly still hungry after eating more than her proper share of bread and cheese, washed down with white wine. She was beginning, by then, to recognize that an

301

occasional glass of wine with lunch or dinner presented neither a physical nor a spiritual danger, but it nonetheless troubled her to see Alison drinking so liberally, even though the wine seemed to have little effect on her *however* much she drank of it. Lizzie wondered if she drank whiskey as well. She wondered, too, how she could ever explain to the WCTU, once she was home, that she had imbibed even the *tiniest* drop of alcohol while abroad. Well, as Alison had said, she was on holiday. There was time enough for a return to abstinence when she was back in Fall River again. And still she could not imagine any of her WCTU friends, or even her co-workers on the Fruit and Flower Mission, behaving as she was now behaving, however far from home they might be. She suddenly thought of Eve and of the serpent in the Garden of Eden.

After their meager lunch, she and Alison sat on wicker lounges on the lawn, taking the sun.

"Delicious," Alison said.

She was wearing a sleeveless, loose-fitting, white muslin garment she said she had purchased on one of her many journeys here or there. She was quite naked beneath it, the sun silhouetting her long legs whenever she rose to pour warm lemonade or to fetch a towel or a cushion. Lizzie—though she had immodestly forsaken corset, petticoat or stockings—felt nonetheless hot and sticky in muslin underdrawers and chemise, a long-sleeved blouse, and a simple dark skirt. Like Alison, she was barefooted; unlike Alison, she was fearful of moving about on a lawn buzzing with hidden bees.

"There are fools, you know," Alison said, her voice a murmur scarcely louder than the hum of the insects, "who insist on coming here only during the winter months, gulling themselves into believing the climate is semitropical—whatever *that* may mean. How they can ignore temperatures in the low forties is quite beyond me. Not to mention the bloody mistral, which can drive one insane within a fortnight. But it's the *fashionable* thing to do, and Lord knows we *must* be fashionable, we British. I prefer the summer months, thank you very much. Are you comfortable, Lizzie? I fear you're overdressed."

"I'm very comfortable, thank you," Lizzie said, though she was not.

"I know people who insist that the summer climate here is

302

blisteringly *hot*," Alison went on, voicing Lizzie's inner thoughts. "You'd think they were talking about darkest Africa. You wouldn't catch a fashionable Englishman here—unless he's ailing or infirm—anytime between the first of May and the end of October. Afraid of missing the London *season*, don't you know. And afraid of the sun. And afraid of God knows what else. Perhaps riffraff like myself who enjoy nothing better than to lie about soaking up the sunshine."

Whereupon she closed her eyes, lifted the hem of her odd garment higher on her legs, and fell into a deep, uninterrupted silence that lingered for the rest of the afternoon.

In her room later, running a tub of tepid water (although she had turned on only the *hot* faucet), Lizzie wondered if this was to be the tenor of her remaining days at the villa. After the whirlwind of the weekend's social activity, however boring it might have been, she felt somewhat disappointed and knew she would soon tire of a routine that seemed premised on an utter commitment to indolence. Well, she thought, perhaps this is only today. Perhaps Alison is resting after the weekend. And surely there'll be something more substantial for supper than there was for lunch.

Instead a sort of high tea was served, consisting of soup, a salad, cold meat, cheese, fruit and—of course—wine. Lizzie was famished when she went to bed that night, determined to mention to Alison—subtly, to be sure—that her convalescence required heartier fare. In fact, she did not feel at *all* convalescent, and she wondered now if Alison's idleness today had been prompted by concern for a guest she felt might still be ailing. As she drifted off to sleep, she imagined all the sumptuous feasts her friends doubtlessly were being served in Italy.

On Tuesday it became apparent that the day before had been no accident. Alison's "holiday" routine became clearly established then as only more of the same: breakfast in bed, bathe and dress, a walk to town (already beginning to pall on Lizzie), a walk back to the villa, lunch, sunshine and lemonade, a late high tea, some conversation before bedtime, and then to sleep at an hour that would have been considered early even in Fall River. Lizzie was beginning to think it might already be time to telegraph Geoffrey. In fact, she was contemplating making the journey to Italy *without* a male escort. Would it really be all that

303

dangerous for a woman traveling alone? She had no desire to offend her hostess—who until recently had been her devoted nurse as well—but surely she hadn't come to Europe to sit about in the sunshine listening to the bees droning in the grass.

On Wednesday there was yet more of the same. When she attempted to break the somnolent routine by asking questions about the nearby towns of Vence and Grasse, Alison answered her only briefly and then went back to reading a novel that seemed to require her complete attention; she was turning quite brown by then, and the garments she wore when taking the sun—all of them looking as though they'd been purchased in some Oriental bazaar—were shorter than would have seemed modest. She smelled constantly of coconut oil, with which she doused her face and limbs and the exposed area above her breasts. She talked idly of excursions Lizzie now feared they would never make. She dozed, she read, she seemed entirely content to lie about like a serpent, utterly unmindful of her guest's wishes. Even before Rebecca's letter arrived in the late-afternoon post, Lizzie had made up her mind to move on as soon as was politely possible.

She read the letter in the privacy of her room.

Dear Lizzie,

You have no idea how happy we were to receive your telegram from Paris with the good news that you had fully recovered and were planning to spend some days with Alison at her villa in Cannes, where I hope this will reach you. It seems a good idea to recuperate in the sun before you once again assume all the rigors of travel, which, though envigorating to be sure, have been exhausting even to those of us in comparatively better health.

I am writing this from our hotel room in Domo D'Ossola (the Hotel de Ville) after a forty-mile journey by diligence from Brieg, which took us all of ten hours on winding Alpine roads that quite scared Anna out of her wits. We had spent the night before, after a seven-hour rail journey from Lake Geneva, in the Three Crowns Hotel at Brieg, which town possesses nothing to detain a traveler, but which served our needs for rest before continuing on into Italy. The town of Domo D'Ossola is equally uninteresting, but the neighborhood is beautiful and affords many pleasant excursions. We went this morning to the marble quarries near Ornavasso, where a guide told us that from hence were brought the stones for the cathedral in Milan, which as you know is our next stop, though we shall be resting at various other places along the way. Well, you have our itinerary.

I am sorry you were not with us in Geneva. The Beau Rivage was delightfully situated, with views of Mont Blanc, and admirably managed, too—although the bees had an annoying habit of getting into the jam pots. I am looking forward to seeing more of Italy than this dreary little town seems to offer. The climate is **so** *delightful, Lizzie! Once we cleared the custom house at Isella, we knew for certain that we were in Italy, so balmy, so lovely!*

We miss you, dear friend, and are hoping you will be waiting for us when we arrive in Milan. Until then, please be assured of our fondest thoughts and affection.

> *Yours sincerely,*
> *Rebecca*

Yes, Lizzie thought, I *shall* be waiting for you in Milan.
All that remained now was to break the news to Alison.

And then, on Saturday morning, Alison seemed abruptly to recover from her lethargy, bursting into Lizzie's room at the crack of dawn, her blond hair falling loose about her shoulders, sunlight streaming through her beribboned nightdress, an excited gleam in her eyes, a wide smile on her generous mouth.

"Good morning, good morning, lazy shanks!" she called cheerfully. "Hurry and eat your breakfast—is the coffee to your liking? If it isn't, I shall have cook whipped in the marketplace! Hurry, you must run your tub and then get into your bathing costume! I shall give you one of my outlandish Arabian smocks to put on over it—no one shall see us but George! Take along the bathing slippers you bought, there may be rocks! Hurry, Lizzie—*oh*, what a glorious day it is!"

An hour later George drove them down into the Old Town, where Alison engaged a fisherman in the port to row them in his dinghy to what she described as a "delightfully deserted sandy beach in a hidden cove." The fisherman seemed to know the spot well, and Lizzie wondered how actually deserted it might be. But the cove was, in fact, quite hidden from sight and surrounded by a semicircle of forbidding cliffs that made it inaccessible except by the sea. Alison extracted promises from the fisherman, sworn to on his mother's eyes, that he would pick them up again at four sharp, and then she waded ashore carrying a blanket, towels and the picnic basket cook had prepared. Extending her hand to Lizzie, she helped her over the pebbles that bordered the small sandy beach.

"I find it peculiar," she said, shrugging out of her tentlike smock, "that bathing in the sea has only *recently* been proclaimed harmless to the health, whereas *I've* been doing it for as long as I can remember." She dropped the white muslin garment onto the blanket she had spread, and stood facing Lizzie, her hands on her hips. She was wearing a dressy bathing costume of navy blue and white alpaca, trimmed with a coarse white piqué lace, and girdled at the waist with a heavy lace-fringed sash. Below the skirt of the costume were pantaloons of the same color and fabric, ending in the same lace trim some three inches below her knee. She wore no cap and no stockings. Her canvas sandals were laced *à la grecque* with white tapes that wound about her ankles and were knotted somewhere below the shin.

"I find it even *more* odd," she said, "that anyone in her right mind should choose to enter the sea as ridiculously clothed as either you or I are," and to Lizzie's great surprise, she unbuttoned the back of her costume and lowered the shoulders, shrugging out of the short, lace-edged puffed sleeves, slipping entirely out of the overskirt, and then dropping the pantaloons over her legs to reveal herself quite naked except for the laced sandals. Laughing, she ran into the sea.

She dove beneath the surface almost at once, and then rose again some short distance further, her arms extended above her head as though she were diving in reverse into the air itself, her blond hair plastered to the sides of her face, a wide grin on her mouth as she turned to Lizzie.

"There!" she shouted exultantly. "Naked to the tail! And, oh, how marvelously refreshing it is! Strip off that clumsy garment and come join me."

She stood grinning in water to her waist, her hands on her

hips now, her breasts fully exposed to whoever with a spyglass should choose to—

Lizzie turned in panic, scanning the boulders above the beach.

"There's no one!" Alison shouted. "Come in, come in, we're quite alone!"

She turned and dove beneath the surface again. This time she stayed under for quite a time longer, frightening Lizzie. When her head once again reappeared, Lizzie let out her breath in relief and took a tentative step toward the water's edge. Even through her slippers the sea felt colder than any stream or lake she'd ever bathed in back home. The water touched her ankles now, and now her shins. She was dressed as fancily as Alison had been, wearing a black sailor-style costume with a white-duck sailor collar and a wide tie embroidered with anchors, the full skirt ending just below her knees. Beneath the skirt she wore black-gartered stockings and full bloomers attached to the waistband. Like Alison, she wore no cap, and her heavy canvas slippers were tape trimmed and tied up her legs to almost the shins.

"You shall feel warmer naked!" Alison shouted. "Take off that silly thing!"

"I couldn't," Lizzie said, and glanced again at the boulders above. She felt the icy cold water touching her thighs through the mohair skirt and bloomers, touching next the recoiling patch of her womanhood, and then her belly and breasts, the sleeves of the costume now as soddenly cold and clinging as the rest of it, and suddenly she recognized that Alison was right, she *would* feel warmer without the oppressively wet garment against her flesh—but no, she couldn't possibly.

She held her breath and dove beneath the surface. The sun disappeared, there was only the cold dark water now, her costume resisting passage through it, scooping water into its neck, flooding it in over her breasts, her nipples puckering in response, the bodice of the costume billowing. She thought—and this took no longer than the five seconds that elapsed as she swam the next little distance under water and reached for the surface—she thought, *But truly I am alone here with Alison, and she's already seen me*. Her head broke the surface. Gasping for air, she stood erect in the water, shivering.

307

Certain she was blushing, she lowered the top of the costume over her shoulders, pulled her arms free of the clinging sleeves, and then stepped entirely out of the overskirt. She waded closer to the beach, wearing only the sodden bloomers, stockings and sandals. She glanced quickly toward the boulders again, lowered the bloomers and hurled the entire costume toward the blanket. Naked but for her gartered black stockings and the white canvas sandals, she lowered herself quickly into the water again and swam to where Alison was waiting.

"My brave Lizzie," Alison said, and smiled.

"I feel like a bawd," Lizzie said, her teeth chattering.

"Nonsense," Alison answered, and rolled over onto her back. "Feel the sun, Lizzie," she murmured. "Let the sun kiss you."

They floated on their backs in the sunshine, their eyes closed, their arms outstretched, their hands almost touching. They bobbed gently on the water. The world was utterly still. Lizzie suddenly laughed.

"What?" Alison said.

"*Should* there be someone on that cliff . . ."

"But there isn't," Alison said.

"But *should* there be, and should he have a spyglass . . ."

"Yes?"

"He shall wonder what on *earth* these four pink-tipped globes are."

"Oh, Lizzie, you *are* a bawd!" Alison said, and both women began laughing as foolishly and as fiercely as they had that day in her Kensington home while the shadows lengthened and the tea grew cold.

The servants left early Sunday morning for their day off, making a frightful clatter of their departure and awakening Lizzie before she felt entirely slept out. In her nightdress she went to the small arched window opening on the courtyard and saw first Moira and then Isabel traipsing across it, each of them carrying small fabric bags similar to the one Lizzie used while shopping back home. In a whisper that must have awakened half the occupants in the adjoining villas, George said from the main gate, "Hurry now, you two!" and she watched as the women quickened their pace. Moira said something to the cook, and both women laughed. She heard the massive entrance doors swinging shut with a loud bang, and then more laughter from beyond them, and the sound of the horse's hooves as the carriage started its descent toward town.

She was ravenously hungry; the fish last night, though fresh, had tasted a bit too much of the ocean, and she had scarcely touched it. She pulled on a combing cape over her nightdress and, barefooted, went silently onto the gallery. Tiptoeing down the stairs to the courtyard, she nonetheless frightened a mourning dove who took sudden flight and soared up over the tiled roof of the villa.

Isabel had squeezed fresh oranges and had set the juice out on the counter alongside the sink. A pot of coffee was steaming on the iron cookstove. A loaf of bread covered with a cloth to keep off flies was on the table, a knife beside it. Lizzie found where the glasses and cups were kept, poured herself some orange juice and coffee, and then rummaged about until she found the sugar bowl in one of the cabinets and the milk pitcher in the top compartment of the square wooden icebox. She found a slab of butter there as well, beside a square block of fresh ice. She was cutting a thick slice of bread from the loaf on the table when Alison came into the kitchen.

"Did the thundering herd awaken you as well?" she asked.

Her blond hair was hanging loose about her face. Her green eyes appeared heavylidded, as though she were not yet fully awake. She wore a muslin nightdress with a frilly collar and sleeves; the early morning sunlight danced through the garment, silhouetting her slender body as she walked barefooted across the tiled kitchen floor.

"Good morning, Lizzie," she said, and took her hands and kissed her on the cheek. "Ah, good, I see they've left something for us to nibble on. They're not always quite so generous on their day off. Have you . . . yes, I see you have, good for you. Did you sleep well last night?"

"Beautifully," Lizzie said.

"And have awakened beautifully as well. I apologize for the stampeding buffalo in the courtyard. Our only consolation is that they'll be gone till Lord knows what hour tonight—the women, that is. The men won't come tumbling in till dawn. What time is it, anyway?" She looked up at the wall clock. Sighing, she said, "Well, we can thank them for a bright and early start." She went to the cabinet, took down a glass and a cup, and then poured herself orange juice and—surprisingly for her—coffee. "I feel dreadful," she said. "I haven't made any plans at *all* for today, and I'm afraid you'll soon find the life here tedious."

"No, not at all," Lizzie said, and wondered why she hadn't seized upon the opportunity to discuss her departure.

"You're too kind," Alison said. "I know I've been neglectful. But I promise, if you like, that I shall take you to any of the social mornings, afternoons or evenings we're invited to from this moment on."

Lizzie suddenly wondered if she had been declining invitations *before* now.

"I shall deck you out in all your finery and introduce you to the very cream of our vast empire—male, female and some who are woefully neuter. Your wish is my command," she said, and made a deep curtsy. "Nor shall I neglect to show you the neighboring sights as well, such as they are. I shall take you to the pinewoods at Juan-les-Pins, and to Grasse and Cap d'Antibes, should you desire. I shall even take you to the fortress on Ste. Marguerite, where that chap in the iron mask was imprisoned. And if one evening you think you might enjoy a visit to Monte Carlo, I'm sure we can find a suitable escort. Do you think you might enjoy that? Wasn't it *beastly* of Albert to have run off just when we might have made good use of him? Didn't you just *adore* the sea yesterday?"

"I loved it," Lizzie said.

"And how charming you looked, *au naturelle* but for your enticing black stockings," Alison said, and rolled her eyes. "Lizzie, you must absolutely promise to tell me the *instant* you're bored, and I shall send for Geoffrey to escort you to wherever your dear friends may be."

Again, the opportunity. And again, Lizzie ignored it.

"I'm perfectly content," she said.

"Good, then," Alison said, and to Lizzie's astonishment, pulled her nightdress over her head and walked naked out onto the terrace and down to the lawn, holding her coffee cup in one hand as delicately as though she were fully dressed and carrying it out to a visiting vicar!

Lizzie watched her long strides across the grass, saw her

310

hesitate, step aside to dodge what was obviously a bee she spied, and then continue toward one of the wicker lounges. She set her coffee cup down, bending over from the waist like a dancer, her back burnished a deep glowing bronze, and then adjusted the cushions on the lounge, spread a towel over them, and lay down on her belly, her arms bent, her head cradled on them, her face turned toward the terrace and the house, her eyes closed.

Well, it *is* her house, Lizzie thought, and the servants are all gone, and certainly if she chooses to wander about nude there's less danger of her being seen *here* than there was on the beach yesterday. And yet there seemed something innately rude about her casual assumption that a guest would accept her nakedness as offhandedly as she herself did, would not in fact find something a trifle—well, yes—*brazen* about a hostess who cared so little for propriety. She remembered, of course, that she herself had been as naked as a sparrow when Alison soaked her with alcohol day and night in Paris, but that had been a situation born of necessity, and illness was certainly ample excuse for such a breach. She remembered, too, that Alison had slept naked on the train to Cannes, but then again the quarters had been cramped and the compartment close, and one might generously suppose that Alison had considered herself as sequestered as if she had been in her own bedroom, which in fact the sleeping compartment temporarily had been. And yesterday, in the sea together, their nakedness had seemed somehow appropriate, an exuberant joining with nature, a celebration of the flesh and spirit under God's own sky and the benign eye of His dazzling sun. (Enticing, had she said? The black stockings? But how? How on *earth*?)

Nonetheless, here in a house—well, on a *lawn*, she supposed, which was not quite the same as a sitting room—but even so, here in her *home*, for such it was, there seemed something inordinately *wrong* about exposing her body as freely as if she were private and alone. That was what troubled Lizzie most, she supposed. The fact that Alison considered herself as effectively *alone* as if Lizzie were a stick of furniture or a blade of grass. And if such were honestly the case, if despite all her protestations of neglected hospitality, Alison felt so truly unmindful of her guest as to shed all her clothing without a by-your-leave, well, then—

Well, then *what*? Lizzie wondered.

Well, then, surely it was time to announce her departure, time to study the routes and the train schedules, time to make her way to Milan. Firmly fixed in her resolve, she walked out of the kitchen and onto the terrace and through the riotously blooming flower garden, and was starting to cross the lawn when Alison opened her eyes and called, "Lizzie, be a dear. Would you bring me my bag? It's just on the table there."

Lizzie picked up the bag. Undoubtedly, it was time for the mistress of the house to douse herself with coconut oil, the better to protect her exposed flesh from the searing rays of the sun. She walked to where Alison was now lying on her side, a smile on her face, her breasts exposed, not quite as tanned as the rest of her body, her hip curving, the blond tufts of her womanhood partially visible at the joining of her legs. Lizzie set the bag down on the grass, and sat in the wicker lounge beside hers. She realized, all at once, that she was *quite* angry, and she could not imagine why.

"There's a dear," Alison said, and sat up fully. Reaching for the bag, she moved it closer on the grass and, unmindful of modesty, opened her legs and set it down between her feet. Lizzie looked away. She heard Alison rummaging in the bag, heard a match striking, smelled the unmistakable odor of first sulphur and next tobacco, and turned to see her—*smoking*!

"It's such a relief when those ninnies are away," Alison said, puffing on the cigarette as though she were a chimney afire. "Do you smoke, Lizzie? These are French, and rather strong, but . . ." Her eyes opened wide. "My dear Lizzie," she said, "your *jaw* is hanging *agape*."

"You *will* try to shock me at every turn of the way, won't you?" Lizzie said.

"But I had no idea . . ."

"What kind of woman *are* you?" Lizzie said. "I have never in my life . . ."

"Oh, dearest, forgive me," Alison said, and at once dropped the cigarette into the grass and started to step on it until she realized she was barefoot. She picked it up again at once, and flicked it into the nearby shrubbery, as though wishing to banish it from Lizzie's sight. "I intended no offense," she said, reaching for Lizzie's hand, taking it onto her palm, patting it wildly with her other hand, "forgive me, please, you surely don't think . . ."

"I don't know *what* to think," Lizzie said. "You take off your clothing, you . . ."

"But surely . . ."

". . . light a cigarette like a . . ."

". . . the sight of me naked . . ."

". . . practiced *tart* . . ."

". . . doesn't offend . . ."

They had been speaking simultaneously, their words overlapping, and now they stopped simultaneously and stared at each other, each of them a trifle breathless.

"Or *does* it?" Alison said.

"Does *what*?"

"Does it offend you? My nakedness?"

"No."

"Then what . . . ?"

"Not in the way you think."

"But in *what* way, Lizzie? Please tell me, dearest. I shall cover myself to my eyes like a *Moslem*, if you desire. I shall wrap myself like a mummy, I shall . . ."

"You promised never to mock me," Lizzie said.

"But do I mock you with my body? How?"

"By pretending I'm not here," Lizzie said softly.

"But you *are* here. I'm only too *aware* of your presence."

"And trying to shock me. I'm not a child."

"I apologize for the cigarette. I really never . . ."

"You should."

"I do."

"A lady smoking."

"I apologize."

"That *is* shocking, Alison. That is truly and *deeply* shocking."

"I shall never do it again."

"In my presence."

"Or beyond it. Never again. If it disturbs you . . ."

"It does."

"Then never again. I promise."

"I don't care *what* you do when you're alone. Once I'm gone, you can . . ."

"Don't say it!"

The words were spoken so sharply that Lizzie physically recoiled from them.

"Please," Alison said softly. "Not yet. Not so soon." And suddenly she moved to sit beside her and took her in her arms and held her close in embrace and kissed her hair and her cheeks and her closed eyes, murmuring, "Please don't leave, I shall do my best, oh dearest, not so soon, we've scarcely, oh, please, please," and kissed her on the lips.

Lizzie's mouth opened in shocked surprise. She tried to twist away, but Alison's mouth pursued her own, more insistently demanding, her body pressing closer, her naked breasts straining against her. She thought at once *No!* and pushed Alison away forcefully, and stared incredulously into her face.

The face crumbled.

Panic stabbed the green eyes, and suddenly they flooded with tears.

Lizzie sat stock still, watching her as she wept into her hands, awkward and helpless and feeling unspeakably cruel. At last she reached out tentatively to touch her friend's hands where they covered her face, and then drew her into her arms, overwhelmed by a sudden wave of unbearable tenderness, pitying her, wanting to comfort and console her. She held her close, her fingers widespread on her back, patting and stroking her, murmuring gently to her, their heads close together, cheek against cheek, the early morning sunlight glistening palely on russet and gold.

When Alison kissed her again, tenderly this time, she felt oddly as if she were somehow distantly and safely removed, an anonymous spectator watching a theatrical performed by two faceless women, merely she and she, herself somewhere else, observing but curiously uninvolved. No longer shocked or even surprised, except by the fact that she was not revulsed, she allowed Alison's gentle exploration of her lips with mild curiosity, the observer still, the silent witness to a shadow play in the sunlight, distantly aware of the buzzing of the bees in the grass and the musky fragrance of the flowers. She did not move (this was not happening to her) when Alison loosened the ribbons of her combing cape and let it fall soundlessly to the grass. She sat silently when Alison's right hand moved to the muslin bodice of her nightdress to linger on her breast, and

314

then caught her breath sharply when she felt Alison's hands gliding up under the muslin.

She thought again *No!*, and the single unspoken word splintered and ricocheted, *No!*, shattering any illusion of asylum, the indistinct performers coming at once into sharp sunlit focus, the she and she unmistakably Alison and herself. She tried to twist away again, but Alison's relentless mouth found her own, and she drew in her breath on a gasp that served only as binding mortar between their lips. Her cheeks were suddenly burning. She felt a rush of blood to her temples, and all at once she was faint, clinging to Alison, dizzily rescuing her mouth, pressing her feverish cheek to hers as she struggled to catch her breath.

Alison took her hands. Silently she drew her to her feet.

She staggered for an instant, almost falling, remembering again the bees everywhere around them in the grass, waiting. Her nightdress dropped whisperingly to the ground. Alison kissed her again. She stood naked and still in the sunshine, her arms limp at her sides as Alison, gently insistent now, found her breasts again, and molded them, delicately caressing the nipples so that they puckered as they had in the water yesterday. Trembling in Alison's embrace, she felt herself being lowered to her knees, and then to the grass where they lay naked side by side, she trembling more violently now, Alison's arms around her, her mouth recklessly upon her own, her tongue incessantly probing. She was not sure whether she thought *no* again, or actually whispered it. She twisted, freed her arms, threw them wide as if in supplication, and then pulled them back when she became aware again of the buzzing of the bees everywhere around them. She did not know what to do with her arms or her hands.

She felt Alison's tongue gliding over her chin and her neck and the hollow of her throat, trailing liquidly to find her nipples and her breasts. She strained toward the flicking tongue, cupping her breasts in her hands, offering them to Alison's passion, writhing beneath her, surrendering her threatened nipples—they would surely *burst* under the onslaught of that savage tongue, she would swoon away and die! She released her breasts abruptly, her hands wildly grasping, her fingers tangling into Alison's golden hair, pulling her head tighter against her.

315

Their legs moved, thighs touching tentatively, parting, inexorably entwining, Alison's limbs becoming her own, Alison's hand behind her seeking, Alison's womanhood pressing toward hers, backs arching, gold against russet below, crisply entangled, silvery moist when suddenly they joined. She heard, or thought she heard, the distant murmur of a surging sea, and the sound grew louder and louder, tumultuous and stormy, and she felt a rush of such powerful intensity where Alison moved against her below, her fingers entreating mercilessly from behind, that now she knew for certain she would die. Her eyes opened wide in terror and anticipation, the sun blinding her. She felt herself crumbling, crumbling in Alison's fierce embrace, yielded in fear and quivering delight to Alison's mouth and fingers and relentless thrust until at last and mindlessly she screamed aloud, and screamed again rather than explode to smithereens.

She sighed deeply then, and closed her eyes against the sun, arms and legs akimbo, Alison above her, their clinging bodies wet with perspiration, she and she. Still throbbing uncontrollably below, she lifted her face to the kisses raining softly on the corners of her mouth and the tip of her nose and her closed eyes and her tear-stained cheeks.

14: NEW BEDFORD—1893

"May it please the Court," Robinson said, "it is not the question today whether in this court from time to time the proper and salutary rule may or may not have been departed from. Your Honors are to inquire today whether, if there *have* been any such departures, they have been rightly taken. I want to say that in a question of this great moment, where the life of this defendant is involved, this Court will not, I trust, take any possible chances resting upon passing decision made in the heat of a trial. We stand today upon the right of this defendant at this hour. And I should be unjust in my opinion of this Court if I did not know that whatever has been said or done upon so important a question as this one before us, that it would have no effect unless it had received the sanction of the highest judicial tribunal of the Commonwealth.

"Now, in order to ascertain where the defendant stands confronting the Commonwealth, we must not lose sight of the exact facts that are before this Court. I have taken the trouble to prepare a brief, a copy of which I now hand to the Court and to the counsel for the Government, presenting the facts—clearly, I hope, and correctly. Let us look those over, to see upon what ground we argue the question involved.

"First: these homicides were committed on August fourth, 1892.

"Second: the accusation of these crimes against the defendant was made by the Mayor and the City Marshal on August sixth, 1892, which was Saturday, the second day after the crimes were committed.

"Third: the defendant was kept under constant observation of the police during August sixth, 1892, and all days following until the conclusion of defendant's testimony and arrest. And there I wish to amplify a little to say that the house was surrounded by the police of the city—we must assume, under the direction of the chief officer of the police force—and it appears also by the evidence that there was no time, day or night, when the eye of the police department was not on this defendant and on all other inmates of the house.

"Fourth: complaint was made and warrant placed in the hands of the city marshal on or before Monday, August eighth, 1892. Your Honors will see by the agreed statement of facts that complaint was duly made, charging her with the murder of these people, on the eighth of August, which was *before* she testified.

"Fifth: the defendant was summoned on or before August ninth, 1892, by subpoena, to appear and testify at the inquest.

"Sixth: before testifying, the defendant made request for counsel at the inquest, and said request was denied, and counsel were not present. Counsel for the Commonwealth—the district attorney—conducted her examination before the inquest. She alone, a woman three days unguided by her counsel, confronted with the district attorney, watched by the city marshal, surrounded by the police.

"Seventh: the defendant, before testifying, was not properly cautioned. That is agreed to.

"Eighth: before the defendant testified, it had been duly *determined*—by complaint made and warrant issued—that defendant had committed the crime of killing the two persons, the cause of whose death said inquest was held to *ascertain*. The significance of this is that, *prior* to her testifying, the fact was ascertained that a crime *had* been committed—in truth, that *two* crimes had been committed—so that the inquest was *not* to discover whether a crime had been committed or not, and its

318

purpose was *not* to determine the fact of crime, but its use and power was devoted to *extorting* from this defendant something that could be used against her.

"See to what extent the Commonwealth, under the direction of the district attorney had gone. They had, under oath, sworn that she had done it and issued warrants for her arrest to the city marshal. And then, rather than to serve it and put her under the protection of the Constitution, they said, 'We will take care of this in our pockets and we will find out what we can from this woman whom we have charged with committing murder. And if we can get anything from her, we will then put away that paper.' Worse than burning a dress! 'Put it away, and we will make up *another* paper later, against which proceeding the constitutional objection will not lie.'

"Now, I am aware that I am discussing a question of law now, and I am not talking to a jury. I trust that I may not have said more than I ought to say. If I do, it is the defendant that speaks to you, Your Honors, out of the fullness of her recognition and remembrance of what happened there in Fall River, out of a jealous regard for her right into which she was born.

"Ninth: the testimony of the defendant began on August ninth, 1892, and continued during August tenth and eleventh, 1892.

"Tenth: when the testimony of the defendant was concluded on the eleventh day of August, she was held, never allowed to depart, never free, always in fact a prisoner, and then arrested two hours later on a similar warrant. For *convenience*, somebody took care of the *prior* warrant—perhaps for the purpose of being able to say that she went later before the District Court upon a warrant which was issued *subsequent* to her testimony.

"I am bound to say, I hope with no unnecessary reflection, that this *must* have been with the knowledge of the law officer of the Commonwealth at that time in charge of the case. At all events, we must reasonably know that had the law officer advised *against* it, or directed otherwise, it would never have been done. So that, without its purpose being intended, it was in fact a colorable evasion of the law, and it might operate to deprive this defendant of the rights that are sacredly guaranteed to her in the constitution of this Commonwealth.

"We hear the Constitution of Massachusetts read, and it

319

passes glibly over the tongue and in and out the ear, and until somebody finds necessity to plant his root upon that Constitution, he fails perhaps to recognize its strength and safety. Lizzie Borden stands upon that venerable instrument today, the Bill of Rights, and she reads in it, 'No subject shall be compelled to accuse or furnish evidence against herself.' What was written when Massachusetts was born. That was the instinct of the hour. That has been the spirit of our Commonwealth's liberty ever since. Shall it be attempted by evasion to circumvent it or to overreach a defendant? And when the Constitution of the United States was drawn, in ran a similar phrase upon this point: 'No person shall be compelled in any criminal case to be a witness against himself.'

"The shield of the state and the shield of the nation are her protection in this hour. If I have given the Court emphasis on it, it is hers rather than mine. I stand by these rights which are hers by the Constitution, and to depart from their preservation will be peril, not alone to her, but to everybody hereafter who may be placed in a similar position, and who may desire to find the Constitution his protection."

He stared in silence at the bench for a moment, and then walked back to where Jennings and Adams sat at the defense table. Jennings nodded almost imperceptibly. At the table beside them, Moody studied a sheet of paper Knowlton handed him, put the paper down and then rose and approached the bench.

"May it please Your Honors," he said, "I have very little to say in reply. I could not help being reminded—as I heard what my friend is pleased to term his argument—a remark of a French general on the charge of the Light Brigade, which I may make suitable to this occasion. I say of the argument generally, 'It is magnificent, but it is not law.'

"I have been trying to find out throughout this discussion precisely what the learned counsel *means*. And so far as I can understand his position, it is that Lizzie Borden's testimony at the inquest is not admissible because it is not admissible. And that declaration is surrounded by a good many vocal gymnastics and fireworks, but so far as any statement of law or citation of opinion upon this question is concerned, I have not seen any. There is not, if I have followed the argument correctly, a single case cited anywhere of an exclusion of such declarations of this sort unless it was when a person testifying at the time was actually under arrest. Not a single case.

"Let us go back a moment to the date of this inquest in order to understand exactly the position of the facts. These two people, Mr. and Mrs. Borden, had been murdered in their house by someone. That, I agree, was a matter so clear that it did not require an inquest to determine. Our statutes then required certain things to be done.

"The first step was the view and personal inquiry of the medical examiner. If he then should be of opinion that the death was caused by violence, he has done his duty. Then the matter, by his report, is referred to the District Court or the district attorney for investigation. *Not* whether there was a death by violence—because the medical examiner determines that—but, assuming that to be true, *how* was that violence committed, and by *whom*? And all the eloquence that has been wasted upon that subject depends entirely upon a misunderstanding of the law.

"It was the *duty* of the Court to do that very thing, to inquire whether this was a death by violence, whether it was a death of violence by human design, *when* the death occurred, by *whom* it occurred. And in doing that very thing, the Court was performing the duty which was imposed upon it by the law of this Commonwealth.

"Now then, a step further. Lizzie Borden is summoned. She appears. She appears by counsel learned in the law—friend *and* counsel both, I may say. A counsel, at least, in whom she well might place great confidence. Counsel asks the privilege of being present at the inquest. It is *entirely* beyond precedent in this Commonwealth, and the district attorney and the Court—in accordance with almost unbroken precedent—declined that privilege. Declined it because the law expressly gives them the *power* to decline it. She is there. She is not cautioned before the magistrate, but her *counsel* is told before she goes in to testify that he may confer with her in respect to her rights as a witness, and the stipulation says that he then *did* confer with her.

"*Now* we are looking at the substance of the thing. At the common sense of the thing. And the substance *and* the common sense of the thing is, Your Honors, that a caution delivered by her friend and counsel *without* the surroundings of the Court, *without* her being in the presence of strangers, would be very

321

much *more* effectual to inform her of her full rights than any caution by the magistrate or the district attorney could be. And Your Honors can have no doubt that the reason why the caution was omitted at the beginning of her testimony was because that subject had been thoroughly talked over between counsel and client, and she knew and understood her rights.

"And after she'd had the opportunity of talking with her counsel, *after*—and I think if we can presume some things about the district attorney, we can presume some things about as learned a lawyer as brother Jennings is. And we can presume that he informed her that she would have the right to *decline* to testify upon a *single* ground, otherwise she must be obliged to go in there and testify what she knew about the matter. She could *only* decline to testify upon the ground that it would incriminate herself.

"And can Your Honors have any doubt that *after* she had talked with Mr. Jennings in reference to her rights thereto, that she went in with a full consciousness that she had a right to decline at the beginning, at the middle, or at the end? And that when she went in there, she testified as a *voluntary* witness in every possible sense of the word, legal or otherwise?

"What, precisely, does this word *voluntary* mean? It means this: if a witness, having the privilege to decline to answer upon the constitutional ground that it will tend to incriminate him, does *not* exercise that right of declination, and testifies, then the testimony is voluntary within the meaning of the law. And in that point of view, there was nothing that occurred here that was *not* voluntary.

"I do not think there is anything else upon this subject in which in any respect I could aid Your Honors. I say that as there is no case to be found, none has been cited, anywhere over the length and breadth of this land or in England, as to an exclusion of the testimony Lizzie Andrew Borden gave at the inquest in Fall River, it should be admitted."

Moody went back to sit beside Knowlton. The three justices carried on a hushed conversation for what seemed an extraordinarily long time. Robinson felt suddenly hotter than the heat of the day warranted.

He had been successful in convincing the judges that whatever Anna Borden planned to say about Lizzie's chance comments on the voyage home from Europe should be excluded from the trial. He had been equally successful in arguing that Eli Bence, the druggist, should not be allowed to testify about her alleged attempt to buy poison on the day preceding the murders. But in comparison to the issue now before them, those other two were insignificant.

After scrutinizing the transcript made at the inquest, he had known for certain that Lizzie's testimony—especially that concerning her whereabouts at the time of her father's murder—was damaging in the extreme. He had carefully prepared the jury for the possible admission of the inquest testimony, questioning Dr. Bowen repeatedly about the drugs he had prescribed—morphine, no less!—for Lizzie in the days preceding the inquest. But he did not know whether this preparation would be enough to convince the jury that in her drugged state she had become confused by Knowlton's questions, contradicting herself repeatedly, losing track of what she had earlier told him, spinning a web that would at best appear deceitful. He simply did not know. And so he waited nervously for the judges' decision, hoping against hope that they would refuse to admit the inquest testimony, for if they did, he suspected all was lost.

Chief Justice Mason cleared his throat.

"The propriety of examining the prisoner at the inquest," he said, "and of all that occurred in connection therewith, is entirely distinct from the question of the admissibility of her statements in that examination. It is with the latter question only that this Court has to deal.

"The common law regards this species of evidence with distrust. Statements made by one accused of crime are admissible *against* him only when it is affirmatively established that they were voluntarily made. It has been held that statements of an accused—as a witness under oath, at an inquest *before* he had been arrested or charged with the crime under investigation—may be voluntary and admissible against him in his subsequent trial. And the mere fact that, at the time of his testimony at the inquest, he was aware that he was suspected of the crime, does not make them otherwise.

"But we are of opinion, both upon principle and authority, that if the accused was at the time of such testimony under

323

arrest, charged with the crime in question, the statements so made are *not* voluntary, and are inadmissible at the trial.

"The common law regards substance more than form. The principle involved cannot be evaded by avoiding the *form* of arrest if the witness at the time of such testimony is *practically* in custody. From the agreed facts and the facts otherwise in evidence, it is plain that Lizzie Borden at the time of her testimony was, so far as related to this question, as effectually in custody as if the formal precept had been served.

"And without dwelling on other circumstances which distinguish the facts of this case from those of cases on which the government relies, we are all of opinion that this consideration is decisive, and the evidence is excluded from this trial."

Could she now begin to believe that what she read in the newspapers reflected a gradually changing tone? Could she further assume that this seemingly new bias in her favor was something shared by the jury? If experienced reporters from newspapers everywhere were beginning to be swayed by the inexorable flow of testimony in this courtroom, was it not possible that a jury composed largely of farmers, simple men all, were similarly being persuaded of her innocence?

The reporter for the *New York Times* had written:

The women who crowd the courtroom and who have been so much annoyed because Lizzie Borden does not cry, possibly felt better when—at the close of the reading of Judge Mason's decision yesterday pronouncing in her favor on the question of the admissibility of certain evidence given by her at the coroner's inquest—she bowed her head to the back of ex-Governor Robinson's chair and wept.

It was not the kind of weeping that would probably satisfy the kind of women who have been criticizing her firm and almost stolid demeanor. There were no sobs, no wild gestures. Probably, indeed, only those who were close to her and who were watching her intently knew that she was crying. But they, if they looked closely, saw that her face was hidden and that it remained low-bent against the back of the chair for as many as ten minutes; that her handkerchief was at her eyes, and that when she lifted her face again her eyes were very red.

Even the *Baltimore Sun*, which had published that hateful word-portrait of her (or so it had seemed at the time), now appeared to have softened its posture somewhat. Only yesterday, she had read:

> Inside the courtroom, the center of all this melancholy business, sits a wretched woman borne down with the weight of an accusation than which in all the record of crime there is none more horrible. A woman of refinement, whose manner and bearing from the moment she took her seat in the prisoner's dock until now have been exemplary. There has not been a look or a gesture, a word or an attitude suggestive of the qualities which she must possess, not vaguely or in small measure but developed in an abnormal and hideous degree, if she is the deplorable creature charged by the state.

Could she now dare to *hope*?

"When did you next receive anything, Professor Wood?"

I received from Medical Examiner Dolan the claw-hammer hatchet—that large hatchet which has been known as the claw-hammer hatchet.

Those two axes which have already been seen.

A large envelope containing three small envelopes, one labeled "The hair of Mrs. A. J. Borden, 8/7/92, 12:10 P.M."; the other labeled "Hair from A. J. Borden, 8/7/92, 12:14 P.M."; and the third labeled "Hair taken from hatchet."

The envelope marked "Hair taken from hatchet" contained when I opened it two pieces of paper. This one, which was sealed and which contained a short hair—it does not now, it is empty now, but that is the paper in which the hair was enclosed—contained a short hair one inch long and containing both the root and the point of the hair. And when they had been examined under the microscope, it was seen to consist almost entirely of the central medullary cavity, which is unlike human hair, and it had a red brown pigment, and it is more similar to a cow's hair than any other animal hair I have ever examined. It is sealed between those two glasses and can be readily seen if the glass is placed on a piece of paper.

325

It is animal hair, there is no question of that, and probably cow hair.

The envelope also contained a piece of paper which I examined very carefully without removing it from the envelope, and then I have examined with a lens every part of the inside of the envelope without finding any hair. It is marked "Hair placed here 1:57 P.M., 8/7/92," and it contains only a mucilage spot in the center. That is, I was unable to find any hair on it at all, and that cow's hair is the only hair which I have had as coming from the hatchet.

I would state that on examination of that stain upon the edge of the hatchet, the cutting edge, I found a good deal of woolen fiber and cotton fiber. That is, in this rough stain right near the back part of the cutting edge, the beveled edge. It contained quite a number of fibers of cotton. Whether that was upon the *other* hair or not, I don't know. I never saw but one hair, and that is the one sealed in the glass.

The hatchet had several stains upon it which appeared like bloodstains, both upon the handle and upon the side and upon the cutting edge.

I observed also that the handle of the hatchet did not set firmly or tightly into the hole of the head of the hatchet. That there was quite a large space, which can be seen now—as I have not disturbed the handle of the hatchet at all—can be seen at this part of the head. Quite a cavity between the handle and the iron of the head, both in front and at the back part.

Now all of the stains on the head of the hatchet were carefully tested.

There is one stain here which has been gotten on since, I see. It looks like an ink stain. That was not on. That was gotten on in court here, some way. It looks like an ink stain, I don't know what it is, it wasn't on before.

All of those stains I subjected to chemical tests and microscopic tests for the presence of blood, with absolutely negative results.

I was unable to detect any blood upon the claw-hammer hatchet.

Either on the handle or the blade.

The two axes I designated as ax *A* and ax *B* in order to distinguish them from each other, and marked those letters

326

upon the end of the handle, so that I would know on referring to my notes which was which. The ax A had a good many stains which might, so far as appearance was concerned, or might not, have contained blood. This ax A has a large knothole in the front of the handle, which on examination with a glass contained some suspicious-looking spots, and it is easy to see a considerable amount of brownish-colored material staining the ax handle near the head.

Now that might or might not, so far as I could see or determine by inspection alone, have contained blood.

But the testing of the stains, both upon the head of the ax and the handle, showed them to be absolutely free of blood.

Precisely the same remarks may apply to the ax B. There was no blood upon either ax, and no blood on the claw-hammer hatchet.

Nor could the hatchet have been washed quickly so that traces of blood might not be found upon it. On account of those cavities in between the head and the handle. Also, the handle is quite rough and torn, ragged. And it will be noticed, too, that the handles of both these axes are exceedingly rough and do not fit into the iron head closely or accurately.

"Captain Desmond, upon the Monday following the murder, did you take part in any search at the Borden house?"

"I did, yes, sir."

"Were you in command of the squad that went there to search?"

"I was, yes, sir."

"What officers were present?"

"Connors, Medley, Quigley, Edson, myself and an outsider by the name of Charles H. Bryant, a mason."

"You say, among others, Officer Medley was there?"

"He was."

"I will call your attention to anything that Mr. Medley showed you during the process of the search in the cellar."

"A small hatchet."

"Did the hatchet which he brought you have any handle?"

"It had a small part in the iron. That is, it had been broken, and the wooden part had been left."

"What do you say to this piece of iron and piece of wood?"

327

"I should say that it was the same thing that he showed me."

"What did you do, Mr. Desmond, after he showed you this hatchet?"

"I looked it over, examined it quite closely."

"Now will you describe everything about the hatchet? Take your own way of doing it, sir. Describe it as carefully as you can, as you saw it at the time."

Well, it had been in some place which was not very clean. It was all dirty. That is, it was covered with a dust which was not of a fine nature. That is, it was too coarse to be called a fine— what I mean is, it wasn't any sediment that might have collected on it from standing there any length of time. It was a loose, rough matter, which might be readily pushed off, or moved by pushing your finger on it.

The dust that we found in general throughout the cellar was nothing at all such as was on that hatchet. It was of a much finer nature, such as any sediment that would form in any cellar. Not the kind of dirt that was on that. This was a much coarser nature. This was a rough dirt here. I could take my finger and rub it off. I gave the hatchet to Officer Medley. I gave it to him wrapped in a newspaper. I got the paper from the water closet there, to do it up with.

"Well," Robinson said, "here's the hatchet," and handed it to him. He went to the defense table, picked up a copy of that day's *Boston Globe*, and carried it back to the witness box. "Won't you wrap it up in about as large a piece of paper?"

"I shall have to get a full-sized newspaper to do it. Much larger than that, sir."

"You got a piece out of the water closet?"

"Yes, sir."

"Brown paper?"

"No, sir, regular newspaper. But a larger paper than that."

"You wrapped it in a newspaper?"

"Yes, sir."

"A very large newspaper?"

"Yes, quite a big newspaper."

"Well, we won't explore for a big one. But as large as that?"

"I think larger."

"Larger than this *Boston Globe*?"

"Yes."

"Well, take that and give us the way you wrapped it up."

Desmond opened the newspaper in his lap. He placed the hatchet head at one edge of it, and then rolled it into two sheets of paper.

"I wrapped it up in some such form as that," he said, "and passed it to Officer Medley."

"That is the way you did it?"

"Yes, sir."

"Rolled it up like that and passed it to him?"

"Yes, sir."

"Made as big a bundle as that, did it?"

"No, sir. Not so large as that."

"It was a bigger newspaper?"

"Yes, it was larger. I don't think there was two sheets."

"Oh, a single folio paper."

"Yes, sir."

"You don't remember what the newspaper was?"

"No, I don't."

"Mr. Medley, how long do you think you were in the cellar before you left with this hatchet wrapped up in paper?"

"I don't think over a half hour."

"You went right off after showing it to Captain Desmond?"

"Yes, sir. I took it down to the city marshal's office. After I wrapped it in paper."

For a moment, Lizzie thought Robinson had missed this. His face showed no expression of surprise, his back did not stiffen the way it had earlier when he'd heard unexpected and conflicting testimony. She almost reached out involuntarily as if to touch Robinson—where he stood too far away to touch—nudge him, alert him to what Medley had just said. It was Officer Medley who had earlier testified that he had seen no footprints on the barn loft floor. If his testimony now could be shown to be in direct contradiction to what *Desmond* had said, would not his story about the barn seem untrustworthy as well? She kept watching Robinson. He had heard, she realized, he had *heard*.

"You wrapped it in paper," he said softly. There was no emphasis on the "you." He delivered his words not as a question but as a statement, a simple repetition of what Medley had just told him.

329

"Yes, sir."

"Where did you get your paper?"

Again no emphasis, the word "your" simply flowing unobtrusively into the rest of the sentence.

"In the basement."

"A piece of newspaper?" Robinson asked.

"I think it was a piece of brown paper. I wouldn't be sure as to that. It was a piece of paper, and that was all I remember surely."

"You wrapped it up in a paper and folded it up," Robinson said, walking back again to the defense table. Again he picked up the *Boston Globe*. "Perhaps you will illustrate how you folded it up in the paper." He handed him the newspaper. "You won't need the piece of wood," he said, "just the hatchet head."

"This is only as near as I can remember doing it," Medley said.

"Well, that's quite right, that's all I have a right to ask you."

Medley set the hatchet head in the exact center of the newspaper spread in his lap. He folded the page over it.

"I'm not very tidy at such things," he said.

He folded the page again. He turned the partially wrapped hatchet head sidewards in his lap, and folded the newspaper over it several more times.

"Now that," he said, "as near as I can think, is about how I did it. Then I put it in my pocket." He looked down at the package. "Nothing stylish about the manner of wrapping it up," he said.

"Well, I'm glad to find a man that's not in style," Robinson said. "Then you carried it off down to the police station?"

"Yes, sir."

"Did you show it to any other officer?"

"Yes, I showed it to one officer as I was passing out. I can't think now who it was. I had it in my pocket."

"Side pocket?"

"Yes."

"Did you wear a sack coat at the time?"

"Yes, sir. A cotton summer sack coat. Not like this one. It was a light-colored coat. And I showed him the hatchet head. I think I tore enough of the paper off, or something, to let him see what it was."

"Did you state that you were a patrolman last year?"

"Yes, sir."

"And are you now?"

"No, sir."

"You've been promoted?"

"Yes, sir."

"When?"

"In December."

"Now, Lieutenant Edson, you participated in the search of the Borden house on Monday, August eighth, did you not?"

"I did."

"Did you or any other party, to your knowledge, on that Monday take anything away from the house?"

"Yes, sir."

"What did you take?"

"Officer Medley had a hatchet head in his pocket."

"Did you see it?"

"He showed it to me partly."

"Do you know where he got it?"

"I do not."

"When did he show it to you?"

"Just as he was about to leave, he came to me and pulled it out of his pocket. It was in a paper."

"It was wrapped in a paper?"

"Yes, sir."

"You didn't see it before that?"

"No, sir."

"Did you examine it?"

"No, sir. Glanced at it, that's all."

"What did he do with it?"

"Went off with it. Away from the building."

"It was only the small hatchet? Had no handle?"

"No handle."

"And he didn't have any handle in his possession, did he? That he showed to you?"

"No, sir."

"You didn't see any loose handle around there?"

"No, sir."

"And you didn't find one yourself?"

"No, sir."

"Well, I don't care for anything else. You spoke of being now lieutenant of police, and last August acting sergeant of police?"

331

"Yes, sir."

"That is a promotion, I take it."

"Yes, sir."

"When were you promoted?"

"February, this year."

"Has Captain Harrington been promoted?"

"Yes, sir."

"Mr. Doherty?"

"Yes, sir."

"What is Mr. Medley's capacity now?"

"Inspector with rank of lieutenant."

"Was he the same last year?"

"No, sir."

"What was he last year?"

"Patrolman."

"Anybody else of those that were around the Borden house that have been promoted?"

"Connors."

"What was he, and what is he?"

"At that time, he was acting sergeant."

"Now lieutenant?"

"Captain."

"Go clear up by *one* promotion?"

"Yes, sir."

"And of the others that you recall?"

"Desmond. Captain."

"What was he last year?"

"At that time, he was acting captain."

"Now he is captain?"

"Yes, sir."

"Anybody else?"

"No, sir."

"Has Mr. Mullaly been promoted?"

"No, sir."

Lizzie smiled.

It was Mullaly who had surprised everyone earlier by testifying that he'd found a second piece of the hatchet handle in that box on the basement shelf.

My name is Francis W. Draper. I am by profession a physician.

My medical education was in the Harvard Medical School in Boston. I have been in practice as a physician since 1869, now twenty-four years. I have been one of the medical examiners for Suffolk County since the office was created by the legislature in 1877. In that time, I have been called upon in a great many cases, nearly thirty-five hundred. All cases of suspicion, all cases of death, where a homicide was suspected or charged.

The first knowledge I had of this matter was the receipt of a dispatch at my home in Boston, which purported to be a telephone message from Dr. Dolan. I came down to Fall River the same day, but I did not at that time go with him to see the bodies. I arranged with him, and the next day—August eleventh—went to Oak Grove Cemetery and saw the bodies with him. At that time, I assisted at an autopsy of those bodies. I made an examination of the wounds upon the head of Mr. Borden, and I drew these marks upon the plaster cast as it is here. They are intended to be an accurate approximation of position and length. I will try to hold it, but I should like to refer to my notes as well.

"How many of the wounds," Knowlton asked, "and which of them, penetrate the bone of the skull?"

"Four of them. The one which cut through the left eye, and the three in this vicinity, above and in front of the left ear."

"How deep was the wound that went through the eye?"

"I don't know, sir. Because it went through the bone behind the eye, and how deep it went into the brain, I don't know."

"How many of the others went into the bone of the skull, without going through?"

"Three of them, sir."

"And which three of them?"

"These in the left temple."

"The short one, and the two on each side there?"

"Yes, sir."

"And the three that went through are the three there, and the one in the eye?"

"Yes, sir."

"Is there anything in the nature or character of the wounds upon the head of *Mrs.* Borden that assists you in determining the size of the instrument or of the cutting edge of the instrument used to inflict the wounds?"

333

"No, sir."

"Is there anything in the nature or character of the wounds upon the head of *Mr.* Borden which would so assist you?"

"There is."

"Would the skull *itself* be of assistance in pointing out such things as occur to you to be important?"

"It would."

"Then in that case, although I regret very much the necessity of doing it, I shall have to ask Dr. Dolan to produce it."

He turned toward Robinson as the medical examiner came from the back of the courtroom, Andrew Borden's skull in his hands.

"I understand it to be agreed," he said, "without recalling Dr. Dolan to the stand, that this *is* the skull of Mr. Borden?"

Robinson nodded impatiently, lifting his hand and waggling it to assure agreement on this point. He was leaning over the back of his chair, in quiet conversation with his client. In a moment Knowlton saw Lizzie rise from her chair. The deputy sheriff rose at almost the same instant. There was a buzz in the courtroom as she made her way out, the deputy sheriff following. Knowlton turned back to the witness box.

"Now, Dr. Draper," he said, "I will ask you whether from an examination of that skull, coupled with the observations of your autopsy, you are able to determine the length of the edge of the instrument which inflicted the wounds."

"I believe I am, sir."

"What do you say it is?"

"Three inches and one-half."

"Will you tell us what it is that leads you to that conclusion?"

Draper reached into his bag and brought out a pie-shaped wedge. "This metallic plate of stiff tin," he said, "is three and a half inches on its longer side." He held the skull firmly in place on the railing of the witness box, and brought the piece of tin to it. "Adjusting it that way," he said, "it fits in the wound in the base of the skull, cutting across the large arteries supplying the brain. It also rests against and cuts the surface of the upper portion, but takes in this edge and no more. I also found another wound in the skull which fits, but not so well. That shows, but not so well as the posterior wound, the same fact."

334

"Are you able to say whether this hatchet head is capable of making those wounds?" Knowlton asked.

"I believe it is."

"Have you attempted to fit *that* in the wounds?"

"I have seen the attempt made."

"Will you do it yourself?"

"I will try."

Knowlton handed him the hatchet head. The courtroom was suddenly quite still. The silence was not lost on Robinson. He turned immediately to the jury box.

"I shall have to ask you," Knowlton said, "to point out to the jury—so that they can see it—the cutting edge to which you refer. And then, after you've done that, to show what you mean by the insertion of the three-and-a-half-inch piece of tin, and then by the insertion of the hatchet."

"If I may go one step further in the demonstrations, I will say a *four*-inch plate does not go into either of those places."

"Will you show us, so that the jury can see it, how that hatchet went in there?"

Robinson's attention was on the jury. As Draper fitted the actual head of the hatchet into the wound he had earlier described, the eyes of each man in the jury box were fastened on that gleaming white skull.

"Now won't you try the *four*-inch piece of tin?"

The attention of the jury was unwavering. Robinson turned to where Draper was now trying to insert the larger piece of tin into the same wound.

"I attempt to get this four-inch in," Draper said, "and I cannot get it in, in any way, into that wound in the base. The same applies to the front, but not to the same degree."

"Now, having shown what you desire to call attention to the jury, what do you say the cutting edge was of the instrument that caused the wound that you have described the borders of?"

"Three and a half inches."

"Are there any *other* wounds, besides those, on which you can make any accurate determination as to the size of the cutting edge?"

"Not so far as I have studied the materials."

"What in your opinion, doctor, was the cause of these wounds?"

335

"Blows upon the head with an edged instrument or weapon of considerable weight, supplied with a handle."

"Would a hatchet be consistent with the description that you have given?"

"Yes, sir."

"In your opinion, could the results you found have been produced by the use of an ordinary hatchet in the hands of a woman of ordinary strength?"

"In my opinion, they could, sir?"

Professor Wood was on the stand again when Lizzie came back into the courtroom, the deputy sheriff following her. Robinson turned to her as she took her customary seat behind him. Their eyes met. She could read nothing in those eyes.

"And who handed the hatchet head to you, professor?" Knowlton asked.

"City Marshal Hilliard."

"Where?"

"In his office."

"Is that the hatchet head?"

"Yes, sir . . ."

. . . it has been in my possession about all the time since. When I received this hatchet, this piece of handle was in the head in its proper position, this fractured end of the handle being close up to the iron. That is, it was in—in that relative position—so far as the upper and the lower end of the eye of the hatchet was concerned. This fractured end was just underneath or flush with the lower edge of the hole in the hatchet, of the *eye* of the hatchet as I have heard it called here.

When I received this hatchet, it contained more of a white film upon both sides than it does now. But it still contains—adherent tightly in little cavities here in the rusty surface, which can easily be seen with a small magnifying glass—white dirt, like ashes, which is tightly adherent and which have resisted all of the rubbing which this hatchet has had since it came into the courtroom. And it is still visible there and gives the side of the hatchet, as you can see, a very slight grayish appearance here in this round part.

That was far more marked on the hatchet on both sides when I first received it than it is at the present time.

336

And that coating there looks as if it might be ashes.

I don't know.

I haven't tested it to see whether it is ashes or not. I couldn't do that. It might be *any* white dirt, so far as I could see, so far as I know.

The fractured ends of this bit of handle, the rough end, had a perfectly white, fresh look, and it was not stained as it is now. And these chips here, these two large chips from the side of this piece, and a little chip from this side also, had not been removed when I had it. When I drove the handle out from the eye, I placed the hatchet in a vise and drove this wood out.

And upon examination with a magnifying glass, that fractured end of the handle was perfectly clean. There was no dust or dirt, no fragments of dirt which could be seen in the angles in this fractured end by means of a magnifying glass. And they cannot be seen there today. It is as clean now, so far as coarse dirt is concerned, as it was then.

In soaking—in order to determine whether there had been any blood upon this handle between the hatchet head and the handle—I placed this to soak in water containing a little bit of iodide of potassium, which removes blood pigment in my experience better than water itself, and allowed it to soak there for several days.

But soaking that bit of wood in that solution darkened the fractured end somewhat so that it came out a darker color than it had been when I placed it in the solution. That's probably due to some of the discoloring matter being soaked off from the outside and absorbed by the wood.

Then I tested that solution—after taking this piece of wood out of it—tested that solution for blood pigment by chemical tests which I need not detail, and found that there was no blood removed from the handle.

Both sides of the hatchet were uniformly rusty, as they are now. And it will be noticed that on the cutting edge here, there are a few smooth pieces in the rust, which I made myself by scraping the rust from the beveled edge. Those smooth spots were done by me in scraping the material with my knife for chemical testing, in order to determine whether there was any blood mixed with the iron rust or not.

There were also several suspicious spots upon the underside

of the hatchet, one of which is plainly perceptible here, three-fourths of an inch from this little notch in the lower edge of the head.

That is a shiny spot which can be easily seen now, and which is not a bloodstain.

It is a stain of some varnish of some kind. There were several other reddish spots upon the side of the hatchet which might or might not contain blood, so far as I could determine by inspection, and which I proved not to be bloodstains.

"Professor Wood," Knowlton asked, "what is your opinion as to the question whether this hatchet could have been used to inflict the wounds which you have heard described, and *then* subjected to any cleaning process to remove the traces of blood? As to whether or not you would be able to find them upon the hatchet?"

"We object to that question," Adams said.

"He may answer."

"Before the handle was broken," Wood said. "Not after."

"I think the question must be answered as *put*," Adams said. "If it *can* be answered."

"If by the question is meant the hatchet head as it is . . ."

"I beg pardon, Professor Wood," Knowlton said. "I don't think my brother has the right to catechize the witness yet."

"I haven't catechized him," Adams said.

"Yes, but you were getting into a colloquy with him, which I do not think is proper. Mr. Stenographer, will you read the answer?"

"'Before the handle was broken. Not after.'"

"That is to say," Knowlton said, "the conditions I named could have existed before the handle was broken off. Why do you make that difference, professor?"

"All this goes in under objection," Adams said. "May it please Your Honors."

"Because it would be very hard to wash blood off that broken end," Wood said. "It would be almost impossible to quickly wash blood out of that broken end. It might have been done by thorough cleansing, but that would also stain the fracture."

"Mr. Seaver, in your capacity as a member of the State District Police Force, did you again go to the Borden house after your visit of Saturday, August sixth?"

338

"Yes, sir. With Dr. Dolan, the medical examiner."

"When was that, Mr. Seaver?"

"My impression was it was the thirteenth."

"Have you a memorandum of your observations?"

"Yes, sir."

"When was it made?"

"It was made at that time. I made it on a paper at that house, at that day, and afterwards copied it into a book."

"Would the memorandum assist you upon a matter of this sort?"

"Yes, sir."

"Please consult it, and then state in your own way, without any questioning, what you found in reference to blood spots."

"There were, on the mop board behind the head of the lounge in the sitting room, five small spots of blood. On the wall just above the head of the lounge, a little toward the kitchen door, we found a cluster of small blood spots, eighty-six in all, within a radius of eighteen inches in length by ten inches in width. On a frame and glass of a picture that hung over the lounge, there were forty blood spots, the highest spot being four feet and ten inches from the floor. The highest spot we found in the room . . ."

She knew she would faint again.

She had absented herself from the courtroom when they were about to show her father's skull, but this now, this gruesome recitation . . .

". . . kitchen door, a quarter of an inch from the south side of the . . . "

Her fingers tightened on the closed fan in her lap. The knuckles showed white where she gripped it. She kept her head bent, staring at the fan and at her own hand clutching it as Seaver went on and on, telling now of the blood he'd found in the room upstairs . . .

". . . marble slab and dressing case, there were fifteen blood spots. On the upper drawer of the dressing case, we found four blood spots . . ."

She took a deep breath. She raised her eyes. One of the newspaper artists was observing her, his pencil moving busily.

". . . faceboard of the bed was besmeared with blood . . ."

She loosened her fierce grip on the fan. She turned her

attention to the witness. She would not faint again. She would *not*.

". . . two blood spots between the dressing case and the window . . ."

Soon, it would be over.

Soon.

"Dr. Draper, if blood, fresh blood, were put upon metal similar to the head of a hatchet, in August, in our climate, on a hot day—would it dry quickly?"

"If it is a thin smear, it will dry quickly. If it is in any considerable quantity, it will take a very much longer time."

"Does blood readily and quickly intermingle with the meshes of clothing and coarse substances like dirt or rust, or anything of that sort?"

"Certain kinds of clothing will absorb blood readily. Clothing of wool or felt will not."

"Cotton clothing?"

"Cotton clothing will absorb the blood readily."

"What do you say in respect to an instrument having rust upon it, and blood striking it and drying on? Would the blood readily intermingle with the rust?"

"I suppose it would."

"And if it intermingled with the rust, would it easily wash off?"

"It would wash off less easily than if it were on a keen, dry blade."

"Assuming that a metallic instrument like the head of one of these hatchets, in August, in our climate, and on a hot day in August, was smeared with blood at ten o'clock, and that the instrument had rust upon it at that time, and that it remained in that condition exposed to the air for an hour—would you expect that the blood would be well dried in with the rust upon that instrument?"

"I should think it likely in a dry day. In a day that was not as moist as today is."

"A *hot* day, I put into my question."

"A hot day, yes, sir."

"And under those circumstances, it could not have been readily washed off, could it?"

"Answering as I did before, not so readily as with a bright surface or metallic, polished surface."

"But I will ask you, whether under those circumstances, you would expect to get the *blood* off unless you got the *rust* off?"

"I think the blood would come off before the rust."

"Before the rust?"

"Yes, sir."

"Do you think it could be effectively removed so that there would be no trace that could be exposed by a subsequent chemical test?"

"I think so."

"You have heard the testimony as to the position in which the body of Mrs. Borden was found?"

"I have, sir."

"And taking that testimony, and the wounds as you observed them, did you form any opinion as to the position of the woman when she was assaulted?"

"I did, sir. I believe that the assailant in the case stood astride of the prostrate body of Mrs. Borden, as she was lying face downward on the floor."

"As to all of the wounds?"

"As to all except the flat wound in the scalp on the left side of the head. I think that was given while Mrs. Borden was standing and facing her assailant."

"From what you have heard of the testimony of how *Mr.* Borden's body was found, are you able to state what *his* position was when assaulted?"

"I have an opinion on it, sir."

"What is that?"

"That the assailant stood above the head of the sofa, above the head of Mr. Borden, and struck downward upon his head and face. I think he was lying on the sofa on his right side, with the face turned well toward the right, and the right cheek concealed in the pillow. I think all the blows could have been received with the body lying in that manner."

"Can you tell what probable effect would be as to the diffusion or scatter of blood from the wounds of Mr. Borden?"

"Mere guess work, sir, in my mind."

"Why so?"

"Because of the nature of the wounds."

341

"Assuming that spots were seen upon the wall immediately over the head and a little to the front of Mr. Borden, in large number, eighty to a hundred; that spots were seen upon a picture upon the wall midway over the body to the extent of forty or fifty; that spots were seen upon the door which was in the general direction beyond his feet; and that other spots were seen upon the door which was in a general direction behind his head and between him and beyond the space where the assailant stood; in your opinion, would the assailant of necessity receive some spatters of blood upon his clothes or person?"

"I should think so."

"What part of the person would have been spattered?"

"The part that was exposed, that was not covered either by furniture or by other protecting substances."

"You have concurred, I believe, in the opinion expressed that the assailant of Mrs. Borden stood astride of her, or over her, when she was lying down."

"That is to my mind the most natural position in which those blows were given."

"And you have heard the testimony about the blood spots. That is to say, that there were many blood spots upon the drawers and the edges of the bureau to her left; that there were a few spots on the sham to her right and upon the upper part of the spread; and that there were some spots upon the mirror of the bureau and the marble of the bureau, quite large numbers. You have heard that?"

"I have heard it, yes, sir."

"Taking into account those spots and the number of injuries that she received, and the appearances of the flowing of the blood there from these injuries, would not of necessity the assailant have been spattered with blood?"

"I should think so."

"What portion of the body of the assailant, in your opinion, would have received those spatters?"

"I should think the front of the dress. Possibly the face. Possibly the hair."

"When you say 'dress,' you speak of the clothing worn by *all* sexes?"

"Yes."

"Any other portion of the body?"

"Well, it is not incredible—it is not inconceivable—that some may have gone into the air and come down upon the back."

"If the injuries had been made with a hatchet similar to the handleless hatchet, having a handle substantially a foot long, would not the assailant, standing in that position, of necessity, in giving the blows, been very near the head in bending over to the head of the assaulted?"

"That would be the natural position."

"And in that situation, giving repeated blows, would not you expect it would follow that the upper portion—the head, the face, the hair of the assailant, assuming that it was not covered—would be spattered with blood?"

"That is reasonable."

My name is David W. Cheever. I reside in Boston. I am a physician and surgeon, educated in the Harvard Medical School. I was also in Europe a little while, at the Medical School of Paris. I've been practicing for thirty-five years and have given attention a good deal of that time to surgery. I was also a demonstrator of anatomy in the Harvard Medical School, and have been a professor of surgery there since 1882. I am a member of the Massachusetts Medical Society, and have been connected with the City Hospital, as one of the surgeons, since 1864. I have been called upon to give my opinion in court in matters in my profession only moderately.

I have heard the testimony with references to the position and surroundings of the bodies as they were found, and the character and color of the blood and the heat of the bodies.

I have also heard Profesor Wood's testimony, and that of Dr. Draper and Dr. Dolan.

As far as my own observations go, they have nothing at all to do with the plaster casts or the cuts, for I never saw the bodies. I was shown the skulls of Mr. and Mrs. Borden, and since then I have made a study of both of them. My own observation was confined to the injuries to the bones.

These indicated that they were made by a heavy, metallic weapon with a cutting edge beveled, with a sharp angle, and with the cutting edge not exceeding three and a half inches in length, and that it was attached to a lever or handle like a hatchet, or some such instrument as that.

343

I have also examined this hatchet head, and I think it could have caused the wounds I found.

The wounds do not *require* that the cutting edge should be any longer than three and a half inches—because the wounds could be made by slashing through the flesh—but *most* of the cuts would seem to show that the edge must have been nearly that length.

I do not think a very narrow hatchet would make them.

I say that it was a cutting edge of not more than three and a half inches because on examining the skull of Mr. Borden, I found that no wider edge than that would reach the carotid wound in the artery, or reach the later wound in the jaw.

Regarding Mrs. Borden's body, I think all the wounds except three were inflicted when she was flat upon her face upon the floor.

I think this scalp wound was inflicted when the assailant was face to face with the victim. It seems to cut from the front; it failed to come out on the other side. My supposition is that when that blow was given, the victim started back, and the hatchet failed to go through, and it glanced.

The other two wounds could have been given in an awkward way, with the head in this position. They would have been more easily given with the person standing up.

Judging from the nature of the skull wounds, the sharpness of the instrument, the weight of it, the wounds of both Mr. Borden and Mrs. Borden, *all* the wounds could have been inflicted by a hatchet of ordinary size, wielded by a woman of ordinary strength. With a handle of sufficiently long leverage. I should think not less than twelve or fourteen inches.

"You would agree that there would be a great deal of effusion of blood in consequence of cutting the carotid artery?"

"It would depend upon the date of that blow with reference to the other injuries. If it was *one* of the last, or *the* last blow that was given, the victim might have been already nearly dead, and the circulation may have been very feeble, and the amount of blood poured out by the heart there may have been small compared to what it would have been if it had been first. It would depend somewhat on that. Usually, the blood from the internal carotid artery is very large and instantaneous."

"Comes with a gush, doesn't it?"

344

"Yes, sir."

"And there are arteries in the head that spurt, are there not?"

"When they are cut into the air on the surface, they spurt."

"And how much in distance do they spurt?"

"Four to six feet."

"Is there in the head a temporal artery somewhere in the region where these injuries were disclosed upon the head of Mr. Borden?"

"Yes, sir. Two of the cuts there would go through it."

"Would you expect a spurting from such cuts?"

"Yes, sir."

"And a spurting of how much distance?"

"Extending several feet."

"Would it throw drops?"

"A spray."

"A spray of drops?"

"Yes, sir."

"Do you perform any surgical operations in the course of your practice, doctor?"

"Yes, I have a good many."

"And you perform many operations upon the head?"

"Yes, sir."

"And when you perform an operation, do you ordinarily put on different outer clothing?"

"Yes, I do."

"What does that consist of?"

"Usually a white linen jacket or a white linen gown, something of that kind."

"Like a duster?"

"Like a long apron."

"Anything else?"

"Sometimes an Indian-rubber apron also."

"And what are those things put on for?"

"Partly to insure absolute cleanliness, and partly to protect my clothes."

"From what?"

"From blood."

"Miss Emma, did any of the members of your family have waterproofs?"

"Yes, we all had them."

"What kind were they?"

"Mrs. Borden's was a gossamer. Rubber."

"That is, you mean rubber on the outside?"

"Yes, sir."

"And black?"

"Yes, sir."

"Where was that hanging?"

"I think she kept it in the little press at the foot of the front stairs. In the front hall."

"Did Miss Lizzie have one, too?"

"Yes, sir."

"Where did she keep hers?"

"In the clothespress at the top of the stairs."

"Do you know where this waterproof of Miss Lizzie's was on the day of the search?"

"Hanging in the clothespress that has been spoken of so often."

"Do you know where it is now?"

"It is there now."

"Been there ever since."

"Every day since."

Every day since, Lizzie thought. Every day since the day of the search and yet before then to the day of the murders themselves, for there had been little rain that August, and no need for a waterproof, no need at all. Every day since that day in August, when the nightmare began, to this sixteenth day of June, ten months and more later, when all was still in the courtroom now as the Government attorneys conferred at their table.

At last, Moody rose.

"As I suggested to Your Honors," he said, "there is one witness on the way from Fall River. His testimony does not relate to a vital part of the case, and we will not insist upon a delay for the expected witness, but will close our evidence at this point."

"The evidence is closed on both sides," Robinson said.

"I desire to say to the jury," Mason said, "that the testimony in this case is now all in. Lizzie Andrew Borden . . ."

She was startled to hear the Chief Justice addressing her. She had expected more—was this all? Yet he had just informed the

346

jury that the testimony had all been heard, and now he was staring at her from behind the bench as she got to her feet.

"Although you have now been fully heard by counsel," he said, "it is your privilege to add any word which you may desire to say in person to the jury. You now have the opportunity."

Lizzie turned to face the twelve men in the jury box. Her head high, her posture erect, her voice clear and unwavering, she said, "I am innocent."

15: CANNES, LONDON, LIVERPOOL—1890

Lost in guilt: the certainty that what Alison had done to her, what she *continued* to allow her to do was Godless and evil, and that she would be punished as surely as had been Eve, whose transgression had eternally doomed all women to a monthly secretion of blood.

"But, why, oh *why*, dear Lizzie, any feelings of guilt? I should sooner slash my wrists than have you experience the slightest remorse. I have loved you from the instant I first laid eyes upon you—oh, that *ridiculous* journey from Oxford to London, where it was all I could do to keep my hands still, patting you and touching you at the merest provocation, smitten like a school-girl! And your own face, Lizzie—admit it—lighting with surprise and delight when first I entered the compartment. Did our eyes meet, or have I only dreamt it this past month and more? Did I see in your secret gray what was most surely in my revealing green? Oh, your radiant splendor! That fair complexion and dazzling red hair, I wondered in the very first instant—I shall blush myself now—whether you were tinted so below, and longed to lift your skirt and petticoats in that public conveyance, causing your Anna to die of mortification behind her veil. How *jealous* I was of your traveling companions! How silly, how hopelessly and immediately in love!

"But, *guilt*, Lizzie? If there truly exists this God you worship, if indeed His all-seeing eye monitors our daily movements, controls them perhaps, then *was* it an accident that He chose to have us meet? And having caused us to be thrown together that way, by the sheerest coincidence, as it seemed—you and your friends on the *worst* possible train to London, Albert and I catching a later train than we'd expected after an *eternal* visit with my cousin and her three squawling brats—no, it could *not* have been coincidence, it was certainly divine *will*, please don't laugh, Lizzie. Your God *chose* to have us meet, chose to inspire our friendship, chose to have us meet again in Paris, chose indeed to have you stricken with influenza so that you might be here this very moment. And chose, my dearest darling, to encourage our intimacy, for which I have nothing but the humblest gratitude. Come to Him enwreathed in guilt then? Nay, Lizzie. Come to Him on your knees instead, in praise and in thanksgiving and in joy. Come to Him as I come to you—in bliss."

Lost in shame: the discovery of herself as someone quite other than what she had supposed herself to be, a proper daughter and sister, a woman who was pious, virtuous, obedient and domestic—a lady.

"But how are you any *less* a lady now, Lizzie? Are your responses not ladylike? I find them exceedingly so. Are your kisses not the kisses a *lady* might offer to her love? Or do you speak of your passion? Is it your passion that shames you so? Then are we, as women, not entitled to the same passion men consider their God-given *right*? Are we any less *ladies* for being passionate *women*? Would it be any more ladylike, I ask, for me to touch, to stroke, to enflame not *your* miniature replica of the male sex organ—I shock my virgin, forgive me, I shall shift to less personal ground, I shall become *objective*. Do you consider it ladylike for *any* married woman to take into her hands a husband's quivering worm and coax it to messy emission? I see that shocks you as well. Be shocked then, Lizzie, for it *is* shocking— to me, it is—and demeaning, and frankly disgusting, and not in the slightest bit *lady*like. Nor can I find anything *ladylike*

349

about a woman spreading her legs to a man's masculine pride, and suffering his brutish batterings. A woman then becomes a beast of the field, and can scarce lay claim to being a *lady*. My hands upon your breasts are ladylike. My body pressed to yours is ladylike. My mouth upon your—if you blush again, I shall *scream*! You may be technically a virgin, but you are no longer a maiden in any sense of the word, so please don't behave as foolishly as if you were Felicity-Twit! Oh, how I *envied* her place beside you in that hotel bed!

"That you should have come through puberty and adolescence, that you could have reached this advanced stage of your own womanhood without once having recognized the erotic potential of that adorable cleft between your legs is a matter of vast astonishment to me. I quite realize that our learned medical tomes prophesize disease or at least nervous prostration as the end result of self-manipulation, but never to have entertained the faintest curiosity about your own anatomy? Never *once*? Never to have *explored* yourself, to have *touched* yourself? Even in this male-dominated prison we share, I find that utterly incomprehensible. I asked you once if there were no looking glasses in all of Fall River. Here, now is a mirror—see how delicately the handle is formed of silver in the shape of a naked woman, her flowing tresses encircling the looking glass itself? Take her in your hands, Lizzie. Open your legs to her. Look upon yourself. Do you see your own lovely reflection? *That* is the lady within you, Lizzie, the *true* lady, known best and only by *other* ladies. Pull back her hood to reveal her pink hard face, lay your fingers delicately upon the center of your pleasure and desire, stroke her, Lizzie, stroke Miss Puss. She blushes as prettily as you do; I shall be compelled to kiss her in a moment."

Lost in fear: the constant gnawing terror of discovery by the servants, for surely they were neither so stupid nor so blind as to not eventually recognize what transpired each night (and often during the mornings and afternoons) in the master bedroom on the second story of the villa.

"But we are careful, are we not, to properly rumple the bedclothes in your room, and to make certain you are there asleep in your virgin nightdress when Moira brings your morning tray? Sherlocks they may be—though I suspect the lot of

350

them are rather dim-witted—but I doubt they have the slightest inkling of our true relationship. I will admit that there's a kernel of truth in the adage that nothing escapes a good servant's eye, be it a mote of dust or a secret liaison. But discretion is the better part of valor, is it not, and none of these worthless clods would be so foolish as to sacrifice a good position for the sake of a gossiping tongue.

"I have no idea what wages your Maggie back home is paid, but Moira earns fifty pounds annually, and cook forty-five. We pay George an additional forty, and Henry, the gardener, earns a hundred a year for allowing my precious orchids to die. As the monkey mentioned while urinating into the till, this certainly runs into a lot of money. Nor are they unaware of the perquisites of the journey to the Continent each summer and the attendant benefits of sunshine and a bit of sport with the local talent. Besides, to whom *would* they gossip, Lizzie? And for what purpose would they risk their good positions here? Should they care to tattle among themselves or to other servants, I care not a fig. Let their tongues wag. Such idle speculation rarely, if ever, reaches the ears of employers.

"I shall tell you something about servants, Lizzie, and you would do well to mind what I say. They are, in many respects, like children: dependent, fiercely loyal if they are treated kindly, and reluctant to believe the slightest harsh truth about mummy or daddy. Should they surprise us *in flagrante delicto* on the lawn—as we shall be careful they do not—they would turn a blind eye to such a glimpse of the primal scene, preferring to believe instead that they were surely mistaken, or else that what they witnessed was a privilege reserved to their wealthy and powerful 'parents.' Like children, so long as they are kept in their proper place, they shall be blindly obedient—which is not to say that they can be trusted with intimacies beyond those they may divine but scarce believe.

"You must be careful, Lizzie, never to submit to the temptation of becoming overly—friendly, shall we say?—with any servant. This general rule goes unobserved by the 'gentlemen' of our time, who are weaned by nannies and often introduced to sex by upstairs maids, and who are not beyond dallying beneath the skirts of any willing household creature who may come within arm's reach. But we, as women, are far more vulnerable and far less powerful, and we cannot afford the luxury of allowing any female employee to believe mistakenly that *she*—because of some indiscretion—is the true mistress of the house."

"I'm not sure I know what you're saying," Lizzie said.

"Do you not? I'm advising you against any intimacy with a servant."

"But who would even *dream* of . . . "

"*I* have dreamt it, and often. You have no idea how I've been tempted by the sight of voluptuous young Moira in her bath, those frisky Irish breasts spattered with freckles . . ."

"Moira!"

"Indeed."

"But surely you've never . . ."

"Of *course* not, have you not been listening to me? Then hearken to my lesson once again. Never, but *never*, let a female employee tempt your fingers or your lips. You shall be eternally sorry if you do, I promise you."

"The very thought that you could even *imagine* Moira as a . . ."

"Hush about Moira now, I regret having mentioned her. I am trying to tell you that our behavior here at the villa, so long as we are discreet and careful, is nothing more than is actually *expected* of us. Indeed, it is our female *obligation* to perform as we do in public. Would you not think it odd if your female friends did not laugh girlishly together, put their empty heads together to exchange delicate secrets, hold hands while walking, embrace in greeting, kiss in farewell? How often have you shared a bed with a lady friend on an overnight visit, undressed in the same room with her, kissed her cheek to bid her a pleasant good night, perhaps even slept in her arms to ward off the winter's chill? None of this is thought upon with the slightest disfavor by the men who govern our lives; they consider it the way of women, the way *they* would have it, the way *they* have trained us to behave.

"They are aware, of course, that Lesbos floats adrift in the *demi-monde*—half the women you saw waltzing together at the Moulin Rouge, cheek to cheek, breast to breast, were undoubtedly lovers. Do you recall the ceiling of the couturier showroom we went to in Paris? On the day you took ill? Do you remember

352

being informed that it had been painted by a Mademoiselle Abbema? Ah, well. Louise Abbema is a great *friend* of Augusta Holmes, a half-Irish blonde who in turn is *chummy* with Colette who, together with the Marquise de Belboeuf—Missy to her *friends*—is not entirely unfamiliar with Montmartre cellars like La Souris, and the Hannenton in the rue Pigalle, and the Rat Mort in the Place Pigalle. Familiar, in short, with the Parisian haunts of the so-called *lesbienne* in her mannishly styled jacket and shirt, though they themselves cannot be considered *demimondaine* in the strictest sense of the word. My point, Lizzie, is that whereas the activities of these conspicuous women might cause the faint lifting of an elegant eyebrow, yours and mine are above suspicion. For all the world to see and admire, we are behaving as proper ladies *should* behave, and whatever happens between us behind a locked door or on a secluded beach is something beyond the imagination of the men who have dictated our narrow ways. But there are more things in heaven and earth than are dreamt of in their philosophy, Lizzie—if you will forgive my borrowing from the bard.

"I am sick unto *death* of their image of us, this myth *they* have created and which *we* are expected to uphold and, yet worse, defend. Our greatest secret, our supreme strength, is that no man on earth, no father, no son, could dare admit to himself that a proper *lady*—his daughter, his sister, his wife—would ever commit a breach that seriously threatened his superior position in the society he has constructed and which he will support with his very life. For should he once believe of any *one* of us that we might so rebel against the absurd rules and regulations proscribing the periphery of our lives, then he must perforce believe that we are *all* capable of bringing down his elaborate house of cards and thereby destroying his faith in the cherished myth of ideal womanhood—the *Lady*, Lizzie. The *Lady* I despise with all my heart.

"Did you know that Louise Abbema wrote a song some years ago, in French to be sure, and that it has become very popular now? I shall sing it for you, if you will forgive my flat English voice rendering her liquid French lyrics:

> *Vers elles, vers elles,*
> *Amour, conduis-nous en battant des ailes.*
> *Vers elles, vers elles,*

Les blondes, les blanches, les belles,
Vers elles, plus loin, là-bas, plus loin encore,
Vers elles, vers elles, les vierges aux cheveux d'or.

"I shall loosely translate the lyrics for you, Lizzie, and in prose that does them no justice, I fear. 'Toward them, toward them, love, take us on your beating wings. Toward them, toward them, the blonde, the fair, the beautiful. Toward them, so distant, there, away, yet farther still. Toward them, toward them—the golden-haired maidens.'

"She calls it 'Hymn to Love,' my dearest love."

Lost in love: a love she had never experienced before, a love beyond filial affection, beyond sisterly concern, beyond (God forgive her!) the love imbued in her for the flesh and the spirit of the savior Jesus Christ, a new and precious love that was in turn giddy and solemn and sacred and nourishing and sad and glowing and present every waking or sleeping moment of her days and nights at the villa. The mere sight of Alison was enough to set her heart tripping, her golden hair in the golden sunlight (though now, in mid-September, there was rain more often than not), her radiant smile, the maidenly perfection of her face and form ("Maiden indeed! I've been mistress of the house for *years* now, your Mistress Puss, Lizzie"), her long-legged stride, her pealing laughter, the scent of her, the coconut oil forsaken now that she was brown as an African, the fragrance of mimosa (or was it only from the hills?). The need she felt for her was incessant, an aching to be held by her, to feel her hands upon her where before now not even her own hands had dared, to seek approval in her marvelous green eyes, to abandon herself utterly to the extravagance of her passion.

Lost in anxiety: the concern that Albert would return to the villa sooner than anticipated, the certainty that *whenever* he returned, his presence would effectively end the ecstasy she shared with Alison.

"But why didn't you tell me this *earlier*?" Alison asked. "It can be settled with a telegram; I shall send one off tomorrow morning."

"A telegram? But how?"

"My darling girl," Alison said, "let me explain the rather

354

dismal arrangement Albert and I have evolved over the years. You must have noticed, though you claimed not to have, that Albert has an eye for the ladies, as revealed through his constant exploration of Felicity-Twit's bottom, and his obvious enthrallment with the prostitute who solicited *une bière Anglaise* from him—or weren't you aware of her occupation?"

"I suspected," Lizzie said, smiling.

"Ah, she suspected, my virgin queen. Accept her sordid trade, then, and accept the fact that had Albert been alone, he would have immediately struck up a bargain with her and followed her to some *hôtel de passe* redolent of disinfectant, where there he would have ravaged her on sheets stinking of sailors' sweat and sperm." She rolled her eyes. "But eet ees zee way of zee men, *n'est-ce pas?*" she said, falling into her broad French accent, "to ex-air-size zee *doigt de seigneur*, pun intentional," she said in her normal voice, "and to *plunge* that raging tumescent beast into whichever rotting hole opens itself before them, however disease ridden, however slippery it might be from the juices of previous conquerors—*amour, amour, toujours l'amour*! I could understand his longings to strip Felicity-Twit to the skin—he confessed this to me one night—but when it comes to his penchant for the bony ladies who . . ."

"What do you mean you can *understand* . . . ?"

"I was tempted to do so myself," Alison said. "*Such* a figure, my God, I would have wallowed in it like a pig in mud."

"But you didn't once really *consider* . . ."

"Oh, I did, I did. More often than once. In fact, had I not been so hopelessly in love with you . . ."

"How can I believe that now?" Lizzie said.

"See how prettily she pouts," Alison said.

"Felicity! The *idea*!"

"A marvelous idea, when one considers it," Alison said, and burst into laughter. "I never so much as touched her even grazingly," she said. "I'd have met Albert's hand halfway there, I imagine. My point, dear Lizzie . . ."

"*Would* you have?"

"Done what? Licked her clean as a platter, had the opportunity been golden? Perhaps. I was so mad with desire for you that I might have leapt upon a broomstick had it chanced across my path."

355

"I shall never believe you again," Lizzie said. "Never."

"To disbelieve truth is to invite deception," Alison said. "My point, dear Lizzie, is that given Albert's lascivious bent, and given my own . . . preferences, shall we say? . . . he is only too eager to seek his pleasure wherever he might find it, and to grant to me a privacy of my own. A civilized arrangement, you will admit, and one that allows for inventive accommodation. I can easily forestall him, if indeed he's the cause of that puckered frown on your . . ."

"My frown has nothing to . . ."

"Most unattractive, I might add. I shall telegraph him in the morning to report that the weather here has turned beastly—as indeed it should within the next week or so—and that he would do well to linger in Germany, or perhaps go on to Italy where there will be sunshine for a good while yet. He will understand completely. You certainly didn't believe that mere *financial* matters would have kept him in Berlin even *this* long? *Die kleinen Puppen* perhaps, but not *die Börse.*"

"So he's had other women," Lizzie said.

"Yes."

"And you knew of them—*know* of them."

"Yes."

"And you?"

"Ah."

"Have there been . . . other women for you as well?"

"The eternal question," Alison said, and sighed.

"Have there been?"

"But honesty so offends you."

"Tell me."

"Yes."

"Many?"

"Enough."

"And other men as well?"

"One before Albert . . . and he not quite a man. None since."

"Who?"

"The man? The *boy*, actually. The women? The lot of them?"

"You make them sound like an *army*!"

"Not quite. A brigade, perhaps."

"Who?"

"See how jealous she becomes!"

356

"*Who*, Alison?"

"The women were a varied lot. A marquise here, a matchgirl there, you know how ferocious my appetite can be, Lizzie."

"And the man? The *boy*, as you call him."

"A boy indeed. Fair-haired and handsome, and as eager to experiment as I myself was."

"Where?"

"In London."

"When?"

"We were both thirteen."

"Both . . . ?"

"My brother. My twin. My dearest love, Geoffrey."

Lost in knowledge.

Eve's sin.

From which, once disclosed, once learned, there was no retreat.

The torrential rains of autumn came early that year, sooner than Alison had expected, although she seemed delighted that now there would be wild daisies on the hillsides. On a Sunday when the servants were gone and the villa was still they lay naked beside each other in Alison's bed, the covers pulled to their throats, the rain beating against the windowpanes as she talked quietly of Geoffrey again. Lizzie listened with the same inexplicable, jealous anger she had experienced when first she'd learned of their reckless adventure, Alison saying now that their early experiments had continued well into their late adolescence and beyond, in fact until the time she was twenty-three and betrothed to Albert by her father, who was then still alive.

"Always the lordly succession to power and control," she said, "male to male, with never a regard for the feelings or wishes of the female involved. I should have been content to have spent the rest of my life in clandestine embrace with Geoffrey—oh, the vast secret we shared in that musty London house my father called our home! I would, in fact, leap into bed with him again in an instant, even now, had not his own interests become so . . . Wilde-like, shall we say?"

"Wildlike?" Lizzie said, consumed with jealousy, her voice angry and tight. "What is *that* supposed to mean?"

357

"Are you not familiar with Oscar Wilde? He's one of our more celebrated authors, and purportedly as 'so' as a turnip."

"As 'so'?"

"As *queer*, Lizzie."

"Odd, do you mean?"

"Odd, yes. But *also* queer."

"I still don't know what you mean."

"Why, homosexual, Lizzie."

"Are you saying *Geoffrey* is homosexual?"

"Oh, quite."

"I don't believe it!"

"Can you believe that *I* am? That you yourself are?"

"But I'm *not*!"

"Lesbian to the core," Alison said, and laughed softly, and suddenly put her hand upon her. Lizzie leaped in surprise. "Have I startled Miss Puss?" Alison said, "There, there," she said, stroking her, "be calm, sweet lady, *stai calma*, I shall smooth your ruffled feathers."

"I'm . . . not at all what you think," Lizzie said. "What you . . . say I am."

"Then you're simply not, of course, and we have no argument," Alison said.

"I should *never* want another woman but you," Lizzie said. "I should never *dream* of allowing anyone else to do to me . . ."

"Never say never," Alison said.

"Though I'm certain that the moment I'm gone, *you* shall tumble into bed with the nearest . . ."

"More than likely," Alison said. "But we have time yet."

"Little more than a month."

"An eternity," Alison murmured.

"Alison . . . if we're to talk . . ."

"Yes?"

"You must stop doing that. Really."

"Is Miss Puss becoming agitated? Then stop I shall, for talk I would. There's nothing I enjoy *better*, in fact, than recalling the days of my wanton youth."

"And now you'll try to make me jealous again, won't you?"

"No, no."

"Oh, yes, *yes*, I know you too well, Alison."

"As well you should. I'm a reflection of yourself, Lizzie."

"Hardly."

"Your very soul."

"Damned to Hell forever."

"For loving?"

"For sinning."

"I've known greater sinners who are doubtlessly strumming harps and floating on clouds this very moment."

"Have you glimpsed Heaven then, to know . . .?"

"*You're* my Heaven, Lizzie."

"As was Geoffrey."

"Indeed. When first we . . ."

"I don't want to hear about it."

"Very well then."

The rain beat upon the windowpanes. There was a harsh wind now, rattling the leaves in the trees outside. From very far away, Lizzie could hear the angry motion of the sea.

"Tell me," she said.

"Have you changed your mind then? A moment ago . . ."

"*Tell* me," Lizzie said.

"Your servant, of course," Alison said, and smiled. "But, oh dear, where shall I begin? We were innocents, you understand, and had not yet been exposed to the witless sexual theories expounded by all those lofty cocks of the walk represented in my father's medical volumes—have I told you he was a physician, my father? The irony of his death, in fact, was that he was unable to diagnose his own disease. But high on a shelf in his library were the dusty tomes containing the sexual secrets of the universe, known by us to be there, of course—there is little that can be kept from bright, inquisitive children—some of which I would rather *not* have learned, believe me. Can you imagine medical practitioners advocating the removal of a woman's ovaries rather than admitting that the natural stirrings she feels in her vagina are prompted by *passion* and not 'female' malfunction? Ah, yes, Lizzie, you have no idea how many women in our day—but that's another story, as our Mr. Kipling might say.

"One rainy afternoon—it's always raining when children make their most important discoveries, isn't it?—one rainy afternoon, my brother Geoffrey mounted a ladder and took down from my father's topmost shelf a book we perused with consid-

359

erable interest. And there, all at once, in full color, and occupying a full page of the volume, were drawings side by side of the male sex organ and its female counterpart. Well! I might add that the drawing of the female organ was rendered in more excruciating detail than that of the male, but perhaps this was due more to the fascination of the artist than to any sense of dedication on the parts of the physicians who'd compiled the volume. But who can say? Physicians today certainly seem steadfast in their dedication to scooping out our insides as if we were melons. I digress.

"Naturally curious, alone in the house—was my mother off to a British equivalent of the *quatre à cinq*? I shouldn't be surprised, for her upbringing was European, and she was surely familiar with the ways of the world, and less bound to propriety than the proper London ladies of her time—nonetheless, alone and curious, the servants God only knew where, the library door locked, we decided to compare against the drawings in my father's text the—how shall I put it?—the real life *articles*. So my brother unfastened his trousers and we examined his penis at great length, no pun intended, and then to correct the gap—again no pun intended—in my own education, I lifted my skirts, and lowered my knickers and opened my legs to him.

"I scarcely had pubic hair then, I don't really recall. A gentle down, I believe, hardly similar to the savage bush I now possess—the 'golden bramble,' Geoffrey used to call it, but that was when we were a bit older. Using a looking glass we took down from the mantel, and much as I showed you to yourself not very long ago, I sat with limbs akimbo while we both stared in wonder at the bewildering labyrinth of fold upon fold of tissue, Geoffrey reciting aloud the anatomical words for what until then I scarcely knew I had between my legs—well, let me reconstruct the scene for you, Lizzie," she said, and suddenly threw back the covers.

"No, don't!" Lizzie cried, and hurled herself upon her. "I don't want to hear another word, I shan't be able to stand it!" Kissing her fiercely, she murmured, "I love you so much, oh God, I love you to death," crushing herself hungrily against her, and knowing in that instant that Alison was as much her own twin as she was Geoffrey's. And suddenly, confronted with this darker knowledge, she wondered which of them—she or Alison—truly controlled their tumultuous joinings, and realized all at once that it was beyond the control of either; they were only what they were; she was all that Alison said she was. She allowed the raging sea to wash over her then, accepting wave after wave, no longer caring *what* she was or might become, no longer trying even to guess who this woman drowning in the arms of another woman might be.

On the twenty-third of October, they returned to London, where Lizzie was reunited with her friends at the Hotel Albemarle. Her letters to them had been full of lies about her continuing frailty, and they were surprised to see her looking in such good health, though, in fact, the color she had picked up in Cannes had faded with the September rains, and the unusually cold winds of October had kept her and Alison indoors much of the time.

Felicity confessed that a gondolier in Venice had pinched her bottom.

Rebecca said that her German had served them beautifully in Munich and Berlin, but that it had not been understood as well in the smaller towns.

Anna complained that the food had been virtually inedible everywhere—"*especially* in Italy."

She saw Alison for the last time on a blustery cold Saturday, two days before she and her friends were to sail home from Liverpool. In the Burlington Arcade that morning, she bought Alison a small pillbox with the sentiment *Thine Forever* enameled in black script lettering on its bright pink top. She gave it to her over lunch at Gatti's in the Strand. Alison's farewell gift was a brilliant red orchid. To the crowds passing by outside the restaurant later that afternoon, the two women in tearful embrace on the sidewalk must have seemed indeed a commonplace. They kissed once more, lingeringly, and then walked off in separate directions, their heads bent against the wind blowing fiercely all about them.

The stateroom she and Anna were to share on the homeward voyage was the same one they had occupied on the outward journey, a luxurious compartment on the promenade deck, fitted with two bedsteads, wardrobes, armchairs, a writing table and a couch. A stained-glass shutter screened the window, and late October sunshine filtered through it, dappling with oranges, reds, yellows and blues the bed upon which Lizzie sat. Across the cabin Anna was unpacking. When Lizzie burst into sudden tears, she could not for the life of her imagine what the matter was.

"Lizzie?" she said, coming to her. "Are you all right, dear? You're not taking *ill* again, are you?"

Lizzie shook her head.

"Then what is it?" Anna asked.

Lizzie choked back a sob, and then dabbed at her eyes with a lace-trimmed handkerchief. "I wish we weren't going home so soon," she said, tears brimming in her eyes again.

"Soon? But Lizzie, we've been gone . . ."

"Oh, Anna," she said, "I've had *such* a happy summer!"

"Well, we *all* have, dear. But that's no reason to . . . "

"I shall never be so happy again," Lizzie said.

"Of *course*, you will. Lizzie, Lizzie . . ."

"Never," Lizzie said. "My home shall be such an unhappy one now, I *know* it! I wish I could stay here forever, I wish I could . . ." and she burst into fresh tears again. "Such an unhappy home," she sobbed into her handkerchief, "such an unhappy one."

Patting her hand, embracing her—but not too closely, for Lord knew *what* she might be coming down with now—Anna tried to understand what Lizzie had meant. A *happy* summer? Why, she'd been sick most of the time! And she'd missed most of France, and all of Italy and Germany!

So far as Anna could see, Lizzie had hardly made *any* journey at all.

16: NEW BEDFORD—1893

"I desire to remind the jury," Chief Justice Mason said, "that there is still a further word to be said before this cause will be finally committed to them. The charge to the jury will be read by Mr. Justice Dewey."

The courtroom today was as crowded as it had been yesterday when Lizzie had listened to Robinson argue on her behalf that the state had failed to prove its case. She could not have imagined then that the courtroom could have held a single person more, but today it seemed as though the crowd, should it take in its breath collectively, might cause the walls to swell and collapse into the street below.

Yesterday morning Robinson had begun his closing argument to the jury at nine o'clock, had spoken until the recess and had resumed his argument at two-fifteen in the afternoon. There were some among her supporters who had felt his address was not quite as eloquent as might have been expected of him, but she had been deeply moved when, in conclusion, he had said to the jury, "Gentlemen, with great weariness on your part, but with abundant patience and intelligence and care, you have listened to what I have to offer. So far as you are concerned,

363

it is the last word of the defendant to you. Take it; take good care of her as you have, and give us promptly your verdict 'Not Guilty' that she may go home and be Lizzie Andrew Borden of Fall River in that blood-stained and wrecked home where she has passed her life so many years."

Knowlton had begun his closing argument yesterday afternoon, had spoken through the remainder of the court day, and had concluded this morning with the words, "Rise, gentlemen, rise to the altitude of your duty. Act as you would be reported to act when you stand before the Great White Throne at the last day. What shall be your reward? The ineffable consciousness of duty done. There is no strait so hard, there is no affliction so bitter that is not made light and easy by the consciousness that in times of trial you have done your duty and your whole duty. There is no applause in the world, there is no station of height, there is no seduction of fame that can compensate for the gnawings of an outraged conscience. Only he who hears the voice of his inner consciousness—it is the voice of God himself—saying to him, 'Well done, good and faithful servant,' can enter into the reward and lay hold of eternal life."

It had seemed to Lizzie, soberly listening to him, that the jury was profoundly impressed by his words. He had ended his address at twelve-fifteen this morning, and it was now two o'clock. The jurors, who had returned after recess to hear Chief Justice Mason's brief opening remark, now turned their full attention to Justice Dewey. He looked uncomfortably hot in his black judicial garments. He consulted the papers before him, looked at the jury once to make certain they were settled and awaiting his words, and then began his charge.

"Mr. Foreman and gentlemen of the jury," he said, "you have listened with attention to the evidence in this case, and to the arguments for the defendant's counsel and of the district attorney. It now remains for me, acting in behalf of the Court, to give you such aid toward a proper performance of your duty as I may be able to give, within the limits for judicial action prescribed by law. And to prevent any erroneous impression, it may be well for me to bring to your attention, at the outset, that it is provided by a statute of this state that the Court shall not charge juries with respect to matters of fact, but may state the testimony and the law.

364

"I may perhaps illustrate this distinction in the course of my remarks. But, speaking comprehensively, I may now say to you that it will be your duty, in considering and deciding the matters of fact necessary to rendering your verdict, not to allow your judgment to be affected by what you may suppose or believe to be the opinion of the Court upon such matters of fact.

"The defendant is being tried before you on a written accusation, termed an indictment, which contains two charges or counts; one count by the use of the usual legal language in substance charges her with the murder of Andrew J. Borden and the other count charges her with the murder of Abby D. Borden in Fall River in this county on August fourth, 1892.

"The Government claims that the killing of Mr. and Mrs. Borden, by whomsoever done, was done with premeditated, deliberate malice aforethought within the meaning of the statute, and it was murder in the first degree. The statute nowhere defines murder itself, and for such definition we must resort to the common law, and according to that law 'murder is the unlawful killing of a human being with malice aforethought.'

"The second main proposition in the case is that the killing of Mr. and Mrs. Borden was done by the defendant. In considering the evidence with regard to this issue, you will need to have certain legal principles in mind and to use them as guides. One such principle is the presumption of law that the defendant is innocent. This presumption begins with her at the outset of the trial, and continues with her through all its stages until you are compelled by the evidence to divest her of it.

"It is competent for the Government to show that the defendant had motives to commit the crimes with which she is charged, and evidence has been introduced from which you are asked to find that she had unpleasant relations with her stepmother, the deceased, and also that her father, Andrew Jackson Borden, left an estate of the value of from $250,000 to $300,000, and that so far as is known to the defendant, he died without having made a will. If his wife died before him, it is not disputed that he left the defendant and her sister as his only heirs.

"It appears that Mr. Borden was sixty-nine years old, and Mrs. Borden more than sixty years of age at the time of their deaths. Taking the facts now, as you find them to be established

365

by the evidence, and taking the defendant as you find her to be, and judging according to general experience and observation, *was* the defendant under a real and actually operating motive to kill her father and his wife?

"Imputing a motive to defendant does not prove that she had it. I understand the counsel for the Government to claim that defendant had toward her stepmother a strong feeling of ill will, nearly if not quite amounting to hatred. And Mrs. Gifford's testimony as to a conversation with defendant in the early spring of 1892 is relied upon largely as a basis for that claim, supplemented by whatever evidence there is as to defendant's conduct toward her stepmother.

"But take Mrs. Gifford's just as she gave it, and consider whether or not it will fairly amount to the significance attached to it, remembering that it is the language of a young woman and not of a philosopher or a jurist. What you wish, of course, is a true conception—a true conception of the state of the mind of the defendant toward her stepmother, not years ago, but later and nearer the time of the homicides. And to get such a true conception, you must not separate Mrs. Gifford's testimony from all the rest but consider also the evidence as to how they lived in the family.

"Whether, as Mrs. Raymond, I believe, said, they sewed together on each other's dresses; whether they went to church together, sat together, returned together; in a word, the general *tenor* of their life. Weigh carefully all the testimony on the subject in connection with the suggestions of counsel, and then judge whether or not there is clearly proved such a permanent state of mind on the part of defendant toward her stepmother as to justify you in drawing against her, upon that ground, inferences unfavorable to her innocence.

"Now, gentlemen, the material charge in the first count of the indictment is that, at Fall River, in this county, the defendant killed Mrs. Borden, by striking, cutting, beating and bruising her on the head with some sharp cutting instrument. In the second count the same charges are made in regard to Mr. Borden. And the government claims that these acts were done with deliberately premeditated malice aforethought, and so were acts of murder in the first degree.

"Now you observe, gentlemen, that the Government submits

366

this case to you upon circumstantial evidence. No witness testifies to *seeing* the defendant in the act of doing the crime charged, but the Government seeks to establish by proof a body of facts and circumstances from which you are asked to infer or conclude that the defendant killed Mr. and Mrs. Borden. This is a legal and not unusual way of proving a criminal case, and it is clearly competent for a jury to find a person guilty of murder upon circumstantial evidence alone. The principle that underlies circumstantial evidence, we are constantly acting on in our business; namely, the inferring of one fact from other facts proved.

"Sometimes the inference is direct, and almost certain. For instance, the noise of a pistol is heard from a certain room in a hotel. The door is unlocked or otherwise opened. A man is found, just dead, with a bullet hole in his temple. Near him is a revolver with one barrel discharged. In such a case, if no contradictory or controlling facts appeared, we should infer—with a very strong assurance—that the death was caused by the pistol. In other cases the facts from which the conclusion is sought to be drawn are numerous and complicated, and the conclusion not so closely connected with the facts or so easy to draw.

"This is illustrated by the case on trial here. You have got to go through a long and careful investigation to ascertain what facts are proved. Then, after you have determined what specific facts are proved, you have remaining the important duty of deciding whether or not you are justified in drawing, and will draw, from these facts the conclusion of guilt.

"Now let me illustrate. Take an *essential* fact. All would admit that the necessity of establishing the presence of the defendant in the house, when, for instance, her father was killed, is a necessary fact. The Government could not expect that you would find her guilty of the murder of her father by her own hand unless you are satisfied that she was where he was when he was murdered. And if the evidence left you in reasonable doubt as to that fact—so vital, so absolutely essential—the Government must fail of its case, whatever may be the force and significance of other facts; that is, so far as it is claimed that she did the murder with her own hands.

"Now, take the instance of a *helpful* fact. The question of the relation of this handleless hatchet to the murder. It may have an important bearing upon the case, upon your judgment of the relations of the defendant to these crimes—whether the crime was done by that particular hatchet or not—but it cannot be said, and is not claimed by the Government that it bears the same essential and necessary relation to the case that the matter of her presence in the house does. It is not claimed by the Government but what that killing might have been done with some *other* instrument.

"Take another illustration. I understand the Government to claim substantially that the alleged fact that the defendant made a false statement in regard to her stepmother's having received a note or letter that morning bears an essential relation to the case, bears to it the relation of an *essential* fact, not merely the relation of a *useful* fact. Now what are the grounds on which the Government claims that that charge is false, knowingly false?

"There are three, as I understand them: one, that the man who wrote it has not been found; second, that the party who brought it has not been found; and third, that no letter has been found. And substantially, if I understand the position correctly, upon those three grounds you are asked to find that an *essential* fact—a deliberate *falsehood* on the part of the defendant has been established.

"Now what answer or reply is made to this charge? First, that the defendant had time to think of it; she was not put in a position upon the evidence where she was compelled to make that statement without any opportunity for reflection. If, as the Government claims, she had killed her stepmother some little time before, she had a period in which she could turn over the matter in her mind. She must naturally anticipate, if she knew the facts, that the question at no remote period would be asked her where Mrs. Borden was, or if she knew where she was. She might reasonably and naturally expect that that question would arise.

"Again, it will be urged in her behalf, what motive had she to *invent* a story like this? What *motive*? Would it not have answered every purpose to have her say—and would it not have been more natural for her to say—simply that her stepmother had gone out on an errand or to make a call? What motive had she to take upon herself the responsibility of giving utterance to this distinct and independent fact of a letter or note received

with which she might be confronted and which might afterwards find it difficult to explain, if she knew that no such thing
was true? Was it a natural thing to say—situated as they were,
living as they did, taking the general tenor of their ordinary
life—was it a natural thing for her to *invent*?

"Now gentlemen, you know that I am expressing no opinion
as to what is proved. I am only trying to illustrate principles
and rules of law and evidence. Referring to the present case let
me use this illustration: suppose you were clearly satisfied upon
the testimony that if defendant committed the homicides she
could by no reasonable possibility have done so without receiving upon her person and clothing a considerable amount of
bloodstain; that when Bridget Sullivan came to her upon call
and not long after some of the other women, she had no bloodstains upon her person or clothing; that she had had no sufficient opportunity either to remove the stain from her person or
clothing, or to change her clothing.

"If these *supposed* facts should be found by you to be *real* facts,
you could not say upon the evidence that defendant's guilt was
to a moral certainty *proved*. So you see that in estimating the
force of different facts, or portions of the evidence it is not
enough to consider them as standing apart, for the force which
they appear to have when looked at by themselves, may be
controlled by some other single fact.

"When was Mrs. Borden killed? At what time was Mr. Borden
killed? Did the same person kill both of them? Was defendant
in the house when Mrs. Borden was killed? Was she in the
house when Mr. Borden was killed? In this connection you will
carefully consider any statements and explanations of defendant
put in evidence by the Government and shown to have been
made by defendant at the time or afterwards, as to where she
was when either of them was killed, and all other evidence
tending to sustain or disprove the truth and accuracy of these
statements.

"Did other persons, known or unknown, have an equal or a
practical and available opportunity to commit these crimes? Is
there reason to believe that any such person had any motive to
commit them? Is there anything in the way and manner of
doing the acts of killing, the weapon used, whatever it was, or

the force applied, which is significant as to the sex and strength of the doer of the acts?

"For instance, the medical experts have testified as to the way in which they think the blows were inflicted on Mrs. Borden, and as to what they think was the position of the assailant. Are those views correct? If so, are they favorable to the contention that a person of defendant's sex and size was the assailant? Is it reasonable and credible that she could have killed Mrs. Borden at or about the time claimed by the Government, and then with the purpose in her mind to kill her father at a later hour, have gone about her household affairs with no change of manner to excite attention?

"Several witnesses called by the Government have testified to statements said to have been made by defendant in reply to questions asked, I believe in each instance, as to where she was when her father was killed, and considerable importance is attached by the Government to the language which it claims was used by her as showing that she professed not only to have been in the barn, but *upstairs* in the barn. And the Government further claims it is not worthy of belief that she was in the upper part of the barn, as she says, because of the extreme heat there and because one of the officers testifies that on examination they found no tracks in the dust on the stairs and flooring. Now what statements on the subject the defendant did make and their significance and effect is wholly for you upon the evidence, and there is no rule of law to control your judgment in weighing that evidence.

"But here, gentlemen, I may repeat to you the language of a thoughtful writer on the law, not as binding upon you, but as containing suggestions useful to be borne in mind in dealing with this class of evidence. He says, 'With respect to all verbal admissions it may be observed that they ought to be received with great caution. The evidence, consisting as it does, in the mere repetition of oral statements, is subject to much imperfection and mistake.'

"Gentlemen, it will be for you to judge whether that extract which I read—which I say I give to you in the way of suggestion and not as a binding authority—expresses a reasonable principle, a principle that is wise and safe and prudent to be acted upon in such a case as this. Whether there is not more danger of some misunderstanding, some inaccuracy, some error creeping into evidence when it relates to *statements* than there is when it relates to acts. Would you not hold that it was a just and reasonable view to take that if a party is to be held responsible in a case like this largely upon statements, that those statements should be most carefully and thoroughly proved?

"Now the Government has called as witnesses some gentlemen of scientific and medical knowledge and experience, who are termed experts, and there has been put into the case considerable testimony from them. I think I may say to you that expert testimony constitutes a class of evidence which the law requires you to subject to careful scrutiny.

"It often happens that experts testify to what is in substance a matter of fact rather than of opinion. A surveyor called to prove the distance between two points may express his opinions founded on his observation, or he may say, 'I have actually applied my measuring chain and found the distance.' So, for instance, Professor Wood may say, 'There are, in science, tests of the presence of blood as fixed and certain as the surveyor's chain is of distance. I have applied those tests to supposed bloodstains on a hatchet, and I find no blood.' This testimony may be regarded as little a matter of opinion as the testimony of a surveyor.

"On the other hand, if Professor Wood shall be asked to testify as to the length of time between the deaths of Mr. and Mrs. Borden, from his examination of the contents of the stomachs, his testimony must perhaps be to some extent a matter of opinion, depending possibly on the health and vigor of the two persons and constitutional differences; upon whether they were physically active after eating, or at rest; upon whether one or the other was mentally worried and anxious, or otherwise.

"Now his knowledge and skill may enable him to form an opinion upon the subject with greater or less correctness; but the question to be dealt with is by its essential nature different from the other. If you should accept his testimony as correct and satisfactory on the first subject, it would not necessarily follow that you should on the second.

"So as to whether certain wounds in the skull were caused by a particular hatchet head or could have been caused by that hatchet head only, if you have the hatchet head and the skull you may think you can apply them to each other and judge as well as the expert. I call your attention to the subject in this way to make clear to you, first, that you are not concluded on any subject by the testimony of the experts, and, second, that it is important to apply to their testimony an intelligent and discriminating judgment.

"Gentlemen, we have given our attention to particular aspects of this case and of the evidence. Let us look at it broadly. The Government charges the defendant with the murder of Mr. and Mrs. Borden. The defendant denies the charges. The law puts on the Government the burden of proving beyond reasonable doubt every fact necessary to establish guilt. The defendant is bound to prove nothing. The law presumes she is innocent.

"The case is said to be mysterious. If so, the defendant cannot be required to clear up the mystery. There is no way, under the law, by which the burden of proof as to any essential matter can be transferred to her. The Government offers evidence. She may rest on the insufficiency of that evidence to prove her guilt, or she may also offer evidence partially to meet or rebut it, or raise a reasonable doubt as to any part of the Government's case. You are not to deal with the evidence in a captious spirit, but to allow it to produce on your minds its natural and proper effect.

"In such a case as this, or in *any* case, you cannot be absolutely certain of the correctness of your conclusions. The law does not require you to be so. If, proceeding with due caution and observant of the principles which have been stated, you are convinced beyond reasonable doubt of the defendant's guilt, it will be your plain duty to declare that conviction by your verdict. If the evidence falls short of producing such conviction in your mind, it would be your plain duty to return a verdict of not guilty. If not legally proved to be guilty, the defendant is entitled to a verdict of not guilty. The law contemplates no middle course.

"Gentlemen, I want to refer at this point briefly to one or two matters, not in a connected way, where it seems proper to me that a brief suggestion should be made. Something was said in regard to evidence tending to show the defendant had made statements in regard to presentiments of some disaster to come upon the household. And you were asked to look upon those statements—which were testified to by one of the witnesses—as evidence tending to show that the defendant might have been harboring in her mind purposes of evil with reference to the household. Statements made only, I believe, the day before this calamity fell on the household, only the day before the deed was done by the defendant, *if* she did it.

"Now, in considering that evidence, you should not necessarily go off in your view of it upon the suggestion of counsel, but, so far as you deem it important, hold it before your minds, look at it in all its lights and bearings, and see whether it seems to you reasonable and probable that a person meditating the perpetration of a great crime, would, the day before, predict to a friend, either in form or in substance, the happening of that disaster.

"Suppose some person in New Bedford contemplated the perpetration of a great crime upon the person or family of another citizen in New Bedford, contemplated doing it soon. Would he naturally, probably, predict a day or two beforehand that anything of the nature of that crime would occur? Is the reasonable construction to be put upon that conversation that of evil premeditation, dwelt upon, intended, or only of evil fears and apprehensions?

"Take this matter of the dress, of which so much has been said, that she had on that morning. Take all the evidence in this case, Bridget Sullivan's, the testimony of these ladies, Dr. Bowen's. Taking the evidence of these several witnesses, considering that evidence carefully, comparing part with part, can you gentlemen extract from that testimony such a description of a dress as would enable you from the testimony to *identify* the dress?

"Is there such an agreement among these witnesses—to whom no wrong intention is imputed by anybody—is there such an agreement in their accounts and in their memory and recollection, and in the description which they are able to give from the observation that they had in that time of confusion and excitement, that you could put their statements together, and from those statements say that any given dress was accurately *described*?

"Gentlemen, I know not what views you may take of the case, but it is of the gravest importance that it should be decided. If decided at all it must be decided by a jury. I know of no reason

373

to expect that any other jury could be supplied with more evidence or be better assisted by the efforts of counsel. The case on both sides has been conducted by counsel with great fairness, industry and ability. You are to confer together; and this implies that each of you, in recollecting and weighing the evidence, may be aided by the memory and judgment of his associates. The law requires that the jury shall be unanimous in their verdict, and it is their duty to agree if they can conscientiously do so.

"And now, gentlemen, the case is committed into your hands. And, entering on your deliberations with no pride of opinion, with impartial and thoughtful minds, seeking only for the truth, you will lift the case above the range of passion and prejudice and excited feeling, into the clear atmosphere of reason and law. If you shall be able to do this, we can hope that, in some high sense, this trial may be adopted into the order of Providence, and may express in its results somewhat of that justice with which God governs the world."

It was now twenty-eight minutes before five o'clock.

The jury had been out of the courtroom since twenty-four minutes past three. Among the articles they had taken with them to assist in their deliberation were the plans and photographs marked as exhibits in the case, the skulls of her father and Mrs. Borden, the bedspread and pillow shams from the guest room, a piece of doorframe taken from inside the dining room, a piece of molding taken from the guest room, the two axes, the claw-hammer hatchet, the handleless hatchet and bit of wood, Lizzie's blue blouse and dress skirt, her white skirt—and a magnifying glass.

Only moments before, Robinson had assured her that there was no need for concern, so convinced was he that upon the evidence submitted to the jury they would never return a conviction. She had said nothing. Nodding, she had merely listened, cognizant of the very real possibility that the jury would not share Robinson's views on the matter before them.

They were coming back into the courtroom now.

Solemnly they filed into the jury box.

"Gentlemen of the jury will answer as their names are

374

called," Chief Justice Mason said. "The crier will count as they respond."

The court crier intoned their names, one after the other.

"George Potter."

"Present."

"William F. Dean."

"Present."

"John Wilbur."

"Present."

"Frederic C. Wilbar."

"Present."

As each man responded in turn, Lizzie studied his face for some clue to the verdict.

"Lemuel K. Wilber."

"Present."

"William Westcott."

"Present."

"Louis B. Hodges."

"Present."

"August Swift."

"Present."

She could read nothing on any of the faces.

"Frank G. Cole."

"Present."

"John C. Finn."

"Present."

Nothing whatever.

"Charles I. Richards."

"Present."

"Allen H. Wordell."

"Present."

"Lizzie Andrew Borden, stand up," the clerk said.

She rose unsteadily, her lips compressed, a rush of blood coloring her face, her eyes vacant. Her heart was pounding furiously.

"Gentlemen of the jury, have you agreed upon a verdict?"

"We have," the foreman said.

She felt her knees weakening. She put one hand on the back of Robinson's chair, supporting herself.

375

"Please return the papers to the Court," the clerk said. "Lizzie Andrew Borden, hold up your right hand."

She lifted her hand from where it had been resting on the chair back. She had difficulty keeping it from trembling.

"Mr. Foreman, look upon the prisoner."

His eyes met hers.

"Prisoner, look upon the foreman."

She returned his steady gaze.

"What say you, Mr. Fore—"

"Not guilty," he said.

There arose from the spectators' benches behind her a cheer that might have been heard in Fall River itself. Her legs suddenly gave beneath her. She sank heavily into the chair, covered her face with her hands, and began sobbing. Robinson came to her and put his arm about her. She looked up into his face. Beyond him she saw the three justices staring implacably out over the courtroom as if totally oblivious to the pandemonium. The sheriff, tears in his eyes, made no move to lift his gavel, although the cheering showed no sign of abatement. Moved, she turned to look toward the spectators' benches. People there were waving handkerchiefs in cadence to their rising and falling voices. She turned back to Robinson again. He was looking at the jury, nodding at the jury, smiling at them, his eyes glowing with what appeared to be almost fatherly pride. Jennings's eyes were moist as he put his hand out to Adams, sitting next to him. "Thank God," he said, his voice breaking, and Adams took his hand and held it tightly, nodding his head speechlessly, his ridiculous mustache bobbing. A full minute must have passed, perhaps more, before there was silence again, and then only because the clerk asked, in a loud, clear voice, "Gentlemen of the jury, you upon your oaths do say that Lizzie Andrew Borden, the prisoner at the bar, is not guilty?"

"We do."

Not guilty, she thought, and covered her face again, and wept into her hands. Oh, dear God, innocent.

"So say you, Mr. Foreman? So say all of you gentlemen?"

"We do."

"May it please the Court," Knowlton said, rising. "There are pending two indictments against the same defendant, one charging the murder which is charged in this indictment on the

376

first count, and the other charging the murder which is charged in this indictment on the second count. An entry should be made in those cases of nol-prossed by reason of the verdict in this case. Now, congratulating the defendant and the counsel for the defendant upon the result of the trial, I believe the duties are concluded."

He was smiling, Lizzie noticed. As though in relief.

"The jurors may be seated," Mason said.

"Lizzie Andrew Borden," the clerk said.

She rose again, though she did not know whether she was supposed to or not. Tears were streaming down her cheeks.

"The Court orders that you be discharged of this indictment and go thereof without delay."

17: FALL RIVER—
AUGUST 4, 1892

For the tick of an instant, she thought the laughter from below was part of her dream, Moira and the cook clattering across the villa courtyard, George calling to them, the women laughing. The laughter came again, Uncle John's, deep and gruff, splintering the dream sunlight, replacing it with wakefulness and the reality of true sunlight slanting through the windows across the room. She lay in her bed listening to the voices downstairs, the room slowly coming into focus.

The clock on the dresser read a quarter past eight.

It was far too early; she had not slept well. Last night—the sound of Uncle John's footfalls on the stairs, awakening her when she had just barely dozed off, the further small sounds of his preparations for bed. And later, the pounding outside, someone pounding on wood. She had known who it was the moment she'd heard the noise. She awakened now with the gnawing knowledge of who it had been.

She lay quite still in her nightdress.

The bedclothes felt damp beneath her and for a moment she feared she might be lying in a pool of her own blood. She sat up and searched the sheets. Nothing. She lay back against the pillows again. She had slept last night with the door closed; the room was hot and sticky now. She watched dust motes climbing the shafts of sunlight that streamed through the windows, and felt the slow ooze of blood between her legs, Eve's curse. She could still hear voices below. She closed her eyes against the morning sun, listening to the droning voices, hoping they would lull her back to sleep again, willing sleep to come again and with it the images, scents and sounds of that summer lost in time.

". . . spend the morning with my nephew and niece," Uncle John was saying.

"Will you be leaving now?" her father asked.

"Not for a bit yet. Give them time to finish their breakfast."

It was no use.

The sounds in this house. Traveling from one room to the next like restless spirits. She opened her eyes and looked up at the ceiling. She did not want to remember what she had done yesterday—*tried* to do, *would* have done—but the memory was full-blown upon her, as though it had been lurking at the edges of her restless sleep all night long, waiting to pounce upon her the moment she was fully awake.

"Never make an important decision when you're flowering," Alison once told her. "Never even try to *think* during your period."

But, oh, this depression had been with her for the better part of two weeks now, long before her courses had begun, the monthly rage of God bubbling in the rank cauldron between her legs, mingling blood and pain with the contradictory passion that overwhelmed her each and every time; never did she so yearn for fulfillment and relief as she did during her term, when it was severely denied her. And yet, she had suffered similar depression before, those months of waiting for word from Alison—but that had been different, the anxiety then had been tinged with hope.

In the beginning, during all of that long, cold winter after her return to Fall River, the letters had been incessant, crossing in the mail more frequently than not, full of passion and ardor, Alison's meticulous hand declaring undying love, promising liaisons in New York or Boston, Lizzie begging her to hurry

379

soon to America, urging her dearest love to join her "in that time of budding . . .

". . . when together and alone we can breathe of the heady air and recapture the harmony and bliss we knew in Cannes. You cannot realize how much I suffer in your absence. The weather here is bitterly cold, and I am headachey and chilled more often than not, though I cannot say for sure whether my malaise may not be caused solely by the nervous strain of my eternal longing for you. I have always been a restless sleeper (as well you know) but I find myself awake now half the night, yearning for the balm of Orpheus and the attendant dreams of that ecstatic time on the Riviera. If my Mistress has the slightest fond memories of her wee lonely Miss, she will book passage at once and fly to her side, **en battant des ailes.** *Hurry, my dearest, I cannot bear the thought of a separation beyond this ghastly winter. Thine forever, Lizzie."*

Alison's familiar stationery arriving at the house some two or three times a week, Lizzie's trembling hand accepting the envelopes from her father—

"I see you're enjoying a nice correspondence with this English lady," he said one day, inadvertently provoking a stab of panic—had he discovered Alison's letters? Had he *read* them? That very afternoon, the house empty save for Maggie puttering about in the sitting room, she'd taken the letters from their hiding place beneath her undergarments in the bedroom dresser drawer, and burned them all in the kitchen stove, an act she regretted later when the flow of mail became a trickle and she longed for the reassuring words and passionate outbursts of the preceding winter.

It had seemed virtually certain that Alison would be coming to New York in May—

". . . primarily to be by your side again, my dearest love, but I confess to an ulterior motive as well. The very **thought** *of enduring the start of another London 'season,' as they would have it, is enough to set me trembling. How shall this season of '91 be any different, I ask you, than that of '90, or '89, or '88, or* **ad infinitum,** *back to the time of William the Conqueror, I dare*

380

say? I should hope to escape it even were it not for the knowledge of my sweet Miss pining, and the expectation of prolonged and blissful quatre à cinqs (cat that sank, indeed!) in some dim and cloistered hotel room while New York's horsecars rumble past our curtained windows. I can scarcely wait, Lizzie!"

—but the trip was postponed until June (this after Lizzie had already booked a hotel for them in New York) and then again till July ("When the heat shall be intolerable, I know," Alison wrote) and then till the fall ("I am aiming for no later than a September 15 departure, and have already made inquiries of the various steamship lines"), the letters less frequent now, once a week, and then twice monthly—and still no definite word that she had booked passage and would soon be on her way.

In October, Alison wrote:

"Oh, my dearest Lizzie, I am forlorn. My wretched husband, the Empire Builder, has decided it is imperative that he visit his money in India, planning on a November departure for arrival when the weather there will be less severely hot than it is just now. Normally, I should have gone dancing barefoot in the streets at news of his departure, but he is insisting this time that I accompany him, Lord alone knows why. Perhaps he wishes me to lead him safely by the hand through the scores of begging lepers in the streets. Perhaps he feels that dallying with twelve year-olds in vermin-infested cribs is less desirable than having his obedient wife by his side to serve as a sometime plaything, though I'm positive he's long forgotten what scant pleasures I may have to offer.

"And you, my love? Have you forgotten the nectar and the spice? Do you long for me as I long for you, my precious, fragile orchid? We will be returning to London shortly before Christmas, and I promise I shall try my utmost to make the journey to America as soon as possible in the New Year. Until then, my darling Miss, be mine forever, as I am surely thine."

There was a card from her at Christmas.
Nothing else.
And then . . . silence.
All through January Lizzie wrote to her daily at the Ken-

381

sington address, suspecting at first that the Newburys had extended their stay in India (but would they not have come home for Christmas, as she'd said they would?), fearing next that Alison had contracted some dread disease in Delhi or Calcutta or wherever they had gone (she had mentioned lepers, hadn't she?), believing then that Albert was intercepting her letters, and then that they had moved and were not receiving forwarded mail, and then that they had gone to Cannes during the winter season Alison so despised (but a letter to the villa was never answered), refusing to accept what was becoming more and more apparent, the unbearably painful realization that Alison no longer *cared* to answer her desperate pleadings.

In the silence of her bedroom, she reread by lamplight the last paragraph of the letter Alison had written before leaving for India:

And you, my love? Have **you** *forgotten the nectar and the spice? Do you long for me as I long for you, my precious, fragile orchid? We will be returning to London shortly before Christmas, and I promise I shall try my utmost to make the journey to America as soon as possible in the New Year. Until then, my darling Miss, be mine forever, as I am surely thine.*

Then what had happened? What was causing the silence now? Should she write to Albert? Had something *truly* dire befallen Alison?

She remembered a rainy afternoon in Cannes, the conversation with Alison that day, the distant sea surging.

"*I should* never *want another woman but you. I should never* dream *of allowing anyone else to do to me . . .*"

"*Never say never.*"

"*Though I'm certain that the moment I'm gone, you shall tumble into bed with the nearest . . .*"

"*More than likely.*"

She refused to believe this. She read and reread the last paragraph of Alison's letter. What was it promising, then, if not a love as eternal as her own? In a blinding snowstorm at the beginning of February, Lizzie walked to the telegraph office in town and sent a cable she hoped would be clear to Alison while

382

remaining cryptic to the clerk who took her hand-lettered message. It read:

Mistress,
Have you changed your mind then?
            Miss

"Miss *what*?" the clerk asked.

"Send it that way," Lizzie said, and the clerk shrugged.

Alison's answer did not arrive until St. Valentine's Day. The same familiar hand on the same familiar stationery. The same Kensington address. And inside the envelope, appropriate enough on this day for lovers, a poem. No date, no salutation, no closing sentiment, no signature, only the poem in blue ink on the paler blue stationery:

The green leaf of loyalty's beginning to fall.
The bonnie White Rose, it is withering an' all.
But I'll water it with the blood of usurping tyranny,
And green it will grow in my ain countrie.

The meaning was immediately clear to her. She read the letter, if such it was, yet another time, and then burned it in the stove together with the letter she'd received in October. The snow lashed fiercely at the windows as the flames licked at the blue sheets of paper. She replaced the lid on the stove and went upstairs to her room, and only then did she begin sobbing with the knowledge that what had happened almost two summers ago had been—for Alison, at least—a passing fancy, something best and soon forgotten, pressed into a memory book like the faded, dry and crumbling orchid she'd received as a farewell gift in London. *Thine Forever*, she thought, and sobbed uncontrollably. Days later, when her father asked if she had stopped writing to her friend in London, she replied simply, "Yes."

Spiritlessly, listlessly, she got out of bed.

There was fresh water in the pitcher on the dresser; she had filled it last night from the tap over the pantry sink before going up to bed—voices in the sitting room, muted, the sitting room dark, she'd had no desire to talk to anyone then, she'd talked long enough to Alice Russell. The fears she'd relayed to her, still with her this morning, vague and nameless, filling her with uncertain dread. The house burning down around them. Perishing in flames. The fires of Hell. Damnation forever.

She poured water from the pitcher into the washbowl.

She dipped her hands into the water.

There's no one! Come in, come in, we're quite alone!

No one then to spy on them from the clifftops as they splashed naked in the gelid sea, no one here in Fall River either to offer her comfort or solace while she waited in vain for a further letter from Alison at home in her own country, her father returning from the post office empty-handed each day, we're quite alone, *Ah, yes*, she thought, *I was quite alone*, and splashed water onto her face, and reached for the bar of soap in the scalloped white dish. Washing her face and her hands, she felt again the steady seep of her own blood, and thought, *Alison was right, of course, so right about so many things*. This was not the time for making decisions, she would be less confused when her monthly sickness had passed.

And yet, yesterday morning, the decision had not seemed at all preposterous to her, lost in hopelessness as she'd been, anonymous terrors consuming her—lost in guilt, lost in shame, lost in anxiety, lost in knowledge, lost in all save love—her menses full upon her and adding to her depression and her contrary passion. Alone in the privacy of the water closet downcellar, she had syringed into herself a mixture of tepid water and carbolic acid, as she did each month to remove particles of dried blood and mucus and to dispel any disagreeable odor. Drying herself, fastening a fresh towel into place between her legs, pinning it before and behind to the band about her waist, her eye had lingered on the word *acid* handwritten on the brown bottle's label in the druggist's careless scrawl, and she had remembered all the talk the day before of poison, her stepmother certain that someone had poisoned the milk, the sounds later of her vomiting behind the closed and barricaded door between their rooms in this prison of a house.

And she had thought, *Yes, poison, why not?* An appropriate end to Eve's sin, the apple poisoned with knowledge, the wrath of God satisfied at last in the completion of the cycle, poison unto poison, carnality purged. "To disbelieve truth is to invite deception," Alison had said, and the truth in this house, be-

384

neath this secretive, deceitful roof, was that whatever transpired here was carnal and lustful, a sinful satisfaction of the tyrannous blood, loveless and doomed. *Yes, poison,* she had thought, and had adjusted her clothing and gone upstairs to tell her stepmother she was going out to do some shopping.

The thought frustrated, the purpose thwarted, the action aborted.

"Well, my good lady, it's something we don't sell unless by prescription from the doctor, as it's a very dangerous thing to handle."

"But I've used it before, you see. Prussic acid, that is. To clean furs. I want it to put on the edge of a sealskin cape. A soiled cape."

The man's obstinance. Her failure at yet another drugstore. The intolerable heat of Fall River yesterday, a century ago. The same interminable heat today, and the same persistent feeling of helplessness and dread. He'd been here again last night, pounding on the lumber pile out back. The same pale young man she'd seen at least a dozen times before, outside the house, in hurried conversation with Maggie. Just after her sister left for Fairhaven, he'd been here again, a shadow on the side steps. She'd seen no skirts; it *had* to have been a man.

She was suddenly confused again.

Her hands hovered over the bowl of water.

She splashed soap from her face, getting some in her eyes, reaching for a towel, her eyes stinging and beginning to tear. And suddenly there were real tears, mingling with the harsher caustic flow, and she buried her face in the towel and murmured aloud, "Oh, dear God, *help* me," and knew He would not hear, knew He would not answer, for whatever codicil she had made with Him long ago had been destroyed forever on that Sunday morning in Cannes. "But I *loved* her," she moaned into the towel, and silently begged God to understand that the secret she shared in this house was not the same at all, was instead carnal and base, lustful and degrading, and prayed for His forgiveness and His guidance, prayed He would deliver her from the flames into which she had thrust a tentative hand last March, when in her loneliness, longing and grief she had reached out to—*Oh, help me, dear God,* she thought, *oh, please, dear God, I beg of you,* and stood quite still by the dresser, the towel covering her face.

"Well, I'll be on my way then."

Uncle John's voice, downstairs.

"What time is it?" her stepmother asked.

"Twenty of," Uncle John said.

"Will you be back for dinner?"

"Oh, yes," he said, "count on me."

"Bridget, have you finished the dishes?"

"Almost, ma'am."

Her voice.

"Have you anything to do this morning?"

"No, not particular, ma'am, if you have anything to do for me."

The Irish lilt of it.

"When you've finished setting the table, I want the windows washed."

"Yes, ma'am. How, ma'am?"

"Inside and out both. They're very dirty."

"Yes, ma'am."

She lowered the towel and looked at her tear-stained face in the mirror over the dresser.

Are there no looking glasses in all of Fall River then?

She had gained far too much weight this past year; her face looked bloated, her eyes puffed and swollen from the tears.

Plump? No, no. You're what my mother might have called wöllustig.

She looked at her skin, far too pale, the fiery coloration of her hair contrasting violently with its ghostly pallor and the lifelessness of her eyes, red from her tears but drained of all other color.

How shall I face each morning without my dearest child to greet me with those pale gray eyes in her round pale face?

She dried her face and her hands, and then sighed deeply and forlornly, and put the towel back onto its rack, and stood uncertainly in the center of the room, as though not knowing what she wished to do next, or where she chose to go. She sighed again, and went at last to the door, opening it and looking out onto the landing to make certain no one was about.

In her nightdress she stepped outside and went to the large clothespress at the top of the stairs. There were nearly a score of dresses in the closet, winter- and summer-weight both. A single, green, summer-weight dress belonging to her stepmother hung at the very front of the closet, but the rest of the garments were hers and Emma's, most of them hers and most of them

386

blue; she favored the color; Alison said it complemented her hair and her eyes. This morning she didn't care what she put on. The dress she took down from one of the hangers was a simple ready-made wrapper, fashioned of chintz and printed with a tiny gold floral figure on a black ground, lightweight enough for the sweltering day. She carried it back into her room, and closed the door behind her again. Moving slowly, as though pushing her way through the miasma of clinging heat, she took off her nightdress, examined it for bloodstains, and then dropped it in the hamper alongside the dresser.

From the bottom drawer of the dresser, she removed a fresh menstrual towel, unfastened the safety pins on her bellyband, front and behind, and then dropped the soiled, blood-soaked cloth into the slop pail she'd had no need to use during the night. She secured the fresh towel, hoisted the bellyband higher on her waist, and then removed from her dresser the fresh underclothing she would wear. A pair of muslin underdrawers. A white petticoat. A white chemise. It was too hot for stockings, and she did not in any event plan to go out today. She dressed hastily, slipping on the chintz wrapper, buttoning it behind and then putting on her combing cape—*Alison's fingers untying the ribbons, the cape falling soundlessly to the grass buzzing with hidden bees.*

She brushed her hair without interest, tucked back a stray wisp, put down the brush and then stood uncertainly again, fearful of going downstairs, knowing she should talk to Maggie, ask her for answers to the questions that were hounding her, and yet fearful of a confrontation, delaying, making up her bed, folding her nightdress and putting it under her pillow, gathering up the undergarments she'd worn yesterday, placing them in the hamper, closing the shutters. There were some handkerchiefs she planned to iron today. She took them from the dresser top, surveyed the room and finally picked up the slop pail containing her soiled menstrual towel. She was almost to the door when she remembered that she was barefooted. She was tempted to go downstairs just this way, but she could visualize her father's raised eyebrows, her stepmother's silent look of disapproval. She found a pair of scuffed felt slippers—the last time she'd worn them had been at the farm—put them

387

on, picked up the slop pail and handkerchiefs again and went out onto the landing.

The door to the spare room across the hall was open. The room empty and tidy, the bed made, the shutters closed. She was passing the open door when she glimpsed the candlestick on the dresser near the bed. She went into the room. It seemed cooler in here, the shutters closed, this side of the house facing north, away from the sun. She stood looking at the candlestick, remembering. *And some of them rather old. One particularly handsome one used to belong to my mother's mother. We keep it in the spare room across the hall. Emma says it's eighteenth century. I would suppose it came from England.*

She had never known her grandmother.

She did not remember her mother at all.

She picked up the candlestick.

There was a fresh white taper in it, and it almost toppled from its socket. She pressed it down firmly, impaling it more securely on the pricket. The antique brass felt silky to her touch, somehow soothing. There was solidity and weight to the long stem and the square beveled base; in a poignant rush, she recalled London again—and Alison. Fresh tears welled into her eyes.

She stood staring at the candlestick for what seemed a long while and then, sighing, put it back on the dresser. Turning toward the door, she stood uncertainly for a moment, forgetting where she'd put down the slop pail and the handkerchiefs, coming dangerously close to tears again. She found the handkerchiefs on the bed, and the slop pail where she'd left it, just inside the door. Sighing again, she went out of the room.

Her father was in the sitting room downstairs, slouched in the large chair near the mantelpiece, reading the morning newspaper. He looked up when she came into the room.

"Good morning, father," she said.

"Good morning, Lizzie," he said, and went back to his paper. He finished the paragraph he was reading and put the paper down. The *Providence Journal*. He rose, turned to the mantelpiece, took down the key to his room and, without saying another word, went out into the kitchen. She could hear him at the pantry sink, the water running there. Through the open dining-room door, her stepmother came into view, a feather duster in her hand.

"Oh," she said, startled. "Good morning, Lizzie."

"Good morning."

"How do you feel?"

"Hot."

"I meant otherwise."

"A little better."

"Will you have some breakfast then?"

"I don't think so."

"There's still coffee on the stove, should you want any."

"Thank you."

"It *does* seem hotter today, don't you think? Than yesterday?"

"Yes."

"Yes," her stepmother said, and nodded. "Lizzie, I'm having company on Monday, and I want everything in order. Please leave the door to the spare room shut, will you? When I've finished up there?"

"Why would I go into the spare room in any case?"

"Well, *if* you should. Remember to close the door again, will you?"

"I'll remember," she said.

"Do you know what you'd like for dinner?"

"Will you be going out?"

"When the room's done. I'll be ordering meat, so if you can tell me what you'd like . . ."

"I don't want any meat."

"What *would* you like?"

"Nothing. I'm still not feeling well."

"I thought you said . . ."

"Yes, but not quite myself yet."

"There must be something going around. A great *many* people in town seem to be sick. I suppose Dr. Bowen was right. I suppose it wasn't poison, after all."

"I should hardly think so."

"I can't imagine anyone wanting to *poison* us, can you?"

"No one I can think of."

"Still, it might have been the milk. With so many people sick, it *could* be the milk, you know." She shook her head, clucked her tongue. "Well, I'll be going as soon as I've done the pillows," she said. "Are you sure you don't want . . . ?"

"Won't you change your dress before you go out?"

389

"Whatever for? What's wrong with this one?"

"It's so hot today. I only thought it might be too heavy."

"No, it's good enough. I've left some wrappers in the parlor . . . would you direct them for me, please? While I'm gone?"

"I will."

"Well, I'll see to the guest room then," she said, and went out.

Lizzie waited. She could hear her father passing through the kitchen again, and then his footfalls on the steps leading up to his bedroom. She took a deep breath and went into the kitchen. Maggie was at the pantry sink, rinsing dishes. She looked somewhat pallid this morning, her pretty face sheened with perspiration, her dark hair braided close to her head, a tall, well-formed woman with a narrow waist, flaring hips and a firm, high bosom. The two top buttons of her dress were unbuttoned. The clock read ten minutes to nine. Above, Lizzie heard her father rummaging about in his bedroom. She set down the slop pail, and put the handkerchiefs on the kitchen table. They had not yet exchanged greetings. She *knows*, Lizzie thought. She's avoiding me.

"What will you want for breakfast?" Maggie asked, coming back into the kitchen.

"I don't know as I want any breakfast," Lizzie said. "I may just have some coffee and cookies."

"There's coffee on the stove. Shall I pour some for you?"

"I'll get it myself."

She went to the cupboard and took down a cup and saucer. At the stove she poured the cup full, and then took a molasses cookie from the jar on the counter.

"Did you sleep well last night?" she asked.

"Not very," Maggie said.

"A bit noisy, wasn't it?" Lizzie said, and looked at her.

Maggie turned suddenly, one hand coming up to her mouth, and lurched toward the kitchen entry and the back porch. The screen door slammed shut behind her. Lizzie rose from the table and went to the back door. Peering through the screen, she saw Maggie near the grape arbor, doubled over, vomiting. Alarmed, she was about to go to her when she heard her father coming down the back stairs. She returned to the kitchen, took the handkerchiefs from the table and carried them and her coffee cup into the pantry. Standing at the sink, she alternately sprin-

390

kled the handkerchiefs and sipped at her coffee. She could hear her father in the kitchen now. She gathered up the damp handkerchiefs, left the coffee cup on the edge of the sink and went out to him. He was standing near the stove, looking down in distaste at the slop pail Lizzie had left beside it. The key to his bedroom was still in his hand. He was dressed for town, wearing a black vest and trousers, black Congress shoes, his black Prince Albert coat.

"Will you be going to the post office?" she asked.

"I'm not sure," he said.

"I have a letter to Emma. I wish you'd mail it for me."

"Where is it?"

"I have it here," she said, and took the letter from the pocket of her dress.

"I may go, I'm not sure," he said, but he accepted the letter.

"When will you be leaving?" she asked.

"In a few minutes," he said. He looked again at the slop pail. "Get rid of this, would you?" he said, and walked out into the sitting room. Lizzie lifted the lid on the cookstove to check the fire. There were coals glowing within. She set her flatirons on the stove top to heat them. In the sitting room she heard the click of the key as her father replaced it on the mantelpiece shelf. She took another cookie from the jar and went out into the dining room, nibbling on it as she stood by the windows. Her father came in again.

"Don't go getting crumbs all over the floor," he said. "And see to that slop pail, will you?" He went out into the kitchen. She heard the screen door slamming shut. She watched him as he came into view on the walk. Across the yard she could see Adelaide Churchill in her kitchen, looking up, glancing at her father where he stood. He walked past the dining-room windows then, on his way toward the street. Sighing, she went into the kitchen, picked up the slop pail, and carried it through the kitchen entry to the back stairs. The stairwell was dark; she went down to the cellar slowly and cautiously.

It was somewhat less gloomy downstairs, where light filtered through the ground-level windows. She found her way to the washroom. There was a pail under the sink there. It contained the soiled menstrual towels she had used these past several days. She shook out the slop pail. The towel she'd replaced

391

earlier this morning fell onto the other blood-stained towels in the pail under the sink. She opened the water tap and rinsed out the slop pail. Water tinted faintly red ran down the drain.

The house was utterly still when she came upstairs again. "Mrs. Borden?" she called.

There was no answer; her stepmother had gone as well. She put the clean slop pail down near the stove, tested her irons, heard a sound outside the screen door and went to it. Maggie was standing there, just outside, holding a brush, setting down a wooden pail of water.

"Maggie," she said, "can you come inside for a moment? I'd like to talk to you."

"I have to wash my windows," Maggie said.

"They can wait. Please come in, won't you?"

"I have to get started."

"He was here again last night, wasn't he?" Lizzie whispered.

"I don't know who you mean."

"You *know* who I mean. He was here pounding on the lumber pile out back . . ."

"I heard nothing."

". . . trying to attract your attention."

"I have to do my windows," Maggie said.

"Come *in* here," Lizzie whispered sharply. "I *won't* talk to you through the door this way!"

"I have to do my *windows*," Maggie said again, and turned away from the door. Lizzie stood watching her through the screen as she walked toward the barn, took the pin from the hasp and opened the door. She was inside the barn for just a moment; when she came out again, she was carrying the long handle for her brush. She closed the door again, put the pin back into the hasp and then came back to where she'd set down her pail and brush. Lizzie stood watching her until she disappeared from her angle of vision, moving past the corner of the house to the other side of the yard.

She stood motionless inside the screen door.

She was suddenly trembling.

And confused again.

She felt an overwhelming need to tell Maggie about what she'd tried to do yesterday, what she would have done if only she'd been successful in her attempt to buy the poison. But at

392

the same time, given her very real decision, acknowledging that she would have made a covenant with death, might still do so if she could not shake free of this persistent depression, why then was she so eager to divulge this to Maggie? Did she expect sympathy? Penitence? What? And why, simultaneously, was she so troubled by the young man's reappearance last night, for certainly it was he, there was no doubt about that in her mind. If indeed she wished to die, had in fact made every effort to purchase the poison that would have accomplished the deed in a convulsive instant—or so she believed—then why should it matter *what* Maggie thought, *what* Maggie did or felt, *how* Maggie responded to the terrible knowledge that her mistress wanted to kill herself?

We cannot afford the luxury of allowing any female employee to believe mistakenly that she—*because of some indiscretion—is the true mistress of the house.*

Alison's words, the oracle of Cannes dispensing wisdom in the privacy of an indiscreet bedroom, the sheets damp with their spent passion, the sunlight streaming through the arched window to touch their naked bodies. But where was Mistress Puss on that cold and rainy day last March—*It's always raining when children make their most important discoveries, isn't it?*—her sister away, her stepmother and father away, the house as empty and as still as it was now, where was she *then* when in her loneliness and need Lizzie had ventured like a child to touch a hand slippery with suds, her heart leaping when Maggie at the sink did not recoil, and discovered in her a longing as deep as her own? *Never, but* never, *let a female employee tempt your fingers or your lips. You shall be eternally sorry if you do, I promise you.*

Ah, yes, Alison's promises, swiftly forgotten. And her own as well, equally fragile, the pillbox she'd bought for her in the Burlington Arcade, *Thine Forever*, though eternity had lasted far too short a while, the summer contract broken on that dank and dismal day when she'd unbuttoned Maggie's chemise to reveal her breasts (*You have no idea how I've been tempted by the sight of voluptuous young Moira in her bath, those frisky Irish breasts spattered with freckles*) the nipples stiffening to her touch, her mouth hungrily receptive.

An indiscretion, to be sure. Even now, she wondered whether she had been propelled less by passion than by a need to strike back at Alison, to prove to the woman who had abandoned her that she herself—now that the green leaf of loyalty had fallen and the white rose withered—was entirely capable of watering their love with the blood of usurping tyranny and allowing her insistent need to grow green again in her own country.

All this, you taught me, she remembered thinking on that day while lovelessly they embraced in the room upstairs, the rain lashing the windows. *All that I am, you made me,* she thought, and knew this to be untrue even as the words found slippery purchase in her mind: she could not blame Alison for what she was; perhaps she could not even blame her for the discovery of herself. The woman shivering beneath her on that stormy day, unskilled, virginal, a servant in every sense, could have been *any* woman, might *indeed* have been had Lizzie found the courage to satisfy her need beyond the four walls of this confining house. In helpless rage, lovelessly, she had ravaged her, suffocating on her peasant aroma, clinging to her when her release— less tumultuous than what she had known with Alison—shuddered through her body to reaffirm her female essence.

Her heart was pounding.

On the south side of the house, she heard the Kelly girl calling, "Bridget! Yoo-hoo!" and she went swiftly through the dining room and into the sitting room where she looked through the window, standing back a bit, not wanting to be seen, not wanting Maggie to think she was spying on her. Maggie put down the brush and pail and walked to the fence where the Kelly girl was waiting for her. She watched as they talked, servant to servant. The Kelly girl giggled. Lizzie watched. She could not go out to her; she could only wait.

She went into the front parlor, found the envelopes her stepmother had left, found as well the handwritten list of addresses, and directed them for her, leaving them in a neat little pile on the table. She went back into the sitting room. She sat in her father's chair, picked up an old magazine, and leafed through it. She looked through the newspaper. The clock ticked loudly. The sitting-room windows were closed, Maggie had undoubtedly let them down before going outside for her water; the house was suffocatingly hot with all the windows closed. Maggie was tossing water up onto the closed windows now. She did not want her to think she was watching her every move. She rose abruptly and went out into the kitchen to test her flats again. They were still not ready; on a day like today, she would do better to set them out on the sidewalk.

On the counter under the windows, she noticed a scrap of paper with an upturned water glass holding it down like a paperweight. She lifted the glass, looked at the paper. It was a note from Dr. Bowen's daughter, directed to Emma, expressing sorrow at having missed her before she'd left for Fairhaven, but promising to call again when next she passed through. She put the note under the glass again, trying to recall when Emma would be home? She could not remember. Maggie was outside the dining room now, splashing water onto the windows. She went into the dining room and rapped on one of the closed windows. Maggie looked in at her. She raised the window.

"Come in here!" she whispered.

Maggie said nothing.

"Do as I say!"

Maggie glanced over her shoulder toward the back yard. She nodded, almost to herself, and put down the water pail. In a moment the screen door opened and clattered shut again. She did not come completely into the dining room. She stood in the open door connecting with the kitchen.

"Did you hook the screen door?" Lizzie said.

"Yes."

"Who is he?" she said.

"I don't know who you mean."

"Your beau."

"I have no beau."

"Don't *lie* to me!"

"He's . . . no one."

"He's *someone.*"

"I scarcely know him." Maggie shrugged. "He comes by sometimes. He talks to me."

"About what?"

"Things."

"What things?"

"Idle chatter," Maggie said, and shrugged again.

"Tell me what he says."

"He . . . he's asked to call on me."

"And what have you said to him?"

395

"I told him he couldn't."

"You're lying again!"

"I swear it's what I said!"

"Then why does he keep coming here?"

"I cannot say."

"Cannot? Or will not?"

"I told him not to, I swear I did."

"Then why was he here again last night? He *was* here, wasn't he? You heard him, didn't you?"

"I heard him, yes."

"Then why did you lie to me earlier?"

"I didn't want to upset you. I didn't want you to think . . ."

"Think what?"

"That I was listening for him."

"You were, weren't you?"

"No, I swear it! But he made such a frightful racket . . ."

"Yes, and what was he clamoring for, Maggie? A bit of Irish pussy?"

"Miss Lizzie, please, I *must* wash the windows, please, oh, *please*," she said, and turned away suddenly and walked swiftly through the kitchen. Lizzie followed her at once, running after her, catching her at the screen door as Maggie was unfastening the hook. She caught her by the wrist. The hook fell loose from her hand.

"Come with me," she whispered.

"Mrs. Borden will . . ."

"Never *mind* Mrs. Borden!"

Still holding her by the wrist, she pulled her back into the kitchen, and then into the sitting room, words spilling from her mouth as she dragged her through the rooms, "Mrs. *Borden*, is it? Afraid of Mrs. *Borden* then? And what will Mrs. *Borden* say when I tell her our sweet Irish virgin, pure as the driven snow, oh yes, oh my, has been hanging on the fencepost like a cat in heat," aware of the uncurtained windows, aware of the neighbors, but refusing to let go of her wrist, "idling with strange men when she should be doing the work she's paid for, what will Mrs. *Borden* say to *that*?"

Her heart was beating fiercely. In the front entry, as they approached the stairwell, Maggie tried to pull away. She gripped her wrist more tightly ("You're hurting me," Maggie whispered) and pulled her toward the stairs, the words still pouring forth in a torrent, helpless to stop the words, wanting to tell her of what she'd almost done yesterday, but instead spewing threats she knew she could not possibly enforce, "Would you like to lose this job, Miss, join the town's Chinamen perhaps, wash the laundry of the millworkers, have the toughs and brawlers pawing you like the slut you are," bitter accusation, "or have they already done so, have you peddled pussy on a stick like a common tart," solemn reprimand, "for shame, for shame, Miss, confess yourself to God for the harlot you've become," the door to the spare room closed, just as her stepmother had left it, "Mrs. *Borden* indeed, we shall fill her ears with more than dirty windows, shan't we? Young men loitering about for a glimpse of our fair Maggie's limbs, or have you already shown him more? Has he lingered there at your maiden well, Miss Puss, get *in* there!" she said, and hurled her through the open door into her bedroom, snapping her out like a whip so that she staggered into the room, almost falling. Lizzie closed the door behind them.

"If you run, I shall come after you," she said.

"I shan't run," Maggie said.

"Undress," she said.

"Miss Lizzie . . ."

"Take off your clothes, do as I say!"

"Miss Lizzie, please. Your mother will be back."

"She's only just left."

"I saw her go at a little past nine."

"Then look at the clock, Miss Puss. What time do you read on it?"

"Twenty after."

"Has she had time to do her marketing and return?"

"What if your father . . . ?"

"He's never back till ten, ten-thirty."

Maggie sat on the edge of the bed. Her eyes darted. To the closed door. To the shuttered windows. There was fear on her face. And something else. Something Lizzie knew well.

"We have time," Lizzie said, and smiled.

They undressed swiftly, aware that this suspended moment was a stolen one, a theft repetitive of all the others over the past five months and more, burglars both, their bodies glistening

397

with sweat, virtually naked to each other now, though Maggie still wore her underdrawers open at the crotch and Lizzie wore like a chastity belt the paraphernalia of her monthly visitation. "I have fleas," she whispered, and Maggie murmured, "Aye," the Irish lilt of it, "You must not touch me there," and Maggie murmured "Aye" again and spread her legs to her, and pulled her down to her and over her, and their lips met.

It was always, and oddly, Alison who moaned beneath her whenever she was with Maggie, Alison whose hands touched her breasts (though the insistent fingers now were surely Maggie's), Alison for whom her nipples stiffened, Alison for whom she throbbed below. She could not distinguish now between the flow of her passion and the interminable seeping of her menstrual blood; they were liquidly mingled, as essentially female as she knew herself to be. And, as when she'd lain with Alison in a past so long ago it seemed never to have happened, her passion now was edged with tenderness. Kissing and fondling this woman she did not love, her voice became gentle, and she apologized for the cruel words she'd hurled at her not moments before, explaining needlessly that this was her time of the month, and that she was always impatient during her flowers, inclined to lose her temper, easily irritated, though passionate as well, she added slyly, and perhaps too ferocious in her ardor (her hand tightening on Maggie's breast to demonstrate, Maggie catching her breath on a small gasp) and so was to be forgiven any outburst, for surely Maggie knew she loved her (the lie sticking in her throat) and would never in her life do anything to harm her.

And then, as if she *truly* loved her—and here she became confused again—she found herself telling her of what she'd almost done yesterday, wanting to share it with her, wanting in this timeless moment to be able to tell someone else about the fears that besieged her day and night, wishing simultaneously that Alison might be here instead, their heads side by side on the pillow, their limbs entangled, their hands searching, Alison with her knowledge and her wisdom, Alison who would offer her the love and guidance she needed.

"I went to buy poison," she said, and watched Maggie's face. "Prussic acid."

398

Maggie caught her breath. "Was it *you*, then, who poisoned the milk?"

"The milk wasn't poisoned," Lizzie said.

"Mrs. Borden . . ."

"No, it wasn't poisoned. Dr. Bowen said it wasn't."

"Then what . . . ?"

"I wanted it for myself," Lizzie said. "To kill myself."

Maggie stared at her.

"Because of you and your beau," she said, lying again, or at least thinking she was lying, no longer certain where the truth actually lay.

"I have no beau," Maggie said.

"For the heartache you and your beau have caused me," Lizzie said, and again wondered if this were the truth. Where *was* the truth in this house? "Do you want me to kill myself?" she whispered.

"No, Miss Lizzie."

"Then you must promise you shall never see him again."

"I promise," Maggie said.

"On your mother's eyes."

"Yes," Maggie said.

"Swear," Lizzie said.

"Yes," Maggie said, in a rush, "on my mother's eyes, I swear I shall never see him again."

Lizzie smiled. "Why are you trembling?" she asked.

"I'm not trembling."

"To your toes," Lizzie said. "Tell me why."

"You know why."

"Tell me. Say it."

"I want you," Maggie whispered.

"It's been far too long, hasn't it?"

"Yes."

"Say it."

"It's been far too long, yes."

"But what is it you want?"

"Everything. You."

"Now? This instant?"

"Yes, now," Maggie said.

"But what of Mrs. Borden?" Lizzie said, smiling, teasing her now. "Surely her marketing is done by now, isn't it?"

Maggie turned swiftly to look at the clock.

"There's time," she whispered.

"But it's almost nine-thirty."

"There's yet *time!*" Maggie said urgently.

"And *Mr.* Borden? Are you not fearful of his return?"

"He'll be at his bank, his banks. We've time yet."

"Then it shall be now, of course," Lizzie said, and again smiled.

"Yes, now," Maggie said.

"Will you not ask for it then?"

"Yes, now, I want it."

"Then ask your Mistress Puss politely," Lizzie said.

"Yes, please."

"Am I not your mistress then?"

"You are, yes, you know you are."

"Then can you not address me as . . . ?"

"Mistress Puss, yes. *Please,* Mistress Puss," she said, and reached out to pull Lizzie to her.

"Lizzie? Is that you?"

Mrs. Borden's voice.

On the landing outside.

"Lizzie?"

Both women sat immediately upright.

Footsteps approached the door.

The door opened.

Mrs. Borden stood in the hallway, looking into the room, aghast at what she saw. She was still wearing the heavy dress she'd had on when she left the house, but another dress was folded over her arm, the green dress that had earlier been in the clothespress at the top of the stairs. *She's come back to change her clothing,* Lizzie thought in an instant. *The heat outdoors has driven her home!* How long had she been standing outside there on the landing? How much had she heard? And what *difference* did it make; her eyes now recorded all there was to see, the two naked women, Maggie reaching for her chemise and clutching it to her breasts, Lizzie's mouth open in surprise.

"Oh," her stepmother said.

Only that.

She continued staring into the room, knowledge narrowing her eyes. She shook her head as though trying to clear it.

400

Maggie was scrambling off the bed now, hurrying to where she'd earlier hurled her dress to the floor, her stockings lying like twisted black snakes beside it.

"Dress yourselves!" Mrs. Borden said sharply. "The *shame*! Your father shall know of this!"

Lizzie leaped off the bed.

"No!" she said. *"Wait!"*

But for what? What was there to say to this dumpy little woman who stood in the hallway like a messenger of God come to strike her dead as surely as the prussic acid would have yesterday? *How* to explain, *what* to explain, to this woman who stood there motionless, her mouth set, her eyes blazing with the discovery she had made? The words delayed her stepmother for a moment, but only that, as though their urgency compelled her to reexamine the evidence of her own eyes, her hesitation allowing Lizzie time enough to rush to the door and out into the hallway where Mrs. Borden, shaking her head again, now turned toward the stairway leading below. Lizzie moved swiftly, blocking her path as if trying to keep her from a father already in the house.

"Get out of my way," Mrs. Borden said.

The women stood there in ludicrous confrontation, Lizzie naked save for her bellyband and the menstrual towel pinned to it, Mrs. Borden sweltering in her heavy dress, the lighter-weight dress still folded over her arm.

"Do you hear me?" she said.

"You mustn't tell him," Lizzie said.

"I shall tell him *all*!" her stepmother said fiercely. "Get out of my way!"

"No," Lizzie said, and shoved out at her, wanting only to keep her from the steps that led downstairs, fearful she might at once go running into the street to search for her father, babble to him what she had witnessed in the bedroom. Mrs. Borden stumbled back from the force of the push and almost lost her balance, arms coming up, the green dress falling to the floor, her eyes opening wide in astonishment. Lizzie took a step toward her, immediately penitent, her hand outstretched.

"I'm sorry," she said at once. "I didn't . . ."

"Don't *touch* me!" her stepmother said.

"Mother, I . . ."

401

"Mother?" Mrs. Borden said. "Don't you *dare!"*

"Please, I meant no . . ."

"Stay away from me!"

"I beg of you . . ."

"Monster!" Mrs. Borden said. "Unnatural *thing!"*

The words were like a physical blow, staggering her.

In blind retaliation against the words, she bunched her fist as a schoolgirl might and struck out ineffectually at her stepmother, the punch only glancing off her shoulder, her eyes nonetheless widening in fear. Lizzie's own fear was suddenly replaced by unreasoning anger. Her stepmother's look of terror, her instantly defensive posture, served only to confirm the hurtful surmise that she was indeed monstrous and unnatural, a creature capable of inflicting serious harm. She immediately rejected this deformed image of herself, blind anger rising to dispel it, suffocating rage surfacing to encompass and engulf the hopelessness of her secret passion, the chance discovery by this woman who stood quaking now against the closed door to the guest room, the fearsome threat of revelation to her father, the unfairness and stupidity of not being allowed to live her own life as she *chose* to live it!

Her stepmother turned away suddenly, fumbled with the knob on the door and threw the door open. She slammed the door shut behind her, tried to hold it closed as Lizzie shoved against it, and then stumbled back into the room, almost falling, when Lizzie shoved against it with all her might, the door banging back against the wall from the force of her fury. Her stepmother regained her footing, backed away from Lizzie as she advanced, darted as though to run toward the windows, rushed instead into the narrow space between the dressing case and the bed, discovered the wall, made a small, squealing sound, turned yet again—and found Lizzie standing there in silent, savage rage, blocking all escape. Unseeingly Lizzie reached for the candlestick on the dresser's marble top, her hand closing familiarly and fiercely around the stem, the base turning up, the taper toppling from its pricket.

"No, don't," her stepmother murmured, and Lizzie struck her.

She swung the candlestick downward from the right, catching her above the left ear and opening a bloody gash some two

402

inches long. Stunned, her stepmother backed away from her, twisting her head to avoid any further blows, and Lizzie struck her again, on top of the head this time, a little back of the crown line, the edge of the candlestick penetrating the scalp and the skull, and yet again immediately, the next blow nearly parallel to the other, blood splashing onto the dressing case's marble slab and upper drawer, her stepmother twisting away, stunned, turning, falling to her knees, blindly grasping the air for support as Lizzie struck her again from behind.

The blow caught her stepmother on the back, to the right of her neck where it joined the shoulders, splashing blood onto the lower drawer and faceboard of the dresser case, and she fell flat to the floor and tried to clasp her hands behind her twisted head, her face close to the wall as Lizzie straddled her and struck her again, and again, and again, blood splashing up onto the northern wall and the faceboard of the bed, Mrs. Borden's fluttering fingers stopping, her body quite still now. And now the candlestick fell with frenzied regularity, a dozen blows raining upon her stepmother's head, opening a large crater in her skull, the cuts radiating out from it like the ribs of a fan or the fingers of a hand, smashing the bones and laying open the brain, drops of blood spattering up onto Lizzie's face and naked arms, her shoulders, her breasts.

Behind her, she heard Maggie's muffled scream.

Breathlessly she sucked in great gulps of air, sitting astride her stepmother, the candlestick still clutched tightly in her fist, droplets of blood on her hand and her wrist. She was drenched with sweat, her hair matted against her blood-spattered forehead. She kept trying to breathe—if only she could catch her *breath*—her chest and her shoulders heaving, her mouth open. In the doorway Maggie was whimpering now, small snuffling sounds like those a frightened animal might make. Lizzie's breathing became more normal. She looked down at her stepmother's shattered skull. She looked over her shoulder to where Maggie, fully dressed, stood in the doorway. She got to her feet. The white candle lay near the dressing case, broken in half, its separate segments held loosely together by the connecting spinal cord of the wick.

"Am I covered with blood?" she asked numbly.

"Some," Maggie said. Her knuckles were pressed to her mouth; she seemed unable to stop whimpering.

"Fetch me some towels," she said. "The bottom drawer of my dresser."

Maggie hesitated, and then turned from the doorway.

She stood exactly where she was, looking down at her stepmother, feeling nothing, knowing only that she must clean herself now, thinking ahead only to that and no further, holding the blood-smeared candlestick in her hand, loosely at her side. When Maggie returned with the towels, she wiped the blood first from the candlestick and then from her hands and her breasts, and then looked at the towels and wondered what she should do with them now. She kept staring at the towels. "The slop pail," she said at last. "In the kitchen. Would you fetch it, please?"

Maggie ran out onto the landing. She heard her footfalls as she scurried down the stairs. She stood where she was only another moment, and then went into her bedroom and wiped the blood from her face and her shoulders and her hair where it was matted to her forehead, looking at herself in the glass, studying her own pale eyes until Maggie returned. She looked at her blankly, and then dropped the soiled towels into the slop pail.

"I shall need to wash," she said.

"Your father . . ." Maggie said.

Lizzie glanced at the clock.

"Yes," she said, "but I shall need to wash."

She put the candlestick into the slop pail, cushioning its base on the towels, and went down the steps into the sitting room, Maggie following her, and through the kitchen and into the pantry. At the pantry sink she washed her face and her hands and her shoulders and her breasts, studying herself for any vagrant blood spots, ascertaining from Maggie that there were none, and then drying herself with yet another menstrual towel which she dropped into the pail. She washed the candlestick as well, the silky feel of it, cleansing it of any blood, leaving it on the pantry counter, and then carrying the slop pail with its towels down to the cellar and over to the wash sink, where she emptied it into the pail containing the towel she had left there earlier this morning.

404

When she came upstairs again, the pantry and the kitchen were empty. The clock on the kitchen wall read a quarter of ten. She found Maggie in the parlor at the front of the house, nervously peering through the window at the street outside.

"What is it?" Lizzie asked at once. "My father? Is he home?"

Maggie shook her head.

She went to the window, stood a trifle behind her so that she could not be seen from outside, and saw first the carriage standing by the north gate between here and the Churchill house next door, the team of horses motionless in the bright sunlight, and then the pond lilies at the back of the carriage, and then Mrs. Manley who lived up the street, and Mrs. Hart who lived in Tiverton but whose sister lived nearby. And then she saw, standing in the gateway, his left arm leaning on the gatepost—

"Why is he here again?" she whispered sharply.

Maggie said nothing.

Outside, the women were negotiating for the purchase of the pond lilies now, selecting them from the tub at the back of the wagon. The pale young man kept watching them boldly, his elbow on the south post of the gateway, his head idly tilted onto his supporting hand.

"Get outside," she said. "Tell him to go away. Tell him never to come back."

"Outside?" Maggie said numbly.

"And then finish your windows."

"My windows?"

"Am I speaking English?"

Maggie went out the front door. Lizzie watched from the window while she engaged the man in brief conversation. Mrs. Manley and Mrs. Hart were gone now. The carriage with its water lilies was plodding its way up the sunlit street. The man smiled, touched his hand to his forehead in a reluctant farewell salute and then began walking away. Maggie stood at the gatepost another moment, glanced nervously up and down the street, and then disappeared around the corner of the house. Lizzie went into the front entry, locked the door again and went upstairs to her bedroom. She put on the same clothing she'd worn earlier, thrown in haste on the bedroom floor: the white underdrawers and chemise, the white petticoat, the black chintz

405

dress with its tiny floral pattern, the felt slippers. She looked at herself in the mirror. When she went out onto the landing again, she saw Mrs. Borden's green dress lying on the floor where she'd dropped it. She picked it up without so much as glancing into the guest room, carried it to the closet at the top of the stairs and hung it carefully on a padded hanger.

She went downstairs swiftly, walking directly into the parlor and looking out at the street. Maggie was washing the windows at the front of the house, the pail and dipper at her feet, the long brush in her hands. Mr. Pettee, who years ago used to live as a tenant in the upper part of the house, was strolling past. He glanced at Maggie and then turned his head away. Downtown she could hear the City Hall clock striking the hour. She counted the strokes: it was ten o'clock sharp. Depending on what business her father had in town, he could be home at any moment. Was he stopping at the post office, as he'd suggested he might? What would she say to him when he returned? What could she possibly *say*?

And suddenly the enormity of what she had done overwhelmed her. Until this moment she had reacted calmly and dispassionately, discounting as a reality the body of the woman who lay upstairs in a widening pool of her own blood, removing herself from the act of violence that had caused her stepmother's death. But now the body upstairs assumed dimension and shape in her mind, the crushed skull, the matted hair in the blood on the floor, and she willed the body to be gone, prayed desperately that it would not be there when next she looked into that room, would somehow miraculously have disappeared so that she would not have to explain it to her father. But *how* explain? How describe the *necessity* of the act without revealing the very thing that had *provoked* it, the discovery of herself and Maggie naked in her room, the fear that her father would be told she was—

A monster.

An unnatural thing.

Remembering the candlestick, she went swiftly into the pantry, picked it up, examined it again for blood, and then carried it with her into the dining room, wondering where she might put it, knowing she could not possibly take it upstairs to the guest room again where it would be discovered and suspected. She

406

wandered into the sitting room, trying the candlestick on the mantelpiece where already there stood a lamp, carrying it at last into the dining room and setting it on the buffet against the wall. It looked quite natural there. Innocuous. Safe.

She went into the kitchen and looked at the clock.

What would she tell her father when he returned?

Nothing, she decided.

We know nothing of upstairs. We heard nothing, we saw nothing. We were going about our normal business, we know nothing. Maggie was outside washing the windows, I was in the dining room, ironing; neither of us—

She tested her flats again, spitting on the bottom of one of them and causing not so much as a sizzle. She wanted to be ironing when he came home, innocently occupied with a mundane household chore. She thought of adding more coal to the stove, decided that wood would provide a faster, hotter fire, and discovered there was no kindling in the scuttle. She went immediately into the cellar and found several old pieces of board near the woodpile, dry and covered with flaking paint, perfect for the instant fire she wanted. She found the hatchet in its usual place, stuck in the chopping block near the furnace. There were other axes and hatchets in the cellar, but this was the only one with a decent chopping edge. The claw-hammer hatchet was as dull as butter, and a third hatchet lay discarded in a box someplace, covered with the crude ashes her father had rubbed on it in an attempt to free it of rust, testing it at last on the chopping block, its handle breaking from the force of his blows.

She started to chop one of the boards into narrow strips, almost nicked her finger in the uncertain light, thought again of her father's surely imminent return and hurried upstairs again carrying the boards and the hatchet. Standing first one board and then the next on the stovetop, she chopped them lengthwise into kindling, put the hatchet into the coal scuttle, and then knelt to feed the wood into the firebox. The coals there had dwindled almost to ashes; small wonder that her flats had never properly heated. Wondering if there was heat enough left to ignite the wood, she closed the door to the firebox, stood watching the stove for a moment and then looked up at the clock again.

From the kitchen closet, she took the small ironing board and

407

carried it into the dining room. She was setting it on the dining-room table when she heard the sound of a carriage outside—had he hired a hack to take him home? She rushed to the window to look out at the street. She saw only Dr. Handy riding by, his head craned over his shoulder for a look up the street toward the Kelly house and Mr. Wade's store. In almost that same instant she heard the screen door opening and then clattering shut again, and she turned toward the kitchen with a start, expecting it to be her father, totally uprepared for him, relieved when she saw that it was only Maggie. Her heart leaped again when she saw the look on Maggie's face.

"He's here," Maggie said breathlessly.

"My *father*!"

"The one you had me send away," Maggie said, shaking her head. "He's up the street, across the street. My God, could he have *seen*?"

"Seen? Seen *what*?"

"What you done upstairs," Maggie said. "He was about the house outside . . ."

"The shutters were closed."

"Then why's he come back?"

"Are you sure it's . . ."

"The same light suit of clothes, yes, the same necktie. Oh my God, if he spied what you done . . ."

"He couldn't have!"

"But *if* he did!"

"No one did!"

"He's acting funny. Swaying . . ."

"Then he's drunk," Lizzie said flatly. "He's been drinking because you sent him away. Don't go outside again. Stay in here, do the windows inside. I want you in here when . . ."

"I don't want to be in here," Maggie said, shaking her head again. "I don't want to see your father. Not with her lying up there dead."

"We know of no one upstairs. Dead or otherwise."

"She's dead up there, you *killed* her!"

"Fetch your handbasin. Wash the sitting-room windows. Nothing has happened, nothing that we know of. They'll ask us where we were and what we were doing. We were going about our normal business, do you understand? We heard nothing . . ."

Maggie was shaking her head again.

"I tell you we heard nothing and saw nothing; we were going about our . . ."

"You can hear *all* in this house," Maggie said. "I can even hear *themselves* when they roll over in bed."

"But *we* heard nothing. And saw nothing. We know nothing but what we ourselves were doing. Whatever else transpired, we did not hear or see."

"Will you tell that to your father?"

"Yes. Now fetch your basin," she said, and Maggie hurried out of the room.

I'll tell him *nothing*, she thought. I'll inquire about the mail, I'll mention that Mrs. Borden is not yet back, I'll—well, wait. I'll say . . . he'll wonder where she's gone and what's keeping her . . . I'll say . . . well, yes, she told me there are people sick in town, I'll say she had a note from someone who's sick and went to visit . . . yes . . . that will explain her lengthy absence. And when later . . . when later she's not yet returned, we'll notify the police in concern for her, and *they* shall be the ones to find her upstairs, the police, and we shall all be astonished and amazed and explain to them that we were going about our normal business with no idea whatever of what horror rested just above our heads, yes, that's how I'll do it, if only he would hurry home before my resolve—

She heard a clicking at the front door.

Someone trying to insert a key into the lock.

Her father!

All she planned to tell him evaporated at once, all the facade she hoped to present to him crumbled in that instant of his imminent entrance, and she fled for the stairs, planning to lock herself in her room, hide from him, and was halfway up the stairs when she heard the doorbell ringing insistently, and then Maggie's voice shouting, "Coming!" and then more softly as she crossed the sitting room and moved toward the front door, "Miss Lizzie?" and the doorbell rang again. She heard Maggie setting something down, the basin she had gone to fetch, heard the doorbell again, the impatient clamor of it, and she stood quite still on the staircase, listening as Maggie fumbled with first the spring lock and then the key.

"Oh, *shit!*" Maggie said, and on the staircase Lizzie laughed, and then suppressed the laugh as she heard the door opening wide and her father saying, "I've forgotten my key. I've been trying the wrong key. Took you long enough to open this door."

"I'm sorry, sir," Maggie said, "I was washing the windows." Her voice was steady and calm. She would be all right. She would behave as she'd been instructed.

"Still at them, eh?" her father said. "Well, then, where's Mrs. Borden?"

They had moved into the sitting room now. Lizzie stood silent and motionless on the staircase, her eyes level with the second-floor landing, her stepmother's body clearly visible through the open door to the guest room.

"I don't know where she might be, sir," Maggie said. "I saw her leaving at nine, somewhat at nine."

"Not back yet, eh?"

"I haven't seen her, sir."

"Well, go about your business," he said. "Will you be long in here?"

"Only a bit, sir."

"I'll use the dining room then."

"Yes, sir."

"Where's Lizzie?" he asked.

"I . . . don't know, sir."

A slight wavering of the voice.

"Well, is she in the house, or has she gone out?"

"I think she's in the house, sir." A pause. "I haven't seen her."

"Well, do your windows; I'll get out of your way."

"Yes, sir, thank you."

Lizzie looked once again at the open door to the guest room. She took a deep breath and went down the stairs. Her father was sitting in the dining room. There was a parcel wrapped in white paper on the dining-room table, and alongside that the mail: several legal-sized envelopes, a larger yellow envelope, a long brown pasteboard cylinder. Maggie was coming from the kitchen now, carrying a stepladder. Her eyes met Lizzie's. Neither of them said a word.

"You got to the post office then," Lizzie said.

410

"Yes."

"Anything for me?"

"Nothing. What's this ironing board doing in here?"

"I'm waiting for my flats."

"Will you be ironing then?"

"As soon as they're hot."

"Looks messy, things lying about this way."

"I'll put it away as soon as I've finished. What's in the parcel?"

"Eh? Oh, an old lock I picked up at the store they're fixing for Clegg." He shrugged. "Might come in handy." He was sorting through the mail now. He picked up the pasteboard cylinder. "I hope this is the survey," he said, and poked his finger into the brown-paper wrapping at one end of the cylinder, tearing it. He eased from the cylinder a rolled document, partially unrolled the stiff paper, said, "Yes, good," and in explanation, "Some land that interests me. Out Steep Brook Way. Where's your mother, do you know?"

"Visiting someone who's sick," Lizzie said.

"Oh? Who?"

"She didn't say. She had a note . . ."

"Oh?"

"Yes. And went out directly afterwards."

"I didn't see anyone with a note," her father said. "This morning, do you mean?"

"Yes."

"I didn't see anyone," he said again, and shrugged. "I'll take this upstairs, all this *work* going on down here," indicating with a hand gesture the ironing board on the dining-room table, and with a movement of his head Maggie on the stepladder. He went into the sitting room, took his key off the mantelpiece shelf and then came back to gather up the mail. In the kitchen he put the mail down on the table, lifted the stove lid over the firebox and dropped the empty document-cylinder into the hole. "Not much of a fire here, you plan on heating these flats," he said to Lizzie. "Your wood's only smoking." He put the lid back on the stove, and looked at the floor. "Splinters all over the floor here," he said.

"I'm sorry," Lizzie said, "I'll sweep them up."

411

"Chop your kindling on the block below," he said, "where you should. And take that hatchet downcellar, where it belongs."

"Yes, father," she said.

"See to it," he said, and picked up his mail and started up the stairs to his room. Maggie turned to her at once.

"Did he . . .?"

"Shhhh!"

They waited.

They could hear his footfalls on the back stairs. They heard the door to his room open and then close. The house was still again.

"Did he believe you, do you think?" Maggie whispered. "About the note?"

"I think so."

"I don't think so," Maggie said. "I'm scared to death, I'm not sure I can . . ."

"You'll be fine."

"He'll want to know what's keeping her. When she hasn't come back . . ."

"Shhh!"

They heard his footfalls on the back stairs again. He went into the kitchen and then the pantry. They heard the water tap running over the pantry sink. When he came through into the dining room again, he said only, "Hot as the devil upstairs; are you about through in here, Bridget?"

"Just finishing, sir."

"Well, hurry about it, would you?"

He went into the sitting room, took off the Prince Albert coat, moved the sofa cushion and tidy to one side and draped the coat loosely over the sofa arm. He seemed about to lie down. Surveying Maggie at the windows, he changed his mind, went out into the front entry where his wool cardigan reefer hung in the small closet and came back into the sitting room. He put on the reefer, pulled a rocking chair over to the light streaming through the windows, and sat in it. Maggie raised the window near his chair. He turned to look at her, annoyed, and then picked up the morning paper again as she carried her stepladder into the dining room. She went back into the sitting room once, to pick up her water pail and her basin, and then began washing the windows in the dining room. Lizzie came through from

412

the kitchen, one of the flatirons in her hand. Their eyes met again. They said nothing.

In the sitting room the clock ticked.

She did not know how long the silence persisted. She was aware of the ticking of the clock, the minutes falling soddenly on the still summer air. At last she said—loud enough for her father to hear, hoping her voice sounded as it always did, everything normal, everyone in this house going about the normal business of the day, washing windows, ironing, chatting—"Are you going out this afternoon?"

"I don't know," Maggie said, her eyes meeting Lizzie's again, a question in them. "I might. I don't feel very well."

"If you go, be sure and lock the door," Lizzie said pointedly. "Mrs. Borden's gone out on a sick call, and I might go out, too."

"Who's sick?" Maggie asked, idiotically.

"I don't know," Lizzie said, a warning in her eyes. "She had a note this morning. It must be in town."

She glanced toward the sitting room again, hoping her father was listening to every word. Maggie went out into the kitchen with her stepladder, washed out the cloths she had used on the windows, and hung them behind the stove. Lizzie came in a moment later, placing the flatiron she'd been using back on the stove, picking up the flat that was still heating there. In a voice loud enough for her father to hear, she said, "There's a cheap sale of dress goods at Sargent's this afternoon, eight cents a yard," and then, in a whisper, "Are you all right?"

"I feel faint," Maggie whispered, and in her normal voice said, "I'm going to have one. Sargent's, did you say?"

"Then go to your room," Lizzie whispered. "There's nothing more to be . . ."

From the sitting room, her father said, "Eh? What's that?"

"Father?" she said, alarmed.

"Were you talking to me?"

"No, sir."

"I thought I heard . . ." His voice trailed.

Maggie gave her a look she could not read, and then went up the back stairs. The stairs creaked beneath her footfalls. She listened to the footfalls, all the way up to the attic, heard the attic door opening and closing. She was carrying the flatiron

413

back into the dining room when she heard her father's voice again.

"What's *this* doing here?"

What? she thought. *Where?*

"This candlestick," he said, and she froze in her tracks. "Doesn't it belong upstairs? In the guest room?"

He turned to her. She stood in the doorway between the rooms, the flatiron in her right hand, staring at him.

"It . . ." Her mind worked frantically. "I brought it down for Maggie to polish. She must have polished it. Must have been polishing it."

"Shouldn't be down here," her father said.

She kept staring at him.

"I'll take it up," he said.

"No . . ." she said, and took a step toward him.

"Eh?"

"I'll take it when I go up again. I have some basting to do . . ."

"Finish your ironing," he said, and turned away from her.

She watched helplessly as he walked from the dining room and into the sitting room again, and then passed from sight into the front entry. She was not prepared for the discovery just yet, had hoped it would be made later in the day when concern for her mother's absence would have necessitated notifying the police. She wanted the *police* to make the discovery and not any member of the household. Nor did she want that candlestick to be found in the room where her stepmother—

The candle!

The broken *candle*!

It still lay on the floor of the room upstairs, an unmistakable link to the candlestick, identifying the weapon, eliminating the possibility that what had been done was anything but a spur-of-the moment act, no assassin lurking about the house with a weapon brought here for the purpose of murder, no, an object at hand instead, an object familiar to the members of this household of which there were but two present at the time of the bloody deed. Herself and Maggie. Only those two. He would make the connection. He could not *fail* to make the connection.

She did not want to be in this house when he came downstairs again, could not face the accusing look in his eyes, could

414

not hope to answer the questions he would most certainly put. Her eyes darted. Like a bird poised for precarious flight, she raised her arms, her hands fluttering, and turned from where she stood in the kitchen doorway, and then rushed into the entry and threw open the screen door, knowing only that she had to get away from here, run, hide, *run*!

Unmindful of whichever neighbors might be watching, she hurtled in terrified flight into the backyard, and then stopped dead when she saw the carriage outside the fence, standing near a tree. An open buggy, a box buggy with a high top seat and a high back. A man was sitting in the carriage. For a shocking instant she thought it was he again, the pale young man returning; *had* he witnessed what she'd done in that upstairs room? But no, the shutters had been closed. And then she saw that *this* man was dressed differently, wearing a brown hat and a black coat, and she dismissed him from her mind as but a passing stranger, her eyes darting again, wondering where, *where*, seeing the barn and running toward it, thinking she would hide in the hayloft, cover herself with hay, hide there forever from the wrath of her father, a witness in effect though he had not been present, a witness the moment he put together candlestick and candle.

She stopped again just outside the barn door, reaching for the pin in the hasp, and then hesitated, pulling back her trembling hand, realizing in a crystal instant that she could never hope to protest innocence if he found her cowering under the hay. She reversed her course at once, turning and starting slowly back for the house, knowing she had to confront him after all, face the wrath of a God sterner than the one who'd banished Eve from the garden, express surprise and shock, grief and concern, claim ignorance and innocence, I know nothing, I saw nothing, I heard—

She heard the sound of horses on the street outside as she crossed the yard from the barn to the house, turned her head to see a team and wagon—the ice-cream peddler, Mr. Lubinsky, his head craned for a look at her as she walked toward the back steps. The team went by, the wagon moved out of sight. She opened the screen door, and went into the house again.

The house was silent.

415

She did not move out of the kitchen. She stood near the cookstove, waiting, listening for the tiniest sound.

She heard his footfalls on the front stairs.

Unhurried, slow, ponderous.

She heard him entering the sitting room.

She did not move from where she stood near the coal scuttle.

He loomed suddenly in the doorframe between the kitchen and the sitting room. There was nothing in his hands, neither candlestick nor broken candle. Had he failed to make a connection? She looked into his eyes and saw there only stricken confusion. Her heart quickened. There was yet hope; he had not yet put it together.

"Someone has killed your mother," he said. His voice was dull, lifeless, his eyes wide and staring.

"What?"

"Your mother . . ."

"*What?*"

"Your mother lies dead upstairs."

"No," she said at once, "that can't be," her eyes opening as wide as his were, hoping that her voice conveyed shock and disbelief. "She's not yet back from town."

"She's slain upstairs," her father said. "Oh, my *God*, Lizzie!"

"Father!" she said, and went to him, and he took her in his arms, and she stood close in his embrace, her heart fluttering; there was yet *hope*!

"We must . . . we shall have to notify the police," he said.

"I'll go at once."

"And Dr. Bowen."

"I'll use his telephone."

"She's slain, Lizzie, oh, dear *God* . . ."

"Come lie down. I'll run to Dr. Bowen's. Come in the sitting room . . ."

"I shall fall if I move. Hold me, Lizzie."

She held him close. He was weeping now. She patted him as she would a child, listening to the sounds of his grief and his shocked mutterings ("Oh, my God, the blood, the blood . . ."), consoling him, "Yes, Father, yes," thinking it would be she herself who sounded the alarm ("Blood on the floor," he said, "the walls, the bed, a broken candle on the . . ."), she who would run across the street to Dr. Bowen's house, telephone the

416

police, alert the neighbors—and suddenly she realized that his words had stopped, and his weeping as well. He moved his cheek from hers and held her slightly apart and looked into her eyes, puzzled.

"The candlestick," he said.

Her heart leaped.

"Whoever did this . . . but you heard no one?"

"No one."

"Saw no one?"

"No one."

"But you were *here*, weren't you?"

"I was here, certainly, but I heard . . ."

"Didn't she scream? When he was bludgeoning her with . . . oh my God, my *God*!"

"Father, please lie down. I *must* fetch the police, we *must* have them here!"

"But how could . . .?" he said, and hesitated, and she saw in his eyes the same puzzlement again. And then he blinked and said, "No, it couldn't have been, you brought it down for Maggie to polish."

"Yes," she said quickly. "Father . . ."

"When did you do that, Lizzie?" he asked gently and in the same puzzled voice.

"Do what, Father?"

"Bring the candlestick down."

"Why . . . this morning," she said. "When I came down this morning. Father, I must . . ."

"I saw no candlestick when you came down," he said, still puzzled.

"Later," she said.

"Brought it down later?"

"Yes."

"Went upstairs to fetch it?"

"Yes."

"And brought it down for Bridget to polish."

"Yes."

"Fetched it from the guest room."

"Yes."

"Did the candle fall from it then?" he asked.

He was working it out, oh God, he was putting it together!

417

"I . . . I really don't . . ."

"When you went to fetch it?" he asked.

"Perhaps . . . well, yes, it must have."

"And you didn't stop to pick it up?"

"Well, I thought of picking it up, yes, I must have, but . . ."

"When you knew your mother would be having company? And had tidied the room?"

"I planned to do it later," she said.

He looked directly into her eyes. They stood not two feet apart in the doorway to the sitting room, he in one room, she in the other. His voice when he spoke was stronger now.

"Was your mother up there when you went to fetch it?" he said. "The candlestick?"

"She'd already left," Lizzie said.

"If the candlestick was the weapon . . ."

"It couldn't have been," she said quickly.

"*If*," he shouted, and she fell silent.

He kept staring at her.

"How came it to be in the dining room?" he said.

"I told you. I . . ."

She hesitated.

"I . . ."

"Did you do this thing?" he asked.

She said nothing.

"Did you do this terrible thing?"

Still she said nothing.

"Why?" he asked. "Dear God, *why*?"

Looking into his eyes, she said gently, "Father, she . . ." and could say no more, for continuing would have meant revealing to him the precipitating act, herself and Maggie in naked embrace, the act her stepmother had called monstrous and unnatural. When he saw that she would offer neither explanation nor excuse, he said, "Go from my sight, *go*!" and turned away from her and went into the sitting room. Like a child accepting punishment, she did as she'd been instructed, dutifully, obediently, going into the kitchen and standing silently by the cookstove, facing the wall, listening to the ticking of the clock. In the sitting room, the sofa springs protested under his weight as he fell back upon it. She heard him say, "Oh, God, oh, dear God," and then all was silent save for the ticking of the clock.

418

Not five minutes had passed since she'd come back from the barn. Within the *next* five minutes, he would regain his strength and composure and go to telephone the police. And when they arrived, they would listen to the logic of candlestick and broken candle, and then go silently and gravely upstairs to look upon her stepmother's shattered, open skull. And they would wonder why. And they would ask her why.

Herself and Maggie in embrace.

The discovery.

The shame.

Is it your passion that shames you so? Then are we, as women, not entitled to the same passion men consider their God-given right?

She looked at the hatchet where she had left it in the coal scuttle.

Chop your kindling on the block below, where you should. And take that hatchet downcellar, where it belongs.

She picked up the hatchet.

She picked it up deliberately, not as she had earlier lifted the candlestick, fully aware of her hand closing around the wooden handle. She went into the sitting room. Her father was lying full length on the sofa, his left leg extended, his right leg bent and dangling over the side, the foot touching the carpeted floor. His hands were folded over his chest as if in prayer. His eyes were closed. Tears were running down his face.

"Father?" she said softly.

He said nothing.

"Are you all right?" she asked.

His eyes opened.

She did not mean to say what she said next, was in fact surprised when it found voice.

"I shall take this downcellar."

Her father looked at the hatchet in her hand.

"Don't tell them," she said. "The police. Please don't."

He looked at her uncomprehendingly.

"The candlestick," she said.

And still he looked at her.

"Please," she said, "*help* me, Father! If you love me . . ."

"*Love*?" he said, spitting out the word as if it were poison on his tongue. "I *hate* you for what you've done! I'll hate you *always* for it! I'll regret *forever* the day I spawned such a foul and murderous creature!" And then, more bitterly, as if he were echoing her stepmother's words in yet another form, he said, "I shall tell them all, everything, *all*! Go from me! You *disgust* me! You offend my *sight*!" and closed his eyes against her, and turned his head into the cushion, concealing his right cheek again.

She raised the hatchet.

He sensed the motion, seemed to sense the motion, and started to lift his head from the cushion, his left eye opening wide, his legs swinging over the side of the sofa as if he would rise. The last thing she saw in that instant before she struck him was that single glaring eye and the silent accusation in it.

She intended the first angry blow to strike that fiercely accusing eye, but she missed the mark and the chopping edge of the hatchet caught her father immediately in front of his left ear, a crushing wound some three inches and more in length, releasing an immediate gush of blood that took her quite by surprise, splashing up onto her face and the front of the black chintz dress. She raised her left hand to ward off the gush of blood, closing her eyes against it, and then opened them at once, and struck him again, slightly higher up this time, above the left ear, a two-inch-long slash sending up another spurt of blood that spattered the wall behind the head of the sofa. And still she struck for the eye though it was closed now, hitting again, and again, and again, at the area in front of and above his left ear, her blows breaking away the skull bone and crushing through into the brain itself.

The eye, she thought, *the eye*, and the hatchet slashed downward to open a wound lost in the left eyebrow near its outer end, the *eye!*, striking again to open a wound above the left eyebrow, blood spattering onto the framed picture above the sofa, and now, *yes*, now the flashing edge of the hatchet passed downward through the eyebrow, cutting deeply through the eye at its outer edge, crushing into the cheek bone on the left side and penetrating the cavity of the skull where the eye rested in the head.

As though blinding that accusing eye had failed to fulfill her purpose or satisfy her rage, she struck out at the other features on that once familiar face, slashing through the nose and the upper lip, hitting him again a fiercer blow that opened a four-

420

inch gash through the left nostril and the upper and lower lips, extending nearly to the tip of the chin. The hatchet felt suddenly heavy in her hand. She struck out less forcefully now, opening a flesh wound above his left eyebrow, and then a short cut in his scalp, and another cut parallel to those, some two inches in length—and all at once she stopped.

She was drenched in blood; she had not expected so much blood. There had not been this much blood upstairs. Her hand where she held the bloodstained weapon dripped blood into her father's own blood flowing from his head onto the carpet. The bodice of the black chintz dress was covered with blood, and she could feel it soaking through to her chemise and her breasts. She realized all at once that killing him had taken no longer than thirty seconds.

The house was utterly still.

"Maggie!" she shouted, "come down!"

Silence.

And then from above in the attic room on the other side of the house, "What's the matter?"

"Come down quick!" Lizzie said. She stood motionless by the sofa, unable to move, fearful of trailing blood through the house, yet knowing that she must wash herself, change her clothes, dispose of them and the gory instrument in her hand before someone else arrived at the door, her Uncle John home for the noonday meal, *someone*, and she shouted again, "Maggie, *hurry!*" and leaped in surprise when Maggie appeared suddenly in the doorway.

"Fetch me some newspapers," Lizzie said. "Quick! The old ones. Across the room. In the bucket."

Maggie stood in the door to the dining room, both hands to her mouth, looking in over the arm of the sofa to where Lizzie's father lay crushed and bleeding. "Oh, God," she whimpered, "oh, sweet merciful . . ."

"Hurry!"

And now all was frenzied haste, though for Lizzie the seconds seemed to drag eternally, the fear mounting that her uncle would barge into the house with a gruff greeting to find her drenched in blood—"Close the shutters!"—Maggie rushing to bring the newspapers and then flying across the room to hurl the shutters closed while Lizzie stripped herself naked save for the bellyband and menstrual towel stained with her own seeping blood. Thirty seconds passed, perhaps a minute—"Burn these in the stove!"—Lizzie running into the pantry, a glance toward the unshuttered kitchen windows, washing and drying herself and the hatchet, Maggie stuffing the newspaper-wrapped garments into the stove, the flames licking up through the open hole.

Lizzie came out of the pantry, put the hatchet on the kitchen table and, without a word, ran through the house and up the stairs to the closet on the landing. She took from its hanger a blue, bengaline silk dress, carried it swiftly into her bedroom, put on fresh underclothing, black stockings, the white underskirt, the dress skirt and dress waist. She studied the felt slippers for bloodstains, found none, and hurled them into her closet. Quickly she put on a pair of low, black tie-shoes, her fingers fumbling with the laces, the clock ticking.

She did not want to go into that spare room again, did not want to see again the evidence of what she'd earlier done. But the broken candle was still on the floor of that room, and so she crossed the landing swiftly and was about to go into the room when she saw the candlestick where her father had dropped it just outside the door, undoubtedly in shock at what he'd seen within. She picked up the candlestick, aware of time, racing against time, not knowing where to put it, not the dining room again, certainly not there, but *where*? Where would they not *suspect* it? She carried it quickly into her own room, put it down on the dresser, and searched in the bottom drawer on the right for a fresh taper. She placed the candle in the socket, pressed it down firmly onto the pricket. She looked at the candlestick once again and then went hurriedly out into the hallway.

The first thing she saw when she entered the spare room was a hank of black hair on the bedspread.

She almost backed out of the room.

The hair, flung up onto the bed by the ferocity of her attack, summarized for her the full horror of what she'd done, and she stood staring at it, unable to move, mesmerized by it, realizing at last that it was only a piece of false braid, a switch her stepmother often wore, the knowledge in no way diminishing the fact that the severity of her blows had sent it flying up onto the bed. She forced her eyes away from it.

The candle lay on the floor where it had fallen, its back broken like a serpent's trod upon. There was no blood on it or near it. She picked it up quickly, studied the carpet for stray scraps of wax, found a rather large piece that had broken off from the base, studied the floor again and then hurried out of the room without looking back at the hank of false hair on the bed or the body on the floor.

In the kitchen downstairs Maggie was still at the stove. She had replaced the lid; Lizzie assumed that the fire had already done its work.

"Burned?" she asked at once.

"All," Maggie said. "But there'll be buttons. From the dress. They'll find buttons in the ashes."

"Then I'll burn another dress in plain sight," Lizzie said.

"The buttons will be different," Maggie said.

"The buttons will be charred," Lizzie said. "Do I look . . .?"

"Fine," Maggie said.

Her voice was low, scarcely more than a whisper. The kitchen, now that a proper fire was going in the stove, was hotter than it had been earlier. Lizzie lifted the stove lid and dropped the candle and the stray scrap into the fire.

"We saw nothing and heard nothing," she said. "We tell them all that we did . . ."

"All that we did," Maggie repeated dully.

"All but what relates. All but what actually . . ."

"What *you* did," Maggie said.

"What *we* did," Lizzie said, and slammed down the stove lid. "You were here in the house. Should either of us stumble, they'll think us *both* murderers.

"I harmed no one," Maggie said.

The same dull voice, a whisper.

"And will not harm me," Lizzie said.

Maggie said nothing.

"Promise me."

"Aye," Maggie said.

"On your mother's eyes."

Maggie sighed deeply. "On my mother's eyes," she said.

"Now run for Dr. Bowen as fast as you can. Tell him what happened here. Tell him we need him at once. Tell him my father is dead."

"And your mother both," Maggie said.

"We know nothing of upstairs. Only my father. It's only my father we've found. You were in your room, resting. I was out in the backyard, near the barn. I heard a groan, and came in, and the screen door was wide open. Do you have that?"

"I have it," Maggie said, and started for the entry. The screen door clattered shut behind her.

Lizzie went into the dining room. From the window she watched Maggie as she ran hurriedly up the path toward the street. *I was in the backyard*, she thought. *I heard a groan; the screen door was wide open*. She turned from the window, began pacing the dining-room floor, going over the falsehood yet another time, refining it, *I was in the backyard, the barn, I was in the barn*, her steps taking her closer and closer to the sitting-room door until she remembered what lay beyond that door, and backed away with a start, almost colliding with the dining-room table.

She hurried into the kitchen, lifted the stove lid again, nervously checked to see that the garments had indeed burned and, satisfied that they had, replaced the lid. She lifted the smaller lid near the firebox, hoping no charred scraps of blood-stained newspaper had drifted that way. She saw only the pasteboard cylinder in which her father's survey had arrived, completely carbonized but still holding its original shape. She replaced the lid—and saw the hatchet still on the kitchen table.

In plain sight where she'd left it!

In a moment Maggie would be back with Dr. Bowen, and the first thing he would see—

She heard hurried footsteps on the walk outside. She picked up the hatchet and turned in panic toward the coal scuttle. The screen door banged open. Maggie came clattering into the house, her face white. She saw the hatchet and stopped dead in her tracks.

"He isn't home," she said breathlessly. "I left word with Mrs. Bowen. She expects him any time; she'll send him over. Are we to stay *alone* in this house till . . .?"

"Do you know where Alice Russell lives?"

"Yes, I think so. Yes."

"Then go and get her." She held out the hatchet to Maggie. "And take this with you."

"No!" Maggie said.

"Take it!"

"I want no part of it! No!"

"Dispose of it," Lizzie said.

"Where? She lives hard by, where would I . . . ?"

"Drop it in the nearest sewer."

"I shall be seen!"

"Then take it to the river. Go by way of Rodman Street . . ."

"The long way round? She lives on *Borden*!"

"They won't ask you how you *went*! Take Rodman to Hartwell . . ."

"There are houses bordering the river there!"

"You can find a way to it. Near Eight-Rod Way, the river's . . ."

"They'll see me; I'll be seen!"

"Would you have them find it *here*?" She thrust the hatchet into Maggie's hands. "A sewer, the river, I don't care which! Dispose of it! Take it *out* of here!"

Maggie said nothing. Silently she wrapped the hatchet in a dishrag, and then went out to the entry. She took her hat and shawl from where they were hanging, carefully lowered the hatchet into her fabric marketing bag and went to the screen door. She hesitated there, turned to Lizzie as if to say something, shook her head instead and rushed outside, the screen door slamming shut again behind her.

Lizzie went to the door. She stood just inside the screen, listening to Maggie's hurried footfalls fading on the street outside, knowing for certain that the moment anyone walked into this house—Dr. Bowen, Alice Russell, *anyone*—she would immediately crumble and confess all that she had done. And then, suddenly, she remembered something Alison had said a long time ago, and she closed her eyes, almost seeing her lips shaping the words, almost hearing her lovely liquid voice again:

Our greatest secret, our supreme strength, is that no man on earth, no father, no son, could dare admit that a proper lady—his daughter, his sister, his wife—would ever commit a breach that seriously threatened his superior position in the society he has constructed and which he will support with his very life. For should he once believe of any one of us that we might so rebel against the absurd rules and regulations proscribing the periphery of our lives, then he must perforce believe that we are

425

all *capable of bringing down his elaborate house of cards and thereby destroying his faith in the cherished myth of ideal womanhood*.

Across the yard she heard a window go up at the Churchill house. She opened her eyes.

"Lizzie?" Mrs. Churchill called. "What's the matter?"

She took a deep breath.

"Oh, Mrs. Churchill," she shouted in alarm, "do come over! Someone has killed father!"

AFTERWORD: CONNECTICUT— 1983

Although this is a work of fiction, much of it is rooted firmly in fact.

The inquest material is factual. It has been curtailed only when Knowlton's questions and Lizzie's responses became overly repetitious. But the words recorded are Lizzie's and Knowlton's own, exactly as they were spoken.

The trial material is also factual, but the full transcript ran to 1930 typewritten pages, and it was obviously necessary to abbreviate. I've deleted the opposing attorney's lengthy opening statements and closing arguments. I've also deleted any testimony that merely corroborated or repeated what other witnesses had already sworn to or that did not bear conclusively on Lizzie's guilt or innocence. In addition, I've severely curtailed Justice Dewey's charge to the jury, without diluting its obvious intent.

In condensing further I abandoned customary American trial procedure in favor of a more novelistic approach. In reality the prosecution presents its case first. There is a *direct* examination of each witness, followed by the defense's *cross*-examination. The prosecution is then allowed a *re*direct, and the defense a *re*cross. After the prosecution has rested its case, the defense then calls its witnesses, and the same rules of questioning and requestioning apply. In taking dramatic license with this fixed procedure, I have often gone directly to the heart of the testimony without identifying a question as being put by either prosecution or defense. Needless to say, whenever anyone's testimony reads as a continuous narrative, it does so because I have eliminated the questions entirely and shaped the answers into what appears to be an uninterrupted flow. Most importantly I have often changed the *order* in which the witnesses actually appeared, sometimes presenting their testimony as an unbroken chain of events arranged in minute-by-minute chronological sequence, and at other times clustering their testimony around the nucleus of a disputed point, so as to achieve greater clarity and understanding on that point. In no instance have I knowingly distorted the meaning of what was said. The words are those of the lawyers, judges, and witnesses themselves.

Lizzie's European trip is premised solely on the various mentions of it made during the inquest and the trial; I searched in vain for further information about it. The reconstructed trip, then, is entirely fictitious, its details culled from newspaper articles, magazine pieces, pamphlets and travel books of the period. I shall be forever grateful to a Mrs. Juliette Adam, who—in writing to the *North American Review* in 1890—provided the inspiration for the American-Girl-as-Orchid metaphor. I should say a word or two about the *quatre à cinq*. I am fully aware that it is currently called *cinq à sept*, but the expression I've used is accurate for the times. In France the *cinq à sept* is still known as *l'heure de femme*—the *hour* of the woman.

While not an entirely unsupported conjecture, Lizzie Borden's lesbianism should also be taken as part of the fiction.

Shortly after the trial Lizzie adopted the name Lizbeth and moved into a new and luxurious home. In 1897 a warrant for her arrest was issued, charging that she had stolen two inexpensive paintings on marble from the Tilden-Thurber Company in Providence. The warrant was never served.[1] According to one

1. Providence Daily Journal, February 16, 1897, p. 1.

source, the paintings were called *Love's Dream* and *Love's Awakening*.[2]

At the turn of the century, a man divorcing his wife on charges of lesbianism named Lizbeth A. Borden of Fall River as corespondent. Judge William Trowbridge Forbes of the Probate Court in Worcester County dismissed the charges as frivolous.[3] Emma lived with her sister in the new house on French Street until 1905, when—after an argument following the midnight entertainment of Lizzie's close friend, the actress Nance O'Neil—she packed her bags and left the house,[4] never to return, never to see Lizzie again. In a later interview, Emma said, "The happenings at the French Street house that caused me to leave, I must refuse to talk about. I did not go until conditions became absolutely unbearable. Then, before taking action, I consulted the Rev. A. E. Buck. After carefully listening to my story, he said it was imperative that I should make my home elsewhere. I do not expect ever to set foot on the place while she lives."[5]

A poem carved into the wood above the fireplace in Lizzie's new bedroom read:

> *And old time friends, and twilight plays*
> *And starry nights, and sunny days*
> *Come trouping up the misty ways*
> *When my fire burns low.*

Carved into the mahogany mantel of the library fireplace were the words *"At Hame in My Ain Countrie,"* taken from a poem by the Scottish poet Allan Cunningham. When Lizzie died in 1927, at the age of sixty-eight, the soloist at her funeral sang a song composed to those words.

Clause 28 of Lizzie's will read: "I have not given my sister, Emma L. Borden, anything as she had her share of her father's estate and is supposed to have enough to make her comfortable."

2. Victoria Lincoln, *A Private Disgrace: Lizzie Borden By Daylight* (New York: G. P. Putnam's Sons, 1967), p. 305.

3. Agnes DeMille, *Lizzie Borden: A Dance of Death* (Boston: Little, Brown, 1968), p. 84.

4. Boston Sunday Herald, June 4, 1905, p. 11.

5. Boston Sunday Post, April 13, 1913, p. 25.

She signed the will as both Lizzie A. Borden and Lizbeth A. Borden.

Her sister died ten days later in Newmarket, New Hampshire.

They are both buried in Fall River's Oak Grove Cemetery, where the remains of Mr. and Mrs. Borden also lie.

Bridget Sullivan died in Butte, Montana, in March of 1948, at the age of eighty-two. She had gone west fifty-one years earlier, had settled in Anaconda, married a man whose last name was also Sullivan and—according to at least one report—had numerous children.